WHEN SHE FALLS

A HALLIE MILLER NOVEL

JEN MURPHY

FIRST EDITION, 2025

LILYKAT PRESS, publisher.

ISBN 979-8-9860219-7-3 (Hardback)
ISBN 979-8-9860219-9-7 (Paperback)

ALSO BY JEN MURPHY

When She Runs. . .
When He Watches

For my siblings, Patti, Jodi, Jimmy, Heather, and Matt
Even though the parents love me the most,
you're all pretty awesome, too.

"It was night, and the rain fell; and falling, it was rain, but, having fallen, it was blood."

– Edgar Allan Poe, 1832

Originally published as "Siope — A Fable"

CHAPTER ONE
CHARLIE

Charlie rolled off the young woman beneath his tanned abs, their shared sweat creating a quiet sucking noise as he lifted off of her and wiped his hand on the bedsheet.

"What's wrong? she asked.

"Nothing. Um, I'm sorry, I can't do this," he said, his voice trailing off as he looked around the small efficiency for his clothes.

"Seriously?" she asked, sitting up and feeling around the bedding for her discarded thong.

He was glad the darkness hid his embarrassment, as the warmth began in his neck and crept up into his cheeks.

He spotted his clothes scattered about the apartment and his phone hiding among the empty Modelo bottles on the white particleboard coffee table, a staple furnishing of modest beach rentals along the Florida West Coast. His jeans lay on the floor next to the sturdy, floral sleeper-sofa, another staple, and he assumed his t-shirt had to be close. He got up and walked naked across the room to retrieve his clothes, the bathroom light illuminating the source of his indignity.

He had been clean for two years, one month, and three days. Although the heroin and sundry other opiates had been out of his system for two years, he continued to suffer the effects of his twenty-year addiction, an addiction that started with an innocent enough experiment when he was thirteen. The most notable lingering effects – and most distressing – occurred in the bedroom. His occasional inability to stay hard, no matter how turned on he may feel, was probably more psychological than physical, according to his counselor, but the cause didn't really matter. When it happened, he was humiliated.

The apartment smelled oddly sweet and musky – a combination of weed, sour beer, coconut suntan lotion, sweat, and failed sex. It turned him on and revolted him at the same time. He needed some fresh air.

When he first got out of rehab, he got a job as a bartender at Marti's, a local beach bar in Key West named not for some former or current owner named Martin but after José Martí, the Cuban poet and revolutionary thinker whose life—and death—changed not just Cuba, but Florida. After a year in the Keys, Charlie returned to the Tampa Bay area, hoping to make amends and reconnect with his family.

With the little bit of money he earned and no longer injected or snorted, he was able to rent a small, dated duplex in Treasure Island and get a job at Middle Grounds Grill, a restaurant-bar on Gulf Boulevard popular to tourists and locals alike. His apartment was in walking distance to it as well as the clear, blue-green waters of the Gulf. Alcohol had never been his issue, so being a bartender didn't summon any of his demons. Working nights gave him the time during the day to go to substance abuse meetings and do other things to stay clean. He started lifting weights, eating healthier, and, despite initial misgivings about it being new-age fuckery, meditating daily. He had put on about thirty much-needed pounds since leaving rehab and his body was toned from his vigorous gym schedule. His mind, too, had regained a clarity and focus he hadn't experienced in years. Women (and men) were hitting on him, including the pretty girl he had met that night, something he hadn't experienced since his early twenties.

"Are you coming back to bed?" she asked without the enthusiasm she had exhibited at the beginning of the evening.

He couldn't blame her. He was disappointed too.

He looked at his phone, scrolling and pretending to check messages, before putting it back down on the sticky, beer-laden coffee table. His ripped physique belied his thirty-four years, and despite the abuse he had inflicted on himself, his face remained young and boyish, especially when he laughed.

Charlie preferred younger women, but only because he felt they judged him less and didn't expect him to have his shit together or didn't care that he didn't. Without responding, Charlie stepped into his jeans and zipped them up, making sure to avoid catching his bare skin in the zipper.

"You're leaving?" she asked, pulling the bedsheet around her.

The air felt heavy, stagnant, and he just wanted to get out of there. He closed his eyes and rubbed his temples before answering her.

"Yeah, sorry, I gotta go, Dana. I'll text you," he said.

"Um, it's Dawn, and you don't have my number," she said, matter-of-factly.

"Dawn, right, not Dana, I'm sorry. My head is just a little foggy right now. Maybe I drank too much," Charlie lied, knowing he had barely gotten through half of his second beer. "What's your number? I'll text you."

"No, forget it. Let's not bother with that. You're not going to text or call so why bother with this bullshit exercise? Just go," she said, unable to hide her annoyance, although Charlie wasn't sure whether it was with him or herself. Probably both, he decided.

He left her AirBnB and began walking the six blocks back to his duplex, passing the now-closed bar where he had met her earlier that night. A warm Gulf breeze swept through his wavy blonde hair, which had been matted to his head with the sweat and humidity of the evening. As he walked under the moonlight on Gulf Boulevard, the sound of the waves lapping gently against the sand in the distance, the faint taste of salt on his lips, even the feeling of the asphalt releasing the day's heat, soothed him. He loved the emptiness of the place before the tourists and spring-breakers took over the street at sunlight.

The band that had been playing at the bar was loading the last of their gear into the back of their cars while a member of the kitchen crew was nearby hosing down the sticky rubber floor mats from the kitchen. Charlie nodded to the guy washing the mats as he walked by, each registering recognition of the other, but neither saying a word.

* * *

"Oh, back so soon? What did you forget?" Dawn asked, unable to hide her annoyance as she got out of bed in response to the knock on her door.

Within a second, there was another knock.

"Hang on," she said loudly, picking up the crumpled peach-colored, floral sundress from its heap on the floor, stepping into it and pulling the front up over her small, perky breasts and the spaghetti straps over her slightly sun-burned shoulders as she headed to the door.

She opened the door with her right hand, her other hand firmly positioned on her left hip to convey the depth of her aggravation; subconsciously, though, she hoped he had come back to apologize and finish what he had started earlier.

Once her brain registered what her eyes were seeing, it was too late.

Her scream was swallowed by the thick, leather glove that slammed against her mouth and shut it as she was pushed violently back into the room. The other gloved hand gripped her throat so tightly that no sound could escape. Worse yet, no air could reach her lungs. Her ears rang and her vision blurred as the door closed quietly behind her.

She was lifted off the ground by her throat, her bubble-gum pink toenails frantically trying to connect with the ceramic tile beneath them, her fingernails scratching and clawing at his hands like she was a wild animal. No, not wild. More than that. Rabid. Her desperation transformed her and pumped her limbs full of bestial frenzy.

But for all this desperate strength, she was no match for him.

As the warmth of her own urine streamed down her legs and her world slipped into blackness against the backdrop of frolicking dolphins and pink seashells, inexplicably, she wondered if she would get her $200 security deposit back.

CHAPTER TWO
HALLIE

Warm air breezed in through the open windows of Hallie Miller's Hyde Park bungalow. The young leaves just coming back to life on the hundred-year-old oak in her front yard rustled. A dog barked in the distance, momentarily disrupting the morning's quiet. Hallie didn't mind, though. She loved to leave her windows open, something one could not do in Tampa during most of the year. This benign weather was the reward for the grueling summer months that would soon arrive without apology or respite. This was likely their last cold spell, if low seventies could count as a cold spell. The mild and fairly dry morning would give way to low eighties by lunchtime and would continue to slowly climb throughout the afternoon until the sun quenched itself in the Gulf, taking the warm air with it. Hallie wished she could keep her windows open while she slept, but she wasn't ready to do that. Not yet. She wasn't sure if she would ever be.

She wandered out to her front porch, stooping to pick up the cushion that had blown off the rocker during the night, the smell of fresh dirt and newly cut grass mingling with the aroma of dark hazelnut coffee steaming out of the mug in her hand. She sat in the rocker and listened to the early morning birds as she enjoyed the serenity of the Sunday morning.

"We can actually accomplish our goals if we break them down into manageable pieces, small tasks that aren't overwhelming," Lisa Demmi, the dynamic speaker and author of *Think SMALL*, had told the crowd of seventy-plus professional attendees, mostly women, the Friday before at the South Tampa Chamber of Commerce monthly luncheon.

Hallie smirked. The simplicity of the advice could probably be applied to anything except practicing law. Everything about practicing law was task-oriented, broken down into constantly changing task lists and accompanying calendar entries, supplemented by the three-a.m. mental checklist to remind herself what she had forgotten to do because she hadn't added it to the never-ending list, a list that was always shifting, always being rearranged, as endless fires erupted. So goes the life of a lawyer, day in, day out, all meticulously reckoned in six-minute increments.

If she was cynical about the utility of Ms. Demmi's message to her professional life, Hallie was a touch more receptive to it as it pertained to her personal one.

"What are my goals now?" she asked herself as she sipped her coffee.

She had always been a driven, if somewhat wandering, person, identifying her objectives without always knowing how she would get there, but always persevering until she did. That was her way.

Relentless Hallie, like a dog with a bone, her father used to tease, affectionately, when Hallie set her sights on something she wanted.

She remembered telling her father she was going to be a lawyer at the age of seven after he explained to her what he did: "I help people," he explained, "in a way most other people can't. As a lawyer, I must know the law and the court system and how to navigate it to get the best outcome or justice for my clients. I am often their last hope before their property or children or liberty are taken away. They depend on me."

It sounded important and powerful to Hallie, and she knew then that she was going to follow in his footsteps. And she did, but, unfortunately, years after her father's death. When Hallie was sixteen years old, he was shot leaving his downtown Tampa office after work one night. Her father was a family law attorney and regularly represented women seeking divorces from their abusive, often powerful husbands. Hallie and her mother had long believed his murderer was an angry husband of one of his clients, and Hallie came close to proving their theory true just last year. After reviewing her father's files and other evidence, she believed Tommy Martino was responsible for her father's death. Martino had died not long after her father, so it didn't seem worth pursuing legally, but she believed knowing for sure would give her family closure. She decided she would review everything again in her free time.

Hallie looked next door and saw Mrs. Butler on her front porch.

"Good morning, Mrs. Butler," Hallie called over as she waved to her elderly neighbor.

"Good morning, Hallie. It's a bit chillier out this morning than I expected," Mrs. Butler returned, clenching her thin blue house dress around her generous frame to shield her from the breeze.

"Hm, I guess it is, but it will be unbearably hot before we know it, so I'll take this *chill* a little bit longer," Hallie said, smiling at her neighbor.

"You're right, dear. By the way, did you get that package that fella said he was leaving for you yesterday?"

"A package? Yesterday?" Hallie asked as she surveyed her front porch.

"Yes, late afternoon. I was out here having my tea and doing my crossword when I saw him on your porch. After all the trouble last year, you know, I like to keep an eye out. You got it, right?"

Hallie looked around her front porch again, more carefully this time, including beneath the wicker rockers and the loveseat bookending the quaint entrance to her bungalow. And there it was, a small manilla envelope tucked behind the rocker, close to her front door.

"Thanks, Mrs. Butler, it's right here," Hallie answered as she bent down and picked up the envelope.

Her coffee mug was just about empty. She set it down on the table next to her cell phone while examining her name scrawled in thick, black handwriting on the outside of the envelope. There was no return address, no stamp, no postmark.

Nothing but her name.

CHAPTER THREE
LINDA

Linda Morgan had never been to Hawaii. In fact, she had never been anywhere outside of Florida. Not really, anyway, because she knew a weekend in Georgia when she was sixteen for her granddaddy's funeral didn't count.

But today, Linda was as excited as she could ever remember being. She flipped through the dresses hanging in the closet of the small, two-bedroom home she had recently rented in Starke, Florida, for the perfect one to wear when the time was right. There were certainly a range of sizes to choose from, although she hadn't lost any significant weight in a few years. She knew there was no reason to get rid of the smaller sizes when she could always go on a diet if she felt like it.

Linda regarded each dress, one by one, the fabrics cool and rich beneath her fingers, until she found *the one*: a pink, A-line dress, adorned with white Hawaiian flowers woven seamlessly into the satin-silky material and finished with a gold hemline. She remembered finding it during a clearance sale at Nordstrom the previous summer about a week after the trial had ended. She bought it right off the rack, no alterations needed.

Even with the heavy discount, it was an unusual splurge for Linda. But that dress belonged to her the moment she saw it. In that dress, she could picture herself far, far away from her current life: enjoying the warm, Pacific breezes, the swaying palm trees, and the forbidding waves thundering against the volcanic cliffs and onto the brown, sandy beaches in the distance. She could almost taste the Pina Colada and smell the suntan lotion Billy would be rubbing onto her smooth, ivory skin.

"You don't want to burn that delicate, ivory skin, my love," he would say, she imagined.

Yes, that was the dress, she thought as she unzipped it and tossed the hanger onto her unmade bed before trying it on.

She smiled as she admired herself in the mirror. When she bought the whimsical floral dress, she struggled to pull the side zipper all the way up: among other things, her DD-sized breasts got in the way. But now, although she still had to wrestle with it a bit, she was able to zip it all the way up without breaking a sweat. She twirled with a giggle, catching delightful glimmers of pink and white and gold in her reflection as she spun around and around.

She had written Billy six letters since his conviction, none of which he had answered. But she wasn't worried or deterred. She remembered her first letter to him, verbatim, as that one was the most important. She had written and re-written it seven times before she finally got it perfect.

Dear Billy,

I hope you don't mind me calling you Billy. That red-headed "female dog" (pardon my French) in the courtroom kept calling you "William" and that just doesn't fit the gentle, sweet man I know you are. In case you haven't figured out who this letter is from yet, I'm the pretty blonde who was sitting in the back row of the jury box, seat number seven to be exact. I also checked the rules and I'm allowed to send you a picture, so I enclosed a recent picture of myself to help you remember me. But you probably don't know my name (I remember them telling us that was one of the rules). So let me introduce myself: I'm Linda. Linda Mary Baker. I am so pleased to make your acquaintance, officially.

I also wanted to apologize for all the stupid, illiterate a-holes (again, pardon my French!) who did not understand the legal system in this great country of ours that you are INNOCENT until proven guilty. And you, Billy, were not proven guilty. I tried to convince the other jurors of your innocence, but they just wouldn't listen to me. Anyway, I know you didn't do any of those horrible things they accused you of, and I pray the truth will set you free one of these days. And when it does, I'll be waiting!

I knew that you were innocent the moment our eyes locked, and I said to myself right then, "Linda Mary Baker, there is no way, as God is my witness (just like Scarlett O'Hara said in Gone with the Wind!), that my Billy Stephens could ever hurt a fly, much less a woman." *I did – I said that, Billy. And I meant it. And right then, I also knew we belonged together. I can't wait for what the future holds for us!*

Forever yours,
Linda XOXO

The next five letters were lighter, as she was always trying to cheer him up and bring a little sunshine to his day. She liked to include something inspirational for him, which usually came from a meme she saw on Facebook posted in one of the animal-lovers groups to which she belonged or by one of her few friends. When she could, she would print the meme or picture, in color, to include in her letter. The last one she sent him was of an orange kitten hanging from a branch with the words "*Hang in There*" just above the kitten's little fuzzy head. That was one of Linda's favorites and it never got old no matter how many times she saw it. She hoped Billy would appreciate it, too, and maybe hang it on the wall of his cell, if the prison allowed that sort of thing.

She sat on the edge of the bed while the gray tiger-striped, stray cat she had rescued three years earlier rubbed up against her pale thigh, which was barely concealed under the slick fabric. The cat purred as she stroked her head.

"Just you wait and see, Carole, you're going to just adore him. Oh, silly girl," she cooed, rubbing the cat's head as the cat rose up to force Linda to keep scratching her behind the ears, "I can't pet you all day, precious; I have to get ready for work. You don't want me to be late on the first day of the job, now, do you, Mrs. Carole Baskin?" she insisted, referring to the cat by her full name as she got up to extricate herself from her fancy dress.

From the speaker on the nightstand, Celine Dion loudly lamented about lost love and heartache. Linda thought the song was depressing and switched to another station where Taylor Swift offered something merrier and upbeat. This would work. She didn't need anything dampening her happy mood. Not today anyway.

Linda hummed along as she squeezed into her department-issued khaki pants, buttoned her department-issued short-sleeved navy shirt with the State of Florida emblem on the breast pocket, and tucked the stiff shirt into her pants before buckling the brown leather belt she had bought that past weekend to complete the uniform. She missed the feel of her silky Hawaiian dress compared to her stiff uniform, but she was excited about her first day.

She swept her ash-blonde hair up onto the top of her head, the darker roots contrasting sharply with the light strands within the bun, and painted her lips with a light pink matte lipstick followed by a clear gloss. She finished her look with a blush that matched her already rosy cheeks, trying to create a contour like the lady at Nordstrom's makeup counter had shown her.

She looked in the mirror and smiled, pleased at how good she looked. She was ready.

"Billy Stephens, my love, I will see you soon," she said aloud as she walked out of her bedroom to begin the first day of her new job in the administrative office of the Union Correctional Institution, the State's maximum-security prison and home to the most notorious and dangerous criminals incarcerated in the State of Florida.

Including Prisoner Number 91752, William Stephens: convicted rapist, murderer, and former judge.

CHAPTER FOUR
THE HUNTER

The Hunter held her by the throat until she stopped struggling. Her brown eyes were wide with terror until she succumbed to the lack of oxygen and lost consciousness. Her urine trickled onto the ceramic floor beneath her, and he held her slight frame away from himself so her piss wouldn't land on his leather shoes. He eased up on her throat and carried her lifeless body over to the bed and laid her down. He removed his black gloves and stuffed them into his back pocket. He retrieved two latex gloves from his front pocket and then easily slipped her sundress off before zip-tying her hands above her head to the bedpost.

He squeezed her nose and gave her a few short puffs in her mouth before administering smelling salts underneath her nose. She inhaled reflexively and instantly started coughing and wheezing. Her small chest heaved with the exertion, and she regained consciousness. The whites of her eyes were blood red where the capillaries had broken when he choked her, and purple bruises were setting in on the pale skin underneath her eyes. Before she could scream, he placed a piece of duct tape over her mouth and watched as the terror returned to her eyes.

The sight excited him.

He reached down and retrieved the steel hunting knife from the sheath strapped to his calf that he always had on him. He had a collection of knives in his truck, but this one was his favorite.

At the sight of the knife, tears started seeping out of her eyes, and she desperately yanked and pulled at her bindings, the zip-ties cutting into her skin.

"Well, hello, sunshine," he said as he looked down at her, admiring her thin frame and perky breasts, tracing the triangular patterns around her nipples with the tip of the knife where her tiny bikini top barely protected her fair skin from the Florida sun.

"You've been a bad girl, Dawn, a very bad girl."

He loved seeing the confusion in her eyes at the sound of her name. He knew she was trying to figure out where they met, how he knew her name.

"All dirty whores deserve to be punished. And I'm here to do the punishing," he said to the terrified girl.

He unbuttoned and unzipped his jeans, pulling them down to his thighs, revealing his erect penis. He used his knife to cut her tiny thong off. Her breathing was becoming erratic but only being able to breathe in and out of her nose with the duct tape covering her mouth, he feared she might hyperventilate.

"Dawn, if you settle down, I won't hurt you," he said calmly. "But if I have to remove the duct tape so you can breathe, I'm going to have to do something else to keep you from screaming, which, I promise you, will be worse than the tape."

He watched as the girl fought to get herself under control. He admired her tenacity. He pulled the knife away from her and put it back in its sheath, which further helped calm the girl's breathing. He wanted her conscious when he fucked her. It wasn't as much fun when they were unconscious or dead; that, he had learned the first few times.

After a few minutes, he effortlessly pulled her body sideways towards him and spread her legs, standing between them, her struggling no match for his brute strength. He thrust himself violently into her, the duct tape muffling her high-pitched wail. Her eyes streamed fresh, wet tears down her flushed, reddening cheeks.

As he was about to finish, he put his large hands around her throat for the second time that night. This time, she wouldn't wake up. He grunted and groaned as he came while strangling her until he felt her body go limp beneath him. He backed away from her, making sure the condom stayed in place.

He went to the bathroom, carefully removed the condom and placed it in the plastic baggy he retrieved from his front pocket. He pulled and zipped his jeans up and stuffed the baggy with the condom into his pocket along with the latex gloves. He put a fresh pair of latex gloves on before returning to the other room. He had made sure, as he always did, not to touch anything in the room other than what he brought with him. He cut the zip ties off the girl with his knife and put those in his back pocket, returning the knife to its sheath. He looked around and found a satin sash on top of the girl's open suitcase on the floor, likely the sash from her robe. After he posed her body exactly how he wanted her to be found, he tied the sash tightly around her neck.

He picked up her white thong from the floor next to the bed and put it into his pocket. They were still damp from her urine and probably sweat. He would sniff them later as he relived the evening before securing them safely in his trophy chest.

The last thing he did before he left the room was fold her sundress and place it neatly on the edge of the bed, and then he retrieved a fresh thong out of her suitcase and folded that into a little triangle before placing it on top of the sundress.

Order amid the chaos, he thought, as he walked towards the beach into the darkness.

CHAPTER FIVE
HALLIE

Her pulse quickened as she opened the letter.

Interested in selling your home for cash? I was driving by and love the curb appeal and everything about this neighborhood. We can close in thirty days! Call me! 877-668-0202
—James

Hallie was relieved, but also admonished herself for being anxious before opening the envelope. Maybe with time, she wouldn't be triggered from the events of the last few years.

Obviously, today was not that day.

She was ripping up the unsolicited offer to buy her house when she heard her phone ringing. She got to it right before it went to voicemail and was happy to see that it was Marcelo calling.

Marcelo. They had just celebrated their one-year anniversary together.

One year, Hallie thought. She had been thinking a lot about their relationship lately.

Hallie had been in longer relationships, including her two failed marriages, but her relationship with Detective Marcelo Garcia was different, more intense. It was hot and passionate, and she felt safe with Marcelo, but she also recognized that maybe it was because of what they had been through that intensified her feelings for him.

The year before, Hallie had been attacked and kidnapped by a deranged sociopath who was stalking, raping, and killing women in the Tampa Bay area. After abducting Hallie, Marcelo found her and was shot trying to rescue her. As he was recovering in the hospital from the gunshot wound, he was attacked again, likely to keep him from identifying the shooter.

Tampa Rico, a local thug, was captured on one of the hospital cameras in the stairwell nearest to Marcelo's room, the same stairwell where a discarded syringe, which tested positive for fentanyl, was found in a trashcan. He disappeared and the police had not been able to find him since. Hallie's abductor, Peter Martin a/k/a Pietro Martino, had also not been seen since. Both had allegedly fled the country.

* * *

"Hey, babe, how's my hot lawyer today?" she heard as she answered her phone.

"Better now," Hallie answered, automatically smiling at the sound of his voice.

"What are you up to?"

"Waiting for you to whisk me away on a sailboat to a deserted island."

"In due time, Counselor, in due time," Marcelo laughed easily. "Will you settle for brunch for now?"

"Brunch sounds wonderful."

"Great, I'll pick you up at 11."

"I can't wait."

Hallie went back inside, locked the front door behind her and placed her mug in the kitchen sink before heading upstairs to shower. She picked out a yellow sundress with tiny white flowers on it, her tan Michael Kors high heel leather strap sandals, which she matched with a small, light brown purse. The purse was just big enough to hold her cellphone, credit card and license holder, and two lipsticks. It also hung nicely from one shoulder across her chest, resting on her opposite hip.

After she was ready, she spritzed herself with her favorite perfume and headed down to wait for Marcelo on her front porch. As she waited, she scrolled through the local news on her phone until one headline jumped out at her. She clicked on the link to the story:

WOMAN FOUND DEAD IN TREASURE ISLAND AIRBNB

By: Jennifer Meister

Sunday, April 7, 2024 / Tampa Bay Times

A 23-year-old woman was found dead last Saturday, March 30th, in an AirBnB on Treasure Island Beach. The owner of the AirBnB,

Ken Gardner, arrived to clean the unit after the guest was supposed to have checked out that day. "When I opened the door, she was on the bed, naked and facing up, with her face beat up real bad and something tied around her neck," Mr. Gardner told a reporter for the Tampa Bay Times. "I backed out and immediately called 911."

EMS responded but the victim, who has since been identified as Dawn Owens from Orlando, Florida, was reported dead at the scene. The Pinellas County Sheriff's office released a statement saying the woman appeared to be the victim of foul play and they are treating it as a homicide. "We have no leads at this time, but we believe she died sometime between 1:30 a.m. and 4:30 a.m. Saturday morning based on our preliminary findings," Detective Jacobs said.

Detectives interviewed people at the six-unit complex and are seeking video surveillance from nearby establishments, but no other information was available at press time. The investigation is ongoing.

Anyone with information should call the Sheriff's Office at (727) 582-6200 or leave an anonymous tip and be eligible for a possible reward by calling Crime Stoppers of Pinellas at (800) 873-TIPS.

Hallie thought about the young victim and wondered how long it would take the police to find her murderer.

She thought about what evidence the police must have gathered, such as the killer's DNA or fingerprints. It was almost impossible not to leave DNA behind at a crime scene these days, and the forensic teams were getting proficient at retrieving it.

Hallie realized her investigative instincts were triggered whenever she read or learned about a murder under suspicious circumstances ever since she found the body of a young coed underneath her neighbor's Hydrangea bushes and a young lawyer was murdered near her childhood home. She found that she enjoyed examining the evidence and putting the pieces together to try to solve the crime. She didn't get the same rush or satisfaction from her cases as a lawyer, and she had recently been wondering how her life might have turned out if she had pursued a career as a detective instead. It was too late for that, she knew, but she was contemplating becoming a private investigator. The thought excited her, and she felt it would counter the burnout and dissatisfaction she felt as a lawyer. She couldn't wait to talk to Marcelo about it at brunch.

The murders of the coed and lawyer ended up being unrelated, but Hallie was partly responsible for identifying the killer of the young lawyer. DNA found under the victim's fingernails was linked to Hallie's daughter, Katie, which confirmed to Hallie the horrible truth that the man who had raped her years before was Katie's biological father. With Hallie's help, William Stephens was convicted of murder and was serving a sixteen-year sentence in Raiford, home of Florida's maximum-security prison. Hallie hoped he would die in prison – sooner rather than later – but she knew there was a chance he would get out one day.

At the sound of Marcelo's truck pulling into her driveway, Hallie closed the news app, tossed her cellphone into her purse, and walked towards the big white truck.

"Good morning, Counselor, muy bellissima."

Hallie smiled as she got into the truck.

"Where are you taking me today?" Hallie asked.

"I made reservations for us at Oxford Exchange, in the atrium."

"Ooh, nice, they make the best French 75 there."

"Is that some kind of fancy French toast?" Marcelo asked.

Hallie laughed, "um, no, it's a drink: Hendrick's gin, a drop or two of simple syrup, lemon juice, and topped with a splash of champagne. It's delicious, like an adult lemonade."

"Hmmm, I might have to try one of those fancy adult lemonades."

"You will love it."

They arrived at Oxford Exchange and had to wait a few minutes for their table. While they waited, Hallie perused the books displayed on the tables and shelves nearby. Oxford Exchange, a two-story building adjacent to downtown, was one of Tampa's coolest spots. The first floor included a bookstore, a quaint café, champagne bar, and the restaurant. The second floor had private offices, workspaces, and conference rooms available to its members. For solo practitioners, it was more affordable than paying the high rent for an office in any of the buildings downtown.

After they were seated and the waitress brought their drinks, Hallie asked Marcelo, "Do you know anything about the woman who was murdered in Treasure Island?"

"No, I haven't heard anything about that case. Please tell me you don't know her," Marcelo said, the concern evident on his face.

"No, thank God. Twenty-three years old, brutally murdered in her AirBnB on Treasure Island, no one arrested yet. Just awful."

"That is awful. But why are you so curious?" Marcelo asked.

"I don't know, really. I was scrolling through the news while I was waiting for you, and it piqued my curiosity."

"Did the article say whether the police have any leads or possible suspects?"

"According to what I read, they have no leads, no suspects, nothing. It intrigues me how that's possible with DNA evidence and forensic science today, not to mention all the cameras everywhere. And I realize I only know what they printed so it doesn't mean that they don't actually have any leads. That's why I was asking if you had heard about it."

"Yeah, most agencies are reluctant to say anything to the press these days until they gather enough evidence to make a case. Everything has to be solid before a suspect can be identified or arrested."

"Right, that makes sense, but, um, well, I've been thinking about something else lately."

Marcelo looked over at Hallie, "Oh boy, I know that look. What are you up to, babe?"

"Just thinking about a career change. That's all."

"A career change? You're a great lawyer. Why would you give that up? I thought you loved being a lawyer."

"I do some days, but a lot of days it's just grueling and stressful. And I have to deal with asshole attorneys on the other side and demanding clients all the time. I think I might be good at investigative work."

Marcelo laughed.

"Why is that so funny?" Hallie asked.

"Oh, you're serious?"

"Yes, I'm serious. I think I would be good at it, and I find it fascinating."

"Um, I get it, you did some research into your father's murder, but,"

"Did some research?" Hallie repeated, cutting him off, her irritation evident.

"Calm down, babe, I didn't mean anything by that. I'm just saying that you can't just decide to become an investigator because it sounds fun. You may be a natural, I don't know, but I do know it takes years of training to become good at it," Marcelo replied.

"I know, Marcelo. I've been reading a lot about it lately, and I've even looked into it. Did you know there's a five-day, 40-hour course offered at Hillsborough Community College, over two weekends?"

"Wow, forty hours? Is that all it takes? Who knew you could become a full-fledged detective in just forty hours," Marcelo said in a tone of condescension followed by a whistle.

"That's not what I said, and I know becoming a detective requires a lot more than a forty-hour course. I'm talking about being a private investigator. That's just the first step in the process. After you finish the course, you have to intern with a licensed PI for two years before you can get your own PI license, but never mind, it was just something I was thinking about," Hallie said, picking up her drink while trying to tamp down her anger.

Marcelo picked up his drink and they sat in silence for a few minutes, both pretending to read the menu.

"Hallie, I'm sorry. I shouldn't have reacted that way. I know you can do anything you set your mind to, but I just never imagined you would give up being a lawyer."

"I wouldn't give up being a lawyer. I just thought it would be something I could do on the side, because it intrigues me, seems more exciting than what I'm doing now. But it's probably a stupid idea. Forget I said anything.

Where would I find the time, anyway?" Hallie said, trying to change the subject.

"Hallie, you were made to be a lawyer. PI work can be messy and dirty, not that you wouldn't be good at it, but you look really hot in your suits. That's what I know," Marcelo said as he winked at her while reaching over to give her thigh a light squeeze.

Hallie was saved from reacting to his misogynistic comment by the waitress arriving to take their order. Hallie ordered another French 75 and the Avocado Toast while Marcelo ordered the Steak and Eggs. They decided to split the Stone Ground Yellow Grits, which consisted of grits, aged white cheddar, crispy bacon, chives, and a maple drizzle, although at that moment, all Hallie could picture was Marcelo choking on the grits, the thicker the better. The thought made Hallie smile.

Hallie wanted to make the most of the day and didn't want to spend it fighting. She decided she wouldn't bring up the Treasure Island victim or her interest in investigative work again. They spent the next two hours talking about random current events, including the latest political candidates, movies, and other random things, the French 75s keeping Hallie's irritation at bay, for the most part.

"So, how's your week looking?" Marcelo asked.

"Not too bad, a few meetings later in the week, but thankfully not insane. I told you I started running again, right?"

"Yes, you mentioned that. Are you sure it's not too soon?"

"It's fine. I was cleared by my doctor. I've started off with a mile, but I'm hoping to build that back up to a 5K soon."

"Don't overdo it, Hallie, please. You have to be careful," Marcelo said, the concern evident in his voice and his eyes.

She knew he was worried about her, but after the way brunch had started, his over-protectiveness annoyed her. Three months before, she would have thought it was sweet, but today she found it suffocating and patronizing.

"I'm fine, I know my limits. I won't overdo it," Hallie said, trying to keep her tone casual. "Anyway, I'm working from home tomorrow and then going for a run after work, but I'll probably be in the office the rest of the week. How about you, busy week?"

"Yeah, I'm working some new cases and chasing some leads on a few old cases."

"Anything interesting you can talk about?" Hallie asked, genuinely interested in hearing about Marcelo's investigations.

"I can only tell you about another case that hit the news this morning. I'm surprised you didn't read about it. The Chief will be giving an official statement at a press conference with the family later today. It's not my case, so I don't know a whole lot about it, but a young woman was found strangled in her hotel room yesterday morning at about

5:00 a.m. when her boyfriend came in after partying with friends all night."

"He found her?" Hallie asked.

"Yeah, that's what they believe so far. The girlfriend apparently got tired and wanted to go back to the hotel to go to sleep. She took their room key with her and told him to wake her when he got back. When he got back to the hotel, after she didn't answer the door or her phone, he went downstairs to get another key. But the girlfriend had reserved the room under her name, so they wouldn't give him a key. After much pleading, they finally agreed to do a welfare check on her. And that's when they found her."

"Oh my God, that's awful. How old was she?"

"Twenty-three, twenty-four, I can't remember exactly. She and the boyfriend went to college in Florida, UF, I think, maybe Florida State, and came back into town for a friend's wedding. They all went out to party after the rehearsal dinner when the girlfriend got tired and headed back to the hotel, leaving the boyfriend out with the groom and his friends."

"Any chance he murdered her, left the key in the room, and pretended like he couldn't get in so that he would have an alibi? Maybe someone should compare this case to the Treasure Island case to see if there are any similarities," Hallie said, her mind racing, running through what she remembered about the Treasure Island victim from the article she had read that morning. "Did I mention she may have been strangled too? Also, they were both about the same age and both from out of town. Was she sexually assaulted? I think the Treasure Island victim was sexually assaulted," she was saying when Marcelo interrupted her.

"Whoa, Counselor, today's my day off, or should I start calling you 'Investigator'?" Marcelo teased.

Her emotions were still too raw from their earlier conversation, and she couldn't hide the agitation she was feeling from his remark.

"Hallie, I'm just teasing you."

"Yeah, I know, but I get it, you're the detective," Hallie said as she poured the rest of her champagne flute into her mouth and swallowed it in one gulp, stopping the lemon twist with her tongue before it went into her mouth.

Marcelo rolled his eyes and groaned, "Babe, can we just enjoy the rest of our brunch and let the detectives assigned to these cases do the work? I promise you if they think the cases are related in any way, they will catch it. Treasure Island is only across the bridge, and it's not like young, murdered tourists are a common occurrence over there or here."

"Of course, you're right. Didn't mean to get ahead of myself. I'm running to the bathroom. Get the check when the waitress comes back, please," Hallie said, getting up and walking away from the table before Marcelo could say another word.

Marcelo was waiting for her in the hallway when she came out of the bathroom.

"Ready?" Hallie asked, as she turned and headed towards the door.

When they got outside, Marcelo broke the silence.

"Hallie, I feel like I've missed something. What's going on with you lately?"

"With me? I feel like you're being very patronizing today. I told you about the girl who was murdered on Treasure Island and how I was interested in investigative work, which you quickly shot down, and then you mentioned this girl in Tampa, and I was wondering whether there were any similarities between the two cases. But as soon as I started talking about it, you made fun of me."

Marcelo held his hands up in surrender, "I'm sorry, I wasn't making fun of you. I just wanted to see you today, have a nice brunch, and forget about my job and the shit I have to see and deal with every day for a little while. I didn't think that was too much to ask."

"You're the one who brought up the Tampa case," Hallie reminded him.

"You're right. Look, I didn't mean to make you feel like I did, but, well, I'm sure if there are similarities between the two cases, the detectives investigating the cases will find them."

"I'm sure you're right," Hallie responded, trying not to sound as annoyed as she felt, "and I'm probably just being over-sensitive."

"Look, if you're really interested in this P.I. thing, I'll talk to some guys I know. Maybe they can give you an idea about what they really do. It's probably not as glamorous as you're thinking it is."

She had to get away from him. Everything he said made it worse, even though she knew, in his own way, he was trying to be supportive.

"No, don't worry about it. It was a stupid idea. Forget I said anything."

They got into the truck and rode to Hallie's house mostly in silence.

When they arrived in her driveway, Marcelo didn't turn the truck off.

Surprised, Hallie asked, "aren't you coming in?"

"I would love to, but I have an early day tomorrow and I have some things to get done before the week starts."

Hallie wasn't sure if she believed him, but she also wasn't disappointed. She wanted to watch the press conference at 5, and then spend the rest of the evening investigating, or as Marcelo called it, "researching" what she could about the Treasure Island and Tampa victims.

"Okay, I understand," Hallie said, "I do too. Dinner this week?"

"Without a doubt, Counselor," Marcelo replied.

Hallie leaned in and kissed him goodbye before she hopped out of the truck. Marcelo waited in her driveway while she retrieved her keys from her purse and unlocked her front door. Before going in, she turned and waved to him. He waved back and then backed out of her driveway.

Hallie stood in her doorway watching the taillights of his truck as he drove down the street away from her. She felt uncomfortable with the way the day had gone and sensed their relationship was changing.

* * *

Hallie changed into her sweats and got comfy on her couch in her living room. She opened her local news app and the article about the Tampa victim popped up immediately: twenty-three-year-old Taylor Reynolds flew into Tampa on Friday morning with her boyfriend for their friend's wedding, which was taking place that weekend. After the rehearsal dinner, a group went out and the girlfriend returned to their hotel room alone where she was found later by the boyfriend and hotel staff, just as Marcelo had told her. She didn't learn anything more from the article other than the victim's name, age, and the name of the hotel where they were staying.

She watched the press conference and learned they were questioning a *person of interest* at the station, but they did not identify who the person of interest was. During the press conference, the Chief reiterated that the public was safe and that they did not believe it was a random attack. The victim's parents and either the boyfriend or a brother stood behind the Chief looking absolutely devastated.

"Chief, Chief, Jennifer Meister from the Tampa Bay Times," one of the reporters called out, getting the Chief's attention, "is there any chance this is related to the tourist who was found murdered in her AirBnB in Treasure Island last weekend?"

Hallie perked up, anxious to hear the Chief's answer. The family also appeared to take notice of the reporter's question, their confused looks at each other making it obvious they hadn't heard of the Treasure Island murder.

"No, not at this time."

"Why not? Both women were visiting the Tampa Bay area from out of town, both were found murdered in their hotel rooms, both victims were about the same age," the reporter was saying when the Chief interrupted her.

"At this time, we cannot comment further on the details of either case, but I have been in touch with the Treasure Island police chief, and we have each independently determined the cases are unrelated. That's all for now."

And with that, Chief Mastandrea ended the press conference and escorted the family out of the press room.

Interesting, Hallie thought.

She took out a fresh legal pad and wrote down the reporter's name. She thought about reaching out to her, but then realized she would seem insane. She had no ties to either victim, and she wasn't a private investigator or law enforcement involved in either case. She had no valid reason to be 'investigating' the cases other than her own curiosity.

She put the legal pad down on the coffee table. She had a pretty good idea why the cases intrigued her, as well as why she wanted to try to solve them, but she needed to consider whether her interest in investigative work was a healthy hobby or something more deep-rooted.

Her face flushed with embarrassment thinking about her conversation with Marcelo earlier.

Maybe it was a stupid idea, she thought.

CHAPTER SIX
HALLIE

After a grueling week at work, Hallie was glad it was over and was looking forward to going for a run. She laced up her running shoes, stretched her hamstrings and calves, and checked the weather app on her phone to make sure the gray clouds overhead were going to hold off long enough for her to get her much-needed run in. When Hallie ran, it was the only time she could completely disconnect from the constant interruptions of life and clear her mind.

She had just started running again after recovering from the head injury she sustained at the hands of Pietro Martino. Since then, she suffered from horrible vertigo and migraines, but with the help of her ENT doctor and the "maneuver" – a horrible rollercoaster-like procedure that knocked the crystals in her ear canals back to where they belonged – she was no longer dizzy and finally able to resume running, albeit slower than ever before.

She finished stretching and was about to put her phone on 'do not disturb' mode when her phone pinged to alert her of an incoming text message.

"We're on tomorrow! 7:00 a.m.! Let's do this!"

"Shit," Hallie said aloud, while glancing down at the text from her always enthusiastic personal trainer, Jason Lane.

She had forgotten that she agreed to the unusually early and unpleasant 7:00 a.m. time slot after her work calendar had filled up and prevented her from making it to her second session during the week. When she agreed to it, she had admittedly gotten sucked in by one of Jason's positive mantras:

"I am confident you will feel good physically and mentally when you continue to invest in yourself as you invest in your clients and family. You cannot be your best to them if you are not your best to yourself first."

He wasn't wrong, but what was she thinking agreeing to such an early time, especially on a Saturday? Hallie had never been a morning person and tomorrow morning was not going to be any exception. But she was also glad she would get her second session in. As a result of training with Jason, Hallie was physically stronger than she had ever been, deadlifting 185 pounds and back squatting 115 pounds, at her best.

Hallie opened the text and typed, "Yup, 7 am – I apologize in advance if I'm surly when we start lol" and hit send before setting her phone to 'do not disturb.' Thanks to Jason, she was never going to be the victim of violence again, at least not without a hell of a fight.

She descended the steps of her porch, hit play on her running playlist, and headed to Bayshore Boulevard for her run. Her Lenny Kravitz Spotify playlist blared in her ears for the next thirty-five minutes. She stared straight ahead, her breathing matching the cadence of her footfall on the concrete beneath her feet. She ran with resolve, feeling the dry, warm air on her face and smelling the salty-sour Bay around her. She navigated the roller-bladers, bikers, and other runners in her path, pleased the climbing heat was starting to send most people to their indoor gyms. She forgot how much she had missed running. She felt strong, stronger than she had in a long time.

Hallie finished her run and walked the few blocks back to her house. She was happy at her overall time and logged the date and time in her notes. She unlocked her front door and was immediately welcomed by the frigid AC as she crossed the threshold, which clashed with the hot sweat dripping down her chest and back. She was thankful that she was only slightly dizzier than when she had started her run and felt her ENT therapy was working. Her doctor told her the dizziness would eventually disappear entirely. She could only hope.

She dropped her running key, a single house key she kept on a band she could slip on her wrist, onto the table in the foyer and wiped the moisture off her neck with the bottom of her shirt. She went into the kitchen and drank a large glass of cold water before running upstairs to take a shower. She put her sweaty clothes in her hamper and wrapped herself in her terry cloth robe.

Hallie was about to step into the shower when she heard the familiar ringtone on her cellphone.

"Hi Mom," Hallie answered.

"Hi Hallie, did I catch you at a bad time?"

"No, it's fine. I just got in from a run and am about to jump in the shower, but I can chat for a few minutes."

"Okay, good, because I want to talk to you about something."

"Uh oh, do I need to pour a glass of wine first?" Hallie asked, only half joking.

Whenever her mother wanted to talk to her about "something" it usually involved something Hallie did not want to talk about.

"I may as well just get right to it," her mother, Becky, started.

"Oh lord, yes, please, by all means, get right to it, don't drag it out," Hallie said, bracing herself for what was coming next.

"Ross is moving in. It's time. We barely spend any nights apart anyway, so why should we waste money with the upkeep of two places? I've talked to Father O'Malley about it, and he agrees we should get married first. It's going to be a small ceremony a few weeks from now, on a Saturday, at St. Paul's in Carrollwood. Ross is Catholic, did you know that? So, we can get married in the church, which you know is important to me. Well, important to us. Ross feels it's important, too. Will Katie be able to come down for the weekend? I really hope so. Anyway," Becky continued before Hallie interrupted her.

"Mom, whoa, slow down. Take a breath," Hallie said. "Congratulations, Mom. I'm really happy for you."

In a rare moment, Hallie's mom was silent.

"Mom? Are you there?" Hallie asked, wondering if the connection was lost.

"I'm here," Becky whispered, and Hallie realized her mother was crying.

"Mom, why are you crying? Is there something else?" Hallie asked, concerned.

"No, I'm happy, that's all. I didn't know how you were going to feel about this. I was so nervous to tell you. I know your father has been gone a long time, but, well, I just wasn't sure," Becky said.

"Aw, Mom, of course I'm happy for you. Dad *has* been gone a long time, and you deserve to be happy. Dad would want that for you, too. If Ross makes you feel that way, then I'm thrilled for you."

"Thank you, darling, he does make me happy. Really happy."

"Good, then I'm happy too. What can I do to help you for your big day?" Hallie asked.

"Well, I know how busy you are, but I did want to ask you for one thing. Do you think you can help me find a dress?"

"Of course, Mom, of course. We can start looking whenever you want," Hallie said, feeling a twinge of guilt at being so wrapped up in her own life that she hadn't really spent much time with her mother recently.

"Maybe next weekend? We're going to have a party afterwards at the Rooster and the Till in Seminole Heights. The owners are Ross's good friends and a lot of our friends from the yoga studio live in Seminole Heights, so it's the perfect location. Have you been there? The chef is amazing," Becky continued, excitedly going through all the details.

It was nice to hear her mom so excited. After her father's death, her mother was devastated and barely held it together. A lot fell onto Hallie's sixteen-year-old shoulders, as the oldest of the three Robinson children. Her brother, Charlie, the youngest of them and her father's namesake, took it the hardest. He lost his father and, frankly, his mother, at the same time, at least for a few years with respect to their mother.

He got in with the wrong crowd, or maybe he was the wrong crowd to them, but either way the vulnerable lot found each other and turned to drugs and alcohol to soothe whatever inequities life had dealt them. By the time Becky Robinson became aware of how bad it had gotten, it was too late. Charlie was gone, at least the sweet, carefree boy who was the spitting image of his father, was gone. And so began the revolving doors of rehabs, stints in juvenile detention centers and ultimately jail, and broken promises. Hallie hadn't spoken to her brother in over two years.

". . . about twenty guests, total, assuming Katie can come home from school and Ross's sister can make it in from Colorado. I've told you about his sister, right? Real hippie but super sweet. She owns one of those marijuana dispensaries out there and is apparently killing it. Isn't that wild? Ross and I took some edibles she sent us one time and let me tell you, it reminded me of the sixties when your father and I tried acid one time. Oh my God, we laughed all night. I'm talking about Ross and I, although come to think of it, your father and I did too. And the sex, well, I know you don't want to hear about that, but, honestly, I thought I may have permanently damaged my what-me-not with our very long evening. I don't think I'll be eating any edibles again any time soon," Becky laughed, finally taking a breath.

"Mom," Hallie said, taking the opportunity to speak, "I definitely don't want to hear about your broken what-me-not, please, oh my God, but other than that, I think the wedding celebration sounds great. We can start looking for dresses next weekend. But I need to jump in the shower before Marcelo comes over for dinner. Can we talk about the rest of the plans tomorrow?"

"Of course, sorry for prattling on as I do, one doesn't get married every day," Becky said, instantly causing Hallie to feel guilty. "Was it because I mentioned my what-me-not?"

"Oh my God, Mom, please stop," Hallie groaned while unable to suppress her own laughter. "I'm going to go now. I need to wash my own what-me-not after my sweaty run," she said, much to Becky's delight.

Hallie loved hearing her mother laugh. When her mother laughed, everyone around her, including Hallie, laughed. Their laughter was contagious – one of the many things she got from her mother. Hallie was smiling as she hung her robe on the back of the bathroom door and stepped into the shower.

The brief mention of her father and the thought of her mother remarrying brought her back to memories of her childhood. While those thoughts made her smile, they also reminded her that she had not resolved the questions she had about her father's murder, or, more specifically, who had murdered him. The night Marcelo almost died, right before he passed out, he mumbled something to her about knowing who killed her father but, after he recovered, he had no recollection of what he said or what he may have learned about her father's murder.

Maybe it was time for Hallie to look into it again – to find out once and for all who had killed her father, or should she say, confirm Tommy Martino had killed him, whether he could be held accountable or not. Not for her mother, who had finally found happiness after years of grief, but for herself and for her father.

It was time.

CHAPTER SEVEN
MONICA

Monica finished the last of her whiskey and tapped the side of her glass while nodding at Marge, the bartender, to signal she was ready for another.

Marge had been slinging strong drinks and draft beers at O'Maddy's longer than some of its patrons had been alive. She had the typical body of a heavy drinker and smoker, the raspy voice to match, and battle scars on her leathery face from her share of bar fights she had broken up over the years.

"He'e ya go, love," Marge said, her Irish-Boston accent still present even after all the years she had lived in Gulfport, as she placed Monica's whiskey on the rocks down in front of her.

"Thanks, Marge, you're the best," Monica said as she slid the empty towards her and picked up her fresh drink.

"This seat taken?" came a voice to Monica's left.

"No, it's a free country, have at it," Monica said.

"Cute place. Come here often?" the man asked her.

"Look, I don't mean to be rude, but I'm not in the mood to chit chat," Monica said, without turning away from her drink.

"Right, didn't mean to bother you," the man said as he got up and moved to an empty seat further down the bar.

She was glad he moved away from her. She had her monthly lunch scheduled with her mother the next day, which always made her surly. She didn't need to make any new friends, and her main goal tonight was to get drunk, go home, and pass out, hopefully in that order.

Marge came over and topped off Monica's drink.

"By yah cha'ming pe'sonality, I'm guessing tomorrow is lunch with Mama Martino."

"Yeah, you know it, Marge, my favorite day of the month," Monica chuckled while rolling her eyes, her own smoker's rasp almost as bad as Marge's.

"Well in that case, this one's on me, because you always have a way of making me feel just a little bit better about my own shitty life," Marge roared, as a few other regulars joined in the laughter.

"Aw, man, fuck you, Marge. And you, too, Mike," Monica laughed, joining in and raising her drink to the chain-smoking regular still in his paint-stained work clothes sitting across from her at the bar. "I don't know why I come in here and put up with this shit."

Marge, too, always had a way of making Monica feel better without making a big deal about it. As tough as Marge was, she had a heart of gold, and once you were in, you were in for good. She looked out for her regulars, and Monica had earned that moniker many years before.

Monica always got anxious before her monthly lunch with her mother, Nina. Nina Martino was a perfectionist, and Monica had never lived, and would never live, up to her mother's exacting standards. Before her father died, she had always been daddy's little girl. She and Nina did not have the typical mother-daughter relationship because of their unrelenting competition for her father's affection. Monica was devastated when he died, as was Nina, although it was not lost on Monica that her Uncle Nicolas, her father's brother, swooped in to comfort her mother shortly after her father's death. Whether her mother admitted it or not, they were in some kind of relationship, although Uncle Nicolas did seem to be more into her mother than she was into him.

Monica finished up her whiskey, paid her tab, and steadied herself after getting off the bar stool.

"See ya, Marge. Wish me luck tomorrow," Monica called out as she walked towards the exit.

Monica was drunk. She had convinced herself that she wasn't, as she often did, but when she got outside, she knew she was. But she was pleased the rain had not started and the temperature was mild, the extreme heat and humidity not arriving for at least two more months. She wanted to walk home rather than spend the money on an Uber or Lyft.

She stumbled out of the bar, catching her square boot heel on the worn floor mat, rancid from years of spilled beer and God knows what else. "Shit," she mumbled to herself as she caught herself.

She didn't fall. She never fell.

She was used to these obstacles. It was the intangible ones in her life that she had trouble navigating. She took a deep breath and searched in her purse until she found what she was looking for: her CBD pen. She took a long, hard hit and held her breath as the welcome taste of strawberry and vanilla settled on her tongue and the chill of the CBD started to work its magic.

As the contents of her pen started to calm her frayed nerves, she changed her mind and decided she should get a ride. She opened the Lyft app on her phone, hoping she had enough money in her account to cover the fare.

The strap of her bohemian bag slipped off her shoulder, catching on her elbow, the sudden jerk of which resulted in her phone, compact and a lipstick falling out of the bag onto the gravel parking lot, missing a puddle by mere inches.

"*Fuuuccckkkk*," she slurred angrily.

As she bent down to retrieve her items, a wave of dizziness overcame her, and she had to steady herself against the car next to her, clutching her head in her free hand while the other held onto the car.

"You all right, Miss?"

She shot straight up at the sound of the voice behind her, relying on muscle memory to convey, once again, that she was not drunk and was completely in control.

"Yes, I'm fine. But they need to fix this damn sidewalk. Someone is going to kill themselves on this deathtrap," she said, pointing to the flawless pathway she had just traversed.

"Can I help you?" the man asked as he pointed to the contents of Monica's bag on the ground while Monica realized he was the guy who originally tried to strike up a conversation with her at the bar.

He was unassuming enough with his dad-bod in khaki shorts and red Budweiser t-shirt, except for his large, muscular arms. Underneath his baseball cap, he had a full head of blonde, wavy hair, bleached from too many years in the Florida sun, which contrasted sharply against his permanently tanned and weathered face.

"Don't worry about it, Marlboro Man, I got it," she rasped, choking back a cough and a laugh at the same time, appreciating her own humor more than the man did, she quickly realized.

"That was a joke, man," she added before the man could answer, the hair on the back of her neck instinctively rising as his gaze never left her as she picked up her stuff.

"Maybe I am the Marlboro Man. I like to smoke things. Maybe I'll smoke you."

"Well, I think you're a fucking weirdo and you can fuck the fuck off and get the fuck away from me," she spat at him, trying to sound tough and unafraid while glancing at the door of the bar to mentally calculate her odds of making it back inside if she had to.

To Monica's relief, the man laughed and started to walk away into the darkness.

As Monica watched him go, he passed under the one light illuminating the parking lot, the yellow glow giving her a better view of the man, including the word tattooed in black ink across the span of his left forearm: *RETRIBUTION.*

She took another hit off her pen, holding the sweet vapor in her mouth for a second before exhaling.

"What in the actual fuck," she said aloud into the darkness. "Retribution? Retribution for what? Being a fucking creep?"

She opened the Lyft app on her phone and realized she had never ordered it. As she put in her address, the app told her it would be twenty minutes before a car could pick her up. She decided she would rather walk the few blocks to her apartment than wait around for Marlboro Man to come back. She closed the app and looked around the parking lot before heading in the direction of her apartment.

"Fuck you, Marlboro Man," Monica yelled into the wind, as she retrieved a real cigarette from her purse to smoke on the way home.

* * *

From his truck in a dark corner of the parking lot, the Hunter watched her walk away from the bar, the orange glow from her cigarette acting as a beacon to let him know which direction she was going.

He never understood why some women had to be so rude, especially when he had been nothing but polite to the bitch.

He started the truck and headed in the direction she had gone, keeping a safe distance so she wouldn't see him or realize he was following her.

A few minutes later, he watched her stumble up the stairs to her apartment. He smiled as he drove past, pleased that he knew exactly where the bitch lived.

CHAPTER EIGHT
THE HUNTER

The Hunter left Gulfport and traveled southbound on I-275 to 75 to Siesta Key after encountering the dark-haired, foul-mouthed beauty in the parking lot of O'Maddy's. He would have to wait until another day to have his way with her, knowing he shouldn't strike so close to the Treasure Island murder in the same county. Traffic was light for a Friday night as he drove down to Siesta Key, and he found his way to SKOB, a/k/a the Siesta Key Oyster Bar, one of the more popular bars with live music in the heart of the little beach town. He had been there before and knew it was the perfect hunting ground, but that had been few years before. He was amped up and glad he had left Gulfport before he did something reckless with Black Beauty.

He sipped his bourbon, watching a pretty blonde sitting by herself at the inside bar as she drank a draft beer and took a shot of something, maybe tequila. Since her friends had left her there about an hour before, she continued to drink as she chatted with the bartender. He had learned the bartender's name was Cassandra, and she was obviously friends with blondie. He had been watching them from a table in the corner until a seat cleared near her at the bar. He made his way over and sat next to her.

Always watching. Always listening. His favorite pastime. Well, almost his favorite.

Cassandra was very different from the voluptuous blonde, yet very attractive in a less overt way. She had long, straight brown hair with hints of gold on the ends, probably lightened from the sun, a slender frame, and an edgy personality. He could tell she was sharp and acutely aware of everything around her, which he knew would make her more of a challenge. He liked a challenge but also thought better to stick with blondie who had been drinking all night. They both seemed to be locals rather than vacationers.

He wanted to strike up a conversation, try to develop a rapport.

"Can I buy you a beer?" he asked when the blonde finally turned and noticed him sitting next to her, her cheeks rosy from the sun, the heat, or the alcohol, or more likely a combination of all three.

"Um, I'm okay, no thanks," she said, turning her back to him and continuing her conversation with Cassandra.

"Can I get you something?" Cassandra asked him less warmly than she had been earlier in the night. It was obvious she was protective of the blonde.

"I'll take a beer, whatever you have on tap," he said, as he drained the last of his bourbon from his glass.

Cassandra poured his beer and placed it in front him as he handed her a twenty-dollar bill. She left his change in front him before returning her attention to the other patrons, including blondie. He sipped on his beer, pretending to watch the Rays game on the television in the opposite corner of the bar so they didn't notice he was listening to their conversation.

"Are you coming home tonight or staying at Massimo's?" the blonde asked Cassandra.

"I'm staying at Massimo's. We're both off tomorrow so we're going out on his boat early in the morning. If you're not working, wanna come with?"

"Aw, I wish I could, Cass, but I work the lunch shift tomorrow. But let me know if you guys are doing anything tomorrow night. I should be off by six."

"If we catch anything decent, we're going to do a fish-fry at Massimo's, but I'll text you after we get back and let you know for sure."

"Okay, sounds good, here's hoping you catch a lot of fish," the blonde said as she raised her almost empty glass into a toast before drinking the remnants of it. "Since you're not coming home, I'm going to go ahead and head out now, before the streets empty out."

"You good to get home by yourself, Stacey? I could ask one of the bus boys to walk you home, we're not that busy tonight," Cassandra offered.

"Nah, it's okay. There's still a lot of people on Ocean and Morton's is open til eleven, so I'll be fine. What do I owe you?"

"Nah, I got this one. You got me last weekend."

"Thanks, Cass."

"Text me when you get home, Stacey. Don't forget," Cassandra said.

As the women said their goodbyes, the Hunter slipped out of the bar so he could be in his truck before she came out. Based on their conversation, he knew she would be walking down Ocean Boulevard, the main strip of Siesta Key, which was lined with restaurants, boutiques, ice cream shops, and bars, towards Morton's Siesta Market, a gourmet deli and market on the corner of Ocean and Canal Road. He headed to Morton's and parked facing Ocean, knowing she would eventually pass by him.

He watched her from the darkness, knowing from experience that she probably forgot about him as soon as she turned her back to him at the bar. Over the years, he had learned a lot about human nature from the victims he pursued. He had also learned a lot about himself from his interactions with his victims, although he hated to use that word. He preferred to call them game, as if he was a hunter on safari. More exhilarating that way.

The first encounter was often the most exciting: the unknown, the anticipation. He could tell within the first thirty seconds whether his target, his *game*, would be a fighter or a flighter. Cassandra was definitely a fighter, and that thrilled him. Stacey, the blonde roommate, seemed like more of a flighter, especially after a night of drinking. To be fair, he liked both kinds. Sometimes the chase was more exciting than the fight: smelling their fear, their sweat, their urine when they pissed themselves, letting them think they were getting away, but he was always closer than they knew, ready to pounce when he was ready, like a lion.

And he always caught them, if you don't count that one bitch who got away before he had perfected his skills. The one he would forever try to replicate or maybe find again – her dark black hair, ivory skin, green eyes – *you always remembered your first*, he thought. Since then, he had a weakness for brunettes, but it was more about opportunity than hair color when he locked in on potential prey.

He was also quite aware that the wretched cunt in his first foster home after his mother died had dark hair and light skin, what he could remember of her anyway, and that damn red smeared lipstick. He would never forget that or the smell of stale cigarettes and cheap whiskey on her putrid breath. His mother was nothing like her; she was an angel. She was beautiful and kind and everything his foster mother wasn't. He remembered whenever she bent down to kiss his forehead, her long blonde hair would tickle his face, which made him giggle. And then she would laugh with him – that's what he remembered most – her laugh and the sparkle in her blue eyes as she laughed; it was like cotton candy and sunshine all bottled up in one, the epitome of happiness.

And then one day, one horrible day, when he was eight years old, she was taken away from him and he had to go live with the cunt who made it a point to beat him on a regular basis.

The beatings were the least of it, he remembered.

He watched the young woman walk away, slightly unsteadily a few times, from the busy bars on Ocean, pass in front of him on Canal, and turn left on Avenido de Mayo, a quiet street lined with Palm trees and quaint beach cottages. He turned down the same street, a safe distance behind her, and pulled over to the curb to watch her. The farther she got down the street, the darker it got, but he could still see her silhouette against the backdrop of the moonlight.

When she was almost out of his sight, he began to drive again, and followed her home, noting her address as he passed. He hoped, like most residents and vacationers in the area, she wouldn't lock her doors. He didn't know what it was about living or vacationing at the beach that gave people such a false sense of security – like somehow crimes didn't happen when you were on vacation or evil wouldn't visit such beautiful locales. That false sense of security was one of the reasons he chose the charming little beach towns as his hunting grounds, another being the abundance of them up and down the west coast of Florida.

He passed under a streetlight, the yellow glow filling the cab of the truck and illuminating the single word tattooed across his forearm:

RETRIBUTION.

* * *

After an hour, he returned to the little blue house and parked a few houses down in front of a house with a For Sale sign, which appeared to be vacant. He appreciated the quietness and darkness of the neighborhood as he walked towards the house and made his way around back. He tried the back door first: locked. He realized it was one of those doors with the code locks on it, so it probably locked automatically as soon as she entered and closed the door.

He looked around the back of the house and was pleased to see one of the windows was open. He peeked into the window and, with the help of the nightlight plugged into the outlet next to the sink, realized it was a bathroom. He slipped his black gloves on and quietly removed the screen and set it up against the house. He slid the window open as far as it would go and was happy to see it would accommodate him.

He grabbed one of the chairs from the outdoor table and placed it just below the window. He climbed in effortlessly, the only noise the creak from the cheap plastic toilet lid under his weight as he stepped down into the bathroom.

CHAPTER NINE
STACEY

Stacey awoke to a sound coming from outside of her bedroom, or was she just dreaming? Her mouth was bone dry from her night of drinking and probably the salty pretzel bites. She sat up and took a big swig of water from the plastic bottle on her nightstand.

She strained to listen.

She thought she heard footsteps in the hallway, but they were so faint she wasn't sure.

Did Cassandra end up coming home? she wondered.

As she listened, she heard the cicadas buzzing outside and the occasional palm frond sweeping against her window from the breeze that was blowing in from the Gulf. She took another swig of her water, believing she had imagined the noises inside her house, or Cassandra had come home after all. Maybe she and Massimo had gotten into a fight.

Wouldn't be the first time, Stacey thought as she got up to pee.

Stacey got up out of bed and padded out of her bedroom in her tank top and panties. She walked around the small house, checking out the kitchen and living room and confirming both the front and back doors were locked. The only other room in the 872 square foot house, besides the bathroom, was Cassandra's room. She opened the door to Cassandra's bedroom and peeked in. She wasn't home.

She went into the bathroom, pulled her yellow panties down, and sat down on the toilet to pee, confident whatever she heard came from outside or she had imagined it.

She washed her hands and noticed the closed shower curtain for the first time since she went into the bathroom. She dried her hands on a hand towel as she worked up the courage to check behind the curtain.

With one quick swoosh, she flung the curtain open, relieved to find the tub-shower empty. She exhaled the breath she didn't realize she had been holding, admonishing herself for being so ridiculous, and returned to bed.

Just as she was starting to doze off, she heard something again.

But this time she knew she wasn't imagining it.

She heard footsteps on the faux wood floor coming down the hallway until they stopped just outside of her bedroom door.

She sat there frozen, paralyzed with fear, listening.

She heard nothing but the blood from her heart pulsating in her ears.

She picked up her phone from her nightstand, cursing herself for not charging it the night before: 1% battery life left. Her hands were trembling as she dialed 9-1-1.

Stacey heard the dispatcher's voice, "9-1-1, what is your emergency?"

Before she could answer, her phone went completely dead.

And then her bedroom door opened.

CHAPTER TEN
MONICA

Monica went out to her balcony to smoke her last cigarette before bed. She was relieved she hadn't encountered Marlboro Man or any other creeps on her walk home. Gulfport wasn't a dangerous city but was not immune from crime due to its proximity to South St. Petersburg and I-275. Monica had to remind herself of that sometimes, because she felt so comfortable in the eclectic, artsy beach community. She fell in love with it when she went to a friend's art exhibition at a small gallery years ago. She found a small, affordable one-bedroom apartment, a stark contrast from her mother's stately Davis Island waterfront mansion, the home in which she grew up.

Her monthly lunch with her mother was scheduled for the next day. Her father, Tommy Martino, had died years before but had established a trust for her benefit, and named her mother as the trustee. One of the conditions to receive her monthly distribution from the trust was that she had to meet with the trustee to discuss her current living situation and goals, financial needs, and anything else the trustee wanted to ask her about. And so, on the third

Saturday of each month, no matter how much she hated it, Monica met her mother at the Columbia restaurant in Ybor City.

Monica looked up at the stars in the clear sky as she blew smoke out into the night. The air was warm and damp, the humidity a reminder that summer was around the corner. She looked up and down the street, relieved not to see anyone. She was a little edgy from her encounter with Marlboro Man earlier in the night. She had a good instinct about people, and her gut told her that he was evil. She made a mental note to ask Marge about him the next time she was at O'Maddy's. Marge knew everyone in town.

Monica's phone vibrated, indicating she had received a text message. She picked up her phone and read it.

"Counting the days until I see you again"

She didn't recognize the number and assumed it was a wrong number. Normally she would just delete and block it, but for some reason she decided to text back.

"Wrong number lol"

She watched the moving dots indicating they were responding. She was amused until the next text came through.

"Silly Monica, I'll see you soon"

"Who is this?" she typed back.

No more little dots. And her message didn't go through. She unsuccessfully tried to resend it. Whoever had sent her the message seemed to have blocked her.

"What the fuck," Monica said aloud as she stared at her phone, looking up and down the street again.

Between her encounter in the parking lot and the weird text, she was more than anxious. She picked up her pack of smokes and went inside, making sure she locked the sliding glass door and put the security pin in place, which she never did. She confirmed the front door deadbolt was locked before going into her bedroom to check for her gun. She pulled the unlocked case out from under her bed, checked her gun, including the clip, to make sure it was ready to fire.

She placed the loaded gun back in the case and put it within reach on her nightstand before climbing into bed.

If anyone came into her apartment, she would put a bullet between their eyes, she thought as she drifted off to sleep.

CHAPTER ELEVEN
THE HUNTER

The Hunter slammed Stacey's head into the back of the heavy oak headboard, dazing her, before wrapping his strong hands around her delicate neck. He felt the charm from her necklace embed into his meaty hand as he held tightly onto her throat until she went limp in his grasp, and he felt her last breath leave her body. He loosened his grip and looked down to admire what he had done, the only light in the room coming in from the streetlight and moon outside her window.

She turned out to be more of a fighter than he thought she would have been from watching her at the bar, and he realized he may have choked her too long. He picked up the lamp that had crashed off the nightstand, put it upright on the nightstand, and tried the switch. The soft light lit up the small bedroom, which was in a state of disarray from her attempt to defend herself. She was stronger than he had expected.

He moved her lifeless body to the hard tile floor so he could bring her back. He blew in her mouth and nose and administered chest compressions until she coughed and inhaled a deep breath on her own. He continued chest compressions for another minute or two and then checked her pulse. It was weak but it was there. He wasn't ready for her to die yet. He was amped up and wanted her semi-conscious when he raped her. Besides the power over her, it was her fear that would excite him most, and he wanted to savor the moment.

He took a zip tie out of his back pocket and secured her wrists together. He wasn't expecting her to recover enough to fight him again, but fear and adrenaline had a way of motivating a person. She coughed and wheezed and seemed to be regaining consciousness.

He took his treasured steel knife out of its sheath and cut her yellow panties off at the hips and then her tank top. She was barely conscious and too weak to resist. He put his mouth on her left nipple and bit down hard, eliciting a yelp and high-pitched scream from her, as a drop of blood trickled down her colorless breast from his bite. He unzipped his pants and straddled her.

Her tanned skin had turned somewhat ashen after he strangled her but now some of her pinkish tones were returning as her heart attempted to deliver the necessary blood throughout her body.

"Well, hello, sunshine," he whispered, "do you remember me?"

Stacey's eyes opened wide at the sound of his voice, the whites around her pupils bright red from the broken capillaries. He watched as her expression went from confusion to the realization of her situation to absolute fear, almost instantaneously. His already hard dick got harder, and the lubricated condom slid on easily. He placed one hand on her throat in case she tried to fight him again and the other on his dick while he jammed it into her. He covered her mouth to stifle her screams until he finished, getting off on seeing the fear and hemorrhaging in her blood-stained eyes. He was so turned on by the sight, it didn't take long.

After he finished, he got off of her and sat next to her, his back against the wall, feeling her battered body trembling beside him. She was whimpering like a sad puppy, which made him laugh.

"Please, please," she begged through raspy sobs, her throat still damaged from being choked, "please don't kill me. I won't tell anyone about you. I promise."

"Oh Stacey, you're being so sweet now, but that's not how you really are. We both know how rude you were earlier, now don't we?"

"Please, I'll be nice. And I'll never tell. Please let me go," Stacey begged through sobs.

"Hmm, we all make choices. Maybe you should have been a little nicer to me in the bar tonight when I offered to buy you a beer. But you were a cunt just like most women are and so I'm not feeling as generous now as I was earlier. You need to be punished."

"Please," she begged, just as he took his knife out of its sheath and slit her throat with the precision of a Japanese master chef, the blood from her jugular instantly coating everything in its path.

He looked around the room and found her yellow panties as she bled out. The soft cotton had a few droplets that had spread out into a flowerlike pattern when it hit the fabric. He stuffed them in his back pocket, knowing he would cherish them later, and then looked through her dresser until he found a set of lavender babydoll pajamas and a fresh, white pair of panties.

Perfect choice, he thought, *the lavender will complement her blonde locks.*

He folded them with the precision of a seamstress before leaving them at the bottom of the bed, neatly placed on top of each other.

He left the room, carefully avoiding stepping into the pool of blood that had accumulated under Stacey's neck and had spread outward towards the door. The red against the sand-colored tile was like a beautiful mosaic. The last thing he did before leaving the room was to snap a picture, with Stacey sprawled naked in the center, and then moved it into his password and fingerprint protected file on his phone.

He left through the back, self-locking door, and walked casually under the moonlight to his truck parked down the street, his cock still throbbing slightly from the encounter.

CHAPTER TWELVE
CHARLIE

Charlie woke up later than usual on Saturday morning, blaming it on the double shifts he had been working the last few days. He liked making the extra money, but he was also lonely when he was home, so when his manager asked him if he could work, he didn't hesitate. He was hoping he would meet someone at the gym, or maybe at work, but he hadn't. And he hadn't been out with anyone since the pretty blonde he went home with a few weeks before.

"Shit, what was her name?" he asked aloud. "Diane? Dana? No, that's not it," he said, shaking his head.

"Dawn! That was it," he smiled, pleased that he remembered.

He blended his usual pre-gym, protein shake and poured it into a plastic Solo cup to take with him for the three-block walk to the gym. He had a bit of a headache, probably from missing dinner the night before. He couldn't eat bar food on his program, and he forgot to pack his dinner for the double shift. He popped two ibuprofens, hoping the protein shake and medicine would work quickly.

He caught and admired his reflection in the full-length mirror on the back of the front door. He was pleased to see his hard work paying off. He was now up forty pounds since he had first checked into rehab.

He looked at the time on his phone. He was a little later than usual and hoped the gym wouldn't be too crowded when he got there. He grabbed his gym bag, shake, and keys from the counter, and left the apartment, locking the door behind him. Nearby, he heard sirens, which he assumed were either racing to a car accident involving a tourist or to a snowbird who was having a medical incident, neither of which were rare in his neighborhood.

Charlie's apartment was at the end of a short block leading to the beach. The sandy, dead-end street was lined on one side with a few dated cottages, the paint chipping and faded from the elements, and the other side with a few, three-to-four-unit apartment buildings. By the time he reached the bottom of the stairs outside of his efficiency, the sirens had stopped. As Charlie walked towards Gulf Boulevard and the direction of the gym, two police cars turned onto his street and appeared to be heading right towards him. Charlie moved onto the sidewalk to stay out of their way.

The first car pulled abruptly onto the sidewalk in front of Charlie, blocking his path. The officer jumped out of the car, shielding his body with the car door, and pointed his gun directly at Charlie.

"What the fuck," Charlie said, unable to comprehend what was happening.

"Drop the bag and get on your knees, hands over your head," the officer yelled while the second car sped up and stopped just behind Charlie.

Charlie slowly put down his gym bag and protein shake, tipping the thick drink over onto the sidewalk in the process. He dropped down to his knees and reached up to the sky to show his hands were empty, believing this had to be a terrible mistake.

The second officer got out of his car and came up behind Charlie. He aggressively pulled Charlie's hands behind his back and cuffed him, while pulling him up to a standing position.

"What the fuck," Charlie squealed, this time louder and more desperate due to the pain in his arms and wrists inflicted by the officer.

"Charlie Robinson?" the officer asked, not waiting for an answer or confirmation. "You're under arrest for the rape and murder of Dawn Owens. You have the right to remain silent. Anything you say can and will be used against you in a court of law. You have the right to an attorney. If you cannot afford an attorney, one will be provided for you. Do you understand the rights I have just read to you?"

"What the fuck," Charlie said again for the third time in the last minute. "I want to speak to my lawyer, Hallie Miller."

CHAPTER THIRTEEN
MONICA

Monica woke up early the next morning, pleased she didn't have a headache or a stranger next to her in bed. She thought about the creep she encountered in the bar parking lot and the weird text she also received. She checked her phone. She had one new text, which was from her mother telling her not to be late. Monica rolled her eyes as she read the text.

She looked down at what she was wearing: red tank top, black thong, mismatched socks, and chuckled at her go-to bed attire. She put her robe on and padded out to the kitchen. She made a double of her Italian caffe and grabbed her smokes on her way to the balcony. As the hot brew started to work its magic and clear the fog from her brain, she lit a cigarette. The warm air smelled of rain and salt from the nearby Gulf, although there wasn't a cloud in the sky. Someone walking by on the street below was talking on their cell about a storm approaching.

Fucking tourists, what did they know, she cackled as she blew smoke out into the air.

She showered and put on one of her less revealing outfits for her monthly luncheon.

Only the best for Nina Martino, she thought.

Forty-five minutes later, Monica walked into the Columbia restaurant in Ybor through the doors on 7th Avenue at precisely five minutes before noon. Ernesto, her mother's regular server, escorted Monica over to Nina's regular table under the atrium. Nina Martino was an attractive woman with shoulder-length, straight platinum hair, olive skin, high cheekbones, and piercing blue eyes. She was already seated, sipping a martini, as she always was. Monica hoped it was her first.

"Hello, Mother," Monica said as she leaned in to kiss her mother on each cheek, making sure not to tarnish her skin with her whore-red lipstick, as Nina liked to call it.

"Darling, so nice to see you. I was starting to worry you weren't going to make it," Nina responded, clasping her hand for a moment, as Ernesto pulled out Monica's chair.

Monica ignored her mother's comment, even though she was on time, and she knew the show of motherly affection was mostly for his benefit, although she did seem in better spirits than other days.

"Thank you, Ernesto," Monica said, smiling at the jockey-sized Colombian waiter.

"Sangria today, Miss Monica, or something else?"

"Um, no, I think I'll have a Bloody Mary today. Double Tito's, thank you," Monica replied while looking down, adjusting her napkin and refusing to look at Nina to avoid her hypocritical judgmental gaze.

"Hmmm, a little of the hair of the dog, is it," Nina said more as a statement than a question.

"No, Mother, I just like Bloody Mary's. Do you have to start on me right when I get here?"

"Start what? Oh my God, stop being so dramatic and defensive, Monica. Speaking of drama, Nicolas got us tickets to Moulin Rouge at the Straz when it opens next year. I'll send you the dates. Tom is coming up from Miami to join us. Make sure you thank your uncle next time you're at the house."

"Don't you think it's strange Uncle Nicolas never got married and he's always at the house, at your beck and call like a sad puppy?" Monica goaded, knowing it would irritate her mother.

"I told you, the Italians are very loyal people, and your uncle made a promise to your father that he would always look after us and take care of me, take care of us. Is it so wrong that he kept his word? Honestly, Monica, you could learn a thing or two about loyalty from your uncle," Nina said, picking up her martini and draining the rest of the glass.

Monica rolled her eyes for the second time since she arrived and was going to respond just as Ernesto returned with her Bloody Mary.

"Do we know what we're having today ladies?" Ernesto asked.

"I'll have my usual, Ernesto. And another martini, please," Nina said, holding her empty glass up in the air for emphasis.

"Very good, Mrs. Martino, the 1905 Salad to start and the Ropa Vieja for your entrée. Miss Monica, how about you?"

"I'll have a cup of the Spanish Bean soup to start and then the Picadillo."

"Excellent. I'll get your orders right in and return with your drink, Mrs. Martino," Ernesto said as he scurried away from the table.

"So," Nina began, "I have some news I think you need to know about."

"What is it? Is it about Pietro?" Monica asked, her blood pressure spiking in a way only her mother could trigger, especially if it was news about her son.

"No, no, nothing about Pietro. I haven't heard from him. This is something else. Christian Kane has been pardoned and released from prison. I thought you should know."

Monica forced herself to swallow the gulp of Bloody Mary that was in her mouth instead of spitting it out all over her mother, which would have been a more natural reaction to what she had just heard. She took a deep breath and tried to process the news. She wanted to throw up.

When she could finally speak, all she could ask was "when?"

"Two months ago. I just learned of it. Nicolas is keeping tabs on him, so you don't need to worry. If he comes to Tampa, we'll know about it. He hasn't contacted you, has he?"

"No," Monica said, recalling the text from the unknown number the night before.

Ernesto brought their starters, and they didn't speak of CK again. Nina droned on about her issues with one of her new neighbors and other things that annoyed her, but Monica was numb, only pretending to listen. Ernesto put her entrée down in front of her and she almost wretched. She wanted to run out of the restaurant, but she knew she couldn't. For the next forty-seven minutes, she tried to listen to Nina and respond or nod when appropriate, but she was on autopilot. She couldn't wait to get out of there to deal with the bomb Nina had just dropped on her.

"You barely touched your picadillo, Moni," Nina said, using her childhood nickname used by her father. "You're not starving yourself again, are you?"

"No, Mother," Monica managed to answer, "I'm just not hungry right now. I'll take it for dinner."

"I hope it's not because of the Christian Kane news. That's water under the bridge. I'm sure he's just happy to be out of prison and hasn't given you another thought."

"I don't want to talk about this. Please, let's just finish our lunch," Monica pleaded, poking her picadillo with her fork to appease her mother while draining her Bloody Mary, the heat from the pepper at the bottom of the glass burning as it went down her throat.

"Of course, I'm just saying, it's nothing you need to worry about."

"I got it, Mother. I understand," Monica interrupted. "Let's talk about something else. Have you heard from Tom? When is he coming up, besides for Moulin Rouge?" Monica managed to ask, trying to direct the conversation away from Christian Kane, the only man she ever loved, the father of her only child, and the man she was responsible for sending away to prison.

* * *

Monica made it through the rest of lunch without further incident, said goodbye to her mother, assuring her she would come to Sunday dinner one day soon, and headed back to Gulfport. But she was anxious and uneasy and didn't want to go home alone to her apartment. She headed straight to O'Maddy's to try to distract herself from her thoughts of Christian.

The news that Christian had been released from prison had hit her harder and in ways she didn't expect. She felt a combination of excitement, dread, guilt, and panic, and her stomach rolled every time she thought of him. She had loved him so much when she was younger, but she never thought she would see him again. He had loved her too, she knew that. But that was a long time ago, and she was responsible for sending him to prison – maybe not directly, but responsible, nevertheless. He could not love her anymore.

When her father found out she was pregnant, and that Christian was the father, he became enraged and forbade her from seeing him again. Christian was ten years older than her, and her father believed he took advantage of his teenage daughter, which was not true. If anything, she had taken advantage of him. She begged her father to let her be with Christian, tried to convince him that he was a good man, but it was no use.

She had tried to warn Christian about her father's anger and to tell him that she was pregnant, but her mother intercepted her messages. Then her parents threatened to cut her off and not help her with the baby if she tried to contact Christian again. Before she could tell him, he was arrested and charged with felony murder for a deal that went south at the Port. Monica later learned her father set him up. By the time she had the baby, she realized that he wasn't going to get out of prison, so she stayed away and moved on with her life.

She had often wondered over the years if that had been the right decision.

And now he was out.

Had he texted her the night before? she wondered.

If he didn't hate her for getting him sent to prison, as soon as he found out that he had a son that she had kept from him, he surely would then. Maybe he already knew.

And for the first time in a long time, Monica was afraid.

CHAPTER FOURTEEN
HALLIE

Hallie made it to her workout right on time Saturday morning. Jason had her doing multiple reps of squats, hinges, and lunges, with varying degrees of weight. She joked that he was punishing her for missing her workout during the week, even though she knew that wasn't true. Her legs were sore from her run the night before and the workout was tough, but she finished it just before 8 a.m., and she noticed she was starting to regain some of her strength that she had lost during her three-month recovery hiatus.

"Great job, today, Hallie. You really pushed it, and I'm proud of you."

"Thanks, Jason. But I felt like you were trying to kill me today," Hallie laughed.

"Never. I knew you could handle it. Strong people problems, remember?"

"Yeah, yeah, strong people problems," Hallie smiled. "Tuesday, regular time?"

"Works for me. Seriously, good job today, Hallie," Jason said to her as she headed out of the gym.

* * *

Hallie showered and dressed and did a few chores around the house before it was time to meet Paige for a late lunch in Hyde Park. They normally met during the week for happy hour, but they had to reschedule to Saturday brunch due to both of their hectic schedules that week. Besides her childhood friend, Bridget, Paige had become one of her closest friends.

Hallie arrived at the restaurant before Paige, a rarity, right at noon, and was seated at a table outside. It was warm, but it was shaded, and they had the fans on. Hallie liked being outside.

"I see you're waiting for one more. Can I get you anything while you wait?" Fabian, the dark-haired waiter who looked like a young Nick Jonas, asked.

"Yes, I would love a glass of the Tua Rita," Hallie answered. "And a water with lemon, please."

Although she preferred Cabernet, the Tua Rita Italian red blend was what she ordered whenever she was at Forbici, one of her favorite restaurants in Hyde Park.

As she waited for Paige to arrive, she opened her phone, automatically scrolling through Facebook and Instagram.

Hallie's phone vibrated in her hand, alerting her that she had an incoming call. She didn't recognize the number. She sent the call to voicemail just as Paige walked up.

"Hey, Hal, sorry I'm late; I hope you haven't been waiting too long," Paige said, as she sat down, dropping her purse onto the empty seat between them.

"Not at all, and besides, I'm the one who's usually late," Hallie responded, putting her phone face down on the table so she wasn't distracted with incoming notifications.

Fabian came over with Hallie's wine and placed it down in front of her.

Without hesitating or waiting for Fabian to ask her, Paige blurted out, "I'll have a dirty martini, Tito's, straight up, light on the dirty. Actually, make it a double."

"That bad?" Hallie asked, laughing.

"You have no idea. Oh my God, this case I have is going to be the death of me," her friend responded.

"What kind of case is it?"

Paige swept her long, dark hair off her face, and twirled it to one side, which highlighted her high cheekbones, bronze flawless skin, and amber eyes. Paige was stunning. She had even enjoyed a brief stint as a model to put herself through law school. She always joked she chose becoming a lawyer over modeling because she didn't want to starve herself for the rest of her career and she liked Italian food too much. She was even more attractive now, in Hallie's opinion, but more importantly, she was a brilliant and fierce litigator.

Fabian came back and placed a large dirty martini in front of Paige.

"Good man," she said, lifting the cocktail up to her brick-red-painted lips.

"Anything to eat, ladies?" he asked.

"We're going to work on these for a bit, and then we'll let you know," Hallie answered pointing to their drinks. "But since she has a double, go ahead and bring me another Tua Rita when you get a chance, please," she said, smiling.

Fabian left and the two friends lifted their drinks while saying "cheers" simultaneously.

"So, tell me about this case that has you uncharacteristically stressed," Hallie said.

Paige brought the martini to her lips, rolling the liquor around on her tongue before answering.

"Ahh, that's good," she sighed, as she placed the glass down in front of her. "It's a family law case," Paige started, as she rolled her eyes.

"What? Why are you working on a family law case? I'm pretty sure that's the definition of malpractice," Hallie laughed.

"I know, I know," Paige said, holding her hands up, "but the daughter of one of my longtime and best clients, a commercial real estate developer, is getting divorced and it's a shitshow, child custody issues, marital affairs, hidden assets, abuse allegations, you name it."

"Oh, is this your client from New Orleans who is developing all that waterfront property near the Port here in Tampa?"

"Yup, that's her, Jodi Trosclair Scott. I handle all of her litigation in Florida, and I review every real estate contract prepared by her business attorneys from a litigation perspective before she'll sign off on it. She's smart and knows more about development and the commercial real estate market than most, but she wants what she wants when she wants it. She's a great client but a very tough woman to say no to. I'm sure it's what makes her so successful."

"I get that, but you don't do family law," Hallie said, stating the obvious.

Paige laughed, "um, I know that, Hallie. I told her I don't do family law. I referred her to Kim Maxwell who is handling the divorce, but Jodi insisted that I work with Kim, as co-counsel, because, in her words, 'I don't trust any damn attorney, 'cept you,'" Paige said, attempting her best Cajun accent.

"Oh, that sounds awful. I could not do family law, too emotional for me," Hallie said. "But Kim is the best, so I'm sure the daughter is in good hands. But why does the case have you so stressed if Kim is doing the heavy lifting?"

"Because opposing counsel has subpoenaed all of Jodi's companies' records, demanding copies of tax returns, bank statements, financial statements, you name it – did I mention her daughter is on the payroll? Anyway, Kim knows family law, but I know Jodi's businesses, and she is relying on me to protect her confidential business information and keep it out of the deadbeat husband's hands. Opposing counsel is a dimwit tool, hired by the soon-to-be-ex-husband's father, who, by the way, is allegedly 'connected,' if you know what I mean."

"Oh shit, who's representing the husband?"

"Stewart Alley, some jackass out of South Florida. Not only is he unethical but he's stupid, and he has some underling associate, Mitch Zaro, who is equally stupid and even more unethical than his boss, filing motions to compel and serving subpoenas on nonparties, which according to Kim are completely improper at this stage of the case. We're getting ready to file a 57.105 motion against them and maybe even a bar complaint. I've never seen such unethical and incompetent behavior from another lawyer."

"Oh wow, this case does sound like a shit show," Hallie laughed.

"You know it; I specialize in shit shows. If I didn't like and respect Jodi so much, I honestly would have declined this case. But she always pays her bills, which are going to be hefty on this one due to the other side's antics, and I admire her."

Hallie's phone vibrated again. Hallie glanced at her phone and noticed it was from the same number as earlier.

"It's either my car warranty expiring or some other rando who I don't want to talk to," Hallie smiled as she declined the call and slipped the phone into her purse.

"I don't want to talk to anyone anymore," Paige concurred.

"Ain't that the truth? Why is this job so soul-crushing?" Hallie asked jokingly, knowing Paige would understand how close her statement was to the truth on some days.

"Girl, we don't have that kind of time or enough drinks to delve into that subject today," Paige responded, both ladies chuckling and raising their glasses in unison.

"Well, okay, here's to the good clients who can afford us at least."

Paige smiled and they clinked glasses, smiling at their shared understanding of the attorney-client dynamic and the love it-hate it aspect of their career choice.

Over the next two hours, the friends caught up on each other's lives. Hallie told Paige all about her mother's upcoming wedding to Ross and her mother's insistence that Paige and Mike attend, which Paige knew she could not decline and assured Hallie they would be there. Paige told Hallie about her husband, Mike Freeman, leaving the State Attorney's office to open his own criminal defense firm.

"Wow, Mike left the State? Now I understand why I haven't run into him at the courthouse lately. I never thought Mike would switch from prosecutor to defense," Hallie said.

"He's adjusting, with my help getting his office set up, of course. Honestly, the man might be brilliant but he's a disorganized mess," Paige laughed. "But I do think he'll be happier in the long run, taking the cases he wants rather than having to prosecute the vilest of criminal cases. He can make a nice living defending non-violent crimes and anything where children aren't involved. Those cases always weighed on him the most."

"I can only imagine. I'm glad he made the move, if that's what will make him happier. Who's taking his place as Assistant D.A.?"

"Amy Stoll. After what she did in the Stephens' trial, she was the obvious choice. She's an awesome trial attorney and prosecutor."

"Yes, she absolutely is," Hallie agreed. "So, I guess it's safe to say she's not coming back to our firm," Hallie laughed.

"No, she's not. This really is her calling, and I think one day she'll run for State Attorney."

The two friends spent the rest of the afternoon eating pizza, catching up, laughing, and venting about various cases, clients, and family. It was a perfect way to end their horrific week and start their weekend. It was exactly what Hallie needed.

*　*　*

After lunch, Hallie drove the two miles to her house feeling good. She had barely gotten in the door when her phone started vibrating in her purse. As she let Juno out front, she pulled out her phone to see who was calling. It was from the same unknown number as the call she received earlier at the restaurant. She let it go to voicemail, but a minute later, the person called again.

"Hmmm, persistent," Hallie said as she declined that call as well, and Juno bounded up the steps and back into the house.

When her phone rang a third time from the same unknown number, she got nervous thinking that something could have happened to her daughter or her mother, so she answered it.

"Hello?"

"Hallie, please don't hang up. It's me, Charlie. I need your help."

Hallie was caught off guard. She hadn't spoken to her brother in over a year.

"Hallie, are you there?"

"Charlie, I have nothing to say to you. I'm certainly not going to help you, after what you did to mom, to all of us," Hallie said, surprised at the anger that instantly rose up within her.

"Hallie, please, I don't know who else to call. I've been arrested."

"Shocking," Hallie said, rolling her eyes. "You know I'm not a criminal defense attorney, Charlie, and even if I was," she started to say before her younger brother interrupted her.

"I've been charged with murder, Hallie."

"What? Murder? Jesus, Charlie, what have you done now?" Hallie asked, trying to process not only what he said but the fact that this was the first time she was speaking to her little brother since she kicked him out of her mother's house.

"Nothing, I swear. Please just help me, Hallie. I don't know who else to turn to."

"Where are they holding you?" Hallie asked, still unsure why she hadn't hung up on him already.

"Pinellas County."

"Okay, Charlie, tell me what happened."

"All I know is that these fucking cops pulled up outside my place and accosted me on my way to the gym, threw me on the ground, handcuffed me, and arrested me for murder."

"Who are you accused of murdering?"

"Um, a girl," Charlie hesitated.

"What girl, Charlie, and how did you know her? I'm assuming this is an overdose, right?"

"It's not like that, Hallie. I'm clean. I've been clean for two years. She was a girl I met at the bar I work at."

"So not an overdose? How did she die, Charlie?" Hallie asked.

"I don't know, but I think someone hurt her. I swear it wasn't me. You know me, Hallie, you know I could never do anything like that," Charlie pleaded.

Neither one of them spoke for the next thirty seconds.

Charlie broke the silence, "Hallie, are you still there?"

"Yeah, I'm here."

"Please help me. I don't know what to do. I know I hurt you and mom, and Trish, too. I'll regret that for the rest of my life, but you know I could never kill anyone. Please, Hal."

"Why do the police think that you killed her?"

"I met her at the bar where I work a few weeks ago. We went back to her place at the end of my shift, had a few beers, hung out, and, well, um, I left there a little while later. One of the officers told me she was found dead the next morning, and they believe I was the last person who was with her. I swear I didn't hurt her, Hal, you know I would never."

"I don't know what I know anymore," Hallie said, trying to make sense of everything Charlie had told her. "Are you sure you weren't high?"

"I promise. I'm clean," Charlie said, the shame evident in his voice. "She was attacked in her AirBnB at the beach. A few blocks from where I live."

Hallie suddenly realized Charlie could be talking about the young woman who had been beaten and strangled to death in Treasure Island.

"Oh my God, Charlie, was this on Treasure Island?"

"Yeah, that's where I live now," Charlie answered solemnly. "Dawn. Her name was Dawn," Charlie said, the irony not lost on him how he couldn't remember her name when she was alive but now, he would never forget it, probably for the rest of his life.

"Oh, Charlie, I read about her murder. It sounded brutal," Hallie said, unable to comprehend that her brother could commit such violence.

"I swear I didn't do it, Hal, please help me," he pleaded again.

Hallie was silent. In her heart, she knew her brother could not have murdered anyone, high or not.

"Hallie, will you help me? I don't know what to do."

"Give me a second, I'm thinking," Hallie said, her mind racing, before finally saying, "okay, I'll make a few calls tomorrow, Charlie. I can't promise anything, but I'll try. I can't promise anything," Hallie repeated.

"I understand. Thank you, sis. I've missed you," Charlie said.

Hallie ended the call without saying another word, a sadness enveloping her. And then all she could think about was how she was going to tell her mother.

CHAPTER FIFTEEN
HALLIE

Hallie spent a restless night, tossing and turning and having nightmares about Charlie and the young girl who was murdered. When her cellphone rang early the next morning, she knew it was going to be her mother. Her mother had a sixth sense that made it impossible for Hallie to hide anything from her.

"Hello?" she answered groggily.

"Good morning, Hallie, did I wake you?"

"Um, no, not really, but I'm not out of bed yet. What's up?"

"Well, that's what I wanted to ask you. I spoke to Trish this morning and she sounded funny. She said she was just tired, but I think she's hiding something. You sound funny too."

"You do realize it's not even 8 a.m., Mom, of course, we sound funny," Hallie countered, admitting to herself that she was stalling.

"You're right, maybe I'm wrong," Becky said, and then went silent as she waited for Hallie to speak.

Hallie knew Charlie and Trish had been talking for the last year, although she only learned about that recently from her sister. Trish, the middle child, had always been closer to their baby brother than she had, and was more forgiving than she was. Trish tried to tell Hallie Charlie was clean, but she wouldn't even discuss it with her, having been down that road so many times before. Trish obviously knew about Charlie's arrest, probably before Hallie did, but she didn't have the heart to tell her mother. Hallie knew she had to tell her. It was just a matter of time before it made the papers, and she would hate for her mother to find out by someone other than her or Trish.

Hallie exhaled, and said, "it's Charlie, Mom, he's been arrested. For murder."

There, Hallie said it, quickly, abruptly, ripped the band-aid off. At least he wasn't dead, and maybe he *was* clean, although Hallie didn't know if she could believe that even if he did sound more coherent and credible than he had in years.

Becky gasped, "Oh my God, no, Hallie, no, there has to be a mistake."

"I agree, Mom, I mean, Charlie is a lot of things, but he's no murderer."

"I knew Trish was hiding something. I just knew it. You both were. When were you going to tell me?" Becky asked angrily.

"Mom, I just found out last night when Charlie called me. I don't even know if Trish knows."

"Of course she does," Becky snapped. "Where is he? Is he okay? Is this drug-related or a DUI? Oh my God, he must have gotten in an accident, and someone died."

"I don't know the details yet, but Charlie says he's been clean for two years. We've heard that before, of course, but he did sound more coherent and more, um, I don't know, clearer, more like the old Charlie, than he has in years," Hallie said, amazed that she was defending him. "I'm sure it has to be a mistake."

"Of course, you're right, it has to be a mistake. Where is he?"

"Pinellas County."

"Can we get him out? Can we see him? Can you defend him?"

"Mom, slow down, please. No, I can't defend him. Even if I wanted to, I'm not a criminal defense lawyer. That would be the worst thing we could do for Charlie. He needs an experienced criminal defense lawyer."

"Oh, right, I don't know what I was thinking. I'm just frazzled. What are we going to do?"

"I'm calling Mike Freeman after I hang up with you. You know Mike, Paige's husband?"

"Isn't he a prosecutor? Can he do something to help Charlie?"

"Well, he used to be. He just opened his own criminal defense firm."

"But how will he be able to help him? He doesn't have any experience defending people wrongfully accused, just putting them away," Becky said, the concern evident in her voice.

"Actually, Mom, he has the best kind of experience. He knows the ins and outs of the prosecutor's office and how to beat them. He's our best chance of helping Charlie."

"Okay, well then, good. Tell Mike that we're thankful for his help."

Her mother stated it as if Mike had been asked to help them and had already agreed to represent Charlie.

"Mom, I haven't even spoken to him yet. I mean, I think Mike will take the case, but I need to ask him first. And we need to see what his retainer and fees will be. This is serious. Before we go spending our life's savings, let's not forget what he did to us . . . to you," Hallie said, regretting the words as soon as they left her mouth.

Becky was silent for a minute, and then said, "your father's death was hard on him. He was just a boy, and I wasn't there for him. I will regret that for the rest of my life."

"You can't blame yourself for Charlie's problems, Mom. We were all grieving."

"But I was his mother. And I wasn't there for him when his father died. And I have to live with that. What wouldn't you do for Katie?"

Hallie couldn't answer that. There wasn't anything she wouldn't do for Katie.

"Exactly. He's my son. And he's your brother, Hallie. And he needs us. He needs you. We need you. Please help him."

And with that, her mother disconnected.

Hallie had a pit in her stomach and felt horrible about Charlie and what his life had been like since their father's death. She also felt guilty about burdening her mother with the news of his arrest even though she knew she had to tell her. She prayed Charlie was clean this time.

Hallie pulled up Mike Freeman's cell phone number in her contacts and called him. As she expected, it went right to voicemail.

"Hey, Mike, it's Hallie. When you get a minute, can you call me back please? It's about my brother, Charlie. Um, well, he's been arrested. So, please call me back when you can, and I'm sorry to bother you on a Sunday."

Hallie got out of bed, washed her face and brushed her teeth. She put her robe on and went downstairs to make coffee and let Juno out.

Just as she finished making her coffee, her cell phone rang. "Hello?"

"Hi, Hallie, it's Mike."

"Hi Mike, I'm sorry for calling you on a Sunday. Thank you for calling me back so quickly."

"So, what's going on, Hallie? Charlie's been arrested? Another drug offense?" Mike asked, familiar with Hallie's family and Charlie's past.

"No, I wish that was it. Hmm, I never thought I'd say those words," Hallie said, the irony not lost on her. "Anyway, did you hear about the murder of the young tourist in Treasure Island? Beaten and strangled, I think. Well, they've charged Charlie with her murder."

"Oh, Hallie, I'm so sorry. Have you talked to him?"

"Yeah, and he swears he didn't do it. Honestly, there's no way – it's just not Charlie. He's never been violent . . ." Hallie trailed off; the words too surreal to finish as she realized she sounded like every other naïve family member defending their loved one of some horrible crime they had allegedly committed. "But unfortunately, he did know her and was with her at her AirBnB the night she was killed."

"Well, that's not good. Where is he being held? Has he had his first appearance yet?"

"Pinellas County. No, not yet. I think it will be today or tomorrow at the latest. He's been in custody for less than twenty-four hours, so I think it has to be scheduled later today or first thing tomorrow morning, if my memory of criminal procedure is right."

"Yes, you're right."

"Can you help him?"

"Of course, Hallie. First, you're my wife's best friend, which means you're like family. She would never forgive me if I didn't help you. Second, I just started my new criminal defense firm, so I need clients," Mike chuckled.

"Thank you, Mike. As you know, I'm not a criminal defense lawyer or even a litigator, but I will help in whatever way I can. And, of course, we'll pay your fees. I just need someone who I can trust."

"No, thank *you*, Hallie. I appreciate your confidence in me. Let me make a few calls to see what I can find out about his first appearance, and I'll file a notice of appearance first thing tomorrow morning. In the meantime, do you know a bail bonds company, or do you need me to recommend someone?"

"Actually, I know Steve Bazarte pretty well. I'll call him when we hang up to see if he can help us in Pinellas, assuming the judge sets bail."

"Great, that will expedite things. I'll send you an engagement letter that outlines my fees to represent Charlie, and if he calls you, let him know you've retained me to represent him. I assume he won't object to that, right?"

"No, definitely not. I really appreciate it, Mike. Thank you."

"I'm sorry you're having to deal with more stress in your life, Hallie. I feel like you deserve a break after the last few years."

"Right? I feel the same way," Hallie laughed lightly. "By the way, how are the new digs? Are you up and running yet?"

"Finally getting settled in. Thank God for Paige, she's been a huge help on the weekends. If not for her, my office would still be filled with boxes, and I wouldn't be able to find my stapler. When I was with the D.A.'s office, there was always someone to call to take care of these things. But yes, slowly but surely, up and running," Mike said.

"The transition is the worst of it, Mike, but once word gets out that you've opened your own firm, you'll be inundated with cases. And then you can hire people to take care of all these things."

"Yeah, looking forward to that day," Mike responded. "Being in private practice has been overwhelming, to be honest, but I just hired an IT person and a good paralegal, so I think I'll be in good shape in no time."

"You will be, I'm sure," Hallie said. "But in the meantime, if I can help in any way, please let me know."

"I might take you up on that. Are you coming over this week? Paige mentioned something about Cubans from Bodega on Thursday night. Man, those are seriously the best Cubans ever."

"That was the plan, but I'll confirm with Paige during the week. Mike, seriously, thank you again for helping with Charlie; it means a lot to me and my family."

"Of course, Hallie, I'll do whatever I can to help, Charlie. I'll be in touch soon."

Hallie was relieved. Mike Freeman had been one of the best prosecutors in the State Attorney's office for years. He was an aggressive litigator but ethical beyond reproach, so he had earned the respect of his colleagues as well as opposing counsel and the judges.

Hallie called her mother and then her sister, Trish, to let them know Mike was going to defend Charlie. And then she called Marcelo to tell him about Charlie.

"Good morning, babe," Marcelo answered, sounding cheerful.

"Good morning, Marcelo."

"What's wrong? I can hear it in your voice," Marcelo said.

"Remember that murder that happened in Treasure Island?"

"Yeah, of course I do, what's going on?"

"Well, it's my brother, Charlie. He's been arrested for it."

"What? What are you talking about?"

"Charlie has been arrested for her murder. He was with her that night, went back to her AirBnB."

"Oh shit, I'm so sorry, Hallie. What can I do to help?"

"Nothing yet, I guess. I retained Mike Freeman this morning, so he's in good hands. I know people always say this, but I know Charlie is no murderer. Drug addict? Yes, absolutely. Thief? Definitely. He stole from his own mother to support his habit. But murderer? No, it's just not possible."

"I'm sorry, babe, I wish there was something I could do or say to make this easier on you."

"Thanks, but I know it's going to be okay because he's innocent. I'll do whatever I have to do to prove it."

"I have no doubt. Your brother is lucky to have you having his back. Do you want to grab a late lunch or dinner later? Or I can bring over a pizza and a bottle of wine?"

"Actually, a pizza and a bottle of wine sounds perfect."

"Great, I'll be there about 4, if that works for you."

"Perfect. Thanks, Marcelo, I can't wait to see you."

"Me too," Marcelo said before they hung up.

She appreciated how caring and supportive he was on their call and was looking forward to seeing him later. Any misgivings or questions Hallie had been feeling recently about their relationship went away.

Maybe they just needed to spend more time together, Hallie thought. *Tonight would be a good start.*

CHAPTER SIXTEEN
LINDA

Linda sat down at the steel desk bolted to the floor and logged onto her desktop computer at precisely 8:00 a.m. Monday morning, punching her virtual timecard.

She was never late.

It had been three months since she started her job as the accounts payable clerk in the administrative department of the Union Correctional Institution, formerly known as Florida State Prison. Union housed male prisoners convicted of murder, rape, and other violent crimes, and was also home to death row inmates, including some of most notorious serial killers in history, such as Ted Bundy, Danny Rollins, Oscar Ray Bolin, and Oba Chandler, all of whom had been executed by the State of Florida. It was now home to one William Stephens, her Billy, who definitely did not belong there.

All requests, orders, and invoices for anything to be purchased for the prison went through Linda's department. She would input the orders and invoices into the computer after they had been approved by her supervisor, Karl Walter. Karl was about fifty years old, had a full head of salt and pepper hair, which he kept short and spiked on top when it wasn't hidden under his Florida Dept. of Corrections baseball cap, and had an old scar that ran the length of his face, starting at the corner of his right eye down to his chin. His close-trimmed beard was more salt than pepper, but it made him look distinguished and hid the severity of the scar. His most recent tattoo, an addition of an eagle's face and crest next to the American flag emblazoned on his strong forearm, was kind of sexy, if Linda was being honest.

But she was devoted to Billy. If she wasn't, she might have been attracted to her boss, the thought of which evoked an unexpected giggle, which she quickly squelched, and caused her face to blush.

Karl stepped out of his office and walked over to the coffee pot to refill his cup. Karl drank a lot of coffee, Linda had noticed. She would have been bouncing off the walls if she drank more than one cup a day. By her calculations, he drank at least five a day.

As Karl stirred his powdered creamer and habitual three sugars into his coffee, he said without turning around to look at her, "Linda, I'm going to need you to head over to the library. The order request is in your daily folder."

When one of the other departments submitted an unusual request, sometimes Karl would send her to get additional backup before he would approve the request. Although she wasn't allowed into the locked-down sections of the prison where the inmates resided, to get to the other buildings she had to walk past the "yard," as they called it. The yard was an outdoor recreation area for the general population inmates, which was enclosed by a thirty-foot, steel fence finished on top with razor-sharp barbed wire, and an armed guard monitoring the activity below from the tower above. At any time of day, there could be thirty to fifty inmates lifting weights, playing basketball, or hanging out in the yard. There was the occasional fight but most of the inmates cherished their time outside and didn't want to risk being sent back to their cell or worse, solitary confinement.

There was a sidewalk that ran adjacent to the yard from the administration building and then jutted out in various directions to the other areas of the prison, including the employee cafeteria, the library, the post office, and the prisoner cell blocks. Linda could only get into certain buildings with her limited access credentials, unlike the guards or her boss, Karl. She could not get into any building or section of the prison where maximum security prisoners might be, which included the library during certain hours.

Her only chance of seeing Billy was if he happened to be out in the yard when she was on one of her errands that took her past the yard. She picked up her daily task folder, which contained the order Karl had assigned to her. Inside she found an unapproved order request from the education/library department with a sticky note from Karl that said, *get backup from Scotty.*

This meant she had to walk past the yard, and her heart fluttered at the realization. Every pass by the yard gave her an opportunity to see Billy.

The sweat started to gather at the nape of her neck and bead on her brow and upper lip. Linda often sweated when she got nervous or excited, like the time she thought that Jordan Jenkins was going to ask her to prom. But then he didn't. She always wondered if it was because he saw the sweat stains bleeding through on the pits of her white Duran Duran T-shirt the day he came up to her in Trigonometry class. He meekly asked her for a copy of her notes from the day before and then walked back to his desk. She guessed he changed his mind.

She was excited at the prospect of seeing Billy, just as she was every time she had to walk past the yard. She feared her mascara was going to start to bleed onto her cheeks. Linda had no problem spending her money on nice dresses or fancy treats for Carole, but she drew the line at mascara. Those expensive brands were no better than the pink and green tube she bought at the drugstore.

She looked across her desk and found her counterpart staring at her.

"I'm sorry, Martha, did you say something?" Linda asked, hoping her question would embarrass her co-worker for staring at her.

"Why are you sweating like that?" Martha asked judgmentally.

"Uh, I don't know, Martha, maybe because we live in Florida and it's a hundred and fifty degrees outside," Linda responded while rolling her eyes and shuffling the papers in front of her on her desk.

"But we're inside in the AC."

"Yeah, but I just came in a little while ago. It takes me a minute to cool down, as if it's any of your business," Linda replied, hoping Martha would turn back to her work and leave her alone.

"What-ev, I guess," Martha replied and appeared to go back to whatever she had been working on before.

The exchange with Martha had distracted Linda from thinking about Billy, her excitement replaced by annoyance, which helped reduce her perspiration. She wiped the back of her neck and dabbed at the sweat on her face with her handkerchief, trying hard not to mess up her makeup.

Once she composed herself, she headed out the door of the administration office, happy to take a break from buttinsky-Martha.

She walked along the sidewalk towards the library. Scotty was usually the only librarian on duty during the day when the non-violent, non-maximum-security prisoners had access. There were also at least two armed guards on duty as well, and only a certain number of prisoners were allowed in the library at a time. Linda had been to the library and had met Scotty many times before, but she had not seen Billy on any of those excursions.

The sidewalk was at least twenty-five feet away from the fence enclosing the yard. Linda was safe walking past it as long as she stayed on the sidewalk, which she had strict orders to do, but it didn't stop the prisoners from whistling and catcalling to her as she walked by. She pretended not to notice, but she couldn't help smiling and blushing at the attention.

The yard was full but not so full that she couldn't make out the faces of the prisoners. She scanned them behind her Jackie-O sunglasses as she had done all the times before since she had started her job at the prison.

But today, *there he was*!

He was sitting alone at a metal picnic table, which was bolted to a concrete slab in the middle of the yard, just on the other side of the thirty-foot fence.

She slowed down her pace in contrast to her racing heart. She was glad she had taken the time that morning to wash and blow dry her hair. Based on the whooping and whistles from the other inmates, she knew she looked pretty good. She casually removed her sunglasses and slipped them into the breast pocket of her crisp uniform shirt.

As she reached the place on her walk that put her in his field of vision, she looked over at him and smiled, slightly lifting her hand in a furtive wave, which was hopefully only noticeable to him and not to the guards in the yard or the tower.

She had been warned more than once not to interact with the prisoners.

"*Linda Mary Baker Morgan, calm yourself,*" she whispered to herself as her heart went *thump, thump, thump* inside her ample chest. She was sure Billy could hear it across the thirty yards that separated them.

Billy looked at her and she almost fainted, having waited for this day for over three months. And there it was, a flicker in his blue eyes, but she saw it: he recognized her. Elated, her pink cheeks flushed with heat, and she picked up her pace to the library, hoping she would make it back in time to see him again before they rotated the inmates in the yard.

It took longer than Linda had hoped to get Scotty's signature and back up paperwork. He was unusually chatty, which annoyed her, but her southern manners required her to be pleasant.

"How you doin' today, Ms. Morgan?"

"Just fine, Scotty. And I've told you, please, call me Linda. We're co-workers, aren't we?"

"Yes, ma'am, we are. It's always such a pleasure seeing you. Has anyone ever told you what a pretty smile you have?"

Linda blushed, "um, thank you, Scotty, but we need to keep it professional, ya know?"

"Oh, I don't mean no harm, Ms. Linda, it's just being cooped up in this library every day, it's nice when a ray of sunshine like you walks in."

Linda was starting to feel uncomfortable from Scotty's compliments and the way he was looking at her. She made a mental note to ask Karl about him.

"Well, you have a good day, Scotty. I have to get back to my post," Linda said as she turned and quickly left the library before Scotty could say anything else.

By the time she got outside, she had started sweating again, and it wasn't just from the heat. She headed back towards the administrative building, and as she turned the corner where the yard came into full view, she could see that Billy was still there. This time, though, he was standing closer to the edge of the fence, precisely where she would cross his path along the sidewalk. As if he was waiting for her.

Thump, thump, thump, went her heart.

Linda glanced up nervously at the tower and was relieved to see the guards focused on the other side of the yard. Understandably, that side posed the greater risk as there were more prisoners congregated on that side playing basketball and using the gym equipment.

She smiled at Billy. He smiled back.

He started walking towards the southwest corner of the yard where the fence and the sidewalk were in the closest proximity to each other. Linda kept walking, pretending to look down at her folder in case the guards looked their way. When she reached the spot where the sidewalk was closest to the fence, she knelt down to untie and retie her shoe while glancing up at Billy.

He was so close, she wanted to smell him, touch him.

"Hello, Linda," Billy said casually, as if he had said her name a thousand times.

His voice was deeper than what she had remembered from the trial.

Linda giggled and nodded, feeling her face blush, which happened when she got nervous.

"I got your letters. And your picture. I enjoyed them very much."

"You did?" Linda asked meekly, still pretending to tie her shoe.

"Yes, I'm sorry I haven't answered them yet. This place is tough on a man's spirit."

"Oh my God, I can only imagine how hard it's been for you. Don't you worry about that one bit," Linda said, as she noticed one of the guards in the yard looking their way.

"I have to go but I'll write you another letter tonight," she whispered, quickly gathering her folder, and continuing on her way towards the administrative building.

"Inmate! Away from the fence!" the burly guard yelled from behind.

Billy calmly backed away from the fence, with his hands up, and winked at Linda as she looked over her shoulder.

*　*　*

Linda sat down at her desk and took a big swig of water out of her forty-ounce pink tumbler she brought with her to work every day as she tried to calm her pounding heart. Unfortunately, she inhaled at the same time as she gulped, sending the water shooting down her airway and causing her to have a violent coughing and choking attack.

"Jesus, Linda, you a'right?" Martha asked, the look of disgust on her face overriding any possible sound of concern in her voice.

Linda held up her hand as she continued to cough and clear her throat to convey the dual message of "I'll be okay" and "give me a second."

"Fine," Linda managed to say after a few more seconds, coughed again, and then said, "wrong tube," as she motioned to her throat while continuing to try to clear it.

"Um, maybe drink a little slower next time," Martha said, shaking her head as she returned to her computer screen, any shred of empathy or concern completely gone.

Linda regained her composure and focused on her breathing to calm herself down from her encounter with Billy. He had gained a few pounds since the trial, which looked good on him, and was even more distinguished than she had remembered. And when he said her name, *oh Lordy*, that was almost her undoing. She could feel her heart racing again as she thought about their encounter.

She looked down at the paperwork that she had brought back from the library, hoping it would give her something to work on to distract her. She also wanted Martha to leave her alone. As hard as she tried to focus, all she could think about was Billy.

Billy, Billy, Billy.

And how she needed Karl to send her on more errands outside of the administration building. She couldn't wait to get home to write Billy another letter. She was proud of herself for having the foresight to use her birth name, *Baker*, in her letters to Billy instead of *Morgan*, her legal name from her brief marriage, which she had never bothered to change back after her divorce.

Billy had recognized her and said her name, she thought, the heat starting to rise within her again.

She took her handkerchief out of her pocket and blotted the sweat off her neck and face. She took her lip gloss out of the clear, regulation seven-by-five plastic bag she brought with her every day and reapplied it. She was glad her hand had stopped trembling.

It was only a matter of time when they would be together – outside of this prison, she thought, almost giddy at the prospect.

She looked up and noticed Martha staring at her – again.

"What, Martha? What? Why are you always staring at me?" Linda asked.

"I'm not always staring at you, but I can't help it when I happen to look over and you're sweating and smiling all by yourself over there and no one is talking to you. Why are you always sweating and smiling like that? It's weird," Martha said as she looked back at her computer monitor.

"I am sorry if I'm just a happy person and you're not. I never knew smiling was a crime around here. And, as I've already mentioned, it's very hot outside. Why don't you just mind your own beeswax, Martha? Jeesh."

"Wow, classic."

Before Linda could respond, Karl came out of his office to refill his coffee.

"Linda, you get that paperwork signed by Scotty?" Karl asked.

"Yes, sir, right here," Linda answered, as she got up to hand Karl the folder with the signed documents.

"Okay, thanks."

"Anytime, sir, I don't mind at all. I like the exercise, so let me know if you have any other errands you need me to run around here," Linda said, trying to sound helpful but not too eager.

Karl mumbled something Linda didn't catch as he went back into his office and shut the door.

Linda looked up and noticed Martha staring at her *again*. Linda stared back and stuck her tongue out at her. Martha rolled her eyes and returned her attention to her computer screen. Normally she would obsess over someone not liking her, but not today. No ma'am, she wasn't going to let Martha or anyone else ruin her excitement over seeing Billy.

Her Billy.

CHAPTER SEVENTEEN
THE JUDGE

Back in his cell, William Stephens smiled as he thought about his good fortune. The juror who had caused the mistrial and had written him all those letters was working at the prison. Had she been working at the prison all this time? During his trial?

No, that was impossible, he realized.

He knew she would never have made it through voir dire, the jury selection process, and both the prosecution and the defense would have stricken her for cause.

He sat on the edge of his bunk and rummaged through the box of personal items he was allowed to keep in his cell. He was relieved when he found Linda Baker's most recent letter in the box, having thrown the rest of them, along with her picture, in the trash. He had never intended to answer her letters, but now she was going to be his ticket out of this place.

He took out a prison-sanctioned pen and writing paper and crafted a quick response. He was careful about what he included, knowing it would be monitored by the prison officials before being mailed, but tried to convey a tone that would garner additional sympathy from her.

My dearest Linda,

Thank you for all of your letters. I enjoyed reading them more than you will ever know. I'm sorry it took me so long to respond to them, but honestly, I was feeling sorry for myself in this hellhole, and I didn't know what to say. I felt so hopeless until I saw your smiling face (in the picture you sent to me). You are like an angel sent from heaven. It has renewed my faith and determination to get out of here, legally of course, so we can be together. I hope you don't give up on me.

All my love,
Billy

Short, sweet, and to the point. That should do it.

He sat back on his bed and closed his eyes. For the first time since he had been convicted and incarcerated, he felt hopeful.

Freedom, and more importantly, vengeance, would soon be his.

And Linda Baker, Juror #7, was just the woman who was going to help him.

CHAPTER EIGHTEEN
LINDA

Linda was so anxious for the day to end, but each time she looked at the clock on the wall, she felt like it was going backwards. The day dragged on slowly but finally ended with no additional unpleasant interactions with Martha. She couldn't wait to get home to write Billy another letter now that she had interacted with him, even if only briefly.

She was excited when she first met Martha, hoping they could become friends. Linda didn't have a lot of friends, certainly none in this town since she had moved there, but it was obvious from the get-go that Martha was not interested in developing any kind of friendship with Linda. She had no idea what Martha's problem was with her, but realized it was probably better now that she and Billy had connected. Linda knew she had to keep her relationship with Billy a secret and that would be too difficult with a best friend to confide in. Luckily for Linda, that wouldn't be a problem.

Linda had a few close friends growing up in Mount Dora, Florida, a small quaint and quiet town about an hour outside of Orlando. From middle school through high school, she had two best friends, Meg and Missi, and the three of them were inseparable. They called themselves the Three Amigas and shared everything from their secret crushes to their dreams. The summer of their freshman year, they had matching t-shirts made at the mall with *The Three Amigas* on the front and their first names on the back. Linda still had her t-shirt, although it would never fit her again, but oh, how she missed those days and her friends.

Meg got married right after college and moved all the way to New Mexico. *What the heck does New Mexico have over Florida*, Linda wondered at the time. Missi left for L.A. after graduating from a prestigious design school in Miami and becoming an interior designer to the stars. They both went away to college and never came back. Linda tried to keep in touch with them for a while, but their lives just went in different directions. Eventually the phone calls and letters were far and few between until they stopped altogether, other than the occasional Christmas card she still received from Meg.

"Oh well, no sense dwelling on the past when I've got Billy in my future," Linda said aloud to herself, smiling, as she walked into her small rental home.

She shed her work uniform, put on one of her comfy house dresses, fed Carol Baskins and fixed herself a cup of raspberry herbal tea. She sat down on the couch with her stationery and favorite purple pen she had recently bought just for Billy's letters. Purple was her signature color, after all.

Dear Billy,

My heart is still fluttering from seeing you. I hope you know my love for you is sincere and that I would do anything for us to be together. As I mentioned in my previous letters, I know you are completely innocent of the heinous crimes they accused you of. I keep praying that one day they catch the real guy who did those things, and you will be set free. I pray for that every night, Billy. Then we can be together. Do you want that too? Oh Lord, I know I'm being so forward, but I just think if you feel it, you should say it. And I feel it, Billy! In my heart, I know you do too! Oh fiddle dee dee, listen to me prattling on like a silly school girl.

* * *

Linda filled the next two pages telling Billy all about her life, including about her beloved cat, Carole, the fact that Celine Dion was her favorite singer and why, and all about her move from Tampa to her little two-bedroom home in Starke that she shared with Carole, although she made sure to leave out details about her job at the prison or anything else that she thought would tip off the mail monitors to her identity or current position at the prison. She finished the letter, sprayed it with a spritz of her *Bombshell* perfume she had gotten from Victoria's Secret, and put the sealed letter in her purse so she could mail it on her way to work in the morning.

"It has been a very good day, Ms. Baskins," Linda cooed, as she went into the kitchen to celebrate by treating her beloved cat with a can of her favorite wet food and herself with a piece of apple pie she had recently bought at Publix.

"A very good day, indeed," she said, as she took a bite of the warm apple pie and replayed her encounter with Billy as Ms. Baskins devoured her special treat.

CHAPTER NINETEEN
CHARLIE

Charlie Robinson sat in his cell, staring at the windowless gray cement wall, trying to figure out how he had ended up back in jail. Two years ago, when he finally got clean, he swore he was never going to be behind bars again. He promised himself he wouldn't even so much as jay walk. At the time, he was committed to staying clean and trying to reconnect with his estranged family.

And now here he was, in jail again, but this time accused of a crime far worse than any he had gotten away with in the past.

*　*　*

Two years before, Charlie went straight from the ER of Tampa General Hospital into one of the scarce, government-funded rehabs in the area after coming very close to dying from a heroin overdose -- not his first, sad to say. His ER doctor very candidly told him that if he was insistent on killing himself, there were quicker and more humane ways he could recommend.

He remembered thinking the doctor was joking, and laughed awkwardly for a moment, before saying, "naw, bro, I'm cool. I just got a bad bag, probably laced with fentanyl. Everybody knows that shit is f-ed up. I'll be more careful," Charlie promised, unsure what he was promising or why.

His body involuntarily twitched, his stomach rolled, and he ached for something he knew he wouldn't get in the hospital. But he hoped they would give him something for the pain and withdrawal symptoms he was experiencing.

He remembered sweating and begging the doctor for some relief, anything to make the *sickness*, as he used to call it, subside.

"Mr. Robinson, um, I don't think you understand the gravity of your situation. A '*bag* laced with fentanyl'," he said, adding air quotes around the phrase, "is the least of your worries. I assure you, a fentanyl overdose will be relatively painless as long as the drug works as quickly and effectively as it usually does, which I have no reason to doubt that it will. You are not experiencing the effects of a fentanyl overdose, which I expect you know. You are experiencing the effects of a heroin overdose followed by the grueling physical and psychological symptoms of withdrawal."

Charlie was speechless, other than the groan he let out as he clutched his body into the fetal position, and knew it was more so from what the doctor was saying to him than the debilitating nausea and stomach cramps he was feeling.

The ER doctor continued, "what you're doing to yourself since, let's see," he paused as he looked down to review Charlie's medical history, which he had obviously already reviewed, "the past twenty years, is nothing short of torture. If you are not trying to kill yourself, I am surprised because you are doing such a damn good job of accomplishing that, albeit at an incredibly slow and painful pace. If you continue on your current path, you'll be dead within six months, maybe less, and it will be an extremely painful journey. Good luck, I'll sign your discharge papers and you'll be back on the street in no time."

The doctor closed the metal clipboard and slid it into the plastic shelf attached to the wall next to Charlie's bed in the ER before he started to walk away.

"Dude, I mean, doctor, wait, . . . please," Charlie pleaded, unsure what he was feeling beyond his normal anxiousness, anger, nausea, and the dreadful panic that if he didn't get a fix soon, he might, in fact, die. "Please help me."

The doctor turned around, his empathetic eyes looking down at Charlie, and said, "Look, I can help you if you really want help. But if you don't, please don't waste either of our time. I can discharge you as you're out of immediate danger, refer you to an outpatient drug counseling program, and free up the bed for someone who may benefit from my years of medical school and insurmountable student loan debt."

The doctor's words had a finality to them that Charlie hadn't felt before, or, he admitted, probably hadn't resonated with him before. He had been in a constant state of denial as to the severity of his heroin and opioid addiction for so many years, convincing himself that he "just liked to party" and could "stop whenever he wanted." But after twenty years of that and having lost everything and everyone who was close to him, Charlie admitted those were lies he told himself.

He was tired, tired of being alone and tired of being sick. And tired of lying. He had been in and out of rehabs, jail, and psychiatric hospitals since he was about sixteen years old, three years after his father's death. Something about this doctor's words scared him. Not the words themselves; he had heard those words or some variation many times before.

But how he said them.

Charlie believed him.

"I do," Charlie stuttered. "I want your help."

And for the first time in Charlie's life, he meant it.

The ER doctor kept Charlie in the hospital for an extra day knowing a bed was opening at the state-funded rehab facility in the next twenty-four hours and gave him something for the withdrawal symptoms. Had he not done that, Charlie would have been using within an hour of being released.

The day he entered rehab, he was thinner and sicker than he had ever been before, more so than even he realized or was ready to admit at the time. He had always been thin, but that day, he weighed about one hundred and thirty pounds, at most, and his 5'11" frame was a literal skeleton.

Before he overdosed, his lowest point, and the catalyst to his estrangement from his family, was when he stole and pawned his mom's wedding and engagement ring the last time he lived at home. When his sister, Hallie, found out, she threatened to have him arrested, but his mother stopped her. They kicked him out of his childhood home, changed the locks, and his mom refused to speak to him *"for her own self-preservation"* she had said at the time. His sisters shut him out of their lives too.

It was the most alone Charlie had ever felt in his life.

But at the time, he didn't care. The only thing that mattered was the high. Anything to avoid feeling *anything* other than physical pain of the addiction, which was always fixed with his next fix.

Through therapy and getting clean, he confronted his feelings about his dad's death that he had been suppressing and numbing for years with drugs. He had been so angry, for so long, blaming everyone for his problems, for not understanding him, not supporting him. He realized he even blamed his dad for leaving him, as if it was his fault he got shot.

And then something miraculous happened one day, after many months of therapy and being completely clean. Charlie forgave himself. And he stopped being angry. He couldn't take back all the grief and pain he had caused his mother and his sisters, but at least he could avoid inflicting any more. He vowed to stay clean for them, even if they never forgave him, and for his father.

He left rehab a month later and had kept his promise ever since.

* * *

The flush of the toilet from his cellmate two feet away from him brought Charlie out of his thoughts. The cell had two bunk beds, one sink, and a toilet that was out in the open and bolted to the concrete floor in one corner of the ten by six-foot cell. Charlie knew it was only a matter of time before the two empty beds would be filled and then there would be four of them crammed in there.

"Man, I need a smoke," his cellmate said.

Charlie nodded without engaging in conversation and returned to the magazine one of his previous cellmates gave to him on the day of his trial. Charlie didn't know what that guy had been charged with, but he knew he either couldn't make bail or wasn't allowed to make bail. He didn't even know his real name. Everyone called him "Big Red" on account of his red hair and large stature, and he had been in for almost a year before his trial. He wondered if he got off or went to prison.

The only thing Charlie had going for him this time in jail was his height and his weight gain from being off the drugs and his rigorous gym training. But Charlie also knew the rules: keep your mouth shut; don't ask anyone what they were in for; and mind your own business. His chatty cellmate didn't seem to know the rules yet. He would learn soon enough, probably the hard way.

"So how long you been in?" the guy asked, looking up at Charlie on his top bunk.

"Long enough," was all Charlie said and pulled the magazine up further in front of his face to give the guy the hint.

"Gotcha, yeah, hopefully my girlfriend will post my bail soon and get me outta here. I really need a smoke. Whatever happened to innocent until proven guilty and basic civil rights and all that shit?"

"I don't think smoking is a basic civil right," Charlie said, regretting as soon as he said it that he had engaged at all.

"Well, it should be," the man laughed nervously. "My name's Barry, how ya doin, man?" the bald, fifty-ish looking man said as he stretched his hand up to shake Charlie's.

"Look, not trying to be rude, but there are some basic rules in here, and the first is don't get too friendly. Keep to yourself and bide your time."

"Anything else I should know?"

"Stay away from the meatloaf. You'll be shitting for days."

CHAPTER TWENTY
HALLIE

Marcelo showed up right on time with a large cheese pizza from Santoro's, one of Hallie's favorites, and a bottle of Rodney Strong Cabernet, also one of her favorites. They spent the evening talking and laughing, both making it a point to avoid talking about Charlie or his arrest. At about ten o'clock, Hallie suggested going up to bed to watch a movie, and was surprised when Marcelo said he couldn't spend the night. He claimed he had an early morning, which seemed strange to Hallie as that had never seemed to stop him before. Their relationship seemed to be shifting but she was too tired and had too much else on her mind to dwell on it. Marcelo left and Hallie went up to bed.

* * *

The next morning, Hallie pulled up Steve Bazarte's number in her contacts and clicked on the message icon.

"Hey, Steve, it's Hallie Miller. When you have a minute, can you give me a call? I need to talk to you about bail for someone. Thanks!"

Steve Bazarte was the best bail bondsman in town. Hallie had met him a few years before through mutual friends and they hit it off instantly. He had a giant personality, which matched his tall and strong physique, and he made Hallie laugh. She hadn't seen him in a while, but she knew he would help her if the judge set bail.

Hallie's phone rang about two minutes later.

"Hallie Miller, long time no see or hear. What's going on?"

"Thanks for calling me back so soon, Steve."

"For my favorite lawyer? Of course."

Hallie laughed, "How many times a day do you give that line?"

"About a hundred times, to be honest," Steve laughed. "And sometimes, I actually mean it. What can I do for you, counselor?"

"Well, it's my brother. He's been arrested and he's being held in Pinellas County. His first appearance and bail hearing should be today."

"What's the charge?"

"Murder, so not sure they'll even grant bail, but his attorney is going to try. I just need to be prepared either way."

"Shit, sorry to hear that, Hal. Text me his name and date of birth. I'll look up the arrest warrant and start working on the paperwork if they grant bail. Are they charging him with first?"

"I don't know."

"If it's first degree, very likely no bail will be set, you know that, right?"

"Yeah, I know."

"Who you got lined up to defend him?"

"Mike Freeman."

"Freeman? From the D.A.'s office? Has he switched sides?"

"Yes, recently started his own firm."

"Well, that's fortunate for your brother. Freeman's good. One of the best."

"Yeah, I know. He's also a close friend, so I know Charlie's in good hands."

"That's good, Hallie. Okay, I'll be ready if they set bail. Text me his info."

"Thanks, Steve, I will. I appreciate it."

* * *

Hallie worked from home the rest of the day or at least tried to work. She was having a hard time focusing on the agreements she was reviewing and found herself daydreaming at her desk. All she could think about was Charlie and the young woman he was accused of murdering. The thoughts ran around in her head until she finally decided to give up on trying to work. She just couldn't concentrate.

She wondered, *was Charlie really clean or was he lying to her, again? Worse yet, was he capable of murder?*

She needed some fresh air and to clear her head. She took Juno for a walk around the block.

By the time she returned home, she had concluded, *Charlie was a lot of things, but he was no murderer, clean or not.*

If he really was clean, and innocent, he deserved a second chance at making something of his life. If he was innocent, which she believed he was at that moment, she would prove it. If he wasn't, she would determine that too.

For the rest of the day, she reviewed the rules of criminal procedure and the processes when someone is charged with murder. As a transactional corporate attorney, this was out of her wheelhouse, and she could only remember what she had learned in law school and studying for the Bar exam, but she wanted to be as helpful in Charlie's defense as she could be.

She analyzed the rules and cases involving discovery, especially the D.A.'s obligations to disclose any exculpatory evidence. Hallie was surprised after reading case after case where the police or investigators had not followed proper procedures with respect to safeguarding evidence or had zeroed in on one suspect while never looking at any others. Often, on appeal, the accused was exonerated based on subsequently discovered DNA evidence or evidence that the police had intentionally suppressed or lost.

By midnight, Hallie couldn't read anymore; she was exhausted. But she also knew what she had to do to help

Charlie. He was her brother, and that meant she was more invested than Mike could ever be. She had no doubt that Mike would be on top of his legal defense, but she could investigate his case, review the evidence against him, and then look for new evidence or holes in the police investigation to prove someone else was responsible.

"C'mon, Jun-Jun girl, let's go upstairs."

The yellow Lab slowly got up, stretched, and then headed up the stairs, as she always did.

Hallie checked the back door, the front door, and shut the lights off before heading upstairs, as she always did.

* * *

Hallie got up earlier than usual the next morning, unable to sleep, recognizing she was probably restless after spending half the night reading all about criminal procedure and thinking about Charlie's case. She sat at the kitchen counter, staring at her laptop screen, as she sipped on her second cup of fresh ground Colombian blend. It was starting to revive her.

She had decided to take the morning off from work to continue working on Charlie's case. She opened a new Excel spreadsheet and inserted everything she knew about Charlie's case so far. She looked up the original article online and included the victim's name, date of the murder, the name of the bar where Charlie worked, and the address of the AirBnB where the victim was murdered, which she had gotten from Charlie.

Hallie watched as Juno got up from her bed in Hallie's office and stretched. She came into the kitchen and looked up at Hallie, wagging her tail.

"Okay, old girl, let's go out," Hallie said, picking up her phone and her coffee as she headed towards the front door.

The yellow Lab bounded past her down the hall with more zest than she had exhibited lately and waited for Hallie by the door. Hallie opened the door, and Juno ran down the steps and into the front yard while Hallie sat down on the loveseat to wait for her, scrolling on her phone. The heat and humidity were arriving earlier each year and lasting longer, and the warm air contrasted sharply with the air conditioning she had just left. How anyone living in Florida could deny global warming was beyond her comprehension.

She used the paper towel she had wrapped around the base of her coffee mug to dab at the sweat accumulating at the nape of her neck, underneath her long, dirty-blonde hair, while trying to remember anything else she could about her conversation with Charlie. She turned her head as she wiped the back of her neck and noticed an envelope nestled behind the rocking chair next to the front door. She picked up the envelope and examined it.

Like the previous one left on her porch, it contained only her name in bold letters on the outside of the sealed envelope. It didn't have her address, a return address, or anything else that could identify the sender. She glanced out at Juno who was busy sniffing every plant in the yard.

"Man, they're persistent," Hallie said aloud, assuming the letter was from another realtor who wanted to sell her house for her.

With the low inventory in the area, buyers and realtors were leaving notes on houses they liked, hoping the home-owner would be interested in selling.

Hallie opened the envelope to find a single sheaf of paper inside:

Well, well, Hallie, how fortuitous to find out that our one blissful night together resulted in a daughter. How I wish you would have told me so I could have enjoyed knowing her as she grew up. But you denied me that opportunity and then to learn during my trial that you used our shared DNA against me to get me convicted of a crime that I did not commit, by the way, is most unfortunate, especially for you. You will regret everything you've done, trust me. The day I leave this prison, which will be sooner than you think, I will come for you. And then I will find Katie. It will be quite the little family reunion, don't you think? Enjoy your days Hallie Miller! – WS

She shivered and glanced up and down her street, hoping not to register a reaction to what she had read in case someone was watching her. She didn't know when the letter was left on her front porch, but whoever had left it there could be watching her. She wiped the sweat from her brow, picked up her phone and coffee cup and called Juno up into the house. Once inside, she locked the door and dropped the letter onto the foyer table.

She had planned to go for a run but decided to skip it. She checked the front and back doors to make sure they were locked and went upstairs to take a hot shower to clear her head. As she showered, she thought about the contents and tone of the letter and what she knew.

She knew Stephens was still in prison. He did not leave the letter on her front porch, at least not personally. The letter had not come through the prison mail system. It was hand delivered with no return address, postage, or anything on the outside of the envelope other than her name. Either Stephens had someone else write it and deliver it for him or it was from someone else who knew about Stephens and was trying to scare her. These were the things she knew, and she tried to analyze it unemotionally.

Either scenario unnerved her, she had to admit, but she was angrier than she was afraid. She thought about reporting the letter to the prison officials, but what good would that do? He would deny he had anything to do with it and she doubted they would be able to find out who did. If she did nothing, he would have to wonder if she even received it, which would drive him crazy if he did have anything to do with it.

As far as hurting her and following through with his threats, Hallie knew Stephens was too much of a narcissistic sociopath to have someone else do his dirty work. As long as he was in prison, she believed she and Katie were safe. She would rely on that belief for now.

After her shower, she texted Marcelo, "Hey, got a letter allegedly from Stephens. I'm fine and you don't need to call me now, just thought I would let you know."

Her cellphone vibrated instantly with an incoming call from Marcelo.

"Hey, you didn't have to call me so quickly. It's no big deal. I know you're busy."

"Of course I did, tell me about this letter," Marcelo responded.

Hallie read him the contents of the letter.

"Is there a postmark on it?" he asked.

"Nope, left on my front porch. Someone is just trying to scare me. It's probably not even from him."

"What makes you think that?"

"Well, it didn't come through the prison mail system, so it really could be from anyone."

"Who else do you think would leave a letter like that just to scare you? Your ex, David? Peter Martino?"

"I can't imagine David would do anything like this. I haven't heard from him since our divorce was finalized two years ago."

"Yeah, that's true, but who else knows about the DNA tests and Stephens' biological link to Katie?"

"Anyone who was in the courtroom during the trial, I would think, but other than that, I can't think of anyone,"

Hallie said. "My name was in the news with the coverage of Stephens' trial and then there were the articles about Peter Martino, including how he attacked and kidnapped me and allegedly other women in Tampa. It would take someone two seconds to find my address on the property appraiser's website. Sickos always have their groupies."

"Well, I think we should consider this a viable threat from Stephens until we determine otherwise."

"I don't want to waste anyone's time with this," Hallie said, regretting that she had told Marcelo about it at all.

"It's not a waste of time, Hallie. Put the letter in a plastic baggie and seal it."

"You don't honestly think you're going to get a print off of it, do you?"

"I don't know, but it's worth a shot, don't you think?"

"Even if there's a print on it, it's not going to be Stephens' print. It had to be written and left on my porch by someone outside of prison. And as far as we know, he's still secure in Florida's finest maximum-security prison. I have no doubt he still has connections on the outside, but would he really go through all that trouble?"

"We won't know unless we check. And if there is a print, then there's a chance we can find out who wrote it and how they're connected to Stephens . . . or you."

Hallie knew she couldn't talk Marcelo out of something once he decided on it, especially when he went into detective mode, so she wasn't sure why she even bothered to argue.

"Fine, I'll put it in a plastic baggie, and you can pick it up next time you're over. When will that be, by the way? I feel like I haven't seen you much lately."

"Sorry, I know, I've been working crazy hours lately. I'm working on a new case, and it's taking up all of my time. I'll try to come by later today or tomorrow to pick it up."

"Okay, I'll leave it on the front table in the foyer in case you come by and I'm not here."

"Okay, sounds good. Maybe we can grab dinner tomorrow night or, if you prefer to stay in, I can pick up dinner on my way to your place?" Marcelo asked.

"I would love that," Hallie said, just before they said their goodbyes and ended the call.

She stared down at the letter in front of her, making sure not to touch it any more than she already had, feeling weird about her conversation with Marcelo. There was something off in their relationship. She couldn't put her finger on it, but lately, Marcelo seemed distant, or maybe she was distant. All she knew is that they were not in the same place as they usually were. They both had busy, stressful jobs, and Hallie was consumed with Charlie's case lately, but she felt there was something more going on. They were drifting apart.

She grabbed two plastic baggies from the kitchen drawer, went out to the foyer and, with one baggie on her hand, she carefully put the note and envelope in the other baggie as Marcelo had instructed. She dropped it back on the table by the front door and returned to the kitchen to continue compiling what she knew about Charlie's case.

* * *

Hallie spent the rest of the day scouring the internet for any cases that seemed like Charlie's: young women who were murdered on Treasure Island or nearby beaches, visitors or tourists staying alone in an AirBnB or other online rentals, and any other similarities she could think of. She was saddened by how many stories she came across about young women murdered, but most of those were by ex-boyfriends or husbands. There were only one or two that seemed remotely similar.

The first was in Crystal River, a Gulf Coast city about an hour and half north of Tampa, which attracts visitors to its beautiful beaches, natural springs, and camping sites. It was also home to the largest manatee population in the State. A young woman had rented an RV in one of the camping parks that was situated between the Gulf and one of the many freshwater rivers. Like the Treasure Island victim, the owner found her body when she went to the RV to clean the RV after the woman was supposed to have checked out.

FOUL PLAY SUSPECTED AT 7 SISTER SPRINGS RV CAMP

By: Laura Giannelli, Staff Reporter

Wednesday, July 14, 2021 / Citrus County Chronicle

An Ocala woman was found dead last Sunday morning in her rented RV in the Nature Coast RV Camp, near the 7 Sisters Springs on the Chassahowitzka River. According to her friends, the victim, identified as 26-year-old, Kaycee Tyler, had spent the week alone kayaking up and down the river, visiting the beaches and wildlife parks, and enjoying being outside after the Covid lockdown in Florida had been lifted. Ms. Tyler, who was immunocompromised due to a childhood illness, had planned the trip alone after spending the previous six months quarantined in her one-bedroom apartment.

"Kaycee just wanted to be outdoors, with nature, and get outside. See, it really wasn't safe for her to be around people yet, cause she could get sick real easy, so she found this great place that wasn't too expensive and not too far away. She could go to the beach, kayak on the river, see the manatees, and not worry about getting Covid. That's all she wanted," her best friend, Misty Smith, said through tears. "Really, was that too much to ask?"

Ms. Tyler's body was found the day after she was supposed to have returned home to Ocala. When her friends and family didn't hear from her on Saturday, they contacted the RV park on Sunday morning. The owner went to the RV to check on her and that's when she found her body.

A person close to the investigation who spoke on the condition of anonymity stated she had been brutally murdered, stabbed multiple times and possibly strangled, and likely sexually assaulted.

The Citrus County Sheriff's Office would not confirm the cause of death, but stated, "We cannot release any information at this time as this is an ongoing investigation. However, we do believe Ms. Tyler is a victim of foul play and we are exploring all possible leads. Anyone with information should contact the Citrus County Sheriff's Office."

Hallie searched for any other information she could find about Kaycee Tyler's case, but all she determined was that no one was ever arrested for her murder. There were a few follow up articles, which didn't contain any new information, and a post on a true crime blog, titled, "*Who Killed Kaycee Tyler?*" with about thirty-seven comments about the murder, the last of which was over a year before. Hallie read through the comments, finding the usual condolences from friends and strangers alike, arm-chair theorists about her murder, and a few random trollers.

There was only one comment that piqued her interest, from an anonymous poster who said: "*She was a ray of sunshine until her last breath left her body. When her light went out forever.*"

Hallie read and reread the comment. It was the last comment on the post, and it was at least six months after the previous posts. There was something about it that bothered her. It was almost taunting, something macabre about posting about her last breath. It said something more about the poster than the victim.

Hallie saved the screen and website as pdfs in a file called "Charlie Research – Similar Cases." Next, she clicked on the link on the blog that said: "*Contact Us*" and sent an email about working with a reporter who was doing an article about Kaycee Tyler's unsolved case and wanted to talk to the blogger. In her email, she added some compliments about the quality of the blog and the research that was done that she thought might play to the blogger's ego to get a response. Whether the blogger knew Kaycee Tyler or not, Hallie knew there were true crime groupies who would become obsessed with victims of crimes or their murderers, to the point that it consumed them. Hallie was hoping the writer of the Kaycee Tyler blog would be able to give her an email address or some other identifying information about that last anonymous poster that she could use to find him or her. It was probably a dead-end, but she had to explore all possibilities.

She added Kaycee Tyler to her spreadsheet, with all of the relevant facts that she knew, including age, hometown, location of death, likely cause of death (unconfirmed), and date of the murder. In the Notes column, she added the blog site and questions she had for the blogger. She didn't want to go too far down the rabbit hole as there was nothing connecting the Tyler murder to the Treasure Island murder, other than Hallie's gut that they seemed similar.

She clicked back onto the tab with the second article she had found:

YOUNG WOMAN FOUND DEAD IN CEDER KEY VRBO

By: Khristen Pello, Staff Reporter

Tuesday, March 21, 2023 / Levy Citizen

A twenty-four-year-old woman visiting from Ohio was found brutally murdered late Saturday, March 18th, after her friends and family couldn't reach her that day. Meliessa "Mo" Kelley had arrived in Ceder Key on March 16th and was scheduled to leave on Thursday, March 23rd. According to her family, she had traveled to Florida to get a break from the frigid Ohio winter and was supposed to meet up with friends who were also staying in Ceder Key.

According to the Levy County Sheriff's Office, Ms. Kelley's murder appeared to have been "sexually motivated", but they would not elaborate further. She was last seen on Friday night where she met her friends at a local bar before heading back to her VRBO. When she didn't show up for a scheduled boating trip the following day, her friends tried unsuccessfully to reach her. After the boating trip when they still couldn't reach her, they contacted her family who also had not been able to reach her. They contacted local authorities who did a welfare check on her, and that's when her body was found in her VRBO.

According to someone close to the investigation who spoke on the condition of anonymity, Ms. Kelley was found with a broken neck and stab wounds, her throat had been slit, and she had suffered blunt force trauma to her head and body.

"What happened to my sister is horrible and no family should have to go through this," Kelley's brother, Todd, told the Levy Citizen. "Some monster did this to her and needs to be held accountable. VRBO also has to take responsibility, because they didn't make sure that rental was safe. There's no way Mo would have let someone in voluntarily."

The Office of Medical Examiner District 8 confirmed they are performing an autopsy of Kelley's body, as required by Florida law when someone dies under circumstances involving criminal violence but declined to comment further on the case. The Florida Department of Law Enforcement is assisting in the investigation, according to an agency spokesman, who also declined to give details on the case. Anyone with information is asked to contact the Levy County Sheriff's Office.

Hallie added Meliessa "Mo" Kelley's name and information from the article to her spreadsheet. A search of her name revealed no one had been arrested for her murder either, although law enforcement had identified a 'person of interest' who was later cleared.

She had been at it for hours and there was nothing more for her to research. It was late. She knew she had to go to bed, or she would be useless the next day. She was surprised she hadn't heard from Marcelo all night, but she hadn't texted him either, she realized. A few months before, they both would have checked in or texted multiple times.

She picked up her phone and texted, "good night, love, exhausted, going to bed. Miss you!"

She waited a few minutes and, when she didn't get a response, put her phone on silent and went to bed.

CHAPTER TWENTY-ONE
LINDA

A few days after seeing Billy for the first time in the yard, Linda came home from work to find a letter in her mailbox with a stamp affixed to the outside of the letter that read: "*From an Inmate at a State Correctional Facility.*" She was so excited she could barely find her house key on her jingling key chain. She held the letter close against her beating heart as she finally unlocked her door and dropped her stuff down on the kitchen counter.

"Carole Baskins, my sweet, we got a letter!" Linda called out excitedly.

She sat down on the couch, her faithful cat immediately joining her and demanding to be caressed.

"Oh, sweety, you're going to have to wait. Oh, heaven to Betsy, I am a nervous wreck," Linda giggled, her hands trembling as she opened the envelope and removed and unfolded the one-page piece of notebook paper.

My dearest Linda,

Thank you for all of your letters. I enjoyed reading them more than you will ever know. I'm sorry it took me so long to respond to them, but honestly, I was feeling sorry for myself in this hellhole, and I didn't know what to say. I felt so hopeless until I saw your smiling face (in the picture you sent to me). You are like an angel sent from heaven. It has renewed my faith and determination to get out of here, legally of course, so we can be together. I hope you don't give up on me.

All my love,
Billy

Linda read the letter over and over, feeling her dreams were finally coming true. His words on that paper validated her move, her job at the prison, everything she had given up in Tampa to be there with him, or at least near him.

"Oh, Carole, fiddle dee dee, wait 'til he gets out, we're going to be a family!" Linda said, stroking the purring cat on her head as a single tear streamed down her cheek.

"There has to be a way to get him out of that awful place," she said as the plump cat climbed onto her lap. "I just know it."

CHAPTER TWENTY-TWO
CHARLIE

Charlie paced around the cell, waiting to meet with his lawyer. Because of the charges against him, the judge had denied bail in his case, so Charlie knew that cell was going to be his home for the foreseeable future. In the last day, two more men were added to his cell, but bald Barry had made bail and had been released within twenty-four hours after being arrested. He was glad bald Barry would not be sharing his cell for longer than he already had. But now there were three men, including himself, sharing a very small area and one toilet. The latest two appeared to be in for drug related charges, probably possession and distribution. Charlie knew the signs all too well. They were edgy and tweaking out, likely from withdrawals, and probably couldn't make bail.

Someone found out that he had been charged with murder, so most of the other inmates he encountered left him alone, which included the tweakers in his cell. Seeing them, he realized how far he had come, but more importantly, how close he almost came to being just like them.

"Robinson, let's go," the guard said as he slid open the cell door with a loud clang.

Charlie walked out, happy for any respite from being locked in the depressing, gray concrete cell with his meth-head cellmates.

He was led through a series of security checkpoints where one locked gate would open in front of him while the gate behind him would immediately close and lock behind him, until he arrived at the conference rooms where the incarcerated could meet with their lawyers. Because he was charged with murder, a violent crime, and denied bail, the guard secured him to the concrete floor with ankle shackles and secured him to the table with cuffs around his wrists in front of him.

Mike Freeman was let in after Charlie was properly secured, and then the guard stepped out of the small room. Charlie had met him briefly at his arraignment.

"Hello, Charlie, how are you holding up?"

"I've been better. But I've also been worse, you know what I mean? Nice to see you again," Charlie said, a weariness in his eyes conveying more than his words.

"Before we begin, I need to set some ground rules. I am going to ask you a number of questions and I need you to be completely honest with me. I cannot help you if you do not answer my questions with absolute candor. What you and I discuss about your case, do not tell or discuss with anyone else, especially anyone in this place.

As long as our communications stay strictly between us, they will be protected by the attorney client privilege. Understand?"

"Yes, I understand. My father was a lawyer, and, Hallie, you know, is a lawyer, so I've been around it my whole life. I should have gone to law school like them, but I fucked everything up after my dad died. No excuse, I have no one to blame but myself for my mistakes, but, yeah, I get it, I understand. I won't talk to anyone but you about my case."

"Good. And as I said, especially anyone in here. Everyone is looking to trade something to get a better deal for themselves and they won't hesitate to use you for that."

"I understand."

"Okay, good. Let's start at the beginning. Tell me when and where you met Dawn Owens and how you ended up in her AirBnB."

"It was a Friday night, I was working, and she came in with some friends to Middle Grounds Grill, the place where I work. Um, I guess I should say, worked. Her friends left and she stayed at the bar and started chatting with me."

"Do you know what time that was?"

"I don't know, I guess about 10 or 11, maybe? She sat at the bar after her friends left until the bar closed."

"Did she leave when the bar closed?"

"Um, no, she waited with me while I finished closing up, and then we left together."

"What time was that?"

"Well, like I said, the bar closed at midnight, so by the time we got out of there, it was probably closer to one."

"Before you closed, did you see anyone else at the bar? Anyone who may have been alone or watching her?"

"No, I didn't notice anything. It was kinda busy and a band was playing. There were other customers sitting at the bar, but I can't recall anyone specific. I was just serving drinks and, in between serving other customers, talking to her."

"And then what happened?"

"After we closed, I cleaned up the bar, counted my drawer, tipped out the bar backs and the kitchen and then left with Dawn."

"Did you go straight to her AirBnB?"

"No, we stopped at a gas station on the way to pick up some beer."

"Which gas station?"

"The one on Gulf Blvd., in between Middle Grounds and her place.

"Was it busy on the street that night? Were other people still out?"

"I guess. I mean, I don't know. There's always people walking on Gulf Boulevard, walking home from the bars or taking late night walks on the beach. So there had to be, but I don't remember anyone in particular."

"What about at the gas station? Notice anyone there?"

"Sorry, man, no. It just seemed like a normal night in Treasure Island. Nothing out of the ordinary."

"And then what?"

"We went back to her place, had a few beers, a little weed, and then I left. I don't think I was there more than an hour."

"So let me tell it to you straight, Charlie. You were arrested and charged because your DNA was found on the bed, next to her body, and fingerprints throughout the place. Witnesses at the bar where you work saw you walking from the direction of Dawn's AirBnB past the restaurant to your place, presumably, around the time when she was murdered. It doesn't look good. Do you have anything you can tell me that will refute the evidence?"

"I told the police, just like I'm telling you, I was there that night. We started to mess around on her bed, but I had to stop. That's probably how my DNA got on the bed. I got dressed and I left. I swear I didn't kill her," Charlie said, burying his face in his hands.

"Why did you have to stop?"

"Oh man, this is embarrassing. Sometimes, I can't finish, if you know what I mean. I get in my head and then it doesn't work. It happened that night, so I just had to get outta there. That's all, I swear."

"Did you get mad when 'it didn't work', as you say? Did she laugh at you or make fun of you? Did you rough her up because you were embarrassed?"

"Oh my God, no, nothing like that. I just got dressed and left. Jesus, I would never do that."

"Okay, Charlie, I'm sorry, but I have to ask you these things and, unfortunately, it's not going to get easier. Our time is about up, but after I leave, if you think of anything at all, I want you to write it down so you can remember to tell me next time I come to see you, which should be next week sometime. In the meantime, I'll request the tapes from the security cameras at the bar, the gas station, and any other places who have cameras in between the bar and her AirBnB."

"Someone had to follow us or showed up after I left because I didn't kill her, Mike. Please believe me. I promise I didn't kill her."

Mike simply nodded and got up to signal to the guards that they were done. He gathered his files and put them in his briefcase.

"I'll see you next week, Charlie."

CHAPTER TWENTY-THREE
HALLIE

Hallie arrived at the office early Thursday morning, determined to focus on her clients and the work that she had been neglecting since getting the phone call from Charlie.

Paige popped her head into her office, "Hey, how are you doing?"

"I'm okay, thanks. I assume you're asking because Mike told you about Charlie?"

"Yeah, he told me, I'm sorry Hal. Anything I can do?"

"No, thanks, I'm good, especially knowing Mike is defending Charlie. Enough about this, how are you doing?"

"You know, the usual, slammed, living the dream, all of the above," Paige said as she rolled her eyes.

"Dinner soon?" Hallie asked.

"Yes, absolutely, let me know when and where and I'm there."

* * *

Hallie worked the rest of the day, not realizing how much time had passed. Only when Nadia, her assistant, said goodnight to her as she left for the day did Hallie realize how late it had gotten. She hadn't even stopped for lunch, and she was hungry. She was looking forward to dinner with Marcelo that night.

She finished the agreement she was working on, emailed the draft to the client to review, and then packed up her files and laptop and left the office. She arrived home about twenty minutes later and went into the laundry room, happy to find a pair of clean sweats and a tank top folded on top of the dryer. She peeled off her work clothes, including her bra, automatically glancing up to the corner where the security camera used to be, before slipping into the comfy sweats and top.

As she went to let Juno out front, she saw the letter from Stephens in the plastic baggie was still on the table in the foyer. She took out her phone and texted Marcelo.

"Hey, still coming over for dinner tonight?"

"Hey, I've been meaning to text you all day, but I've been tied up on that case from last week and now another one came in."

"Need to cancel dinner?" Hallie wrote back.

"Would you mind? I've got a domestic that turned deadly in Carrollwood, murder-suicide, and I need to interview a couple of witnesses in the neighborhood."

"No problem, I've had a long day, too, and I'm exhausted."

"Okay, I'll call you tomorrow. Sorry about dinner, I'll make it up to you."

"No need to apologize," Hallie texted back, "I understand."

Hallie did understand. Both of their jobs were demanding and they often had to put work first, but this didn't help assuage her uneasy feelings of late. He was distracted and it seemed like it was due to something more than just his cases. More importantly, however, she realized, she wasn't as disappointed as she would have been in the past. She was actually a little relieved to have the night to herself to decompress.

She didn't have the energy to make anything for dinner, so she stood at the kitchen counter eating Cool Ranch Doritos that she dipped into a tub of cream cheese. It was one of her guilty pleasures and favorite snacks. That would suffice for dinner. She fed Juno and cleaned up the few dishes in her sink before retreating to the living room.

She sat down on the couch to watch the latest *Only Murders in the Building* episode, one of her favorite series when she had the time to watch TV. She watched the recap and started watching the newest episode. She had no idea when she fell asleep, but she bolted awake to an entirely different show on her screen. Juno was lying on the floor next to the couch, snoring peacefully, and she had no idea how long they had both been out.

She got up and made herself a cup of decaf hot tea. While her tea steeped, she called Juno to the front door to let her out one last time before they went upstairs. While

Juno sniffed around in the front yard and did her business, Hallie looked around the front porch, relieved not to see any new letters left for her. Juno looked up and uncharacteristically growled and barked at something or someone down the street.

Hallie looked down the street in the direction Juno had been looking, but didn't see anyone or anything, but she felt uneasy.

"Juno, c'mon, girl," Hallie called without diverting her gaze from down the street.

The obedient Lab bounded up the front steps and into the house. Hallie locked the front door behind them before looking out the glass pane one last time but saw nothing. Juno seemed fine, completely oblivious to whatever had alerted her a few minutes earlier, but anxious for her treat before heading upstairs to take her position for the night in her bed next to Hallie's, their nightly routine. Before heading up, Hallie checked the front and back door one last time to make sure they were locked, picked up her tea, and shut the lights out in the kitchen on her way up.

She went upstairs, with Juno in tow, and went into Katie's bedroom at the front of the house before heading into her room to take a warm bath before going to bed. She looked up and down the street, relieved that she didn't see anything, or more importantly, anyone. Juno was getting older, so for all she knew, it could have been a stray cat or a raccoon that spooked the old girl.

When her bath was ready, she turned on her Zen playlist on her Boze player, lit her favorite candles, and climbed into the tub. She turned the jets on low and soaked in the warm water, the lavender and Tea Tree oils soothing her skin while the aromas relaxed her.

But she couldn't stop thinking about Juno's unusual reaction outside that night combined with the letter she had received from Stephens, allegedly.

This can't be happening again, she thought as she closed her eyes.

She had finally healed, at least physically, from her injuries of the last two years, but she had not completely recovered from the psychological traumas that still triggered her. Receiving a threatening letter, whether it was from Stephens or not, brought it all back to the forefront, and as much as she had dismissed it the day she received it, it had since started to weigh on her.

But she refused to allow him *or anyone* to have that power over her. She refused to be intimidated or frightened by his threats.

After her bath, she put on a large t-shirt and climbed into bed. She drank her tea, which had cooled to the perfect warmish temperature, and began reading Lisa Unger's latest book, *Close Your Eyes and Count to Ten*.

She could barely keep her eyes open after only a few chapters, and when she found herself re-reading sentences, she closed the book, shut her light off, and fell fast asleep.

CHAPTER TWENTY-FOUR
MONICA

Monica finished her second martini and felt her nerves starting to settle. She reminded herself that Christian had been out of prison for two months and hadn't tried to find her, as far as she knew. She also tried to convince herself that the text may not have been from him. Maybe the text had been from her son, Pietro, or someone from O'Maddy's trying to fuck with her as a joke. And maybe her mother was right: Christian was probably so happy to be out of prison, he hadn't given her a second thought.

"You okay, Monica?" Marge asked her.

"Yeah, thanks, just stressed from my lunch with my mother. I'm fine," Monica lied as she dropped her credit card onto the bar, signaling she was done.

Marge cashed her out and Monica headed out of the bar. The yellow-orange glow of the sun was beginning to sink into the Gulf as a throng of people gathered on the small beach across the street to watch the sunset. Monica thought about watching, too, but then decided she wanted to get back to her apartment before it got too dark.

She walked the few blocks home, checking over her shoulder every few minutes, not sure what she was expecting to see. She had to admit she was more anxious than usual after hearing the news about Christian's release. She made it home safely, and, after making sure the front door and slider to her balcony were locked, she got ready for bed.

Just before she went to sleep, she pulled her cherished nine-millimeter Glock 26 out from underneath her bed, opened the case, which she always kept unlocked in case she needed the gun in a hurry, confirmed the gun was loaded, including a full clip and one in the chamber, just as her father had taught her, before returning it to its case. She placed the case on her nightstand and fell fast asleep.

* * *

Miami, Florida, 8:37 a.m.

CK looked outside past the uncharacteristic gray sky over the blueish-turquoise sea below as the unrelenting rain pelted the hurricane-enforced glass pane of his hotel room window. The tall palms swayed vigorously while in the distance he saw a shredded Cuban flag flapping in the wind, no doubt a casualty of the last storm that had pummeled Miami. The naked woman in the bed next to him stirred as the light peeked in from the gap in the curtains, revealing her flawless, umber skin.

His head was pounding, and he thought he might throw up.

Again.

He had to get out of that room, away from the smell of perfume, alcohol, cigarettes and possibly sex or vomit or both that was lingering in the stale, humid air.

He had met her the night before in the hotel bar after, admittedly, drinking too many Don Julio 1942 Añejo tequilas, his regular drink of choice since he had gotten out of prison. She was sitting alone at the end of the bar, pretending not to have noticed him just as he had pretended not to have noticed her. He drained the last of his tequila, the ice clinking against his teeth as he tipped the glass back while taking her beauty in: her shoulder-length, curly black hair falling loosely onto her smooth, bare shoulders; the corners of her mouth turned up, slightly, as she laughed easily with the bartender; and the gold in her eyes flickering like a flame when the light from the moon hit them at just the right angle. She saw him watching her, got up and walked towards him, self-assured and without a hint of diffidence.

"Is this seat taken?" she asked, her voice betraying a whisper of a South African accent and something else he could not place.

Without waiting for a response, she sat down on the bar stool next to CK and motioned to the bartender, "Jimmy, two more, love, on my tab."

When the bartender brought their drinks, she turned to CK and, while smiling and raising her glass to his, said in the same sultry voice, "Hello, I'm Anika, and you?"

The rest of the night was a blur. More tequila for him, more rum for her. Talking, laughing, arms brushing against each other, his hand on her knee, her hand on his crotch. And then nothing. No memory. CK had no recollection of paying the tab, leaving the bar, nothing. And then he woke up that morning with Anika, her name the only thing he remembered, next to him in his bed, both naked, and his head feeling like someone had put a sledgehammer to it.

He took a quick, cold shower and brushed his teeth, but that was all he could muster. He had to get out of that room, get some fresh air. He opened his wallet and dropped two twenties on the nightstand and slipped his wallet into his back pocket along with his room key. It had been a long time since he had been with a woman, and he was anxious to get out of the room before she woke up. He hoped the cash on the nightstand would pay for her Uber or breakfast or something, if she even took them. But hopefully she would be gone before he returned.

In the lobby, he poured himself a Cuban coffee from the complimentary self-serve station and popped three ibuprofens before walking out into the rain towards the beach. As he walked, the pain relievers, the strong coffee, and the smell of the ocean began to work their magic. His stomach was no longer churning, and his headache was beginning to subside. The cool rain pelting his face was also a welcome relief.

He started to gain clarity on why he was there and what he needed to do next. His thoughts turned to Monica, as they often did in the past few weeks. He had loved her – there was no question about that. He never thought he would feel anything but love for her. Even knowing that her father had set him up to get him away from Monica, he never blamed her for that.

But now he felt something very different: *rage. Deep, searing, unbridled rage.*

He would punish her for what she and her family had done to him – but most importantly, for what she had kept from him. All those years, for keeping his son from him.

Finally free, he was going to make up for lost time, and first on his list was connecting with their son – *his son* – the son he never knew he had.

Then he would find Monica.

He checked his phone. No messages. He opened his contacts and clicked on the contact saved in his phone as *Sis*, although he hadn't spoken to his sister since shortly after he went to prison. She had only reached out to him once – to tell him that their mother had died. But even then, she hadn't come in person. She sent a letter. With the delays caused by inspections and bureaucracy, CK learned of his mother's death a month after she died. He never blamed his sister for abandoning him after what he did – that he understood – but he would never forgive her for telling him about their mother's death in a cold, emotionless letter. If she had come in person, he may have been able to get a furlough to attend the funeral. Probably not, but it was possible. She took any shred of a possibility away from him.

CK had a lot of scores to settle now that he was out of prison.

He clicked on the messages box, pulled up the number he knew by heart, and typed "Here. ETA?"

After about a minute, his phone vibrated in his hand. He lifted his phone and swiped up to trigger the face ID before reading the response, "Landed. Meet at hotel at 11."

He was still getting used to the new technology since he had been out. In prison, he could only get old burner and flip phones. The so-called smart phones were too smart: easily detectable and traceable with GPS locators within the prison so no one used them. Old school was better on the inside. But he was amazed at the new technology as well as the insecure and unblocked internet service. There really wasn't anything you couldn't find online, whatever your kink.

Times had certainly changed, he thought.

He checked the time again: 9:42 a.m. He hoped it was safe to return to his room. He had a little over an hour before he had to meet his associate and he needed to get himself together and jot down his notes.

He made his way back across the hotel lobby towards the elevator, refilling his coffee on the way. The door to the elevator opened and he found himself face to face with the beautiful Anika.

"Um, g-g-good morning," he stuttered awkwardly, as he backed up to allow her to pass by him as she got off the elevator.

At first, she said nothing as she passed him, barely registering that she recognized him. She had been asleep when he left the room earlier, and it was quite possible that she didn't recognize him, especially if she was as drunk as he was. He hoped that was the case.

But then she turned back to him, as if he was an afterthought, and came in close for an embrace or a kiss. Her musky perfume instantly reminded him of the far too many tequila shots he drank last night, and his stomach recoiled at the memory.

Instead she stuffed the twenties he had left on the nightstand into the breast pocket of his shirt before whispering into his ear, without a hint of the South African accent she had exhibited the night before, "Darling, next time save us both the trouble and buy yourself a cheap, twenty-dollar whore – she'll be happy to get paid whether you can get it up or not."

She turned and walked away, never looking back at him.

He stood there for a moment, feeling the heat rise in his face as his embarrassment quickly turned to rage.

The ping on his phone notifying him of an incoming text saved her, for now. He shook his head and stepped onto the elevator, thankful she was not going to be in his room when he got there.

But if their paths crossed again, he would not be as polite, he thought as he clenched his hands into fists.

He was back in the lobby an hour later waiting for Ray.

CK watched the stocky man with the receding hairline and pasty pale skin approach the hotel lobby. The man wore a leather jacket, which was out of place in the hot Miami sun, and walked with a slight limp. Most people probably wouldn't notice the limp, but CK was there when a guard shattered the man's kneecap with a swift and hard swing of his baton, instantly debilitating him. CK intervened and stopped the guard from smashing in his skull, which brought its own punishment to CK, including broken ribs and a month in solitary.

As he came through the automatic doors, the man flicked his burning cigarette butt onto the pavement and exhaled a plume of smoke that followed him into the lobby. He dipped his sunglasses below his dark eyes and scanned the room until he spotted CK. As he walked towards him and picked up his pace, the limp became more pronounced.

"Ray, been a long time, brother," CK said as he reached out to shake the man's hand.

"Fuckin-A, as I live and breathe, the Broker, in the flesh! How in the hell are you, buddy?" he said, pulling CK into a bear hug.

"Can't complain," CK said as he gestured to the scenery around them. "This beats the fuck out of our previous cage in Raiford, don't it?"

"Hell yeah, it does. How'd you get out? I thought you were a lifer?"

"Long story. I'll tell you over some tequila one day. Let's just say a powerful family did me right after a lifetime of wrongs. They owed me."

"Got it, brother, just happy to see you on the outside," Ray said, clamping down on CK's shoulder in a warm grip.

"Me too," CK replied. "For both of us. How's the leg?"

"About as good as it's ever gonna get, but it could be worse, right?"

"Yeah, everything can always be worse. No fuckin doubt about that."

"So, what's the job boss? Who's the mark?" Ray asked.

"Well, not really a mark this time. My son. He was born when I was inside, and I've never met him. Hell, I don't know if he even knows about me. I certainly didn't know about him until a few months ago. But I want to find him."

"He's here in Miami?"

"Maybe. I'm not sure. I traced him to Santo Domingo, but after a few weeks scouring the island, I came up empty. I know where he's been, but not where he is. Through some of my old contacts, I learned he's either here or in Cuba. It might be harder to stay oblivious in Cuba these days. My gut tells me that he's hiding out here."

"Hiding out? Who's he hiding from, Boss?"

"Everyone, I think. He may have done some bad things up in Tampa. But I want to find him and meet him. And maybe I can help him, get him on the right track."

"Got it. And then what?"

"And then I have a score to settle with his mother and her family."

CHAPTER TWENTY-FIVE
HALLIE

Hallie scrolled through her social media and the latest local news on her phone while enjoying her morning coffee when a headline caught her attention:

SIESTA KEY WOMAN FOUND MURDERED IN HOME

By: Jennifer Meister

Friday, April 26, 2024 / Tampa Bay Times

Stacey Morris, 31, of Siesta Key, was found dead in her home last weekend by her roommate, Cassandra O'Leary, who became concerned when she learned she hadn't reported to work on Saturday morning. According to the police report, Ms. O'Leary tried texting and calling Ms. Morris, but she didn't answer or respond to her texts, prompting her and her boyfriend, Massimo Tini, to go to the home she shared with Ms. Morris. They found her body in her bedroom and immediately called the police.

The Medical Examiner has not released the official cause of death but has characterized it as a homicide. A source close to the investigation, who spoke on the condition of anonymity, indicated that it was one of the grisliest crime scenes they had seen in their career and the victim was likely tortured. "A literal blood bath," according to the source. The police are asking anyone in the area who saw or heard anything unusual to call the Criminal Investigations Division of the Sarasota Police Department at 941-. 263-6073.

As she finished the article, she thought about the Treasure Island victim Charlie was accused of murdering and the other two woman who were murdered under similar circumstances and whom she had just read about.

And then she thought about the young woman who was found strangled in her hotel room in downtown Tampa. She had initially wondered whether the Treasure Island and Tampa murders could be related: both were young woman in their twenties, both from out of town, both strangled, both had been partying. But a few days after the press conference, the police arrested one of the groomsmen who apparently had been obsessed with the victim. He was caught on one of the security cameras walking her into the hotel shortly before she was murdered. When shown the video during questioning, he broke down and confessed. He was drunk, and after walking her to her hotel room, he tried to kiss her. She rejected his advances, and he became aggressive. According to his statement, he *"lost it and didn't mean to hurt her."*

Bullshit, Hallie thought. *You meant to hurt her; you just didn't mean to get caught.*

Hallie knew the downtown Tampa victim was not related to the Treasure Island victim, but she now knew about three other murdered women, including this latest Siesta Key victim, and the Crystal River, Citrus County and Ceder Key, Levy County victims. All were beach towns, catering to tourists, and all within a few hours of Tampa and each other. Hallie, understanding the way law enforcement worked, especially in some of these small towns, found it interesting that each murder took place in a different county. That would certainly make it harder for local law enforcement to connect their own investigation to an investigation in another county.

The murders weren't identical, but similar enough, especially the age of the victims and the fact that they all happened in quaint beach towns along the west coast. Hallie believed they were connected, even though, admittedly, the Tampa case sounded more similar to the Treasure Island case than the Siesta Key case did, at least what Hallie had read online, but there was something about the cases that struck her, especially after discovering the Crystal River and Ceder Key cases.

It was worth looking into for Charlie's sake, she thought.

CHAPTER TWENTY-SIX
LINDA

Linda had seen Billy three times in the yard over the past month. Each time he smiled at her and blew kisses to her with his back to the guards in the yard, which she would pretend to catch and hold against her heart. She got a new cellphone just for his calls, and he would try to call her every Saturday. She would regularly add money to his prison phone account from an untraceable prepaid Visa card. They knew their calls were being recorded, so they made sure never to say anything that would identify her, including her name, or about their plans.

She had received four more letters from him, each sweeter than the last, including the one she received the day before:

My dearest Linda,

Every time I receive a letter from you, my heart skips a beat. You are the love I have waited for all my life. I am so thankful that God brought you into my life. My lawyers are filing an appeal on my behalf this week. I am confident that once the higher court sees how all of my constitutional rights have been trampled on, they will either set me free or at least award me a new, fair trial. Your support in my quest to prove my innocence means more to me than you will ever know. If there is ever a chance for us to be together, I know you will do whatever you can, as will I, to make that happen. Until then, I remain,

> *Faithfully yours,*
> *Billy*

As with most of his letters, she read them over and over again until she had practically memorized them. She longed for the day they would be together in real life. In the meantime, she looked forward to going to work every day, always hoping that Karl would send her on an errand so that she might get a glimpse of Billy in the yard, and then she couldn't wait to get home to see if she had received a new letter from Billy. For the most part, she was happy in her new life, but she prayed his appeal would go through or something would happen to allow them to be together in person.

She sat at her desk, looking again at the clock on the wall, thankful Martha was keeping her snarky comments to herself for a change. She wasn't in the mood for her that day. She finished inputting all of the invoices from her daily folder in the system, disappointed that none required her to leave the administration office. Her thoughts were interrupted by Karl's voice.

"Listen up, we're going to keep monitoring this storm. It's early in the season, but it's possible, and if it heads our way after it hits landfall off the Gulf, like Hurricane Charlie did back in '04, we're going to have some bad weather in this area. I just emailed you both the prison's emergency policies and procedures – review them before you go home tonight and be prepared."

"What storm?" Martha asked, looking nervously at Karl and then back at Linda.

"Right now, it's only a tropical storm, but it's expected to turn into a hurricane, Hurricane Alice, after it hits the warm waters of the Gulf," Karl responded.

"Wait, is it really heading our way?" a dumbfounded Martha asked.

It was Linda's turn to roll her eyes.

"It's possible, Martha," Karl answered, "How long have you lived in Florida?"

"Um, about a year."

"Okay, so as a lifelong Florida resident, here's what you need to know: watch the local news or listen to it, get batteries and a flashlight, plenty of water, and if they tell you to evacuate, do it. Otherwise, hunker down and ride it out, unless you're in a mobile home. Are you in a mobile home, Martha?

"No, my boyfriend and I live in a little house in Starke."

"Okay, good, then you should be fine as long as they don't order your area to evacuate. The prison will send an employee-wide text alert if we close the office, which we will do if it's not safe for you to come into work. How about you, Linda, you prepared?"

"Yes, sir, I'm good. Lifelong resident of Florida, too, so I'm very familiar with what to do in a hurricane. I lived near the water on the West Coast during the last two."

"Okay, good, so you know what to do. Why don't you both finish up whatever you're working on and head out early today. That way you can get whatever supplies you need. People start to panic and buy up all the water as soon as we're in the cone of uncertainty, so make sure you get you some water on the way home, Martha."

"Cone of uncertainty?" Martha asked, her normal glibness gone from her ashen, freckled face.

"Watch the weather channel when you get home. They'll be showing the various projected tracks of the storm, also called the spaghetti models because all the lines look like a bunch of spaghetti noodles, meaning no one has a damn clue where the storm is going to hit. And to hedge their bets, they create a cone of the projected path with the eye of the hurricane at the center of the cone, which will shift and wobble left and right, as the storm gets closer to landfall. As I've always said, prepare for the worst and hope for the best. I've also always said the projections are a bunch of horseshit," Karl chuckled, donning a goofy smile on his face.

Linda and Martha looked at each other, exchanging an unspoken, rare moment of alliance at Karl's strange behavior.

"Anyway, since we're administration and not essential personnel during an emergency event, if the storm continues on its current path, our office will be closed until after the storm has passed and it's deemed safe to return. Martha, watch for uprooted, fallen trees and downed power lines. And don't drive through standing water, ever. After you read through the procedures, you two get on out of here," Karl barked, the weird smile no longer on his face.

Linda and Martha did as instructed, silently reading the prison emergency procedures Karl had sent to them before gathering their stuff and heading out of the office. The sun was bright and relentless in the cloudless sky, and it seemed even hotter than usual. They walked across the parking lot towards their respective cars. The blazing asphalt trapped the heat on its surface the way a log in a fire pit glowed red long after the flame had died out. The air was sticky and still and the idea of an impending wet and windy storm seemed improbable in that moment, but not to Linda who had grown up with such weather all her life.

"Stay safe, Martha," Linda yelled after her co-worker, to which Martha gave a thumbs up over her shoulder without turning around, got into her blue Kia, and drove away.

Normally Linda would feel annoyed at Martha's aloofness and poor manners, but not today. No sir, neither Martha nor an approaching hurricane could dampen her spirits today.

She had plans to make, she thought excitedly. *It wouldn't be long before she and Billy would be together.*

The storm was still at least 24-48 hours away, depending on its speed once it hit the warm waters of the Gulf. There was no reason to get all worked up about it this early, she knew from experience, but she also knew as it got closer, the stores would run out of everything, so it was a good idea to stock up on her hurricane supplies on her way home. Besides water, batteries for her flashlight, candles, matches, and a few nonperishable food supplies, she was also going to treat herself to a nice Pinot Grigio. She felt like celebrating.

Linda stopped at the Winn Dixie in Starke on her way home. Linda made her way around the store, thankful there were still pallets stocked high with cases of water. She hoisted two cases into her cart and added a few, one-gallon jugs as well.

"Linda?"

She turned around at the sound of her name.

"Oh, Scotty, hi," Linda said, surprised to see him outside of the prison library.

"Gettin' ready for the storm?" he said, glancing into her cart.

"Yup, better safe than sorry," Linda replied nervously.

"Yeah, me too," he said.

Scotty was always polite and nice to her, but she always felt like there was something bubbling just under the surface that wanted to come out. She couldn't put her finger on it, but it unnerved her. He had a strong build, his muscled forearms adorned with tattoos, and short blondish-brown hair. He wore thick, black-rimmed glasses, which magnified his blue-green eyes, giving them a buggy effect.

"If you need help securing anything at your house or boarding up your windows or anything, I'm happy to help. You don't live too far from me," Scotty offered.

"Um, th-th-thank you, Scotty, that's super sweet of you," Linda stammered. "But I don't think the storm's going to be that bad, do you?"

How does he know where I live? Linda wondered.

"You never know, with this damned global warning. And look what happened with that last one that hit down in the Naples and Ft. Meyers area. They didn't see that one comin' either. As you said, better to be safe than sorry," Scotty replied.

"Well, I think I'm all set, but I appreciate the offer, Scotty. I better be goin' so I can get the rest of my stuff before they run out of everything," Linda said as she pushed her cart in the opposite direction.

"You stay safe now, Linda," Scotty said as he stood in the middle of the aisle watching her walk away.

Linda picked up her pace, trying to shake her uneasy feeling. She finished her shopping, relieved that she didn't run into Scotty again. She perused the celebrity magazines in the checkout line, decided on the one with Taylor Swift on the cover, and paid for her groceries and left. By the time she arrived home, her focus had returned to the storm, and she didn't give Scotty a second thought.

Power outages and tornadoes were the only real concerns with a hurricane this far inland, unlike the flooding and storm surge that the coastal cities would get. The storm, if it hit, was expected to be a Category 1 or maybe even a Category 2, which probably meant a lot of wind and rain, but nothing catastrophic.

Linda had been through worse.

A lot worse.

CHAPTER TWENTY-SEVEN
HALLIE

Over the next few days, Hallie's focus shifted from Charlie's defense, her research into other murdered victims, her mother's wedding plans, and the letter from Stephens to preparing for the first hurricane of the season headed towards Tampa Bay. The current tracks had it heading up through the Gulf of Mexico towards the west coast of Florida, which included the Tampa Bay area. Hallie had been through many hurricane preps in her life growing up in Tampa, although it was rare for a hurricane to hit the area dead-on, especially this early in the season.

Hallie grew up hearing about the Tocobaga, a native Indian tribe who legend had it protected the Tampa Bay area from storms. The Tocobaga lived in small villages from the nine hundredth century to the fifteen hundreds until the last of them died out from disease and violence brought by Spanish settlers during the seventeenth century. Before they were eradicated, the Tocobaga built mounds out of layers of shells and sand, which they used as temples, homes, and burial grounds, with the oldest remaining known mound located in Phillippe Park near

Old Tampa Bay. Locals believed the Tocobaga and the sacred mound have protected the Tampa Bay area from major storms for centuries.

It was hard to argue against the folklore as there were only two direct hits to the area in the last two hundred years: the Great Gale of 1848, which made landfall in Clearwater, Florida, and the hurricane that hit Tarpon Springs in 1921. Tampa had been spared time and time again, creating an attitude of indifference – or worse, disregard – among most residents whose hurricane preparation consisted of stocking up on alcohol and snacks. Hallie had to admit she had done the same over the years, but this one seemed to be on a direct path to Tampa, and she was nervous about it.

The impending storm was approaching fast and, unless it deviated from its current track, Hallie knew it had to be taken seriously. She had gone to Publix the day before to stock up on water, wine, batteries, and things to eat that wouldn't require electricity before everything ran out, including bags of ice for her coolers. She packed up a few files from her office in case the storm impacted the Tampa Bay area, and she was stuck at home for a few days afterwards. She left the office and called Marcelo on her way home.

"Hey babe," Marcelo said as he answered his cell phone.

"Hi," Hallie responded. "I'm worried about this storm. I think it could be bad. What do you think?"

"I'm watching it, but it's too soon to tell. It's going to wobble east and west until it's a lot closer and we get a better idea of the track. It could turn, you know, like Hurricane Charlie did."

"Yeah, I remember that one. Do you think this one will turn?"

"No way to tell until it gets a lot closer, so we should prepare as if it isn't going to turn."

"Yeah, that's what I was thinking. Do you think I need to board up my windows?"

"How old are they?" Marcelo asked.

"Um, let me think. They're about ten years old. I had to replace them after all my air conditioning was seeping out of the old original flimsy windows."

"Nah, you don't have to board up then. Your windows are new enough that they should sustain hurricane force winds under the new code requirements that went into effect about twenty years ago," Marcelo said.

Hallie wished she felt as confident as Marcelo sounded.

"Are you going to come protect me?" Hallie asked playfully.

"As soon as work ends today, I'll be there. I've got mad hurricane-protecting skills."

"I can't wait," Hallie replied, smiling, looking forward to seeing him that night. She still wasn't sure why they seemed to be drifting apart, but if it took a hurricane to get them back in synch, she was okay with that.

"Me either. Do you have enough supplies, or do you need me to pick anything up on my way?" Marcelo asked.

"I think I have enough of everything, including water, ice, nonperishable food, and, of course, adult beverages, but I can stop somewhere on my way home if you think we need anything else. Anything come to mind?"

"Just you, Counselor," Marcelo said, making Hallie smile, which had not been happening lately.

* * *

She decided to stop at Publix on her way home to pick up a few more things, just in case they lost power for days. It was an absolute madhouse with people scrambling to prepare for the storm. There was barely anything left on the shelves, but she got the additional supplies she wanted, including a loaf of bread, a jar of peanut butter, a long stemmed click lighter, more candles, and charcoal and lighter fluid for her grill. By the time she got home, Juno was anxiously waiting for her at the front door.

"C'mon, sweet girl, I'm so sorry you had to wait so long," Hallie said as she let her out and watched her in the front yard.

She remembered her leftover rotisserie chicken in the fridge and decided she would give Juno an extra treat for dinner.

"Are you my sweet girl? I have a special treat for you tonight," Hallie cooed, petting Juno on the head as they came back into the house.

Hallie fed Juno, adding the left-over rotisserie chicken to her dry food and mixing it up. Juno stood at her side and wagged her tail, excited about the feast she was about to have. Hallie set the dish down, checked to make sure she had locked the front door, and poured herself a glass of wine. She then turned on the TV to watch the latest storm coverage, switching between her local news station and the Weather Channel.

Jim Cantore from the Weather Channel was reporting live from Tarpon Springs as the Tampa Bay area was in the latest cone projections. If the storm stayed on track, it could be a direct hit.

It is never a good sign when Cantore shows up in your city, Hallie thought.

She flipped back to her local station and was comforted hearing the voice of Denis Phillips, the local Chief Meteorologist, who was famous for his weather preparation rules, the most important of which was Rule #7: "*Don't freak out unless I tell you to.*" Denis, clad in his signature suspenders, was showing the latest track of the storm and calmly explaining the most likely impacts of the storm on the Tampa Bay area. She, like most residents in the area, trusted Denis and appreciated his calm demeanor and accurate reporting during a storm.

She was about to go upstairs to change out of her work clothes when she heard the familiar buzz vibration on her phone signifying she had received a text.

"Hey, Counselor."

"Hi, I just got home."

"Ready for company?"

"As long as it's you, absolutely," Hallie responded with the devil emoji.

"Be there in ten minutes. Open a bottle of wine," Marcelo responded with the red heart and wine glass emojis.

"Well, you're in luck, I already did. Are we starting our hurricane party early?" Hallie teased.

"I miss you. I can't wait to see you."

"I miss you, too," Hallie said.

Maybe we're okay, she thought, thankful the strangeness of the last few weeks was not there. She picked up her glass of wine, grabbed her briefcase off the kitchen counter and dropped it on her desk before heading up the stairs to change and freshen up before Marcelo got there. She stripped out of the skirt, blouse, and bra she had worn to the office that day. She put on a fresh thong, tank top, and jean shorts, brushed her teeth, and replenished her lipstick just as she heard Marcelo's truck pull into her driveway.

He was at the door when she came down the stairs. When she opened the door, he immediately took her in his arms and kissed her, hard.

"Mmmm, minty, Counselor," Marcelo said, still holding onto her waist, and licking his lips.

Hallie felt herself melt. If he had taken her right there, she would not have resisted.

"You are so sexy," he whispered in her ear, his tongue grazing her earlobe, her body automatically reacting to him as she started to throb, and her hips rose up into him. She could feel his heat and his yearning against her. She felt her own too.

He backed her up into the living room, and unbuttoned and unzipped her shorts, letting them fall to the floor. She lifted her tank top over her head, revealing her supple, bare breasts, her nipples hard and longing for his mouth to be on them. He gripped her ass in his strong hands and lifted her onto him as she straddled him. He sat back onto the couch, pulling her on top of him. Her body responded instinctively, almost primitively, grinding on top of him as her mouth took his into hers. She thought she was going to explode.

He moved out from underneath her and stood up to take off his shirt, revealing the perfect patch of dark hair on his well-defined pecs. He unbuttoned his jeans and slipped them off, never taking his eyes off her. When he took his black boxer briefs off next, he revealed how much he wanted her in that moment.

Her heart was pounding.

Her body was throbbing.

He sat down and lifted Hallie back on top of him. She straddled him, one knee on each side of him. She felt all of him, harder than before, and she ached for him to be inside of her. She had never wanted anyone so much in her life as she wanted him in that moment.

"Please," she begged, "please."

"Baby," he whispered in her ear, his warm breath tickling her earlobe and exciting her even more.

"Please," she said again as she guided him into her.

They devoured each other for the next hour, taking turns pleasing each other, in perfect rhythm, until they both climaxed a final time before collapsing next to each other on the couch.

"Wow," Hallie said.

"Wow," Marcelo echoed.

"We really need to start our evenings off like this more often," Hallie laughed.

"No objection from me, Counselor."

"Can we go away somewhere soon? After this stupid hurricane passes?" Hallie asked.

"Where do you want to go?"

"Anywhere, an island, a cabin in the mountains, anywhere secluded, the more deserted the better, for a long weekend. Tonight reminded me that we need to make time for us, get away from all the bullshit here," Hallie said.

"Yes, I agree. Let's do it."

Before long, Hallie fell asleep with her head on Marcelo's chest, dreaming of pina coladas and aquamarine waves crashing against a sandy beach with Marcelo by her side. It was the best sleep she had had in a long time.

* * *

Marcelo checked his phone, making sure not to wake up Hallie. He had two missed calls and four texts. He was glad he remembered to silent his phone before he got out of the truck.

He knew who they were from.

He turned his phone off, placed it on the end table, stroked Hallie's blonde hair and closed his eyes.

CHAPTER TWENTY-EIGHT
LINDA

The weather channel continued to track Hurricane Alice as it traveled up the Gulf. It was expected to make landfall somewhere north of Pinellas County, and from there, to travel northeast across the State, which put Raiford, where the prison was located, and Starke, where Linda lived, directly in its path. If it hit as they predicted, they could expect heavy rain, wind gusts up to eighty miles an hour, and tornadoes. It was less than seven hours away, but the outer bands had already started to make landfall on the western coast of Florida. Linda wasn't particularly nervous, but she also knew that she had to have a plan because it was looking more likely that she was going to be somewhere in its path.

She did a load of laundry, ran the dishwasher, and took a shower, in case she was without running water and electricity for a few days. Next, she filled as many empty pitchers and old water jugs as she had on hand with tap water and lined them up in the bathroom, the only windowless room in her house, and stacked the bottled water she had just bought in there as well. She charged every electronic device she had, including the two portable chargers she kept for emergencies, and placed them on the bathroom counter next to the portable AM-FM radio and extra flashlights.

She gathered her important papers and sealed them in plastic baggies and added them to the plastic bin in the bathroom. She added a change of clothes, cat food, protein bars and other snacks for herself, and a few other valuables she didn't want to lose should the worst happen. She piled a comforter on top of some couch cushions on the floor so she would have something comfortable to sit on and put an extra litter box next to the toilet. She was all set. She and Carole Baskins could easily ride out the storm in the bathroom if it got too bad.

For the next few hours, Linda sipped on her glass of Pinot Grigio and watched old episodes of *Friends*, intermittently switching over to the weather channel to keep an eye on Hurricane Alice. Before long, she couldn't keep her eyes open and went to bed hoping the storm would take a hard shift north by the time she awoke the next morning.

* * *

BOOM!!

Linda jolted awake at what sounded like a bomb going off outside. She shot up, her heart pounding, and listened as the trees swirled in the howling wind and the branches slapped against her window. She heard multiple car alarms going off up and down the street, which she thought must have been triggered by the loud noise that woke her. She reached for the lamp on her nightstand and fiddled to find the switch in the dark.

Click.

Click.

Nothing.

The power was out, and Linda realized the sound she heard was likely a transformer blowing, knocking the power out to the whole street.

"Oh, heavens to Betsy," Linda exclaimed, grabbing her phone and flashlight from the nightstand, finally breathing normal again.

She looked at her phone, thankful for the light it emitted into the dark room. It was 11:23 p.m. She opened the local weather app, including the live radar, and could see the eye of the storm hadn't made landfall yet, but it was a large storm, and they were getting hit by the bands from the east side of the storm. The east side of a hurricane, also called the dirty side, was the most dangerous side to be on, and it was no surprise to Linda that there were reports of tornadoes touching down in the area. As the next gust came through, she thought the trees were going to shatter her windows, and she knew it was time to retreat to her windowless saferoom she had prepared.

She turned on her flashlight to look for Carole Baskin. It didn't take long to find her hiding behind the chair in the corner of her bedroom, the flashlight beam illuminating her golden-yellow eyes. She scooped up the terrified cat and brought her into the bathroom. Before settling in herself, she closed the door behind her and went out to the living room to look out the front window.

All the streetlights were out, and she could see that a large tree had uprooted itself out of the soaked ground and fallen onto the street, blocking the entire roadway. Her neighbor was lucky it didn't fall onto his house, which she could barely see through the torrential rain, wind, and darkness.

As she stared out, trying to see if there was any other damage, flying debris whacked against the window, sending Linda running back into the bathroom. She made sure not to let Carole escape and quickly shut the door, her hands trembling as she locked it. She grabbed another flashlight and the portable radio and sat down on the seat she had made for herself earlier. Carole was pacing and meowing loudly but seemed to calm down after she was able to climb onto Linda's lap.

"It's okay, muffin, I know you're scared," Linda cooed as she scratched the cat behind her ears. "I'm a little scared, too, but we're gonna be okay. We just have to wait for this nasty old storm to pass, and then we'll get out of this dag-gum bathroom, pardon my French."

She turned on the radio and turned the knobs until she finally connected to a station reporting on the storm.

"A tornado has touched down at the maximum-security prison in Raiford and one of the buildings has been badly damaged," the newscaster reported before she lost the signal and could only hear heavy static.

Linda turned the knobs left and right, frantically trying to tune back into the station. When she finally connected, Linda heard, "at least seven prisoners from . . . *[static]* wing . . . *[static]* escaped. . . . *[static]* . . . possibly dead."

"What in the world? Oh, my lamb," Linda said aloud while clutching her chest.

She stayed in the bathroom for the next few hours, trying to discern what was happening outside. It would be eerily quiet and then it would howl and rage, with branches or debris clacking against the house. She prayed the little concrete block house would hold up. She was also worried about Billy. She adjusted the tuner on the AM-FM radio, trying to see if she could learn anything else about the storm or what happened at the prison. She picked up the local UF radio station, which was broadcasting live about the storm and its impacts on the area within its broadcast footprint, which included Starke.

Growing up in Florida, Linda remembered at a young age having to choose between the two power houses, Florida State or University of Florida. It was never about the universities but about their football teams. Most of her current neighbors had "Gator Nation" bumper stickers and other Gator adornments on their houses and cars to show their allegiance to the University of Florida football team, which was about twenty miles south of Starke.

"What are you, a Seminole or a Gator?" she remembered Joey Larson asking her on the playground during recess in the third grade.

"Um, neither?" Linda timidly replied, not having any idea what he was talking about.

"C'mon, Linda, you have to pick one. It's the rule."

"It's a rule? I never heard of that rule. What's the difference?" Linda asked, bewildered.

"Well, a Seminole is an Indian, like the Seminole Indians, and a Gator is, you know, just an alligator, get it?" Joey asked without waiting for her to answer. "So you have to pick, do you want to be an Indian or an alligator? Because once you pick, you're that for life. That's the rule, my dad said."

"Well, if I have to pick," Linda said slowly, looking up at the sky as she thought, "then I want to be an alligator."

"Ugghhh," Joey said as he smacked his forehead dramatically. "Really, Linda? Did you listen to anything I said?"

"I did. You told me I can be an Indian or an alligator. I want to be an alligator."

"Suit yourself. Me and my dad are Seminoles. But it's *gator*, not alligator. Why did you pick gator anyway?"

"Well, my Aunt Betty gave me a green stuffed alligator when I was six and I named her Allie. She's so cute and I still have her. She sits on my bed. So that's why I would rather be an alli . . . I mean, a gator than an Indian. I don't have any Indian stuffed animals."

"I guess that makes sense. I don't have any alligator stuffed animals. But everyone knows it's cooler to be a Seminole. That's what my dad says. I like alligators too but don't tell my dad. He'll get mad."

"I won't, I promise."

"Do you think I could see your alligator next time I'm at your house?" Joey asked, looking down at his feet in case Linda said no. She did not.

From that day forward, as decided on a sunny afternoon on a playground in the third grade, Linda became a Gator and Joey, true to his word, was a die-hard Seminole for as long as she knew him. She wondered where Joey was today.

The little radio crackled, and the newscaster's voice interrupted her reverie, "one wing has been completely destroyed, but the full extent of the damage is not yet known. At least three inmates and one guard have died from a roof collapsing on them, and many more have been injured. At this time, they have accounted for all but seven prisoners who they believe have escaped. A spokesperson for the Union County Sheriff's office said they are working with the Florida Dept. of Corrections to track the escaped prisoners. They warned that these individuals are extremely dangerous, possibly armed, and should not be approached. If you live in the area, keep your doors and windows locked and if you see anyone suspicious, call 9-1-1 immediately.

This is a developing story. We will keep you updated as we receive new information."

"Oh dear, Carole, I pray our Billy is okay," Linda said aloud as she stroked the tiger-striped cat curled up on her lap.

She listened to the radio for the next hour but didn't hear any further updates on the missing prisoners. The storm continued to rage outside in fits and bursts as the bands swirled overhead. She checked the radar again. The eye seemed to be further east but the worst of it did not appear to be subsiding anytime soon.

She clutched her beloved cat to her chest and closed her eyes.

CHAPTER TWENTY-NINE
MONICA

She looked at her phone. It was 4:30 p.m., and the outer bands of the hurricane had started to arrive in waves. She checked her weather app and learned that the eye had shifted again, and was now far enough north that they wouldn't receive the worst of the weather. She called O'Maddy's to see if they were open and was comforted at the sound of Marge's gruff voice answering the phone.

"O'Maddy's," Marge answered.

"How long you staying open with this damn storm coming?" Monica asked, knowing Marge would recognize her voice.

"What fuckin sto'hm?" Marge cackled. "A little wind and rain has eve'yone's panties in a wad. This ain't no No'theaste'neh, I tell you what. Now that's a fuckin sto'hm. This is nothin, just a little wind and rain; c'mon down. The regulars are all here."

"Perfect, on my way," Monica replied, thankful she didn't have to wait it out alone in her apartment. She didn't like to admit it, but storms made her anxious.

Since the wind and rain were coming in gusts, she decided to order an Uber instead of walking. She called her ride and was surprised she only had to wait about three minutes for her driver to get there.

She arrived at O'Maddy's and dashed inside shielding herself from the rain with her hoodie.

"How you doin' tonight, love? Stayin' dry?" Marge asked.

"Yeah, trying. But couldn't sit home alone waiting for the power to go out, so I figured I would come here," Monica replied.

"I hea' ya," Marge said, "What em I gonna do, sit in my apa'tment out back doin nothin? Nah, I figu'ed I might as well open up to give some of these losahs a place to ride it out. Mike ova thaya lives in a tent. He's not makin' it through one of ouwa nahmal sto'hms much less this one," Marge teased.

Mike, the house painter, tipped his bottle of beer and nodded as they all laughed.

Monica sipped her dirty martini and watched one of the TVs above the bar. All the stations were broadcasting about the storm, the one in front of her no exception. The reporter, clad in her plastic raincoat, was reporting live from St. Pete Beach, which was about four miles away from Gulfport. Gulfport wasn't directly on the Gulf, despite its name, and was protected, somewhat, by the Boca Ciega Bay that separated it from St. Pete Beach. The Bay acted as a buffer, at least from the worst of the storm surge that St. Pete Beach could get.

"Marge, I'll take another," Monica said, pointing to her empty glass.

"I got ya," Marge replied.

As she fixed her drink, Monica asked, "Marge, you got any kids?"

"I do," the hardened bartender responded with a hint of uncharacteristic softness in her eyes. "Two boys and a girl. A few grandkids now too."

"Are you close? Do you see them much?" Monica asked.

"Naw, they got thea' own lives now, still up in Boston. They don't need me fuckin' up thea' kids lives like I did thea's," she laughed in her gruff way, but with a sadness Monica hadn't recognized before. "My kids let me talk to my grandkids at Easta' and Christmas and I send gifts, but they won't let me visit. It's okay, my life is hea' now."

"I'm sorry, I get it. I have a son. I fucked him up, too," Monica said as she looked down into her martini glass, seeking absolution from a source that could never grant it.

Marge seemed to shake it off, any softness replaced by her regular surly and acerbic personality, "Why you bringin' all this shit up tonight? Shut the fuck up and drink your drink or get the fuck out, Moni. I love ya like a daughta' but I ain't got time for this bullshit."

Monica lifted her hands in surrender, signifying she understood. Marge's life and apparent estrangement from her kids made Monica sad. Marge was about twenty years older than Monica, but she saw herself in her. The resemblance frightened her, and she wanted desperately to be better: better than Marge; better than her own mother; better than the mother she had been to Pietro.

She paid her bill and walked home, bracing herself against the wind, the rain mixing with her tears, vowing to make changes in her life.

CHAPTER THIRTY
HALLIE

The eye of the storm was still offshore and north of the Tampa Bay, but it continued to gain strength as it traveled northeast over the warm waters of the Gulf of Mexico. The outer bands had already begun to land, and the Bay area was feeling its effects. Marcelo had left early that morning to place sandbags around his house in case the river breached the banks and to check in at the precinct. He had promised to be back before the worst of the storm arrived, if he could.

The wind howled outside Hallie's windows while sheets of rain and branches thrashed against the old house with each strong gust. She hadn't lost power yet, but she knew it was only a matter of time. She had her candles and flashlight ready and was doing her best to keep Juno calm.

Juno hated storms. And she hated to get her feet wet, so whenever it rained, Hallie had to put her on her leash to force her to go out.

Hallie had strapped Juno into her thunder vest earlier in the night and given her one of the anxiety pills the vet had prescribed for her. Both helped, but she was still too anxious to leave Hallie's side. Each time another wave of wind and rain came through, Juno trembled and scooched closer to Hallie, trying to climb into her lap.

"It's okay, June Bug," Hallie cooed to her beloved lab. "This too shall pass."

Hallie checked her phone, relieved to see she still had service and a full battery.

"Hey, how's it going?" Hallie texted Marcelo.

After about ten minutes, Hallie's phone pinged.

"Mom r u ok? I'm worried @ this storm that's hitting Florida," came the text from her daughter, Katie.

"Hi love. I'm fine. This old house has been here for over a hundred years. She's got this," Hallie responded, happy to hear from Katie.

"Dad says it's a bad one. Worst one Tampa has seen in a long time. Is Marcelo w/ u?"

"No baby, but I'm fine. He'll be here later. You know your dad always worries too much lol," Hallie responded, trying to put her daughter at ease.

"Juno must be freaking out. Is she ok?"

"Glued to my side lol but she's ok. How are you? How are classes?"

"Fine and fine. Promise me you'll evacuate if the storm gets worse – before it gets too bad that you can't leave. You know how bad it floods there," Katie directed.

"I promise. I'll call you after the storm has passed."

"I love u Mom."

"I love you more," Hallie responded, her eyes moistening for a second.

She knew Katie loved her, but her sometimes aloof daughter didn't express those emotions often. In that way, Katie was more like her father. Kevin was logical and self-assured, not one to exhibit emotions that could show any vulnerability.

Hallie ended the thread with a heart emoji just as the power went out. She got up and walked to the window, which elicited a whimper from Juno.

"It's okay, old girl, it's just a little wind and rain," Hallie said, trying to reassure them both.

Hallie lit the candle on her nightstand, grabbed her flashlight and headed towards Katie's bedroom at the front of the house. Looking down the street, she could see the power had gone out on her entire block and the water from the Bay was covering the street. The only light came from the moon and the heat lightening behind the angry clouds in the distance.

Thwack!!

The sound was so loud Hallie jumped, and Juno growled, uncharacteristically, while looking up at the ceiling.

"Holy shit, that was loud," Hallie said, wondering if a large limb from the giant Oak in her front yard had fallen onto her house.

She looked out the window. The old Oak was still intact, but something must have landed on the roof, maybe a large branch breaking off from the Oak or debris flying through the air.

She checked her cell phone again. Still fully charged and two bars. No reason she wouldn't receive a text from Marcelo if he texted her. She decided to reach out again.

"Hey, you good? Getting a little tense over here but we're fine. Can't wait until you get here."

Hallie watched as the dots on her message app lit up, signifying he was typing an answer.

And then they stopped, and no text came through.

The lights in her bathroom flickered for a moment, but then went dark again. Hallie looked out the front window, confirming the rest of the houses on her street were also still without electricity. Large gusts of wind rattled the windows and shook the branches, before getting eerily still and quiet. Juno was alert and still looking up at the ceiling in the direction of the original loud noise.

"Don't get squirrely on me now, girl. I'm nervous too," Hallie whispered, hoping that Juno would settle back down.

Hallie's phone vibrated in her hand, signifying she had a message.

"Sorry, working on something but I'll be there soon. You ok?"

"Yeah, no power, but we're ok," Hallie typed back.

"I should be done in about an hour. I'll text when I'm on my way."

"Okay, see you when you get here," Hallie sent, hoping he didn't change his mind.

She climbed into bed and pulled the comforter up around her. The house was cool but would warm up quickly the longer the air conditioner wasn't running. Juno did three circles next to Hallie until she curled up in a ball next to her and started to snore.

Hallie started to doze off too.

CHAPTER THIRTY-ONE
LINDA

Linda was startled when her cellphone rang. She must have dozed off, and Carole Baskins was sound asleep in her lap.

She looked at the number but didn't recognize it.

"Hello?" she answered, timidly.

"Is this the voice of an angel I hear?" came the recognizable voice through the phone, causing Linda to sigh in relief.

"Oh, my word, I've been worried sick about you. I heard the news reports. Are you okay?" Linda asked.

"Don't you worry about any of that nonsense. Are you ready to head to the mountains just like we planned?"

"Now?" Linda asked, her mind spinning from all the emotions she was feeling in that moment: excitement, trepidation, confusion.

"Well, my love, this storm is the answer to our prayers. When that tornado ripped that prison wall down, I believe God was forging the way for us to be together. I know it's sooner than we planned, but do you have everything ready to go like we talked about?"

"Um, yes, I think so. I just have to gather a few more things but mostly everything is already packed up in the car.

Except Carole Baskins, obviously," Linda giggled nervously. "I need to get her in her carrier and get all of her stuff."

"Oh, now darling, do you really think it's a good idea to bring a cat with us? Just fill a giant bowl with food and water and she'll be fine."

"William Henry Stephens, no sir! You bite your tongue. You know good and well I am not leaving Carole Baskins behind."

"Okay, okay," Billy relented. "Well just hurry up because we need to get out of Starke. Do you know where the Krystal is on Temple near the fairgrounds?"

"Um, yeah, I know it. I pass it on my way to and from work."

Linda knew the Krystal all too well as she stopped there often on the way home from work to pick up a bag of their delicious square burgers.

"Meet me there in an hour."

"What, now? Are you serious? It can't be safe for me to drive in this weather," Linda protested nervously.

"Honey, the worst of the storm is over in this area. It's no worse than a typical summer thunderstorm now," Billy said, trying to reassure her. "There might be a few more bands coming through, but you'll be fine. Just make sure you look for any trees in the road and downed powerlines. Avoid those. See you soon, my love."

She went to respond, to voice her concern about leaving the safety of her home, but Billy had disconnected.

Linda sat there trying to figure out what to do. Wasn't this what she had wanted? She thought about the letters they had exchanged and their phone conversations where they talked about their future together. They also talked about what they would need to start that life together, which she had gathered and packed in her trunk over the last few months. But she always believed that the truth – the truth that he was innocent – would set him free. It was important to Linda that he got out the right way.

She admitted to herself that exchanging letters and talking about their future together was probably a violation of her employment agreement, but she hadn't done anything that would be considered a law violation. At worst, she could be fired, but nothing more. Now he wanted her to pick him up, a convicted and now escaped felon.

"Oh Lordy, Carole Baskins, are we ready for this next adventure? Should we do this?" Linda asked the gray cat purring on her lap.

Linda had never gotten so much as a speeding ticket, if you don't count what happened to poor Donnie Morris. And she never counted that as that really hadn't been her fault.

The most she had ever done, by mistake, of course, was return her library book two months late. In all fairness, she had checked out five books at the time and she thought she had returned them all in the overnight return bin outside the library, but low and behold, Laura Lippman's *Prom Mom* had slipped under her passenger seat. She didn't find it until she got the overdue notice from the library and had to go searching for it.

Was she really ready to do this? She sat on the floor of the bathroom with Carole in her lap, rubbing the cat behind her ears while she purred, trying to figure out what to do. She thought about her life and how lonely she had been for the past few years. She always tried to do the right thing, and where did it get her? She thought about the things Billy said in his letters to her. No one had ever spoken so sweetly to her. How could it be wrong when it felt so right? Maybe Billy was right, maybe the hurricane was God's way of helping them be together.

She made up her mind. For once in her life, she was choosing what was in her heart, even if it might technically be against the law. If they could just clear his name, then it would all be okay. And that's what she would do as soon as they were together.

"I'm game if you are," Linda declared to Carole as she picked her up and guided her into her pink carrier. "Nothing ventured, nothing gained, right sweet girl?"

Linda sat behind the wheel of her blue Ford Escape under the carport, relieved the strong winds from earlier seemed to have subsided, and started the car. Carole meowed loudly from her carrier in the backseat. The only good thing about Hurricane Alice seemed to be that it was a fast-moving storm and was passing through the state quickly.

"I know, sweetie, I know," Linda cooed, "it's all going to be okay," she said, trying to convince herself more than her feline friend.

It had not taken Linda long to load the remaining items, including her suitcase and Carole Baskins, into her car. She already had the trunk packed with everything Billy had told her get before the storm arrived: a backpack filled with a pair of men's jeans, sweatpants, three t-shirts, a pack of underwear, pack of socks, two baseball caps, toiletries, and two prepaid phones. She also had two 24-packs of water, snacks and canned goods to last them a week, sleeping bags, a tent, a portable grill, and blankets. Linda didn't particularly like camping but thought she had done a good job preparing. The last thing she placed on the floor of the front passenger seat was a bag filled with a woman's button-down house dress, a gray wig, a razor and shaving cream, a bottle of water, a washcloth, and a small make-up bag that contained foundation, lipstick, and glasses.

She tuned the radio to the local station to see if there were any updates as she backed out of her driveway, making sure to avoid the large branches and debris behind her.

"Wow, it's a mess out here," Linda said aloud, stopping in the middle of the road to take in the downed trees and random patio furniture in her path. "Maybe we should turn back, Ms. Baskins? Oh, fiddle sticks, I don't know what to do."

She drove slowly down her street, relieved to see that none of the homes around her appeared to be damaged. She took a deep breath and let it out. This was it. She stopped at the stop sign, knowing she had a choice to make. After a few minutes, she made it.

She chose Billy.

She turned left out of her street and towards her new life with him, whatever that entailed. She knew after tonight she couldn't go back to her life as it was before. She felt bad for deceiving Karl. He was a nice man and a good boss. But that little bitty, Martha, she didn't feel bad about her at all. Martha would be delighted with the drama.

When Linda didn't show up for work after the hurricane passed, someone would try to call her, she figured. When she didn't answer or respond, would they go to her house to check on her? Maybe. Probably. But she wouldn't be there, and hopefully by then, she and Billy would be long gone. How long would it take before they figured out she was with Billy? Maybe not immediately, but eventually, she thought, especially after they reviewed the tapes of his phone calls and their emails and letters and figured out it was her. It wouldn't be hard.

The roads were mostly empty as she headed towards the meeting place. Billy was right, the winds had died down considerably and it wasn't any worse than a normal summer rainstorm. It took her about fifteen minutes to arrive at the Krystal. She pulled into the deserted parking lot and did a loop around the building. Billy was nowhere in sight. She backed into a space at the end of the building and faced the highway to watch for any cars approaching.

She had been waiting for about fifteen minutes when she saw a figure emerging from the trees that lined the back of the parking lot.

Billy.

Linda unlocked the doors and waited for Billy to get in the passenger seat. She thought he looked thinner than the last time she saw him, but that could be because his clothes were soaked and stuck to his frame.

"Let's go," he said, looking around nervously.

"Which way?" Linda asked, as she headed towards the exit of the Krystal.

"Head south on 301 to I-75. They're probably expecting us to head north to get out of Florida, judging by the state troopers I've seen heading in that direction for the past hour. Watch your speed. Don't go over the speed limit, especially on 301."

"Where are we going?"

"We need to get to a populated city where people mind their own business and won't pay us any attention. We're heading to Tampa."

"Isn't there a chance that people will recognize you there?"

"Not if you brought the things I told you to get," Billy responded, "and besides, I have some unfinished business there."

Linda input Tampa into her GPS and saw they had about fifty miles to go before they got to Interstate 75. Those fifty miles were going to be the riskiest part of their trip. If they could make it to 75 without being pulled over, she believed they would make it. The rain never stopped and would go from really strong and almost blinding to a light mist. Linda knew they were probably driving through some of the outermost bands as they headed southwest towards Tampa. The sweat started to bead on Linda's upper lip, and she felt her blouse sticking to her, despite the cool air blowing from the vents. Her knuckles were white with how tight she was gripping the steering wheel.

"Just relax, Linda, and go the speed limit. There's no reason for them to pull you over unless you give them a reason."

"What if they have a roadblock set up?"

"Don't worry, I'll be ready."

Billy reached into the bag at his feet and pulled out the razor, shaving cream, water, and washcloth. After he finished shaving, he applied the foundation, lipstick, and put on the wig and glasses. Linda looked over and started giggling.

"See? I'm just a sweet little old lady," he said as he pulled the house dress over his head and prison jumpsuit to complete the disguise. "If there's a roadblock, I'm going to pretend to be asleep and you just tell them you're returning from a trip with your mother."

"Okay, but let's just hope there's no roadblock."

"Fingers crossed, my darling."

"Where are we going to stay when we get to Tampa?" Linda asked.

"There's a motel on Nebraska Avenue in Seminole Heights that a buddy of mine in the joint told me about. His sister owns it. She's discreet, and so are the other motel guests."

"Nebraska Avenue? That sounds sketchy. The only motels I've seen on Nebraska have hourly rates and I think we both know what that means," Linda said.

"It's only temporary, hon. We need to go somewhere where no one asks any questions, and, more importantly, where they don't like talking to cops. As soon as I finish my business, we'll be heading north to the mountains, just as we planned."

"What kind of business do you have to finish?"

"Don't worry about that."

"I want to help."

"You can help by keeping your mouth shut and doing what I say. Now shut the fuck up and drive," Billy snapped.

Linda was taken aback. His anger was so unexpected and came out of nowhere. She had never seen that side of Billy. She felt the heat rise in her cheeks as she blinked back fresh tears and swallowed the lump in her throat. Linda hated to be yelled at, and it triggered memories of her childhood when her stepfather used to berate her and her mother. When he drank, which was all the time, he did more than yell. Linda shuddered at the memory while she tried to focus on the road ahead.

They made it to I-75 without encountering a roadblock or any police officers. Linda was relieved but still hurt by the way Billy spoke to her. She tried to remind herself how much pressure Billy was under, and that he probably didn't mean to be so harsh with her. Once they reached I-75, Billy wiped off the makeup with the damp washcloth and removed the wig, glasses, and dress. They had been driving for over two hours and were almost to Tampa when Billy finally spoke.

"275 South is coming up. Make sure you don't miss the exit. Where are the other clothes I asked you to get?"

Linda didn't answer and just remained silent, focused on the road ahead.

"Look, I shouldn't have yelled at you earlier, hon, but I was stressed, and I can't have you asking about things you have no business asking about. Really, I'm trying to protect you," Billy said as he reached over and patted her plump hand on the steering wheel.

At his touch and what sounded like an apology, Linda started to feel a little better.

"Well, it hurt my feelings, Billy, but I understand. You're under so much pressure, and sometimes, I admit, I can be a real buttinsky, that's for sure. My mother was always saying that to me when I was little. She would say, 'Linda, mind your business and stop being such a buttinsky, always sticking your nose where it doesn't belong.' I'll do better, Billy. I promise."

"I know you will. Okay, there's the exit for 275. We're almost there. And then the fun begins."

Linda didn't know what he meant about that, but she instantly had butterflies in her stomach and was ready to forget all about the way he snapped at her. After all, neither one of them had been on the run before. And she really was asking too many questions. She had to have faith that he knew where they were going and why. She promised herself that when they got to Tampa, she would relax and be much more supportive of what he was going through.

Twenty minutes later they were pulling into the parking lot of the El Rancho Motel on Nebraska Avenue in Tampa, the seediest motel Linda had ever seen.

She would rather sleep in the car than venture into this place, she thought to herself.

"Um, Billy, this can't be the right place. I'm scared we're going to catch MRSA or something worse if we stay here," Linda said as she looked around, trying not to make eye contact with the people loitering around the parking lot.

"I told you, it's only for a few days. I'll wait in the car. Check in at the office and pay in cash. Ask for Maria and tell her Johnny sent you. You have the cash I told you to get, right?"

"Yes, I got it."

"Good girl," Billy said, which made Linda cringe.

What was she some kind of dog? Well, if they slept here that night, she had no doubt they would end up with fleas, she thought but didn't say, not wanting to make him mad again.

Linda reminded herself that Billy was under a lot of pressure, and she needed to be more cooperative. They could work out all of these minor things when they got to their cabin in the mountains and could put this unfortunate experience behind them. Linda unclicked her seatbelt and started to get out of the car.

"Hon, don't forget, don't use your real name. If they ask for ID, tell them you lost it and give them another twenty-dollar bill. That's how this works."

"Um, okay, got it," Linda said, trying not to sound as nervous as she felt. She didn't want to disappoint Billy, after all.

As she got out of the car and headed towards the office, she was hit with a strong odor of weed coming from the direction of a group of people sitting outside one of the rooms off the parking lot. The motel room door was open, and Linda noticed two young children running in and out of the room. Linda tried to not to look their way as she made her way to the office door.

The small, gloomy office reeked of cigarette smoke, the walls stained permanently yellow. The woman behind the counter was completely engrossed with something on her phone and didn't acknowledge Linda when she walked in.

Linda cleared her throat, "Um, hi, um, I'm supposed to see Maria. Johnny sent me."

At that the woman looked up from her phone and cackled, smoke billowing out of her mouth from her filterless cigarette, "Bitch, you know Johnny?" she coughed as she continued, "No fuckin way, oh man, *Johnny sent you*, now that's some funny shit," as she continued to laugh, but not in a 'we're all in on the joke' way, but menacingly.

Linda was scared.

"Um, sorry, um, yeah, I mean, you're right, I don't know your brother. But my boyfriend does. He's in the car. He said you would be able to give us a room here. I have cash."

"Well, I do like cash," the woman laughed again, "but I don't know if I have a room for you. Who's your boyfriend?"

* * *

A few minutes later Linda returned to the car with a key. The woman gave them a room on the opposite end of the motel from the office and a few doors down from the weed smokers.

"How did it go?" Billy asked as she opened the door.

"Fine."

Linda's cheeks were flushed, and she was sweating.

"Fine? Everything okay? You don't seem '*fine*'."

"Yes, it's fine. She didn't believe me at first. But I did what you told me to do. I told her Johnny sent us, and I put the cash on the counter, including the extra $20."

"Did she ask for ID?"

"No," Linda said, "she didn't ask for my ID," realizing she had given Billy's name out of nervousness. There was no way she was going to tell Billy that.

"So why are you being so weird? Is there something you're not telling me?"

"Um, well, excuse me, but this is the first time I've checked into an establishment of this sort, and I'm a little nervous. But I did what you said. I gave her the cash, and she gave me the key. Can we please go to the room now? I want to get out of this car and parking lot, and I know Carole Baskins wants to get out of her carrier," Linda said, looking around the parking lot again.

"Fine. I've got the backpack, and I'll grab your small bag from the back seat but don't open the trunk or bring anything else into the room. We need to be as unmemorable as possible and the less stuff we bring into the room, the better."

"Well, I'm not leaving Ms. Baskins in the car, and we need to bring her litter box and the bag with her food and stuff in it. So I'll take her and you get the other stuff," Linda said, more authoritatively than she expected.

She put her oversized purse over her shoulder, picked up the pink cat carrier with Ms. Baskins meowing loudly, and headed towards room #7 at the El Rancho Motel, the name of which Linda had already changed in her mind to the *El Rauncho Motel.*

"Oh, my dear, Carole, I do not know what I have gotten us into, but whatever it is, I will also get us out of it," Linda whispered to her beloved cat as she walked towards room #7 behind Billy Stephens.

CHAPTER THIRTY-TWO
MONICA

Monica had fallen asleep after the eye of the storm had made landfall much further north of Gulfport and the outer bands that had been delivering wind and pelting rain in her area had started to dissipate. She was jolted awake at the sound of a garbage truck in the alley behind her apartment slamming the contents of the trashcans into its large trunk followed by the buzz of its mechanical arm.

Hmm, the County didn't suspend trash pickup today. That must be a good sign, Monica thought as she got up out of bed to look out of the window to assess the storm damage. She was surprised she had not lost power either.

She looked up and down the alley and the next street as far as she could see. There were a lot of palm fronds strewn throughout the alley but other than that, it didn't look too bad. She ventured onto her front balcony and realized when she saw her ceramic ashtray smashed to pieces in the parking lot below that she had forgotten to bring it inside before the storm. Luckily it didn't crash through anyone's windshield.

She went back inside to grab her broom and dustpan. She didn't need any grief from her landlord, so she wanted to pick it up before anyone noticed. She slipped on her cutoff jean shorts and slipped her bare feet into her slides. She headed downstairs with broom, dustpan, and a plastic bag, and quickly swept up the broken ceramic pieces and the few wet cigarette butts that hadn't blown away. She deposited the trash into one of the bins nearby and returned upstairs, relieved she didn't run into her landlord or any of her neighbors.

Just as she came inside, her cellphone was ringing.

"Hello?"

"Monica, dear, how did you fare through the storm? Everything okay?"

"Hi Mother, yes, I think everything is okay. Just a bunch of palms down but other than that, from what I can see, it's all good. How about you? Did you flood? Any water in the house?" Monica asked, referring to the fact that Davis Islands flooded under normal summer rain conditions, much less under a hurricane and storm surge from the Bay.

"Yes, typical flooding, but luckily no water in the house. Your Uncle Nicolas had someone bring in a ton of sandbags, so the back of the house was pretty secure. But, as you know, if we ever get a direct hit, sandbags won't make a bit of difference."

Monica rolled her eyes at her mother's reference to 'Uncle Nicolas.' Monica had figured out years ago, long after her father's death, that her mother and Nicolas had gotten together, although her mother never admitted it.

Poor Uncle Nicolas, one of her father's two brothers, was desperately in love with her mother. Monica sometimes wondered when he had fallen in love with her.

"Well, thank God you didn't get a direct hit, and the sandbags did their job," Monica said.

"Lunch this Thursday, darling?"

"Mother, it hasn't been a month already. I think our regular lunch is next week."

"Would it kill you to see your mother more frequently than once a month? I'll see you on Thursday. The Columbia at noon."

And with that, her mother hung up. No more questions, no waiting for an answer, just her directive. Monica sat there for a moment confused. Did her mother have something to tell her? Unless it was a holiday or someone's birthday, they stuck to their regular monthly schedule. And Monica didn't buy the "can't you see your mother" guilt line. Her mother was not the maternal or sentimental type. Was it about Pietro? CK? She would have to wait until Thursday to find out as her mother would never tell her in advance.

She made her Italian caffe, grabbed her smokes, and remembered the ashtray she kept on the balcony was gone, having just cleaned it up off the driveway below. She made a makeshift ashtray out of aluminum foil and brought her coffee and cigarettes out to the balcony along with a towel to dry off the wrought iron chair. She sat and enjoyed the morning, relieved the storm had spared the area once again.

Monica knew Pietro had been accused of horrible crimes, but she didn't believe he could do what they said he did. She was proud of her son and the man he had become. He had a good job as the IT Director at a prestigious law firm, well, before the accusations that caused him to flee the country. She did not believe his running was a sign of guilt, but rather something he had to do until he could clear his name. The press and the police always made it sound so much worse than it was and regularly framed people for crimes they didn't commit.

She wasn't worried though. As soon as he came back, her uncle would retain one of the several attorneys the family kept on retainer, and, hopefully, they could put this behind them. She wanted Pietro home so she could try to make up for the years she had failed her son. As he got older, she realized how much he reminded her of her father, both in looks and personality. She felt guilty about a lot of things she had done in her life, but abandoning her son with her mother was at the top of the list.

Maybe it wasn't too late to make things right, she thought.

She sipped her caffe out of the delicate demi cup and lit her second cigarette of the day as she sat on her balcony and watched as her neighbors began to clear the debris from the storm. The street was littered with branches and other wreckage from the storm, but nothing that made it impassable. She was relieved about that. She hated to feel trapped and always made sure she knew where her exits were in any situation.

Her phone pinged, notifying her that she had an incoming text.

She opened the text, from a new unknown number, and read it:

"Hello, my sweet Monica, are you ready for me?"

"Who the fuck is this?" Monica sent back.

"You really don't know?"

"No, who the fuck is this?"

"Three more days. Counting down the minutes . . ."

CHAPTER THIRTY-THREE
HALLIE

Hallie had no idea how long she had been sleeping when she woke up in the dark room, the only light emitting from the candle on her nightstand and the screen from her cellphone. Her phone pinged to alert her to an incoming message. She rubbed her eyes as she picked up her phone, trying to shake the fogginess from her brain. She saw she had four missed texts from Marcelo.

His last text said, "on my way, babe. I'm sure you fell asleep. I'll let myself in."

She was wondering how far away he was when she heard his key in the front door, the one she had given him the month before after they celebrated their one-year anniversary.

She felt a wave of relief knowing he was there. The lavender candle she had lit when the power went out was flickering and emitting a sweet scent that was competing with the mustiness of the old house, which was getting warmer from the air conditioning being off.

Hallie got up and grabbed her robe off the chair in the corner, wrapping it around her as she started down the stairs with her flashlight. She heard Marcelo in the kitchen, fixing a drink.

"Hey, how is it out there?" Hallie asked as she came into the kitchen, surprised but at the same time not surprised to see the professional-grade lantern on the countertop fully illuminating the kitchen. He was like a boy scout on steroids. She turned her flashlight off and slipped it into the pocket of her robe.

Marcelo looked up as he poured a healthy shot of whiskey into an ice-filled glass, rubbing his temple with his free hand. He looked tired. He attempted a smile, but his eyes conveyed something Hallie hadn't seen in them before. She didn't know what it was, but it worried her.

"That bad? Should we evacuate? Will it get worse?" Hallie asked, genuinely concerned while hoping she was misreading the situation.

"No, the storm's not the problem, we're fine. The worst is past this area. Hallie," Marcelo began but then stopped, picked up his whiskey and took a long pull.

"You're scaring me," Hallie said.

"The storm hit Raiford. A tornado damaged the prison, took an entire wing out. About ten prisoners escaped. Seven are still unaccounted for, including Stephens. Stephens is on the run, Hallie," Marcelo said matter-of-factly.

"What? Wait, what?" Hallie said, confused, hearing the words but unable to comprehend what Marcelo was telling her. "Oh my God, Katie," Hallie started to say.

"Katie is safe. I've already called the locals in Rhinebeck – don't worry, they're on it. They put a few plains-clothes on campus to watch her. Stephens can't get on a plane in this weather, even if he's got fake identification, so we have the benefit of time. We can get Katie home as soon as the storm passes and they re-open Tampa Airport."

"Oh my God," Hallie said, "how can this be happening? I can't believe this. You're sure Katie is safe?"

"I promise you; Katie is safe. They have eyes on her – she's safe in her dorm – and they're going to stay there for the rest of the night and tomorrow. They also put a uniformed officer at the door of the dorm. No one gets in without showing ID. Katie's safe, babe," Marcelo said, trying to reassure her.

"I need to let Kevin know."

"Of course, I'll be in the living room," Marcelo said, picking up his whiskey and a candle, leaving the lantern with Hallie.

"How long?" Hallie asked.

"How long what?"

"How long has he been out?" she asked, knowing the drive from Raiford to Tampa was about two and half hours under non-hurricane conditions.

"At least five hours. Maybe a little longer."

Hallie called Kevin and broke the news to him about Stephens but assured him, as Marcelo had assured her, that Katie was safe. They agreed to talk in the morning to decide what to do about bringing Katie home.

* * *

Hallie didn't sleep much the rest of the night, her mind consumed with Stephens. She could tell that Marcelo hadn't slept any better, his thoughts probably similarly occupied. Neither of them would probably sleep well again until Stephens was back behind bars.

Hallie's power had come back on at about five thirty that morning, and she was relieved that the house had already started to cool down. After making landfall, Hurricane Alice had passed across the state and, by the time it had reached Jacksonville had been downgraded to a tropical storm. When Hurricane Irma hit, Hallie had been without power for five days, and it was so unbearably hot, she stayed at Paige's. She was glad she wouldn't have to leave her house this time.

Kevin called her as soon as the sun was coming up. He likely hadn't slept either. Her inclination, as she told Kevin, was to fly Katie home on the first available flight. But after much back and forth, Kevin, always the voice of reason, suggested he and his wife, Jodi, would fly up to New York to take Katie away somewhere until Stephens was back in custody. Stephens could find her in Tampa or at school, but he couldn't get to her if Kevin and Jodi took her somewhere he didn't know about. Reluctantly, Hallie agreed, and they called Katie together that morning to tell her that her father and Jodi were flying up later that day to take her on an impromptu trip.

"What's going on?" Katie asked, the dread evident in her voice.

They told Katie the truth about Stephens' escape while trying to reassure her that they were just being overly cautious. They had not told Katie about the letter from Stephens mentioning Katie by name and the not-so-subtle threat. There was no need to worry her more than they already had.

Hallie made herself a much-needed cup of coffee, thankful she had enough ice and a large cooler that she didn't lose everything in her fridge overnight, including and most importantly her half and half. Coffee in hand, Hallie went outside to survey the damage on her street and around her house, Juno in tow. A large, thick branch from the oak in her front yard was dangling precariously off the roof, caught up on the gutter, which it had ripped partly away from the house. That explained one of the loud noises she had heard during the storm. She hoped only the gutter was damaged and not the roof itself.

Hallie looked next door to Mrs. Butler's house and down the street. Other than a lot of branches and palm fronds scattered through the yards and on the street, the damage did not appear too serious. It seemed the Tocobaga had protected Tampa once again.

Juno was back at the front door, waiting for Hallie. The storm over, the old girl's appetite had returned, and she knew it was time for her breakfast. Hallie patted her block head as they went into the kitchen. After feeding Juno, Hallie turned on the local news to see how the rest of the city had made it through when her cellphone rang.

Hearing her mother's familiar ring, Hallie answered immediately, "Mom, how are you? Is everything okay at your place?"

"Yes, we're good. Lost a few screen panels on the pool cage and a lot of debris around the neighborhood, but if that's the worst of it, I can't complain. How about you?"

"Good, I'm so glad, Mom," Hallie said, genuinely relieved. "A large branch took out the gutter on the front of the house, but hopefully the roof is unscathed. I think that's it, but we'll inspect more carefully later. Everything looks okay though."

"Like my pool cage, a gutter and even a roof are replaceable. We have a lot to be thankful for," her mother responded.

Not that she didn't agree, she did. But Hallie knew what was coming next.

"Mom, I agree. I am thankful. Very thankful. How is Trish? Did you talk to her yet?"

"Yes, she's safe too. The lake came up into her pool but not into her house. The dock has some damage and they don't know about the boat yet but all of that is replaceable too."

"Yes, it is. Thank God we're all okay. I'll call Trish later," Hallie said.

"Well, maybe you and Trish should meet me at church this Sunday so we can express our gratitude properly. I can put on a nice pot roast for dinner. You know Ross would love to see you, too," Becky said.

Hallie suppressed the audible groan that would usually follow her mother's attempt to guilt her into going to church. Her mother had a way of saying a few things in one breath, one of which always included some request to get her to church. Hallie hadn't been to church in years and had no intention of breaking that streak anytime soon.

"Mom, it's not a good weekend for that, and there's something else," Hallie said, hesitating, not wanting to scare her mother, but at the same time knowing that she had to tell her about Stephens' escape before her mother saw it on the news. She felt a little guilty knowing that the news she was about to deliver would abruptly end any further discussions about her attendance at church.

"What is it, Hallie?"

"Stephens escaped from Raiford last night, during the storm. But try not to worry. I'm safe and so is Katie. Kevin and Jodi are flying up later today to take her somewhere until Stephens is back in custody."

"How?" was all her mother asked, and she could hear the concern in that one word.

"A tornado damaged the prison and some of the prisoners escaped. Some died too, but Stephens was one of the ones who escaped."

"Oh Hallie, are you sure you're safe?"

"Yes, Mom, I promise you, I am. Marcelo is here with me, and he said every law enforcement officer in the State is looking for Stephens. If he's smart, he's heading north and out of Florida, not to Tampa." Hallie said, trying to reassure Becky.

"Okay, I hope you're right. I will say extra prayers for you until he's caught. Please tell Marcelo I'm counting on him to keep you safe."

"I will, Mom, but I can take care of myself. Try not to worry about this. I'm sure Stephens will be back in custody in no time. As I said, every law enforcement agency in the state is looking for him."

Hallie finished her phone call with her mother just as Marcelo came into the kitchen.

"Good morning," Marcelo said. "Who was that?"

"Becky," Hallie said, referring to her mother by her first name, a habit she had developed whenever she talked about her to Marcelo or her close friends. It made them laugh, not at her mother's expense, but everyone delighted in Hallie's stories about Becky and their interactions, which she always told with love and humor. Hallie realized this was not one of those times, but she was trying to deflect from the seriousness of the moment, one of her other bad habits.

"And? How are she and Ross? Is her house okay?" Marcelo asked.

"Yes, house is fine. But I told her about Stephens," Hallie said, wringing her hands and cracking her knuckles because she didn't know what else to do with them.

"How did she take it?"

"As expected, worried but stoic. That woman is a rock."

"Hmmm, like mother like daughter?"

"I don't know about that, but what I do know is I hate that I have to keep testing her strength."

"I know but hearing about Stephens from you is better than if she hears or reads about it on the news."

"Yeah, I know. I just need her to be extra vigilant until Stephens is caught, you know, just in case . . ." she paused and didn't finish her thought. "Well, anyway, I'm glad Ross is living with her now."

Instinctively she stopped cracking her knuckles and crossed her arms over her chest.

Her father used to admonish her for cracking her knuckles so she would cross her arms to stop herself. It made her look angry. She sometimes was angry. But almost never at her father. Most of the time she was just fidgety and nervous.

It's a tell, Hallie, you don't want your opponent to have the upper hand, see any weakness. Cracking your knuckles is a tell, her father would say, *and so is crossing your arms.*

She never wanted to show any weakness.

"Did you sleep at all last night?" Hallie asked, changing the subject as she uncrossed her arms.

"Not much. I think I finally dozed off about five thirty this morning. How about you?"

"Off and on. Not restfully, that's for sure."

"Have you been outside yet? How does it look?" Marcelo asked.

"Not too bad, thankfully. A huge branch hit the roof and took out a gutter on the front of the house, but I think that's it. The water is starting to recede too."

"Good, gutters are easy to fix."

"Well, I hope that's the worst of it," Hallie said, as she thought about Stephens being out there somewhere.

"Don't worry, Hallie, we're going to get him."

"Speaking of which, any updates?"

"I'm checking in with the Chief now," he said, waving his cellphone in the air as he poured himself a cup of coffee and headed towards Hallie's front porch to make his calls.

Hallie poured herself a second cup of coffee with a healthy pour of half and half and brought it out to the living room to watch the local news. All the local stations were reporting on the storm damage, ongoing rescues, and bridge and road closures, but for the most part the Tampa area had fared better than originally expected.

* * *

Hallie was glued to the TV for the rest of the day, flipping between the local stations who were covering the storm damage and national stations who had picked up on the prison escape. After updating Hallie on what he learned from the Chief, Marcelo had showered and left. Although there were reports of sightings of Stephens in the Tampa Bay area, none of them panned out. According to Marcelo, the more reliable information they received was that Stephens was as far north as Tallahassee and as far west as Pensacola. She could only hope that the information he had was accurate.

The only good news and best bet at catching Stephens was that the prison escape had made national news, which would make hiding out for him more difficult. Contributing to the heightened media attention was due to escaped prisoner, Julian Modesti, hijacking a car at a gas station in Lake City and taking a young man, the car owner, hostage. Modesti had been serving a life sentence, no possibility of parole, for the deaths of three people whose bodies were found buried on his property just outside of Tampa, in Riverview, Florida. Julian, known as Ju-Ju or Bad Ju-Ju on the street, maintained that he had never killed anyone but readily admitted he was an organ broker on the black market. It had taken the jury less than two hours to convict him of capital murder.

"Insurance in this country is a racket," Julian had said during an interview from prison after his conviction. "Unless you're super rich and have good insurance, you're not going to get that liver transplant or kidney transplant that you need. That's bullshit and that's where I came in. I was trying to change the system and help people who needed it like my sister."

While Julian never admitted to killing anyone, he never explained how he came into possession of the three bodies found buried on his property. The State was able to prove he had sold their organs on the dark web, and that was enough for the jury to find him guilty on all counts as well as other crimes, including the sale of human body parts.

At his sentencing hearing, in a heart-breaking plea to the jury to spare her son from the electric chair, Julian's mother explained that his younger sister had died five years earlier at seven years old from a rare genetic condition. She was on the transplant list, but without insurance, they didn't have the money for the expensive treatments that would have given her more time until a match could be found. She cried that her Julian had never recovered from his sister's death and blamed the insurance and healthcare industries for her death and Julian's bad decisions. It worked and her son was spared the chair.

After kidnapping the man in Lake City, Modesti had driven north. The man was found hours later, tied up and blindfolded in his car in the parking lot of a Days Inn near Interstate-10, luckily with all of his organs intact. But Modesti was gone. Cameras from the Days Inn showed a man fitting his description getting into a blue Ford Bronco and driving out of the parking lot towards the east-west interstate. The Ford Bronco had been reported stolen by its owner and was later found just outside of Pensacola. The police learned that Modesti had ties to the New Orleans area and believed that's where he was headed.

As Hallie continued to watch, she learned Julian 'Ju-Ju' Modesti was Stephens' cellmate in prison. She could only hope they were together, and Julian was harvesting and selling Stephens' organs, but she knew that would be too good to be true. More importantly, if Stephens was with Julian, they were heading northwest and away from Tampa, and that gave Hallie some comfort.

She shut the TV off and let Juno out one last time before locking up and heading up to bed, Juno right behind her. After not sleeping the night before, she was exhausted. She brushed her teeth, slipped on a loose tank top, and climbed into bed. She texted Marcelo goodnight and put her phone on silent as she sunk into her pillow and pulled the comforter up around her.

* * *

"I think she went to bed. All the lights upstairs went out about ten minutes ago. Do you want me to keep watching her? . . . . Okay, boss, heading home for the night. I'll check in tomorrow for my next instructions."

CHAPTER THIRTY-FOUR
LINDA

Her mouth felt like dry leather and tasted like a combination of a dirty ashtray and metal. Her head was pounding, and she tried to remember where she was. Linda looked around and recognized the drab surroundings: the orange and brown plastic drapes covering the large rectangular window, the only window in the small room, the television mounted and bolted to the wall above the faux-wood, flimsy dresser, and the small round table with two chairs directly in front of the window. She remembered she was in a motel room in Tampa but had no idea how long she had been there or why her head hurt so bad.

She tried to think. The last thing she remembered was having one glass of pinot grigio with Billy the evening they checked in, to celebrate making it to Tampa and finally being together. Billy had a glass of scotch. She remembered him kissing her softly on the cheek, his breath so close she could smell the warm, woody aroma of liquor on his breath. The bottle of scotch was one of the items she had been instructed to get in the letters he sent her embedded with a secret code.

One day when Linda was on one of her errands for her boss, Karl, she received a message from Billy through one of the guards. The guard walked past her and dropped a small piece of paper just in front of her. Linda started to speak up to let him know he had dropped something when he looked over his shoulder for a moment and mouth-whispered, "from a mutual friend," and kept walking, never breaking his stride.

Linda bent down pretending to tie her shoe, placed her folder on top of the note, and picked it up when she picked up the folder. She knew it was from Billy. Her heart was pounding a mile a minute, she remembered, from the excitement and adventure of it all. When she was sure she was out of camera view, she slipped the note into her Florida State regulation khaki pants, determined to wait until she got home to open it. She felt like it was the longest day of her life.

When she finally opened the note, she was delighted and giddy. She felt like she and Billy were on a rom-com mystery show, and she was the lead character, like Kristen Bell in Veronica Mars, one of her favorite series she had watched when she was younger.

The note said, "*Who doesn't love a crossword puzzle clue? Every 3rd and 7th letter brings me closer to you.*"

She read and reread the note, having no idea what it meant. At one point her heart sank, believing the guard might have dropped it by mistake and it had nothing to do with her. But it all became clear in the next letter she received from Billy. He quoted Shakespeare and Justice Ruth Bader Ginsberg from the U.S. Supreme Court and made other ramblings that seemed to loosely respond to Linda's letters but without any order or intelligence, which was so different than his previous letters. She took out the scrap of paper and circled the third and seventh letter in every word of Billy's previous letters and jotted them down on a notepad. After the third letter, it started to make sense.

It was a list!

He had figured out how to tell Linda what she needed to compile to prepare for the day when he would get out and they would be together without alerting the mail monitors to their plans.

And now they *were* together, but he was different. He was not the same man that he was in his letters to her. Something was off, less affectionate, angrier.

Maybe it was just the stress of the situation, she thought, *she was stressed too, after all.*

She looked over and saw the bottle of pinot grigio on the small table next to the window where she had left it. The bottle of scotch was gone. She felt so strange and couldn't understand why her memory was so foggy. She hadn't drunk more than one glass of wine, as evident from the mostly full bottle of Pinot left on the table. Had she switched to scotch? She hated scotch; she couldn't imagine that she would have done that.

She tried to remember anything from the night before; any sliver of a memory or a feeling or anything. She could not.

Nothing, not one single memory.

She looked around the depressing motel room for Billy. Her brain was so fuzzy, and her head was aching beyond any headache she had ever experienced. She would deal with the pain first and then figure out where Billy was. Maybe he went out to get them coffee, the thought of which sent her stomach reeling. The smell of it would probably make her retch. She held onto the sides of the bed to still her spinning head and the wave of nausea.

She spotted a bottle of water on her nightstand and looked around for her purse. She knew she had put a new bottle of Tylenol in it before she had left her house. She saw her purse on the floor next to the bed, thankful it was within her reach without too much effort. She painstakingly pulled it up next to her on the bed, and lifted herself up onto her elbow while noticing she was in the same outfit she had arrived in. She rummaged around in the large bag until she found the bottle of Tylenol amidst crumpled fast food and gas station receipts, assorted lipsticks and eye makeup tubes, individually packaged moist towelettes, and a few snack bags of dried fruit and mixed nuts.

She removed the childproof cap, poured three capsules into her trembling hand, and swallowed all three at once with a swig of the room temperature water. She sank her throbbing head back onto the pillow, closed her eyes and prayed the pain reliever would kick in quickly.

She must have dozed off. When she woke up again, she was relieved to find the pain had mostly subsided. She still had the weird metallic taste in her mouth, which was adding to her nausea, but at least the excruciating headache had waned. She sat up, which caused her head to spin and stomach to flip, but she steadied herself until it passed. She couldn't for the life of her understand why she was so groggy and feeling so sick.

After a few minutes, she made her way to the bathroom, brushed her teeth and washed her face while the shower warmed up. She leaned against the bathroom counter until the latest wave of queasiness and dizziness passed before stepping into the hot shower.

Where is Billy? she wondered as she attempted to dry her body off with the small motel towel.

Unable to wrap the towel completely around her body, she shielded her front with the small towel and left the bathroom to put on clean clothes. She looked around the small, dank room. Everything seemed to be in order. Linda's open suitcase was where she had left it on the luggage rack and Ms. Baskins was curled up on top of Linda's clothes inside of it. She put on a fresh bra, panties, and a cotton sun dress, warm from Ms. Baskins' heat, and started to feel a little better.

Her eyes swept the room again, looking for anything that would give her a clue about the night before or where Billy may have gone. Maybe he had left a note.

And that's when she noticed it.

All of Billy's stuff was gone.

Every last bit of it.

CHAPTER THIRTY-FIVE
THE HUNTER

The storm had passed, and the Hunter was on the move again. He didn't like to be cooped up like a caged animal. He needed to be free, free to go wherever he wanted, with no restraints, other than the ones life required to maintain his normalcy and an income to afford his safaris, as he liked to call them.

He never understood how animals in zoos didn't revolt against their keepers at every instance. He assumed they were drugged, overfed, or beaten into submission, or possibly a combination of all three, to keep them obedient and well-behaved. In the past, he had used similar tactics with his victims, at least the ones he kept for longer than a few hours. But with the Mrs. never traveling to see her mother in Port Charlotte anymore, he never got the house alone. Now he had to torture and kill his catches within a few hours of meeting them, which seemed so uncivilized, in his opinion.

If he could prolong it now, would he even be able to? he questioned himself. *He had to admit that he wasn't as patient as he was when he was younger.*

He drove down his latest target's street in his white Ford Explorer, surprised to see her on her balcony. He lowered his baseball cap as he drove past, confident she would have been too drunk when they met for her to remember what he looked like. But he didn't care if she remembered him or not.

At least not yet.

When they did meet again, he would make sure she remembered him. She would never forget him, at least for the remaining few hours of her life. Maybe he would be more patient with her, keep her alive for a few days like he used to do in the past, to give her the false hope that if she obeyed him and was a good girl, she might live.

So naïve and stupid, he laughed to himself, *just like they all were.*

He looked in his rearview mirror to admire his latest obsession. She was sitting on her balcony, smoking a cigarette, the white smoke floating up and enveloping her witchy, black hair and ivory skin. She wasn't wearing her signature red lipstick he had come to expect, but she was still attractive. He looked forward to their next meeting. It would have to be somewhere private, where he could take his time with her.

She may not remember him now, but she would when he held her throat in his strong hands and crushed her larynx while she stared up at him, pleading for her life with her terrified eyes. He loved how the blood vessels burst in the whites of their eyes as he choked them out.

He would take his time with her, he promised himself.

He smiled thinking about all the things he was going to do to her, the thought of which excited him. He shifted in his seat to give himself a little relief from the tightness in his pants. He turned up the radio, smiling as a classic John Denver song played. He hummed along as he continued to watch her in his rearview mirror, pleased to see her watching him with a curious look on her face.

Maybe she did remember him after all, he thought.

"Soon, my sweet," he said aloud as he turned right at the next corner and headed back towards the interstate.

CHAPTER THIRTY-SIX
CHRISTIAN KANE

The Florida airports opened the day after the storm had made its way into Georgia. It had been downgraded to a tropical storm and was no longer a threat, at least not in Florida. CK took the first available flight out of Miami and arrived in Tampa. He retrieved his bag from the overhead compartment and got off the plane to wait for Ray. They headed for the baggage claim level even though neither of them had checked a bag. CK walked quickly, anxious to get outside for a smoke and to look for his ride, with Ray limping closely behind him.

They walked straight outside, and both lit up a cigarette as soon as they cleared the automatic doors.

"What's next, boss? Where we going?" Ray asked.

"To see an old friend."

"Does this have anything to do with your son?"

"Yeah."

"Is that why we left Miami? Did he come here?"

"Ray, no disrespect, but shut the fuck up. No more questions."

Ray was very good at following orders and didn't say another word.

Within a few minutes, a dark blue Denali pick-up with dark tinted windows pulled up to the curb in front of them. The driver got out to help them with their bags.

Before throwing the two bags into the back, he reached out to shake CK's hand, "Nice to see you again, Boss. It's been a few years."

"Yes, I think you could say that," CK chuckled. "Nice to see you, too, brother," CK said warmly. "This is my associate, Ray; Ray, this is one of my former colleagues, Miguel, from my Port of Tampa days. What were you then, twenty-one, twenty-two?"

"Yeah, that seems about right. Nice to meet you, Ray."

"You too, man," Ray said as the two men shook hands.

"I was surprised you found me," Miguel said, returning his attention to CK.

"I'm amazed at what and who you can find with the internet and social media platforms I've had access to since I've been out of the joint. I think you can find anybody or anything."

"Well, that's true."

They exited out of the airport onto W. Spruce Street, which turned into Boy Scout Blvd., and headed towards Dale Mabry Highway. CK looked around as they drove, noticing all the restaurants, condos, and high-rise office buildings that had gone up since the last time he was in Tampa. They passed a large mall that included expensive-looking restaurants and stores like Nieman Marcus and Nordstrom.

"Holy shit, this place is unrecognizable since I was here last. I know I've been away for a while, but this is crazy. None of this was here. I think that used to be a cow pasture or an orange grove or something over there," he said, pointing out his window to what looked like an office complex.

"Just wait, the whole City is like this. Wait until you see downtown. Everything is exploding. Bro, it's nothing like it was when you left."

"Do you see anyone from the old gang around?" CK asked.

"Just my cousin, Rafael. We're still partners, and our wives are sisters, so we're joined for life, unless one of us dies or gets divorced, and if one of us gets divorced, we're probably going to die anyway," Miguel laughed.

"What line of work are you in, Miguel," Ray asked, trying to join the conversation.

"Import export, just like the old days, right Boss?" Miguel said with a wink.

CK nodded and smiled but was otherwise preoccupied with something on his phone.

Miguel continued, "Bro, when you got popped, it freaked everyone out, man, and most people scattered. If they could get to you, any one of us could be next."

"Nah, I was set up. They weren't interested in any of you. But I would have done the same thing."

"Glad you're out, man, glad you're out."

"Me too, my friend," CK said sincerely.

"So, where are you staying? Should I take you there first?"

"Nah, let's grab some food first. What's good around here?"

"Boss, I got you. I know just the place and it's not too far."

They pulled into the parking lot at Rick's on the River, a pub on the Hillsborough River known for its oysters, wings, and other traditional Florida fare, including gator bites. They sat at one of the picnic tables overlooking the river as a medium-sized gator floated quietly by. The waiter, a blonde kid who looked like he was barely old enough to be in high school, brought them menus and took their drink order. Since being out, CK had a whole new appreciation for an ice-cold beer served in a mug.

After the waiter walked away, Miguel took a piece of paper from his jeans pocket and slid it over to CK.

He glanced at the piece of paper and asked, "You sure this is it?"

"Yeah, I'm sure."

"Where's Gulfport?" CK asked.

"Just over the bridge, close to the beach."

CK slipped the paper into his pocket and smiled as he took a swig from his cold beer the waiter had just delivered.

Soon, Monica, soon, he thought.

CHAPTER THIRTY-SEVEN
MONICA

Monica woke up early the next morning and checked her phone right away. She was relieved she hadn't received any more texts from the unknown sender during the night. She needed something to keep her mind off the texts, including who had likely sent them to her. Recently, she had started painting and throwing clay again and had returned to the community art center in Gulfport where she used to go. The hours were limited but it was free and had a decent kiln. Until she sold a few pieces, she didn't want to incur the extra expense of renting a formal studio. It got her out of her apartment and was a more productive way to pass her time than getting hammered at O'Maddy's.

She made a cup of coffee and sat on her balcony with her smokes, her morning ritual. A large white truck turned down her street, easily navigating the debris that still hadn't been completely cleared, as it slowly went past her apartment. Monica looked down at the driver. The darkly tinted side windows and glare from the sun ricocheting off the windshield made it difficult to see him clearly, but Monica felt a pang of recognition at the man's silhouette. There was something about his profile and strong jawbone that struck her. She took a drag of her cigarette just as the truck turned the corner and drove out of sight.

She showered, got dressed in a pair of old jeans, a t-shirt that didn't matter if she got paint or clay on it, tied her hoodie around her waist, grabbed her art tote and headed out to the studio. Lily, the manager who was also an artist, was already there.

"Hey Monica, how did you do through the storm? Is your place okay?"

"Yeah, thank God. Just some branches down and other debris, but nothing worse. How about you?"

"Same. We dodged it again, thankfully. I'm sure we won't always be so lucky."

The women nodded in agreement and then Monica set herself up at a workstation at the far end of the room near a large window that offered the most natural light. She was working on an abstract oil piece of the ocean against the backdrop of a dark and ominous sky inspired from the recent hurricane rolling across the Gulf. Monica kept to herself and appreciated the quiet of the studio, the only noise coming from a speaker playing softly in the corner and the occasional conversation between other artists who had lingered in throughout the day.

By 7 p.m., when the studio was supposed to close, Lily and Monica were the only two left, and both were still working. Sometimes, when there were only two or three artists left, Lily would lock the doors and let them stay for a little bit longer. Tonight was one of those nights.

By the time they both packed up and cleaned up their areas, it was after 9 p.m., and the parking lot was dark and empty. Monica pulled her hoodie on and hoisted her art bag over her shoulder.

"Hey, do you feel like grabbing a kava at Kat's place?" Lily asked as she locked the front doors.

"Hmm, is that champagne? I'm more of a vodka girl," Monica said.

"It's not alcohol, silly," Lily laughed. "It's a plant-based drink and very calming."

"Seriously? Non-alcoholic? What's the point?" Monica joked.

"Well, if you suffer from anxiety or trouble sleeping like I do, it's actually very helpful. C'mon, you should try it."

"What does it taste like?" Monica asked skeptically.

"Honestly, it takes a little like mud, maybe with a little pepper," Lily giggled.

"Um, that sounds disgusting," Moni responded, smiling, intrigued. "Please tell me why I would want to drink this kava shit voluntarily?"

"Because it's calming, all natural, and doesn't have the bad stuff alcohol has in it. I actually prefer kratom, which is also plant-based, but tastes better, fruitier. Trust me, you'll sleep like a baby tonight."

"Okay, so maybe I'll try the fruity one, but not the mud one," Monica laughed as she took her vape pen out of her bag and took a hit.

She liked Lily. And she liked that they were starting to develop a friendship. Monica didn't have a lot of friends. She looked around the parking lot, noticing all the empty parking spaces, and the overall desertedness of the area. It made sense. It was late enough for the law students to have gone home for the summer, but still too hot for the snowbirds to have arrived. Normally, she was relieved when summer came, enjoying the reprieve from the crowded restaurants, bars, and streets in Gulfport, but lately the emptiness made her feel uneasy. Maybe this fruity mud drink would be just what she needed to calm her frayed nerves.

Lily finished locking the rec center door and said, "C'mon, come with me. I'll introduce you to the world of plant-based beverages and to Kat, the owner. She's an amazing tattoo artist when she's not running the kava shop; you'll love her."

"Okay, you sold me at fruity mud," Monica chuckled, preferring not to go home by herself yet anyway.

They arrived at the kava shop, which was more crowded than Monica expected it would be. She had passed it a thousand times, but had never stopped in. As they entered, everyone seemed to know Lily, and she introduced Monica to various people as they made their way to the counter, where Kat, the owner, greeted them.

"Kat, this is my friend, Monica; Monica, Kat."

"Nice to meet you, Kat," Monica said.

"You hang out at O'Maddy's, don't you?" Kat asked.

"Um, yeah, sometimes."

"Yeah, I've seen you there. Marge is a good friend of mine," Kat said, as she wiped the counter down in front of them. "What can I get you?"

As Lily ordered their drinks, and continued chatting with Kat, Monica caught a glimpse of someone walking out of the kava shop.

Holy fuck, is that Marlboro man? Monica asked herself as she spotted a man in a baseball cap leaving.

It was only for a split second, and she couldn't be sure it was him.

Ugh, what a creep, she thought. *I hope he doesn't live around here,* remembering the truck that drove down her street that morning and the eerie feeling she had.

"So, what do you think?" Lily asked, interrupting Monica's thoughts, as she watched her try her kratom drink for the first time.

"Um, it's okay, I think. A little strange, but not terrible," Monica said honestly.

"The more you drink, the more you'll like it. And seriously, if you have anxiety or are unusually stressed, it really does help."

"You just described my constant state of being," Monica said.

"Same," Lily laughed.

* * *

Monica was ready to leave about midnight, but Lily wanted to stay longer. Monica said her goodbyes to everyone she had met and headed out alone. She wrapped her hoodie a little tighter around her and pulled the hood over her head, despite it being warm and finally dry outside. She walked across the parking lot and headed towards her apartment. The dark street was lined with palm trees and other tropical fauna, overtaking the sidewalks in some places, with some still strewn about from the storm. As she reached the other end of the parking lot, she heard an engine start somewhere not far behind her. She looked back over her shoulder but didn't see any headlights.

She picked up her pace.

The street was eerily quiet and devoid of the normal tourists and law students that would usually be out bar hopping, but after summer began, the snowbirds left, most of the students returned home, and Gulfport was left to the locals. With the recent hurricane, even the locals weren't out.

She opened her phone to check the time and to have it ready if she had to call for help. Not that anyone could get to her in time, but it made her feel safer having it ready. She cursed herself for not charging her phone before she left O'Maddy's when she saw that her battery life was down to 1% and likely wouldn't last for the three blocks she had left to go.

When she was almost to her apartment, she heard a dog barking and the sound of laughter and music coming from the balcony of a nearby apartment as she passed. The sounds made her feel less anxious, as if she wasn't completely alone, even though at that moment she was.

Or so she thought.

CHAPTER THIRTY-EIGHT
HALLIE

Things had mostly returned to normal since the storm had passed: the debris on Hallie's street had finally been picked up, her handyman had replaced her broken gutter, and her calendar was filled with meetings and phone calls with clients. There were no recent sightings of Stephens, and for all Hallie knew and hoped, he had left the State of Florida. She didn't care where he went as long as he stayed the hell away from her and Katie.

Katie was still in Canada with Kevin and Jodi on a ski trip but would be returning to school the following week. They couldn't live in hiding from Stephens for the rest of their lives, and she and Kevin agreed they would hire a private security company to watch Katie until Stephens was caught and back behind bars.

Hallie went into the office early that morning. She worked all day, including through lunch, happy she kept a stash of protein bars in her desk. By the end of the day, she was relieved to see she had made a dent in the work that had suffered because of the storm and her distractions from Stephens' escape and her brother's case. But today she had managed to bill a solid, eight-hour day, and she was ready to go home. She texted Marcelo.

"Hey, how was your day? Can you chat?"

"Sure, call me."

She called Marcelo and he answered immediately.

"Hey, babe, how was your day back in the office?"

"Productive, thank God. Put out some fires and got some really old stuff off my desk, so I feel good about that. How about you? How was your day?"

"Busy, but not too bad. Working on a new armed robbery case in West Tampa, but I don't think it's going to take long to solve. We have camera footage and a few likely suspects to bring in. One of them will probably flip on the others to cut a deal, so I should be able to wrap it up pretty quickly."

"So, I guess that means you're working late tonight?"

"Yeah, they're bringing two of them in within the next hour and I need to conduct the interviews. I'm not sure how long they'll hold out but could be a long night."

"I get it. I'm exhausted anyway, so I'm going to go home, take a hot bath, and crawl into bed."

"Now you're making me jealous. I would rather be there with you than with these scumbags I'll be spending the evening with," Marcelo chuckled.

"Well, you know where I'll be if anything changes, Detective. Maybe they'll crack quickly under your relentless questioning," Hallie teased.

"I can only hope, but doubtful. I won't bother you tonight so you can get some sleep. Call me in the morning?"

"Absolutely."

Hallie hung up, gathered some files for the next day in case she decided to work from home, her laptop bag, and headed out of her office. The office cleared out on most days by 6:30, but she could see that a few attorneys and paralegals from the litigation group were working late in one of the conference rooms. They must be preparing for a big hearing or trial because it was already after 7.

By the time she got into her car, she realized how hungry she was. All she had eaten all day was two hardboiled eggs for breakfast and the protein bar she found in her desk. She was too tired to cook but didn't want to eat fast-food either. She called Forbici to place an order as she pulled out of her building so that it would be ready by the time she got there. Forbici was an easy stop on the way to her Hyde Park bungalow.

She headed out of downtown towards Hyde Park, happy there was no traffic. She couldn't wait to get out of her clothes, especially her shoes, and get comfy. She hoped a new episode of *Only Murders in the Building* was out. She stopped at a redlight at Kennedy and N. Boulevard and glanced down at her phone while she waited for the light to change. She was reading an email from a client when a sporty, silver Lexus behind her honked after she hadn't noticed the light had turned green. She waved her hand

above her head in the universal apology signal and pro-
ceeded until she turned left onto Willow. The Lexus stayed
behind her and also turned left on Swann. He could have
easily passed her on Kennedy to get in front of her, so this
seemed intentional and made her a little nervous.

Too tired to deal with some impatient, road-raging jerk,
she decided to pull over on Willow to let him pass.

At first, he pulled over too, right behind her, but then
must have changed his mind and quickly zipped around
her, honking his horn again and yelling something out of
his window as he shot her the middle finger.

"What an asshole," she said aloud.

She sat there a minute stunned. *What was this world
coming to*, she thought. She delayed him maybe twenty or
thirty seconds at a stop light and that's how he reacted? No
wonder more people were carrying guns on them, especially in their cars. People were insane.

She drove a few more blocks, relieved not to encounter
the silver Lexus again, and pulled into the reserved curbside
to-go spot at Forbici. She picked up her dinner and headed
home, checking her rearview mirror from time to time as
she drove the two miles to make sure the crazy Lexus driver
wasn't following her. She couldn't wait to eat, take a bath,
and go to sleep, and hopefully forget all about the lunatic
in the Lexus and all of her other worries.

* * *

Hallie bolted awake. The air in the room was still and everything was quiet. She felt her pulse racing, as if she had had a nightmare, but she couldn't remember what she had been dreaming about. She felt uneasy and anxious. She looked at the time on her phone: 2:37 a.m.

Then she thought she heard a noise from downstairs. But she wasn't positive. Her mind could have been playing tricks on her, as she was still not fully awake. She held her breath and listened. She couldn't hear anything over her own heartbeat. She looked down at Juno. If Juno was sleeping, then she would know it was just a bad dream, PTSD from the events of the previous two years, the hurricane, Stephens' escape from prison, and her encounter with the lunatic Lexus driver earlier that night.

Except Juno wasn't lying in her usual spot.

The blood from her heart pounded louder in her ears, but she tried to stay calm. She scanned the room, her eyes adjusting to the darkness, thankful for the nightlight emanating from her bathroom.

Her bedroom door was open. She usually closed it when she went to bed each night, but maybe she forgot. She had been so tired the night before.

She sometimes forgot.

She tried not to hyperventilate.

Maybe Juno had gone downstairs to get water, she told herself.

Maybe she had heard Juno going down the stairs. Maybe that's what woke her up.

Maybe she was safe, and no one was in her house.

Her breathing and heartbeat had almost returned to normal when she heard something again, but this time she was awake, and she knew what she heard. It was subtle. But this time, she had no doubt. Unfortunately, she knew exactly what she had heard.

Hallie had lived in her 1920 bungalow for over fifteen years and knew every one of the old girl's sounds: the creak of the floorboard in front of the fridge in the kitchen when someone was sneaking a late-night snack; the clackity-clack in the attic when the air handler kicked on during the warmest summer months; the back door rattling for a split second when the front door was opened or closed.

And the creak of the third step up from the bottom of the staircase under the weight of someone coming up the stairs.

These were the sounds she knew.

Hallie could tell if it was Katie, or Juno, or when it used to be David, and now Marcelo, based on the sound of the creak on that damn third step.

And that is what she heard. It was not Katie or Juno. It was someone the size of David or Marcelo and she couldn't breathe.

But Marcelo would have texted her if he was coming over. She glanced over at her phone. She didn't have any text notifications. It wasn't Marcelo.

Where was Juno?

Hallie's mind raced, almost as fast as her pulse was racing. She held her breath and tried to listen, praying it was her imagination.

Creak . . .

She heard it again. Closer.

Fifth step.

Where was Juno??

Three seconds passed. Maybe seven.

Creak . . .

Closer.

Creak . . .

Closer.

Her heart was pounding so hard in her chest she thought she might have a heart attack. She was sure whoever was coming up the stairs could hear her heartbeat. She slid as quietly as she could out of her bed, the wood floor under her feet thankfully not betraying her as it did the intruder on the stairs. She grabbed her phone off her nightstand and quickly made her way into her bathroom, silently closing and locking the door. She sat down on the floor with her back against the wall opposite the door and stretched and locked her legs against the door so whoever was out there could not get in, or at least not very easily.

She called Marcelo.

He answered on the first ring.

Before he could speak, Hallie whispered, "someone is in my house."

"I'll be right there. Where are you?"

"In my bathroom, upstairs. Hurry. I think he's in my bedroom," she whispered, cupping her hand over her mouth as she tried to whisper into the phone.

"Call 9-1-1 and leave your phone on. Now!" Marcelo demanded.

"Okay. Please hurry," Hallie whispered, not wanting to disconnect from Marcelo but knowing he was right.

Hallie listened for a second before dialing 9-1-1. She heard nothing. She tapped the three numbers on her screen, her hand shaking uncontrollably. The dispatcher answered immediately.

"9-1-1, what's your emergency?"

"Someone is in my house," Hallie whispered, trying to speak as quietly as she could, her voice trembling.

"What's your name?" the dispatcher asked.

"Hallie Miller," she answered.

"Allie Miller?"

"No, Hallie, with an 'H'," Hallie said, praying whoever was in her house would realize she was on with the police and leave.

"Okay, Hallie, what's your address?"

Hallie gave her address, listening to the sound of the dispatcher typing onto her keyboard in the background with each answer she gave.

Hallie listened to the sounds in her house.

Nothing.

Where was Juno?

She kept her legs locked straight against the bathroom door, focusing intently on the door handle, fully aware how easy it would be to smash the door open, possibly breaking her ankles or legs in the process if they used enough force.

The dispatcher continued to talk to her in a soothing voice, trying to reassure her that the police were on their way and would be there soon.

Hallie stayed silent.

"Hallie, are you still there? Are you okay?"

"I'm here," Hallie whispered, as she finally heard sirens and hoped whoever was in her house heard them too.

Please, God, let those be coming for me, she silently prayed.

"They're almost there, Hallie, everything's going to be okay," the dispatcher said reassuringly.

Hallie knew the dispatcher could not promise that, but she appreciated her for saying it, and it was exactly what she needed to hear in that moment.

Within seconds, the sirens stopped in front of her house. A minute or two after that the police were in her house, and she could hear them coming up the stairs towards her – no creaks this time, but instead heavy boots pounding loudly up each step of the old wooden staircase – while simultaneously yelling "clear" and calling out her name.

Hallie didn't stand up or open the door until they were in her bedroom, right outside of the bathroom door, and she was sure whoever she had heard before was not there.

She shakily opened the bathroom door, relieved she had worn one of Marcelo's oversized t-shirts to bed that night.

"Ms. Miller?" the uniformed officer asked, as he backed up to allow Hallie to come out of the bathroom.

Behind him Hallie could see and hear the other officers going through the rest of the rooms and closets on the second floor while simultaneously calling out to their colleagues.

"Is my dog downstairs? Is she okay?" Hallie managed, the growing lump in her throat making it almost impossible to speak.

As the adrenaline drained from her body, she thought she might faint. She must have faltered because the officer reached out, took her arm, and guided her to the chair in the corner of her bedroom.

"Please, I need to know if my dog's okay. Please," Hallie pleaded, feeling she might pass out or hyperventilate for the second time that evening.

"I'm sorry, ma'am, I don't know, but I'll check," he said, while taking his radio off his belt and speaking into it, "hey, it's Koster, anyone find the dog? Also, we need EMT up here."

"I'm fine," Hallie said, her voice getting stronger as she regained her composure, "I don't need EMT. I just need to find my dog."

Hallie heard the officer speaking but she couldn't make out what he was saying other than she heard him say something about a dog. Her heart was pounding in her chest, and she just wanted to find Juno.

"I'm sorry, what?" Hallie heard the words coming out of her mouth as if she was having an out of body experience.

"EMT is standard procedure, ma'am," Officer Koster repeated, "in this type of, um, situation."

"What type of situation is this, Officer? Someone broke into my house, but they didn't get to me and I'm fine. I told you, I don't need EMT. I just need you to find my fucking dog," Hallie said, exasperated, and immediately regretting taking her fear and distress out on the young officer trying to help her.

She was about to apologize when the officer's radio interrupted and the voice on the other end said, "Koster, we found the dog."

CHAPTER THIRTY-NINE
THE JUDGE

Former Judge William Stephens watched from his car down the street as the police swarmed Hallie Miller's Hyde Park bungalow. A long time ago, he had spent an amazing evening with her. She was a young associate, he was the managing partner, and she had been flirting with him and sending him all the signals that told him she wanted him: she laughed at his jokes, listened intently to his stories or opinions, brushed her hand across his forearm when she reached for the bread that last night, and, of course, wore that hot black suit, which he knew was for his benefit.

Sitting next to her, he looked down as she crossed and uncrossed her legs at various times as he imagined what she had on underneath that short skirt. Her jacket and cream-colored silk camisole barely contained her ample, natural breasts, which he had admired many times when he summoned her to his office, sometimes just for that reason.

He knew Hallie was married, and because of that, she might have some hesitation to cheat on her husband, even though he knew she wanted him. He needed to relax her, so he slipped a roofie into her drink at the Law and Liberty dinner. Normally when he did that to one of his dates, they were willing participants, thanking him afterwards for a great evening, whether they remembered the night or not, especially when he slipped a few hundred bucks into their hands as he said goodbye. The combination of the drinks and the roofie caused Hallie to go out almost immediately, but he fucked her anyway as soon as he got her up to his room. He knew that if she was awake, she would have not only loved it but begged for it. How could it be considered rape when he was so good at what he did?

He always wondered that and felt "enjoyment" should be a defense to rape, just as truth was a defense to slander or libel.

Alas, he could not change the law, but he could punish Hallie Miller for sending him to prison. She also kept his daughter away from him, but he didn't mind that so much as he never wanted kids and never had to pay child support. But now he knew Hallie's weak spot and could use the little bastard child against her.

It felt so good to be out of prison. Two things he knew for sure: one, Hallie Miller had to pay; and two, he was never going back to prison, no matter what.

He drove away, smiling at all he had accomplished that night.

CHAPTER FORTY
HALLIE

Hallie held her breath, afraid of what she was going to hear next out of that horrible little black box in the officer's hand, when she heard, "Dog seems okay. We found her locked in the downstairs bathroom."

Hallie let out a sound from deep within her that sounded like a cross between a groan and a sob, having expected the worst but so relieved to hear that Juno was okay. She bolted up from the chair and headed towards the stairs.

"Ma'am, we really should have an EMT check you out," the officer was calling after her.

Hallie was already through her bedroom door and halfway down the stairs, never stopping to answer or even look back.

She got to the bottom of the stairs and saw Juno sitting next to the officer who had apparently found her in the bathroom. As soon as Juno saw Hallie, she got up and started wagging her tail, letting out an uncharacteristic bark. Hallie dropped to her knees and hugged her as Juno licked the warm tears off her face. Hallie started to laugh.

"You're okay, old girl, you're okay," Hallie whispered to her loyal, four-legged friend, as tears continued to pour from her eyes. "What would Mama do without you?" she asked, as Juno continued to lick her face.

"Ms. Miller? Would you mind if we went into the living room? We want to ask you a few questions so we can understand what happened here tonight."

"Um, yes, okay," Hallie said cautiously as she got up and dried her face with the bottom of her t-shirt, suddenly realizing she was half naked as she headed towards the living room. She wrapped a throw blanket around her as she sat down on the couch, Juno by her side, her faithful friend refusing to let anyone between them.

Just as the officer was about to ask her something, Marcelo came through the front door. Juno barked once and wagged her tail familiarly at the sight of him but wouldn't leave Hallie's side.

"Hallie, are you okay?" Marcelo asked as he rushed towards her. She stood up and he took her in his arms in a strong embrace, which almost made her lose it again.

She cleared her throat as she sat back down on the couch, "yeah, I'm okay, just still shaky from the whole thing."

"Detective Garcia, may we have a word?" one of the officers in the hallway asked as he motioned to Marcelo.

Marcelo looked down at Hallie before answering.

"Go, I'm fine. Juno and I are going to chill right here on the couch after all the excitement tonight, isn't that right, my sweet girl?" Hallie said as she stroked Juno's big, block head, pleased that her hand had finally stopped trembling.

"I'll be right back," he said, his concern evident in the uncharacteristic deep crease etched in his forehead.

Hallie watched as Marcelo gathered with the officers in the foyer before they went out to her front porch.

They did not want her to hear them, she thought. *What had they found?* she wondered.

Her blood pressure started to rise again, and she had to take deep breaths to try to calm her racing heart. For a moment she heard Marcelo raise his voice, but then the voices returned to a whisper. They came back in, and Marcelo looked angry.

"Ms. Miller," the officer who was about to ask her questions before Marcelo came in started again, "um, on Detective Garcia's request, because of all you've been through tonight, we're going to forego asking you anything tonight. But we would like you to come to the station at your convenience tomorrow to fill out a report, if you don't mind."

"Of course, thank you," Hallie said, looking at Marcelo, trying to understand what had transpired outside.

Fifteen minutes later, the officers left, and Marcelo locked the front door as he came back into the living room.

"How are we doing, Counselor?" he asked lightheartedly as he walked towards Hallie.

"Better now," Hallie managed. "What did they find? Do you think it was Stephens?"

"Um, they didn't find any signs of a break in or anything else," Marcelo stammered.

"Wait, that doesn't make any sense. Someone was in my house. Probably Stephens."

"They said the front door was unlocked when they got here. That's how the officers were able to come in."

"That proves someone was here. I locked it after I let Juno out last night right before I went to bed."

"Are you sure?"

"Of course, I'm sure," Hallie snapped, her fear being replaced by anger.

"Well, they didn't find any evidence that the door or the lock had been tampered with. They know about Stephens, but they don't think it's him. He's probably out of Florida by now, and without any damage to the door," Marcelo began.

"Are you fucking kidding me? Do they think I made this up? Is that what you think?" Hallie interrupted, her anger quickly rising.

"No, you didn't let me finish."

"Go on," Hallie said, crossing her arms across her chest, trying to remember that Marcelo was on her side.

She silently gave Marcelo credit for not telling her to calm down, as all of the previous men in her life would have done in that moment, which always had the exact opposite effect as soon as the words were spoken.

"Look, all I'm saying is that you've been under a lot of pressure lately, with Charlie's case and Stephens' escape. Anything is possible. But I also know *you*, and if you heard someone in your house, then someone was in your house. Since the locks on the front and back doors don't look like they were picked or tampered with, whoever it was either has a key or came in another way."

"What if it was Stephens?" Hallie asked.

Before Marcelo could answer, they heard another car pulling up outside. Hallie looked out her front window and saw an unmarked, nondescript, black sedan pulling into her driveway behind her BMW.

"That's Detective Johnson," Marcelo said looking out the window. "I asked her to come by to try to lift some prints. She's the best in the department and I don't want to rely on the responding officers to have done their jobs properly. Wait here a minute while I brief her."

Hallie was relieved he was having someone he trusted look for more evidence. She knew someone, most likely Stephens, was in her house. She wasn't sure whether Marcelo actually believed her, but she knew the other officers did not, and, because of that, they hadn't bothered to do a thorough search.

Hallie looked out the front window as Marcelo met the detective on her driveway. He touched her elbow as he leaned in and whispered something in her ear, which seemed very familiar, almost intimate. She wasn't a jealous person but there was something about the interaction that bothered her. She headed towards the front porch, preferring not to wait inside like a helpless victim.

As she walked outside, she heard Marcelo giving the attractive detective the background on Stephens, including Hallie's history with him, his trial, the contents of the threatening letter she had received from him, his recent escape from prison, and what had happened that night.

Detective Johnson had reddish-brown hair, the ends naturally highlighted from the sun, which matched the light freckles speckled on the cheeks of her ivory skin. She was young and pretty in a girl-next-door way, and her warm smile instantly made Hallie feel at ease.

"Hallie, this is Officer Alicia Johnson; Johnson, this is Hallie Miller. As I mentioned, Johnson is one of our fingerprint experts in the department."

"Nice to meet you," the auburn-haired officer said as she extended her hand to Hallie.

"You too," Hallie said, "thank you for coming out so late."

"No problem, I'm happy to help," Detective Johnson said. She looked down and then said, "Um, I knew Naomi Banks. We were friends," referring to the young lawyer Stephens was convicted of murdering.

"Oh, I'm so sorry," Hallie said.

"Yeah, me too. Thank you."

After the introductions, Detective Johnson silently and meticulously went about her work. She dusted the chair, doorknob, and other places on the front porch where someone could have touched. After that, she went into the house and started in the bathroom, dusting everything where Juno was found, followed by the back door and everything in between.

Hallie mentioned that she heard someone coming up the stairs, which is what prompted her to call the police. The detective went over to the staircase with her kit and dusted the banisters leading upstairs.

After about an hour, she had finished and gathered numerous specimens, which she had placed in individual plastic bags. She took a set of Hallie's prints to rule them out against the others collected and placed them in a bag and marked it 'H. Miller' with a black sharpie. She placed them all in one larger bag and said, "I'm going to head back to the precinct now to drop these at the lab to see if they can get anything we can use. I marked them 'urgent' so hopefully they'll process them tomorrow, depending on what else they have."

"Sounds good, Johnson, I really appreciate it," Marcelo said as he walked her towards the front door.

"Nice meeting you, Hallie, hopefully we'll get something; all we need is one," Detective Johnson said as she walked out and headed towards her patrol car.

"I hope so, thanks again for coming out tonight."

"Of course, no problem at all."

Marcelo walked the detective out and Hallie retreated to the living room and curled up on the couch, pulling her knees up into her body and wrapping the blanket around her. She was exhausted.

"How are you doing, babe? Want a nightcap?" Marcelo asked after he came back inside.

"Yes, please. I'm tired but I'm too wired to go to bed yet."

"I get it, believe me. Wine or something stronger?"

"Wine, please. There's a bottle of Faust on the counter that's open from the other night."

"You got it."

Marcelo came back out to the living room with a glass of wine for Hallie and a glass of either bourbon or scotch on the rocks for himself. Marcelo sat down next to her, and they both sipped on their drinks in silence.

Hallie broke the silence, saying, "I thought he was on his way out of Florida. I thought I was safe."

"For all we know, he is on his way out of Florida. We don't know this was him. He would be crazy to come any-where near Tampa."

"Who else could it be?"

"I don't know. But we're going to figure it out."

"I hope you're right. Thank you for believing me," Hallie said.

"I know you, Hallie Miller. I'll always believe you and in you."

"I appreciate that. How do those officers think Juno got locked in the downstairs bathroom? Do they think she did that to herself?"

"Well, they think you could have locked her in there by mistake or maybe before you called 9-1-1. I told them that was ridiculous and impossible. As I said, they don't know you, and they do come across some crazies out there. I set them straight."

"Oh my God, that's so ridiculous. Why would I do that? Are they even going to investigate this or take it seriously?"

"Yes. I will make sure they do. But it doesn't matter, because I'm going to investigate it myself, which is why I had Johnson come out right away. If Stephens or anyone else was in here and left a print, she'll have found it," Marcelo said, the wariness in his eyes evident for the first time to Hallie as she looked up at him.

"Okay, I'm sorry, I know you're doing everything you can and I'm grateful that you believe me."

"Always," Marcelo said as he gently massaged her neck and shoulders.

"I can't believe this is happening, again," Hallie said, somewhat defeated.

"We're missing something," Marcelo said, thinking aloud as he was obviously churning things over in his head, "and I'm going to figure it out."

"All I know is someone was in my house. I don't know how they got in, but there is no question in my mind."

"I know."

And then another idea came to her.

"Marcelo, I need to be able to protect myself. You can't be with me 24-7, and you know that. Someone was in my house. I need you to teach me how to shoot," Hallie directed.

"Um, I know you're upset and scared, but I don't know if that's such a good idea. You've always been against guns, for obvious reasons, which I completely understand and respect," Marcelo said.

"Because my father was shot? Is that what you're alluding to? Or is it because I'm too emotional?" Hallie interrupted, her irritation returning.

"Whoa, Counselor, we're on the same side here," Marcelo responded, putting his hands up in mock surrender.

Hallie took a breath, realizing Marcelo was right, "I know, I'm sorry," she said, rubbing her temples, and taking a few seconds to regain her composure. "But I can't live this way: in constant fear, looking over my shoulder, feeling like I'm not safe in my own home. So, I'm asking you, will you please take me to the gun range and teach me how to shoot?"

"Okay, Counselor, you've made your case. Do you want to go tomorrow?"

"Thank you, yes, right after my work out," Hallie said, feeling like she was taking some control back in her life.

"You got it, Hallie," Marcelo replied.

"Can you stay?" Hallie asked, the exhaustion creeping in as the adrenaline waned and the wine relaxed her.

"I planned to. You need to get some sleep. Let me walk you up to bed."

* * *

Marcelo walked Hallie up to bed with Juno in tow, and slid in next to her, gently stroking her forehead as he watched her drift off to sleep in less than five minutes. After he was sure she was sound asleep, Marcelo went downstairs and pulled out his notebook. He wrote down everything he knew as well as the questions he needed to answer. Marcelo was determined to figure out the answers to his biggest questions: *How did someone get in and out without leaving any evidence of a break in? Do they have a key? Was it Stephens or someone else?*

Marcelo walked the perimeter of the inside of the house, examining every door and window, double checking each one twice. He went outside and walked around the outside of the house with his flashlight, shining it on the ground beneath every door and window to look for footprints or any sign of disturbance, which was futile, he quickly realized, as the officers who responded had already done the same and left their own footprints in the process. It would be impossible to tell which ones were theirs and which ones belonged to an intruder.

He heard a car alarm going off on the next block, but other than that, the neighborhood was quiet. He looked up and down the street but didn't see any unusual cars or anything out of the ordinary.

Marcelo was frustrated. He knew he was missing something. He sat down on the wicker loveseat on the front porch, the beam from his flashlight sweeping across the railing across from him. The air picked up and rustled the leaves in Hallie's yard. At the same time, the light from the flashlight reflected off something on the ground just on the other side of the railing.

He got up and leaned over the railing to get a better look. It took him a few minutes, but then he saw the tip of a metal object sticking out from under the leaves and storm debris remnants that hadn't been completely cleared up yet. He descended off the porch, wrapped his sleeve around his hand so he wouldn't leave prints on it if it was anything important, laid on the ground and stretched until he was able to grab it.

After retrieving it, he shone the flashlight on it and saw it was a tool, although he didn't recognize what kind of tool it was. The thin tool was rounded and smooth on one end while it tapered into a sharp, course edge on the other end, like an ice pick. It was dirty but not rusty, so there was no telling how long it had been outside, but probably not too long. He brought it inside and dropped it into a plastic bag. First thing tomorrow he would figure out what kind of tool it was and whether it could be connected to the break in at Hallie's house.

Marcelo put his phone on 'do not disturb' and made sure the ringer was on silent before going upstairs to lie down next to Hallie. He knew he probably wasn't going to be able to fall asleep, at least not easily, but he knew he had to try. Tomorrow would be a busy day. He closed his eyes, but his mind kept thinking about the metal file he found and how it could have been used to pick Hallie's lock. He was stumped by the fact that there were no tool marks on the door itself, so he concluded the metal file was probably unrelated. But it wasn't rusty so it couldn't have been there for a long time. He had to rule out any connection to the break in before he mentioned the metal file to Hallie.

Maybe Alicia would find a print or something else on the evidence she had collected.

She was one of the best detectives he had worked with in a long time, and he knew she would put aside any personal feelings she had to do her job.

At least he hoped she could.

CHAPTER FORTY-ONE
LINDA

She was confused. And sad. But she was also starting to get angry. Where had he gone? Why did he leave her there, all alone? It felt like déjà vu, and she didn't like it.

"Are you kidding me, Billy Stephens?" Linda yelled into the empty motel room, immediately regretting how much the volume of her own voice hurt her pounding head.

She couldn't believe he had left her there. That it was happening to her again. There had to be a logical explanation. He wouldn't have just left, would he? No, he would be back. Or he would call or text her.

He loved her, didn't he?

That's what he told her in his letters, on their phone calls.

She believed him.

But what if he didn't love her? What if it was all lies?

Linda had been down this road before. She had been married to Toby Morgan. She had met him online and he seemed perfect . . . until he wasn't. He moved to Tampa from Oklahoma to be with her, and they got married two weeks later. Six months after that, he was gone. After clearing out her bank account and stealing the truck she had bought for him. She waited seven years for him to come back. When he didn't, she finally obtained an uncontested divorce and moved on with her life. The only thing she kept from him was his last name. That was three years ago. She swore to herself then, she wasn't going to let another man do this to her.

And then Billy came into her life. And she never thought she would be feeling this way again. She had believed him. But now what? Was he doing the same thing to her that Toby did? Was he just using her like Toby had? Why did he take all of his stuff with him and leave her there? And why did she feel so bad and not remember anything from the night before?

Linda wasn't stupid.

She felt used. And she didn't like that.

Nope, not one bit, she thought to herself.

She always tried to see the goodness in people and give them the benefit of the doubt at least once. And when someone hurt your feelings or did you wrong, maybe they didn't even realize it. Linda believed you had an obligation to let people know how they had hurt or wronged you and give them the opportunity to apologize and make it right.

She waited seven years for her ex, Toby, to do that. He never did. She wasn't going to wait another seven years for Billy to make things right, but she could certainly give him a few days. He said he had a plan, and she had to trust him.

Linda took comfort in seeing Ms. Baskins resting obliviously on top of her clothes in her open suitcase. She peeked out of the heavy curtains, the sun momentarily blinding her, and was relieved to see her car parked just where she had left it when they had arrived the night before.

At least he hadn't stolen her car like Toby had, she thought.

She closed the curtains and lied back down on the bed. Her head was still throbbing, and she was still feeling groggy. She turned the TV on, and, although it didn't get many stations, she could watch the local news to see if there was anything about Billy. At some point, she drifted off to sleep again.

*   *   *

Four days had passed, and she had still not heard from Billy, and he hadn't come back to the motel. She had survived on the snacks and waters she had packed in the car for them, not wanting to venture out of the room in case he came back. But she was tired of waiting, and it was obvious he wasn't coming back for her.

She had promised herself that she was never waiting around for a man again. And, she had learned that if you wanted something, you had to go get it yourself. She was determined to find Billy to ask him to his face why he left her there in that seedy, nasty motel room, all alone. And if she determined he had used her and didn't really love her, she was going to turn him in herself. Or worse. But until then, she was going to give him the benefit of the doubt.

"Okay, Carole, we're putting on our big girl panties and we're going to go find Billy. Maybe he's trying to protect us and is in danger. We're going to find out, aren't we, my precious? One way or another, we're going to get to the bottom of this. We're a family, after all," she said as she scratched the cat's head and peeked through the vinyl curtains out to the parking lot, "and you don't abandon family."

She packed up her belongings, loaded Ms. Baskins into her pink cat carrier, and headed out to her car in the parking lot.

"Let's go find daddy, my sweet."

CHAPTER FORTY-TWO
HALLIE

Hallie awoke before her alarm went off. Marcelo was sleeping soundly next to her, and she was grateful he had spent the night with her. She got up, brushed her teeth, washed her face, put her hair up in a ponytail, and put her workout clothes on. She was meeting her trainer, Jason, at the gym for a 7 a.m. session.

"Hallie?" Marcelo asked in a groggy voice.

"Go back to sleep. I'm going to let Juno out and then head to my workout session with Jason. I'll be back in an hour or so."

"I should get up anyway," Marcelo responded as he looked at his watch. "Do you have time for coffee?"

"Sorry, hon, I need to be there at 7."

"Okay, go kick some ass, Counselor."

Hallie kissed Marcelo on the forehead and went downstairs, Juno right behind her. She let her out and then fed her while she made a cup of coffee for the road. She felt more determined than she had the night before and, with Marcelo beside her, had slept soundly. She arrived at the private gym at 6:45 a.m. and waited in her car for Jason to arrive. Before today, Hallie was never early and was often a few minutes late. But she felt different today, knowing Stephens was out there, somewhere, and had possibly been in her house the night before.

She had to get as strong as she could, with Jason's help, so she could defend herself against him or anyone else who came after her. She believed in her gut that Stephens was the one who broke into her house, and, if he came back, she was going to be ready for him.

While she waited for Jason to arrive at the gym, she stretched her calves against the curb, her nerves and muscles buzzing.

"Well, this is a first, look who's the early bird this morning," Jason said, carrying his backpack and clipboard with Hallie's training sheet, as he unlocked the padlock to the gym. "This is exciting," he said.

"I'm ready, Jason. You need to make me strong."

"You are strong, Hallie," Jason smiled.

"Well, you need to make me stronger."

"You're getting stronger with every workout, but why the urgency today? Do we have an event coming up? I'm sensing a newfound commitment," Jason teased.

"No, I wish it was something like that. Someone was in my house last night," Hallie said, flatly, "I think it was Stephens."

Jason knew all about the trial and who Stephens was.

"Oh no, seriously? I saw on the news that he had escaped from prison during the hurricane, but I didn't think he would be stupid enough to come back to Tampa. Why do you think it was him?"

"I received a threatening note, allegedly from Stephens, not too long ago, and now with his escape, I think it has to be him, but I don't know anything for sure."

"Why 'allegedly' from Stephens?" Jason asked.

"Well, an envelope was left on my front porch when Stephens was still in prison, but I know it was from him. He must have had someone else write it and leave it there. The only other possibility is that someone else who knows about him wrote it and wants to scare me. I don't know anymore. I feel like I'm going crazy."

"I'm sorry, Hallie. You're not crazy. What happened last night?"

"I was sleeping but something woke me up and then I heard someone coming up the stairs. I don't know who else would want to hurt me besides him."

"Obviously he didn't get to you, because you're here, so what did you do?"

"I locked myself in my bathroom and called 9-1-1. By the time the police got there, he, or whoever it was, was gone."

"Thank God you're okay. Do they know how he got in?"

"That's what's weird. No sign of a break in, but when the police arrived, the front door was unlocked, and Juno was locked in the downstairs bathroom. I know I locked that door before I went to bed."

"Besides Stephens, could it be anyone else? Anyone who might have a key?"

Jason knew Hallie's history. He knew about the attacks on her by Stephens and Martin a/k/a Pietro Martino and all about her creepy ex-husband, David. Hallie had been training with Jason for years and they had become friends.

"I changed the locks after David moved out, so it can't be him. I honestly don't know."

"Hallie, let me help you."

"You are helping me, Jason. You're making me stronger, and I'll be able to defend myself," she said as her eyes conveyed her determination.

"Yes, I will continue to help you with all of that, and you will continue to get stronger and be able to defend yourself, but I can offer you more. You're dealing with dangerous people, bad people. Um, well, I have another line of work, private security but kind of super private, not available to the general public. Please let me help you," Jason pleaded.

"Private security? I don't think I need that, but I appreciate the offer. I have Marcelo and the police are on it, I think I'm okay."

"Hallie, please don't take this the wrong way, but I've heard some things about Marcelo, from other cops. I don't trust him."

"What do you mean, *you don't trust him*? What kind of things have you heard about him?"

"Nothing specific, but that he may not always follow the rules, may not be the straight arrow you think he is."

"What does that even mean?"

"What do you know about his family?"

"They're from Colombia originally, two of his brothers still live there, I think; he doesn't talk about them much."

"There's a reason for that. The brothers you mentioned are soldiers in one of the biggest and most violent Colombian cartels. There are rumors that Marcelo is affiliated with them too, or used to be, at least."

"No, Jason, you're wrong about Marcelo. Colombian cartel? That's crazy and impossible. But even, for argument's sake, if his brothers are criminals, that doesn't make Marcelo one. I'm sure he's rubbed some people the wrong way, he has a strong personality. But I know him. He's a good cop."

"How long have you known him? What do you really know about him? His past? We've known each other, what, three, maybe four years? You trust me, right?"

"Well, yes, but I don't understand what you're saying. I trust Marcelo, too. We've been together for over a year. I mean, he's my boyfriend, I love him. I don't understand where you're going with this. I don't care what his brothers do in Colombia. He's not a part of that life."

"I'm just worried about you. What if the break in at your house has nothing to do with you but something connected to Marcelo or his family? That's how the cartels work; they go after loved ones to send a message."

"No, no, that's impossible, Jason. I appreciate that you think you're trying to protect me, but you're wrong about Marcelo," Hallie said, her voice rising angrily. "And I can protect myself. I'm going to learn how to shoot and get a concealed weapons permit. I don't want to rely on him or you or anyone else to protect me. If Stephens or anyone else, including the fucking Colombian cartel, comes for me, they will need protection from me. That's why I'm coming to you, to make sure I can protect myself, do you understand?"

"Yes, I understand, and I'm sorry, Hallie. I've said too much and overstepped. I'm just worried about you. Forget everything I said, and you're right, I probably have the wrong information about Marcelo. He should not be judged by his family. Let's restart, if you're ready, and get you stronger."

"Thank you, Jason, yes, please, let's do this," Hallie said, trying to shake off what Jason had said about Marcelo.

"Okay, let's do it. We start now," Jason took out his clip board and wrote some notes, crossing some things out and adding others, before saying, "Give me a number."

"Solid seven, maybe a seven and a half," Hallie responded, to indicate how she was feeling, mentally and physically, with ten being the highest.

"Okay, not bad. Which playlist do you want me to play today?" Jason asked, falling into their normal rapport, each of them trying to overcome the awkwardness of the previous ten minutes and pretend it never happened.

"Eminem. No question," Hallie said, knowing Jason would understand her choice.

She was angry. And she was not going to be a victim. And now she was also confused about the things Jason had said to her, but she couldn't think about those things now. She had too many other things on her mind, including Stephens or whoever broke into her house the night before

* * *

After her work out, Hallie met Marcelo at the gun range. They spent over an hour getting Hallie comfortable with holding a gun and introducing her to the various mechanisms of a gun, including the safety, the magazine clip, the chamber, how to load a gun and how to tell if it's loaded. After handling many different models, sizes, and calibers, Hallie found she was most comfortable with the Walther PDP F-Series, 4-inch, 9-millimeter pistol, specifically designed for a woman's smaller grip.

Hallie filled out the Florida background check application to purchase the gun and signed up for a training course to obtain the certificate of completion she would need to obtain her concealed weapons permit. Florida had a three-day waiting period for her to purchase the gun, but Hallie was able to rent the same model that she could use that day for her first lesson and training session.

"Babe, I'm sorry, but I need to get to the precinct. We've covered a lot today. Maybe we could wait to schedule your first training session in a couple of days?"

"No, I don't want to wait. It's okay, I'll be with the instructor. I want to do it today. You go on. I'll check in with you later."

"Are you sure?"

"Yeah, go ahead, I'm good. I learned so much from you today, and I appreciate you helping me so much, but I don't want to lose my momentum. I want to proceed with the training class now, since they have the slot and the trainer available."

"Okay, I get it. Be careful, be safe, and call me later."

"I will," Hallie said as Marcelo leaned down and gave her a peck on the cheek before she returned her attention to the unloaded handgun in her hand.

She had to admit she felt powerful with the sleek, black steel gun in her hand. Maybe this was what she needed to feel safe, as long as she would be able to use it if and when the time came. As she waited for the trainer to bring her back to the shooting range, a sign over the doorway caught her eye: *"Never point a gun at anything you don't intend to shoot. Never shoot at anything you don't intend to kill."*

If someone was trying to hurt her or Katie or anyone she loved, and after what she had been through, she was confident that she would be able to pull the trigger. She re-read the sign over the doorway, committing the words to memory.

"Words to live by," she whispered to herself.

CHAPTER FORTY-THREE
LINDA

Linda couldn't sit and wait around in the grungy motel for Billy one minute longer. She had already called into work to let them know she had evacuated to stay with family in Tampa before the storm hit and would not be able to return until the following week. She wanted to buy some time so no one would connect her to Billy's escape. When she had called the office, she was relieved to get Karl's voicemail. She knew she wasn't a good liar so leaving him a message was easier than having to speak to him. She hoped her message would give her enough time to find Billy and figure out what to do next without becoming wanted herself.

Linda packed up the Ford Escape and placed Carole Baskins in her carrier on the passenger seat beside her. She returned the only key card she had to the front office and checked out. Maria, the woman who had checked her in, appeared amused. Linda got the impression that most guests didn't formally 'check out' of El Rancho Motel but rather absconded in the middle of the night, just like Billy had.

"Thanks so much for your hospitality, Maria, I appreciate you," Linda said as she sashayed out of the motel office.

She heard Maria cackling and coughing behind her as she left the musty, airless office.

Linda got into her car, fastened her seat belt, and turned to the cat next to her, "Okay, Carole, here we go."

She reversed out of the space, put the car in drive and turned right onto Nebraska and headed towards downtown Tampa as she tried to think of where she might begin to look for him. She had been driving for about ten minutes, still unsure where she was heading, when she passed a public library on her right, which gave her an idea. She made a U-turn and pulled into the parking lot of the public library on Nebraska Avenue.

She didn't want to leave Carole in the car but knew they wouldn't let her into the library with a cat.

Was there such thing as a service cat? Emotional support cat? Dogs were allowed everywhere these days, why not cats? Linda wondered.

She looked in the back seat and spotted the big cloth beach bag she had filled with sheets, blankets, and towels, which she figured they would need if they made it to a cabin in the mountains as they had originally planned. She emptied it out and placed the carrier into the bag, making sure airflow to the slats were not blocked. She hoisted the straps of the bag over her left shoulder, grabbed her purse and phone, and locked the doors with her key fob, making sure she heard the double beep to signify it was locked.

"Oh Ms. Baskins, we are on an adventure, aren't we?"

The cool air of the air conditioning and the distinct smell of old books hit her as soon as she walked through the automatic doors. She smiled at the librarian at the front desk as she walked by, trying to keep the beach bag on her opposite side.

"Good morning," the older lady at the desk said cheerfully.

"Good morning," Linda said cheerfully back, and then added, "do you have computers available for public use?"

"Yes, we do, dear. It's first come, first serve, but you picked a good day. I don't think anyone is on them today. They're just over there," the woman said as she pointed across the room to a row of connected desks on the left. Each desk was separated by a partition for privacy and contained an antiquated desktop monitor on top of it.

"Perfect, thank you so much," Linda said, quickly heading towards the computer stations before Carole decided to meow or otherwise blow their cover.

She clicked 'guest' at the login page and opened Google. She entered "Judge William Stephen Tampa" in the search field. The search results included numerous articles, all of which she had already read, and most of which contained false information about Billy and the trial. She was looking for a specific video. She entered a few additional search combinations, each time scrolling the result list. She had done this so many times after the trial, wanting to learn everything she could about Billy. She knew she would recognize the link when she saw it.

She tried again. This time she typed "William Stephens judge plea life sentence lawyer DNA" in the search field and hit enter. This time, links to articles as well as video clips about his plea deal and sentencing came up. Linda scanned down the results until she found the one she had been looking for.

"Bingo," Linda said, a little too loudly, garnering the attention and judgmental eye of the front desk librarian.

Linda silently mouthed the word 'sorry' and returned her attention to the monitor screen.

She opened the video, making sure the volume was on the lowest level possible where she could still hear it, but front desk gestapo could not, before she hit 'play.'

"Ms. Miller! Ms. Miller! What do you think about the sentence?"

The cameraman zoomed in on a pretty, blonde walking down the courthouse steps. She paused, looked to a gentleman dressed in a dark suit to her right, probably a lawyer, before looking back at the reporter and answering: *"For the sake of Naomi's family, I think the sentence is a fair and just result. He deserved more but Naomi's husband and young son should not have to endure another trial."*

"Is it true that you were the one who connected Stephens to the DNA found on the victim through your own DNA?"

"No comment," she said, as she resumed her descent.

"Hallie, how is your DNA connected to Stephens?" another reporter in the crowd of reporters shouted at her, as another one yelled, "Hallie, is it true you and Stephens have a child together?"

Linda continued to watch the video. The man in the dark suit held up his hand to the reporters who were shoving microphones in the blonde's face.

"We're done here," he said, as he escorted the blonde down the rest of the steps towards a waiting car.

"Hallie Miller, that's right; that's your name. Hmmm, let me see what I can find out about you on the ole' inter-web," Linda said, remembering that during the trial the prosecution claimed that Billy was the biological father of her daughter. They had used the child's DNA to connect Billy to DNA found under the murder victim's fingernails, but Linda didn't believe all of that science mumbo-jumbo. Even if he was the child's father, how did that make him a murderer? It didn't make any sense. She knew all of that could be manipulated, which it obviously was.

But now she needed to know more about this woman. Was this woman and her child Billy's "unfinished business" in Tampa that he mentioned? She had no other leads to go on, so she decided she might as well start there.

She cleared the history in her Google search and typed in "Hallie Miller Tampa" and hit enter. Links to numerous articles dated over the past few weeks popped up. Apparently, the woman's brother had been charged with murdering a young girl on the beach.

"Yeesh, that's some family," Linda whispered to herself.

Linda kept searching and found the older articles about Hallie, and Linda started reading each one of them. After about an hour and a half of going down internet rabbit holes, exploring public social media posts, and reviewing available public records, she felt she knew all she needed to know about this Hallie Miller, including where she lived in South Tampa.

Linda wished she had her regular cellphone with her so she could save the address in a note on her phone, but she had left that phone at her house in Starke, and her burner phone didn't have that capability. She left her bag with Ms. Baskins in it next to her chair at her computer station and went to the front desk to ask the librarian to borrow a piece of paper and a pen or pencil.

"Hi, so sorry to bother you, honey, but do you have a piece of paper and a pen or pencil I can borrow for a few minutes?" Linda asked, trying to pour on her southern charm.

"Aren't there any over there?"

"Um, no, I didn't see any," Linda said, looking back over to the computer area.

"Okay, let me see what I can find, but usually it's first come, first served – that's our policy, so if there are no supplies over there, then someone else must have used them, or stolen them as they're apt to do around here."

"I don't need much," Linda said, "even just a pen or pencil would be great, I can probably find a scrap of paper in my bag."

"Well, hang on, give me a minute," the librarian said as she rummaged through a drawer below the counter. "Okay, here we go," she said as she pulled out a yellow legal pad.

She handed Linda the legal pad and then retrieved a blue pen from the cup next to the register, and said as she handed it to her, "I need this back when you're done."

"Of course," Linda said, reaching out to take the pen from her.

The librarian hesitated for a moment before handing it over to Linda. She thanked her and took the pen and legal pad back to her station. At the top of the page, she wrote Hallie's name, address, law firm information, and cell phone, all of which she found easily on the internet. She couldn't find anything about Hallie's daughter, including on any social media, which was unusual, especially for a girl her age. But she found Hallie's mother's name, sister's name, and both of their addresses and wrote all their information down on the legal pad.

She knew where she was going to start.

She tore off the sheet she had just written on, folded it, and slipped it into her purse. Then she tore off the next two blank pages just as a precaution and threw them into the shredder bin next to the printer-copier. She had watched her share of true crime shows and knew a thing or two about not leaving a trace. She returned the legal pad and pen to the front desk and headed out of the library with Ms. Baskins and her plan in tow.

CHAPTER FORTY-FOUR
THE HUNTER

He watched her from the back of the quaint neighborhood bar. He had been thinking about her since the night he followed her out into the parking lot a few weeks before and tried to help her pick up the contents of her bag. Instead of being thankful, she was rude to him. He could tolerate a lot of things, but rudeness was not one of them. He had been a perfect gentleman to her. Just like Dawn and Stacey, both of whom he had offered to buy a drink. And how did that work out for those cunts? Exactly as it should have.

This one, though, wasn't like Dawn or Stacey, or any of the other women he had followed home from beach bars. She was older and seemed more confident, more street savvy. She was thin, about five-six, with high cheekbones. The contrast of her long, jet-black hair against her ivory skin and red lipstick was striking and reminded him of his foster mother.

He hated that fucking bitch.

This one was a lot prettier than his foster mom but seemed just as surly and possibly even more of a drunk than his foster mom was, if that was even possible.

Likely just as much of a whore, too, he thought.

Listening to her conversation with the bartender the first time he had watched her, he knew her name was Monica.

Oh, Monica, I am going to take my time with you, he thought, *you will be worth the wait.*

He would punish her for her abhorrent behavior, just like the others.

He shifted in his bar stool and adjusted his baseball cap so the camera over the bar wouldn't capture his face.

He watched her as she slammed back her martini and motioned for another. She didn't seem interested in anyone or anything other than the drink in front of her. She seemed agitated, upset about something, not that he cared, and she kept checking her cell phone.

He had to be patient and plan her attack meticulously, he thought.

There was no doubt she was scrappy and a fighter. The thought excited him. But when he pounced, he couldn't take the chance of her getting away or arousing the attention of a neighbor.

He needed to get into her apartment when she wasn't home, learn more about her habits and the layout of the apartment. He always learned a lot about his victims from his initial interactions with them or listening to their conversations with others, but he always learned the most from breaking into their homes.

He left a twenty on the bar for his tab, pulled the bill of his baseball cap down, and left the bar. He drove a few blocks away and parked his truck in the driveway of a vacant condo that was being renovated near Monica's apartment. He was about to get out of his truck when his cell phone rang.

"Hello, everything okay?"

"Sorry to bother you, hon, but was wondering if you were coming home anytime soon?"

"Unfortunately, no, it doesn't look like it. With everything that's going on, I may end up being here half the night. Everything okay at the house? Need something?"

"Well, we need creamer for your coffee in the morning, and I'm already dressed and washed up for bed. But if you forget or you're too tired, I'll run out in the morning before you get up."

"Okay, I'll try to remember. Gotta get back to work now. Get some sleep, darlin'."

The Hunter ended the call, making a mental note to pick up a pint of sweet cream on his way home. He looked up and down the street before getting out of the truck and walking the short distance to the apartment.

He couldn't wait to feel her take her last breath. There was such power in that moment.

He easily picked the lock and went inside, locking the door behind him.

Hmmm, let me see what I can find out about you, my lovely whore.

CHAPTER FORTY-FIVE
MONICA

At the end of the night, Monica called an Uber to take her home. She hadn't received any more texts, but she had convinced herself that they were from Christian, and he was coming for her. It was just a matter of time. She would talk to her mother and her uncle about hiring protection.

She unlocked her apartment door, relieved as the cool air hit her and that she had remembered to turn her window AC unit on in her bedroom. It was loud but the cheap landlord hadn't installed an adequate unit to cool the entire apartment in the hot summer months, so the window unit her cousin Tom installed for her helped. She wanted to get into her comfy clothes, curl up on the couch, and watch something mindless.

She kicked off her shoes and headed towards her bedroom to change. On her way, she unhooked her bra from the back under her shirt while reaching in to pull her left strap over her shoulder. As she headed into her bedroom, she noticed some of her thongs caught hanging out of her underwear drawer. That was unusual.

She tried to think about how things had looked when she left earlier that day, but her mind was foggy from the martinis. She had been in a hurry and was no neat freak, she acknowledged, but she knew she didn't leave her drawer that way.

Someone had been in her apartment.

Whoever it was could still be in there, she quickly realized.

She stopped instantly and did not continue through her bedroom door.

She stopped taking off her bra and pulled the strap back over her shoulder, keeping her breathing steady.

She backed up into the small galley kitchen and grabbed the largest knife from the too expensive knife block from Williams Sonoma, one of the first purchases she made for her kitchen when she first got her apartment. She wished she could get to her bedroom to get to her gun. Before she left earlier, she had placed the unlocked case containing her loaded Glock back underneath her bed. If she could get to it, she knew how to use it.

Her father had taught her how to shoot guns, including his Glock when she was younger. She was a dead-on shot and rarely missed her target. Her father wanted her to compete, professionally, but that ended when he died. When she moved out of her mother's house, she bought a newer model of her father's Glock for protection but mostly because it reminded her of him. As she had confirmed a few nights before, it was loaded: one round in the chamber, seventeen in the clip. When she was carrying on her person, she would take the round out of the chamber because you never wanted to shoot yourself or anyone else accidentally. She had learned that the hard way when she was sixteen.

She shivered at the memory of Charlie Robinson sprawled, face down, on the sidewalk, a crimson stain appearing on his back and spreading out like the black ink on a Rorschach test. She shook the thought from her head and returned her focus to the present moment.

There was no doubt someone had been or still was in her apartment, she thought, holding tightly to the thick black handle of the largest knife from the butcher block. *Is it a random burglar or, oh my God, is it Christian?* Monica's mind raced as she thought about what to do next.

She opened her phone and texted her cousin, Tom.

"Tom, someone broke in. Might still be in here. Call 9-1-1. I don't want them to hear me on the phone."

She put the phone on the counter and backed herself against the wall in the galley kitchen so that no one could come up behind her. She thought about running out of the apartment, but where would she go? And there was no guarantee that whoever had come in hadn't left and was outside watching her, waiting for her to come running out. She felt her chances were better inside, with the large knife, unless, of course, they had a gun, or worse, her gun.

A few months before, one of the maintenance workers was using his master key to enter women's apartments in the building when they weren't home, including Monica's, to go through their belongings and do God knows what with them. Apparently, he was *only* a voyeur, his biggest crime being that he stole women's panties and lingerie, but Monica knew voyeurs often progressed to more serious sexual crimes. He had been fired and charged with breaking and entering and other crimes after someone caught him in their apartment. The landlord changed all the locks on everyone's units after he left, and Monica never saw him around again. The current maintenance guy was a sweet older man who lived on site with his wife and often had his grandchildren visiting him.

Monica did not believe that he had broken into her apartment, but who the fuck was it? she wondered. *Christian? Marlboro Man? Some rando who followed her home from O'Maddy's?*

Her hand around the knife was sweating, and she let go of it, one hand at a time, to wipe each hand on her jeans. She stayed backed against the counter, listening for any sound coming from her bedroom. The window AC unit was so loud, she couldn't hear a thing. She held the sharp knife in front of her with two hands, ready to defend herself. She had never used a knife for anything other than cooking, but it was all she had without being able to reach her Glock.

She waited and listened.

Nothing but the whirring and buzzing of the AC wall unit.

She heard a ping on her cellphone, alerting her to a new text message. She held the knife steady in her left hand as she picked the cellphone up off the counter to read the text.

"Hang tight, Moni, help is on the way."

Monica replied back, typing with her right thumb, "K hope they hurry."

Within five minutes, someone knocked on Monica's door at the same time she received another text from her cousin.

"You're okay, open your door."

Monica ran, knife still in hand, and opened the door, expecting the police or one of her uncle's thugs, but instead found a good-looking man in gym shorts, running shoes, and a tight-fitting, black t-shirt, which emphasized his rock-hard abs and muscular arms, emblazoned with the slogan: "You Gotta Want It."

"Um, hello?" Monica said more as a question than a greeting, confused, thinking her cousin had made a mistake.

The man put his pointer finger up to his lips to signal to her to be quiet as he moved past her towards the back of the apartment. She noticed the gun in the waistband of his shorts, which seemed out of place with his outfit and which he took out as he walked towards her bedroom.

She texted to her cousin, "he's here, will call soon."

The man checked every inch of Monica's small apartment, confirming that no one was inside. He checked her windows and examined her front door lock. Then he checked the sliding door leading out to her balcony, which was locked, and she watched as he confirmed the security pin was in place, before he unlocked it and went out onto her balcony.

When he came back in, Monica said, "You think I'm crazy, don't you? I'm telling you someone was in here."

"I know," the man said calmly as he took out his phone and made a call.

"Hey, it's me. Yeah, I'm here, it's clear, he's gone. . . . Yeah, lock was picked and entry was through the front door . . . . No, I don't think so but I'll have her check to see if anything is missing. I'll call you when we leave," he said before putting the phone back in his shorts pocket.

"How do you know the lock was picked?" Monica asked after he hung up, while also trying to process everything she heard, including his comment, 'when *we* leave.'

"I found fresh scratch marks in the metal around the keyhole. They're faint, but they're there. Look around and see if anything is missing, but I doubt you'll find anything."

"What makes you think that?" Monica asked as she started looking around her apartment.

"Because we're dealing with a different motivation here."

"What kind of motivation?" Monica asked, not sure she wanted to hear the answer.

"It's personal."

"What do you mean, it's personal?"

"This wasn't a random break in. They broke in because you live here."

"How do you know that?"

"Let me try to explain. If this was random and your average robbery, your place would be destroyed because the intruder or intruders don't have a lot of time, so they pull out every drawer and open every cabinet and closet looking for valuables."

He pointed at her tv in her small living room and her laptop on her dining room table, "see those? You're tv and laptop, those are easy things to grab, even if you have to leave on the fly. But whoever broke in here didn't take those. Why would that be?"

"Maybe they saw me coming up the street and left before they could take anything," Monica said hopefully, knowing it was highly unlikely.

"That's fair. But let me ask you this: have you had anyone over lately? I mean, when you left today, did you leave a male friend behind?"

"I think that's a little personal."

"Just answer the question. I honestly don't care who you are or are not sleeping with, but trust me, it will make sense when you answer."

"Okay, fine, no, I was alone last night and did not leave anyone here when I left earlier today."

"So that confirms it. Someone was going through your lingerie and nightstand drawers, that's obvious. But as you'll notice when you go into your bathroom, they also left the toilet seat up, unless you regularly pee with the seat up. Do you?"

"Oh my God, what are you talking about? No, I don't lift the seat to pee."

"Okay, so no one is in the apartment, and they entered and exited the same way, through the front door, which you found locked when you came home, I assume, so you did not surprise him. Was the front door locked when you came home?"

"Yes, yes it was," Monica said, seeing the logic in everything this person standing in her living room was saying and starting to feel queasy at the implications.

"Leaving the drawers with your lingerie spilling out as he did and the seat up on your toilet was intentional. He wants to scare you. He wants to make sure you know he was here. And he'll be back."

"What the fuck, how do you know all this?" Monica asked, using anger to hide her fear.

"Before I went private, I used to be a detective in the sex crimes unit in Miami. I learned a lot about human nature, and let's just say, I know what motivates certain types of men."

"And what motivates this one?"

"Fear."

Monica didn't know how to respond to that, other than it had worked. She didn't scare easily, but she felt a chill go up her spine and her hands started to tremble.

"I know this is difficult, Ms. Martino, but I recommend you check to see if anything is missing and then we can decide what to do next. I'll wait out here."

She went into her bedroom to check for her jewelry and any other valuable possessions, including her Glock. All of her jewelry appeared to be in her jewelry box on her dresser and nothing seemed to be missing or out of place, other than her underwear, bras, and lingerie cascading out of her drawers. She could see now how staged it looked and not haphazard, which further alarmed her.

Next, she checked for her Glock. She pulled the gun case out from under her bed and placed it on her nightstand. As she opened the case, she was relieved to see the matte, black pistol where it was supposed to be, but when she picked it up to inspect it, she instantly noticed it was lighter. She removed the clip and, as she suspected, discovered someone had unloaded the seventeen bullets from the magazine, replacing it with an empty clip. Next, she checked the chamber and confirmed whoever had emptied the clip also removed the bullet from the chamber.

They found her gun and removed all the bullets but didn't steal it, which meant the guy standing in her living room was right: whoever had been in her apartment intended to return. Reaching for an unloaded gun in the middle of the night with someone standing in her bedroom would have been useless.

What did he want? she wondered. *He wanted her to know he had been in her apartment, that was obvious. He probably didn't want her to notice the clip had been emptied, or he would have just stolen the gun, maybe even the case, too. But he didn't. Just the bullets. Which told her one thing: he wanted her to reach for her gun and pull the trigger with no ability to protect herself. In that moment, he would have the upper hand and see her fear.*

She looked around the rest of the room and noticed something else odd. There was a nighty from her lingerie drawer, folded neatly at the bottom of her bed with a thong, also folded neatly, placed on top.

The man poked his head into her room, "Are you almost ready? I'm supposed to drive you to your mom's house on Davis Island."

"And if I decline?" Monica asked, knowing she had no intention of staying alone in her apartment that night, but at the same time detesting being told what to do.

"I can't force you, obviously, but I recommend you don't decline. Let me do my job, Ms. Martino. You'll be safer at your mom's."

Monica knew it was pointless to resist. If she did, as soon as her mother and cousin, Tom, got the word, they would be on the phone with her. She wasn't in the mood for an argument with either of them that night. She was also very uncomfortable knowing someone had broken into her apartment, went through her things, and then removed all of the bullets from her gun.

She packed a small bag with enough clothes for a couple of days, packed up her toiletries, and tossed a few new vape cartridges into her makeup bag. She also retrieved a fresh box of 9mm cartridges from the top shelf in her closet and put those in her bag with her Glock, which she had secured back in its case. She made a mental note to order one of those new gun safes that opened with facial recognition.

"Okay, I'm ready. You don't have to call me Ms. Martino, by the way. Please, call me Monica. I didn't catch your name," Monica said more as a question.

"It's Jason. Jason Lane."

CHAPTER FORTY-SIX
HALLIE

After her shooting lesson, Hallie went home, showered, and then went into the office. Sitting at her desk, she remembered the weird conversation she had with Jason that morning. She tried to shake what he said to her, but she kept hearing it in her head:

"How much do you know about Marcelo and his family?"

There was no way Marcelo was connected to a Colombian cartel. But what if his brothers were? Would Marcelo look the other way or cover up for them? He was a regarded detective, and she trusted him, but when it came to family, would he do the right thing? Hallie didn't know the answer, but she knew she needed to talk to Marcelo about it when the time was right.

She couldn't think about it any longer. She had so much work to do, so she pushed all of her thoughts away so she could focus on the work she had to get done. She reviewed and answered all of her unanswered emails from the past few days, spoke to a number of clients, and drafted and revised various agreements she had promised clients or opposing counsel. She opened her time management portal to enter her time and realized she had been there for and billed over seven hours, despite not getting to the office until after eleven. It was late and she was ready to quit for the day when her assistant brought a file box into her office.

Nadia, her latest assistant, was young, smart, and ambitious, with dreams of moving to New York City where her parents had met and grew up. She was of Russian and Puerto Rican descent, which contributed to her striking beauty and unique look. Although she grew up in Tampa, people assumed she was from somewhere in Europe with her thick, shiny black hair, large brown-green eyes that had speckles of gold in them, and warm, olive skin. Hallie knew it was only a matter of time before Nadia left Tampa to pursue a more exciting life in New York. She couldn't blame her.

"What's that?" Hallie asked, looking at the box in Nadia's hands.

"Hmm, not sure. Courier just dropped it off at reception for you," she said as she placed the box on the credenza next to Hallie's desk and looked down to read the label. "Oh," she said, pausing for a second before continuing, "it's from the Law Offices of Michael Freeman."

By then her brother's arrest for the murder of the young girl on Treasure Island had made the news as well as that he was being represented by the former prosecutor, Mike Freeman. Due to the brutality of the crime, the State had charged Charlie with first degree murder and the judge denied bail. The news articles also mentioned that he was the younger brother of Tampa attorney, Hallie Miller, who had her own brush with sensational news after being kidnapped by a serial rapist/killer the previous year. For a few days, the old stories about Hallie resurfaced online, especially since there wasn't much more to report about Charlie or his victim.

As Mike had promised, he had promptly filed a Notice of Discovery with the court and served it on the D.A.'s office. He explained to Hallie that the State had fifteen days after that to provide a list of their reports, witnesses, and other evidence, which would be made available to the defense to review and copy, and he would send her copies of everything he received.

"Ah, the initial discovery in my brother's case," Hallie said, noticing her assistant's uncomfortableness. "It's okay, Nadia, I'm sure you read about the case."

"Um, yeah, sorry, Hallie. You can't seem to catch a break."

"Doesn't seem like it, does it?" Hallie laughed awkwardly. "Anyway, just leave the box there, that's fine, thanks."

"Need anything else?"

"Actually, yes. Please clear my calendar for the next two days. Unless it's urgent, reschedule everyone to next week. I'm going to work from home for the rest of the week. If you need me, you can email or text me, of course."

"You got it, and then I'm going to head out, if you don't need anything else," Nadia said.

"No, that's it, and it's late, get out of here. You can re-schedule everything first thing tomorrow morning," Hallie said, sensing the young woman's relief not to talk any further about Charlie's case.

"Okay, thanks," she said as she quickly left Hallie's office.

Hallie opened her rolling hand cart and placed the box on the base of it. She gathered her files and laptop and placed them in her briefcase and placed that on top of the box before securing the box and briefcase to the back rungs of the cart via the attached bungee cords. She grabbed her purse and left her office, pulling the cart behind her.

She got home, and after taking care of Juno, went upstairs to change out of her work clothes and into her uniform, as she liked to call it: black tank top, sweatpants or leggings, and pair of socks. She returned downstairs and rolled the hand cart that she had left by the door into the living room. She went into the kitchen, opened a bottle of Rodney Strong, and poured herself a glass just as Juno was finishing up her dinner.

She returned to the living room, Juno in tow, and sat on the floor next to the coffee table, her back leaning up against the couch. She unhooked the bungee cords from around the box and pulled a fresh legal pad and pen from her briefcase so she could take notes as she went through the discovery.

"Alexa, play my Sting playlist," Hallie said to the device in her living room as she opened the top of the discovery box. The speaker came to life and started playing *Shape of My Heart* softly in the background.

Hallie was surprised at how little there was in the box. She expected it to be filled with a lot more files and documents, but all it contained were a few manila folders. Juno got comfy next to her and fell asleep as Hallie pulled the first manila folder from the box, which was marked '*Crime Scene Photos.*'

She took a deep breath and a few sips of her wine before opening the folder. She set her wine glass on the coffee table and opened the file.

It took her a minute to understand what she was looking at. And then she couldn't unsee it, and she audibly gasped. Juno picked her head up and looked at Hallie.

"It's okay, baby," Hallie said, patting Juno until she rested her head back down.

The first picture was a close-up of the victim's neck, which showed she had been violently strangled with some type of ligature, possibly a piece of clothing or something else owned by the victim, which was still wrapped around her neck. The next few pictures showed the victim as she was found on the bed, various angles, and the room overall. Everything in the room seemed to be in disarray except Hallie noticed a floral tank-top or sundress folded very neatly on the bottom corner of the bed.

"That's odd," Hallie thought, as she made a note on her legal pad to inquire as to the folded clothing when everything else seemed to be strewn about haphazardly.

She went through the rest of the pictures and other information provided by the State, and she understood why there wasn't more in the box. They had everything they needed to convict Charlie, and they didn't need anything more.

The DNA analysis and other evidence found at the scene, combined with eyewitness accounts, were all damning. Charlie's DNA was found throughout the small apartment, including his semen found on a sheet underneath the victim and his hair on the bed and victim's clothing. Charlie's fingerprints were also found on the coffee table, a Modelo beer bottle, and the bathroom counter. Hallie read through the analysis and noted results that didn't seem to match Charlie. As she didn't have experience reading these types of reports, she flagged the report to discuss what the findings meant with Mike Freeman.

In addition to the physical evidence, there were two eyewitnesses who identified Charlie as the person they saw walking by them that night from the direction of the victim's place within the time frame of when she was murdered. One was a kitchen worker from the bar where Charlie worked who was rinsing mats in the parking lot at the time and the other was the drummer from the band that had played at the bar that night and was loading up his equipment at the same time.

Hallie was sick to her stomach. *Was it possible Charlie was a murderer?* She shook her head and dismissed the thought as quickly as it had entered her brain. It was just not possible.

After reviewing the initial discovery from the State, she decided to research everything she could about Dawn Owens, the victim, Charlie, and Ken Gardner, the AirBnB owner. He was the one who found her, but according to the report of the first officer on the scene, had an alibi for the night before. Since Ken Gardner found her, alibi or not, Hallie wanted to talk to him.

She also decided to do another internet search to see if she could find any other similar murders besides the other ones she had initially found. Since then, she had learned from Marcelo through his police connections that Dawn Owens was raped and strangled, with strangulation ruled as the ultimate cause of her death, which was confirmed by the medical examiner's report in the discovery file.

She expanded her search, but this time did not include the words *vacation* or *beach*. She found an older case from 2021:

Gainesville Woman Found Murdered

By: Deb Gardner

June 15, 2021 / Gainesville Sun

Kristina Dillard, 27, of Gainesville, was found dead in her home on Sunday after her neighbor, Laura Singleton, called the police requesting a welfare check on her. Ms. Singleton said she heard the woman's small dog barking more than usual and she realized she hadn't seen Ms. Dillard in a few days. "Look, I'm not one to judge, but she was a strange woman. And she had certain habits: walking her little yappy dog was one of them, and not picking up the dog's business was another one – I mean, I'm not saying that's what got her killed, but people don't take kindly to inconsiderate people around here. But, oh Lord, a murder in this neighborhood, what is this world coming to?" Ms. Singleton said.

Ms. Dillard was last seen leaving Loosey's Downtown, a local bar and restaurant where she worked, on Friday, June 11th at about 1:00 a.m. Management said she left after her shift and wasn't scheduled to work again until the following Monday.

On Sunday, she was found with a stocking tied around her neck and had been beaten and sexually assaulted. The Gainesville police have not identified any persons of interest but are seeking the public's help. The police are asking anyone who was in downtown Gainesville on Friday night who may have seen Ms. Dillard or any suspicious activity to contact the Gainesville police non-emergency line.

Hallie opened her spreadsheet on her laptop and added Kristina Dillard to the list of victims, including date, location, and what she knew of her murder. She was starting to see a pattern. She opened her calendar on her phone and confirmed each of the victims had been murdered late Friday or early Saturday morning.

"Hmmm, always on the weekend," Hallie said aloud.

The Siesta Key victim had bruises on her neck as if she had been strangled, but her throat was slit, including her carotid artery, which was the official cause of death, although she had other significant wounds as well. The injuries of all of the victims didn't match each other exactly, but had enough similarities that Hallie felt they belonged on the spreadsheet.

Even though the injuries and causes of death were not identical, each of the victims had been attacked in their residences or vacation rentals at night on a weekend, were in their twenties, and, except for the Crystal River victim, which didn't say, had been last seen at a local bar on the night they were murdered. Also, with the exception of the Gainesville victim, each had been living or staying in popular beach towns where transients and vacationers went unnoticed. But Gainesville, home to the University of Florida, as a busy college town, would also allow someone to slip in and out unnoticed, so it also fit.

Someone could have followed each of them home, Hallie thought, trying to picture the last few hours of each girl's life.

Charlie had told her that he met Dawn at the bar where he worked. She had been there with friends, but they left, and she stayed by herself, sitting at the bar to talk to him. He couldn't remember anyone else at the bar as it was a busy night. He didn't see anyone talking to her or bothering her, but he was busy so he couldn't say for sure that she didn't talk to anyone else.

The Gainesville victim had left the bar where she worked on the night of her murder, and Hallie remembered reading that the Siesta Key victim had a roommate who was a bartender at the bar where that victim had been on the night of her murder.

Maybe it's time to take a trip to Siesta Key, Hallie thought. She would love to talk to the bartender, if she still worked there, to see if there were any other similarities with Dawn Owen's murder. She believed they were connected and if she could find the connection, it could prove Charlie was innocent.

Hallie opened her AirBnB app and started searching for places within walking distance to Siesta Key Village and to the beach. If she was going down there, she might as well make a mini vacation out of it. And then she got another idea.

She wanted to see if Ken Gardner had any AirBnB rentals in Siesta Key, but AirBnB doesn't provide the house address until after the tenant books the property and never provides the host's last name. But she thought she could find the information out another way.

She opened the Pinellas County Property Appraiser's website and searched for properties in Pinellas County owned by Ken or Kenneth Gardner. She found two, one was a residential home in Pinellas Park and the other was the rental on Treasure Island. She wrote down the address of the Treasure Island property and then went back onto the AirBnB site to search for rentals in Treasure Island until she found one rented out by a host named "Ken" which seemed to match the general location of the address from the property appraiser's site.

Clicking on the link, she knew she had found the right property and host based on how Charlie and the detective writing the initial report had described the rental property. Also, the property dates were blocked out as unavailable for the next few weeks, which seemed consistent with the police not releasing the property until their investigation was complete. She clicked on the host's link to see if he owned any other properties.

"Found you," Hallie said aloud, pleased with her sleuthing skills.

She clicked on a condo located in Siesta Key that rented for $282 a night, was a block from the beach, and was walking distance to Siesta Key Village. She was confident "Ken," the super-host who owned the Siesta Key condo was the same Ken Gardner who owned the AirBnB in Treasure Island where Dawn Owens was murdered. Since he was the one who found Dawn Owens, Hallie wanted to talk to him to see if there was anything else he knew or could tell her that hadn't ended up in the papers or the discovery provided by the D.A.'s office that might help Charlie.

Hallie checked her calendar on her phone and then clicked on the dates she wanted on the AirBnB app, pleased to see the next weekend was available. She would head down on Friday afternoon and come back on the following Sunday morning. Lately, Marcelo was working all weekend, so she knew he wouldn't be able to go with her. She also preferred not to tell him the real reason she was going, because he probably would not approve. She decided to ask Paige to go with her.

She entered her credit card information on the site and booked the Siesta Kay condo. She would go whether Paige could go or not, but she hoped she would be able to.

She texted Paige, "Did someone say road trip? Girls' weekend on the sandy white beaches of Siesta Key this Friday? Drinks on me! You in or out? Please say yes."

Hallie waited about two minutes until she heard the familiar sound on her phone of an incoming text.

"You had me at 'drinks on you' – I'll start packing now!" Paige texted back.

"I knew I could count on you! I'll give you the deets tomorrow, but we should leave no later than three on Friday to beat the traffic."

"Perfect! Can't wait."

Paige was Hallie's most spontaneous friend and was always up for an adventure. Before she married Mike, Paige was always planning a trip somewhere. Now that she was with Mike, she didn't travel as much but was always game for a spur of the moment girls' weekend.

Hallie was thrilled that Paige was going with her. She would tell her about the real motive for the trip on the hour and half drive down from Tampa. Knowing Paige, she already suspected there was an ulterior motive for the sudden trip, but she appreciated that she hadn't asked.

CHAPTER FORTY-SEVEN
HALLIE

Hallie arrived home at about eight-thirty. Katie was back at school and Stephens had not been apprehended, but there continued to be reports of him being seen as far away as New Orleans and Nashville. Hallie didn't care where he was as long as he was far away from her and Katie.

She unlocked her front door, dropped her purse and mail on the table in the front foyer, and her briefcase with files and her laptop on her desk in her office. It was then she realized that Juno hadn't greeted her at the door and wasn't lying on her bed in her office.

"Juno, girl, I'm home, wanna go out?" Hallie called, feeling sad at the realization that Juno seemed to have aged more rapidly in the last few weeks than she had in years.

She heard her whimper, and her heart dropped.

"Juno, honey, where are you?" Hallie called as she prayed Juno hadn't fallen and hurt herself.

She went towards Juno's whimper and found her in the downstairs bathroom with the door closed shut.

She let her out of the bathroom, trying to figure out if there was any way that Juno could get stuck in the bathroom on her own and close the door. After examining the bathroom and the door, Hallie was confident that it was impossible.

Someone had to have locked her in there.

Again.

And could still be in her house.

Hallie headed towards the front door with Juno following close behind her. She grabbed her purse and keys and headed out the front door. After getting safely in her car with Juno, she called Marcelo. He showed up in less than fifteen minutes with an unmarked car pulling up behind him.

The pretty, auburn-haired detective Hallie knew as Detective Alicia Johnson got out of her car and waved to Hallie. Hallie waved back, noting to herself that Marcelo and the detective must have been together when Hallie called him since they arrived at exactly the same time.

Marcelo motioned to Hallie to stay in her car with Juno while they went inside to check out the house. Only because someone could still be in her house, Hallie complied and stayed in her locked car.

After a few minutes, they came out with several plastic evidence bags. Detective Johnson placed all the bags in a larger clear bag and wrote something on the outside of the bag with a black sharpie and placed it on one of the steps, just as she had the last time she was at the house. She then appeared to be dusting the doorknob and other areas of the front porch, including the railing and any other places an intruder could have touched, Hallie assumed.

Marcelo came out a few minutes later, and the two convened in the front yard again. Hallie couldn't hear what they were talking about, but she saw Marcelo motion to the house and then to Hallie as he talked. It seemed they had gathered everything they needed, and any threat inside the house was gone, so Hallie decided to get out of the car. As soon as she opened her door, Juno stood up and barked when she saw Marcelo, wagging her tail and alerting Marcelo and Johnson to their presence.

"Settle, girl," Hallie said, petting her beloved Juno on her big, yellow block head.

Marcelo looked over when he heard Juno and nodded and smiled in Hallie's direction. Hallie let Juno out of the car, who immediately ran to Marcelo.

"Hey there, Juno girl," Marcelo said as he dropped down to one knee to give Juno the attention she wanted.

"Thank you for coming over so quickly," Hallie said. "I hope I didn't pull you away from anything important," she said, looking at both detectives.

"Hallie, this is important," Marcelo said, before turning to the officer next to him, "Hallie, you remember Detective Johnson, don't you?"

"Of course, nice to see you again," Hallie said, reaching out to shake the detective's hand.

She shook her hand, smiling warmly, and said, "I'm sorry you're going through this again."

"Thank you," she answered a little embarrassed. "I keep thinking there must be another explanation for how Juno keeps getting locked in the bathroom. Maybe she goes in there and somehow hits the door with her tail or lies down and kicks it. I don't know what to think anymore. Maybe I'm crazy."

"For what it's worth, I don't think you're crazy. I would be doing the same thing as you," Detective Johnson said.

Before Hallie could respond, Marcelo said, "Hallie, we found a note in the kitchen, on the counter."

"A note? Who is it from? What did it say?" Hallie asked anxiously.

Marcelo opened a picture of the note on his phone since the original was in one of the plastic evidence bags collected by Johnson. The picture was of a plain piece of paper on Hallie's kitchen counter with a handwritten message in thick, black ink:

Count your days bitch.

Hallie gasped reflexively before regaining her composure. She locked her jaw and gritted her teeth as she stared at the picture of the note.

"What in the actual fuck," Hallie said.

"Hallie, I promise, I'll figure out who broke into your house and who left this message on your counter, and I'll stop them before they get near you."

"You can't promise that, Marcelo. This one was left *inside* my house, on my fucking kitchen counter to be exact, and you weren't here. Whoever left it knows how to get in, probably knows my routine, and knows how to get to me if he wants to. All he has to do is wait for me. I promise you; he'll be back and he's making sure that I know that. Maybe Stephens and Peter Martino have teamed up together to get even with me."

"We don't know that it's either of them, Hallie. As far as we know, Martino is still out of the country and Stephens . . . well, last we heard, he was heading to New Orleans," Marcelo said.

"Really? How many other psychopaths are after me? One of them left this note in my kitchen, and frankly, it could be either one of them at this point," Hallie said angrily, taking out her frustration on Marcelo when she knew it wasn't his fault.

She felt vulnerable, and she hated feeling that way. She knew Marcelo was trying to come up with a plausible explanation that might ease her fears about Stephens or Martino, but nothing made sense. Either way, they both knew he couldn't keep her safe 24-7, not as long as both were still out there.

"I dusted everything and lifted a lot of prints, including from the back door. Maybe we'll get lucky this time," Johnson said, trying to sound optimistic and to alleviate the tension. She turned to Marcelo, "I'll drop these at the lab tonight, Garcia, and mark them urgent. Hopefully they'll process them this week, but I know they're pretty slammed."

"Thanks, Johnson. Call me when you hear anything," Marcelo said.

"You got it," Detective Johnson replied as she headed towards her car with the evidence she had gathered. "I'll be in touch as soon as I hear from the lab," before stopping and turning to Hallie and saying, "I can only imagine how stressful this is for you. I'll do whatever I can to help you and catch this son of a bitch."

"Thank you, Detective, I really appreciate it," Hallie said.

Marcelo walked Hallie and Juno into the house as Johnson drove away. Hallie poured herself a glass of wine, her hand trembling slightly, and sat down at the kitchen counter. Marcelo sat down next to her.

They sat at the counter in silence before Hallie asked, "Anything else?"

"Yeah, um, one more thing, the back door was unlocked this time," Marcelo said.

"Ah, that explains how they may have gotten in, or maybe how they left. Great," Hallie said, sounding defeated, "but I promise you that door was locked when I left this morning."

"Did you let Juno out the back door when you got home tonight?"

"No, I never made it past the bathroom. And there is zero chance I left it unlocked. First, I always lock the back door, if I even use it. But I haven't let Juno in or out of that door in weeks and I check the deadbolt every single night before I go to bed."

"That's what I thought, but I had to ask. And when you came home, you're positive the front door was locked, right?"

"Yes, I'm positive. I used my key. I would have noticed if the deadbolt was unlocked. The bolt would have already been in the unlocked position so my key wouldn't have turned it. And besides, even if I didn't notice somehow, someone put Juno in the bathroom and someone left me a threatening note on my kitchen counter," Hallie responded calmly, the exhaustion hitting her.

"Hallie, I know you're upset, but I wouldn't be doing my job if I didn't ask the questions. I'm just trying to explore all possibilities," Marcelo said.

"I know, but it's just so frustrating. You know I always lock the doors, checking them multiple times, compulsively, especially after what I've been through. Do you honestly think I'm going to all of a sudden get careless? I'm terrified after the last few years, much less the last two weeks. I can't even sleep with my windows open. I have to take Xanax just to sleep sometimes. I promise you there is no way I have ever forgotten to lock the doors."

"I'm sorry, babe, I know how careful you are. I didn't realize it was still that bad for you, I'm sorry," Marcelo said, sounding genuinely sad for her.

"No, don't do that. I'm fine. Don't pity me or treat me like I'm a victim. I'm fine. But I'm not stupid or careless either and that is why I can say with one hundred percent certainty that the fucking back door was locked, and so was the front door."

"Okay, Counselor, the doors were fucking locked. Tell me exactly what you did from the time you came into the house until you called me."

"I brought the mail in with me when I came in, and I may have scanned through it before I tossed it on the table in the foyer. I dropped my briefcase and purse on my desk and that's when I realized Juno wasn't by the front door waiting for me or on her bed in my office. I called to her and that's when I heard her whimper. I never went into the kitchen. After I found Juno locked in the bathroom, I grabbed my purse, and we went out to my car to call you."

"I thought I had figured out how they were getting in, but I was wrong. It was just a hunch anyway, but I feel like I'm on the right track. I just need to figure it out," Marcelo said.

"How? What were you thinking?" Hallie asked, her interest piqued.

"Okay, so I found this tool outside the other night, off the front porch under the leaves by the railing. I wasn't sure what kind of tool it was, so I took it with me. I've learned that it's called a pinner file, which very experienced locksmiths use to create new keys from locks when they don't have the original key."

"Go on," Hallie said, intrigued.

Marcelo explained the process to her, based on his discussions with one of the detectives in the forensic unit who investigates high-end, professional robberies and was a noted expert on locks, including getting past them.

"It's not your average locksmith, Hallie, but someone specialized, especially a lot of criminals. They use this filing tool, starting with a blank key that they insert into the lock, and by twisting the blank key back and forth, the pins in the lock make tiny scratches, sometimes only visible with a magnifying glass. They remove the key, file it down where the scratches are, and then repeat the process, until eventually the key works and the lock unlocks. It takes patience and precision."

"Holy shit, that has to be it!" Hallie exclaimed.

"Not so fast, Counselor. I thought I was onto something, too, but then I learned that you can't make a key using that method on a deadbolt, so it would only work on your pin-lock, your bottom lock, in this case, and you said yourself, quite clearly, you always deadbolt the doors. So, I'm back to square one. I sent the tool off for fingerprints anyway, just in case, but it's probably a longshot. That tool could have been laying in your bushes for years."

"Wait, tell me more about this pinner file and how they can make a key from a regular lock. I understand it won't work on a deadbolt" Hallie said, her mind racing. "But with the regular pin-lock, how long does the whole process usually take?" Hallie asked.

"Maybe about thirty minutes up to an hour and a half, depending on the age of the lock and the expertise and experience of the locksmith. But you have deadbolts, Hallie."

"Marcelo, I use the same key for my bottom lock and my deadbolt," Hallie said calmly, watching as the impact of her words hit Marcelo.

"Fuck, oh my God, I can't believe I didn't realize that. I should have known, or at least asked you. You only gave me the one key, which I always use on the deadbolt, and the bottom lock is never locked when I come over. I assumed it was a different key," Marcelo said, cursing himself.

"The back door locks, both top and bottom, are always locked, and use the same key as the front door, but the truth is, anyone can pick a normal lock, but not a deadbolt. So, I don't always worry about the bottom lock on the front door, because only the deadbolt is going to keep someone out. Unless they have a key to it, of course," Hallie said.

"God, I'm so stupid, I don't know why I didn't think of that. Okay, so that's it. They made a key of your bottom lock, which works on both the bottom lock and deadbolt. But how would they have known that?"

"All they had to do was watch me, with binoculars. They would have seen that I use the same key for both locks. So, whoever it is, maybe Stephens or whoever he hired, has a key to my house," Hallie said, the implication of her words hitting her.

Marcelo didn't respond.

Hallie knew there was nothing she could say to make him feel better about the fact that he didn't realize or hadn't considered that the same key opened both locks. And she didn't have the energy to try to comfort him when she was trying to process the fact that someone had a key to her house and could come and go as they pleased. She was frazzled.

They sat in silence while they both contemplated what to do next.

"Can we leave?" Hallie asked, mentally numb and unable to make any decisions.

"Yes, let's go to my house for tonight. We'll get the locks changed in the morning."

"Okay, yes, let's do that. I'll grab some clothes. Can you get Juno's bed, dogfood, and bowls while I pack?"

"Of course. Anything else?"

"Yeah, grab a bottle of wine, please."

CHAPTER FORTY-EIGHT
THE JUDGE

William Stephens dropped the key into the center console of the car. Stan, one of his former lackies, had made a key for him to get into Hallie's house. Stan was an expert locksmith, a skill he had used and perfected over his lengthy career as a burglar. When Stephens had been a judge, he let him off with probation numerous times in exchange for his services over the years. He had reached out to Stan from prison, promising him a hefty payoff for a simple job: all he had to do was deliver a handwritten note, dictated by Stephens, to Hallie Miller's house, and to make him a key from the lock itself. Stephens knew Stan could do the job with his eyes closed.

He met up with Stan his first night back, after dropping a roofie in Linda's glass of wine. He couldn't wait until she passed out. The cat annoyed him less than that insufferable woman. If he heard her say '*fiddle dee dee*' or '*heavens to Betsy*' one more time, he may have strangled her on the spot. The only reason he didn't kill her, and had decided to roofie her instead, was because her death would bring attention to her, which in turn, would bring more attention to him.

It would not take long before the police would realize she worked at the prison and connect her to his escape, and then they would know he was in Tampa. So far, based on the news reports, they thought he was in New Orleans.

He was also confident that when she woke up, she wouldn't go to the police. She had more to lose than he did, because he had nothing to lose. He had no intention of going back to prison. *Ever.* But she would be arrested and tried as an accomplice for anything he did while he was out.

He insisted on making sure the key worked before turning over the cash, which he had retrieved from his storage unit in Ybor City. Years before he was arrested, Stephens had set up an LLC and rented a storage unit under the LLC's name to keep his safe where he stored all the cash he received from his illegal activities, including bribes and other payoffs. He also stored other illicit items he didn't want to keep at his house, including his porn collection of young girls, weapons, and enough cash to sustain him for years. Before he went to prison, he paid the storage fees for the next three years so he could keep his things safe and undisturbed until he was able to get out of prison. He knew he could get someone to pay the fees for him after that if he wasn't out by then.

Stan met him at Hallie's house, and the key worked perfectly. He paid Stan the ten thousand dollars for his services and they both left. Stephens watched her house for a few days and nights to learn her routine. That first night he let himself in, he made sure the boyfriend wasn't there, and Hallie had gone to sleep. The dog came down the stairs, and he bribed the dog with steak he had in his pocket before locking her in the bathroom. He was prepared to kill the dog if she barked, but lucky for her and for him, she didn't make a sound.

He started up the stairs, his intention to rape Hallie for old times' sake before killing her, but those damn creaky steps tipped her off. He knew she would be on the phone with her boyfriend and the police before he could make it to the top, and it wasn't worth getting caught before he could exact his revenge. He casually went out the front door and walked through one of the yards across the street to the next street over where he had left the car he had bought from a lot on Nebraska Avenue. He paid $2,000 in cash for it and threw in an extra $500 for the unregistered license plate. He heard the sirens approaching as he headed in the opposite direction towards Bayshore Boulevard.

He realized that getting to Hallie in her home wasn't going to be ideal. There would always be the chance the boyfriend could show up or a neighbor could hear her screams. It would be better to follow her or lure her somewhere and then grab her. He came up with a plan. He wanted her to feel vulnerable, to know that her house was not safe. She wouldn't want to stay there, and that would give him more opportunities to follow her and get to her. She would be out of her routine, out of her comfort zone.

He entered Hallie's house a second time when he knew she wasn't home, this time locking the front door behind him, locking the dog in the bathroom again just for kicks, and then leaving her a note on her kitchen counter. Then he let himself out the back door, purposely leaving it unlocked, and watched the house from down the street until he saw Hallie run back out and jump in her car, the dog in tow.

The scene made him laugh as he drove away, knowing it wouldn't be long before the boyfriend and police showed up again.

So predictable, he laughed.

He was going to miss this game when it ended.

And he knew exactly how it was going to end: *with Hallie Miller dead.*

CHAPTER FORTY-NINE
LINDA

Linda pulled down Hallie Miller's street and parked in front of a vacant lot undergoing construction a few doors down from her house. There was a black BMW and a white truck parked in the driveway and a black sedan parked on the street. Linda knew the black sedan was law enforcement of some kind from her experience at the prison, because the detectives and undercover officers who came to the prison all drove similar cars. She also knew from the news articles she read about Hallie, the guy who owned the white truck was a detective, Detective Marcelo Garcia, with the Tampa Police Department. Linda had figured out from watching Hallie and the detective for the last few days that they were a couple. She watched the black sedan leave about fifteen minutes after she had arrived. She had hoped the truck would leave too, but it was still there.

She had spent the last two days driving around Tampa, from downtown to Ybor City and all the way to Carroll-wood, and back again. She even went back to the El Rancho Motel to ask Maria, the very unhelpful desk clerk or owner or whatever she was, if she had seen Billy or heard from him, which prompted another round of laughter from Maria. Honestly, Linda was beginning to think maybe Maria couldn't comprehend what she was saying from the years of obvious substance abuse.

She had no leads, didn't know who any of his friends or connections were, other than Johnny's sister, Maria, who was out of her mind, and all she had to go on was this damn lawyer whom she believed was the reason they were in Tampa instead of in a secluded cabin somewhere in the mountains of Tennessee. So, she sat, waiting, watching, and hoping Billy would show up, so she could talk to him. Maybe if he saw her there, he would understand how much she loved him and would do anything for him. And maybe he would realize how much he loved her too.

After many conversations with Ms. Baskins on the subject over the last few days, Linda was convinced that Billy had left her at that horrible motel to protect her. He didn't want to get her in trouble as he dealt with his 'unfinished business,' as he had called it, which she believed to be somehow connected to this woman, Hallie Miller.

So, there she would sit and watch until Billy showed up. Or she would follow her when she left. She had come to the realization that this woman was her only way to find Billy, because he was going to show up to finish his business with her eventually. That was all she was sure of when it came to him.

And when he did, she would be there, too.

* * *

Linda watched Hallie Miller carry a small overnight bag and a leather briefcase out to her car. The detective boyfriend came out behind her carrying the dog bed and a shopping bag, likely filled with the dog's supplies, while a yellow lab followed closely behind them. After they loaded up the car, she watched as they helped the dog into the back seat. She could tell the dog was old and, as an animal lover, immediately had a softness in her heart for the fur baby. Maybe even a little bit for Hallie, but she quickly shook that off.

"No time to get soft now, lady," she reminded herself.

Just because the woman had a dog didn't mean she was a good person, and she needed to remember that this woman was responsible for Billy being sent to prison, according to Billy.

She watched them lock up the house. Hallie got into her car and the boyfriend got into his truck. They were obviously going somewhere, but it couldn't be far or for long as Hallie had packed very lightly. Linda waited while they both pulled out of the driveway. The boyfriend pulled ahead, and the little black BMW followed. Linda waited until they got to the end of the street and turned right before she started her own car to follow them. Between the big truck and fancy BMW, she knew she could follow them at a distance and still be able to see them without them spotting her.

She followed them as they headed north on Howard Avenue and crossed over Morrison, Swann, and eventually Kennedy Boulevard. With the UT students and other young people in South Tampa crowding into the bars on Howard Avenue, the busy, two-lane road made it very easy to follow them without being detected. After they crossed Kennedy, the traffic thinned out and she knew she had to back off to be less conspicuous. She intentionally pulled into the gas station on her right and waited a few minutes before pulling out again, while never losing sight of them.

She watched as they got caught at the next light. She easily caught up with them, but stayed a safe distance behind, keeping a few cars between them.

"Oh, Carole, we're in it now, aren't we? We're like regular PIs, like Nancy Drew or Veronica Mars, in hot pursuit of the bad guy," Linda giggled. "Or should I say, '*bad gal*'?"

Linda's adrenaline was pumping, and she wasn't sure what she was doing. She just believed that if she followed Hallie Miller, and knew where she was, it would lead her to Billy eventually.

They got in the right-hand lane, and she watched as the truck turned right with the BMW following closely behind it. Linda thought it would be too obvious if she turned too, so she passed the street they turned onto and turned right at the next block. She took the next right onto Albany and stopped at the corner of Albany and Cass, the street on which they had turned. She looked down the street to her left and saw the taillights of the BMW at a stop sign a few blocks down. She waited a minute and then turned left, maintaining a generous distance.

The truck pulled into a small driveway just past the stop sign in front of quaint, yellow house with white shutters, and a red door. It was in need of a paintjob but was still cute. The little black car came to a stop in front of the house and parked next to the curb on the street. Linda was at the stop sign and decided to turn right to avoid being seen. She could circle back later now that she knew where the boyfriend lived. She had no doubt that Billy knew where the boyfriend lived, especially with his connections.

It was only a matter of time before he showed up.

It had been a long day and Linda was tired and hungry. She remembered passing a hotel on Howard Avenue not too far away. It would be the ideal location, in between the boyfriend's house and Hallie's house. She drove around the block to check the boyfriend's house one last time. The truck and BMW were there. She hoped they were in for the night because she needed to rest and let Carole out of her carrier.

She headed back towards Howard Avenue, stopping at a McDonald's drive through on the way. The hotel she had seen earlier, the Hyde Park Hotel, was quaint and seemed like the perfect place to stay. She left Carole in the car while she went into the office to check for vacancies and room rates. She was pleased to find that they had a room available for just under $200 for the night, with a king size bed, smart tv, and complimentary breakfast, and booked it for three nights.

A lot more than a night at El Rauncho, she giggled to herself, *but at least she wouldn't catch MRSA or have her organs stolen during the night.*

She registered under her real name and paid with her credit card as the hotel didn't take cash. She wasn't worried, because Billy wasn't with her, and she hadn't seen him in a few days. And, after all, she told her boss, Karl, that she was in Tampa, so this was consistent with that. She needed a hot shower and a clean bed.

She went back to her car and placed Carole's carrier back in the beach bag so she could bring her up to the room undetected. She placed her McDonald's bag on top of the carrier inside the large bag and hoisted the straps over her shoulder. She carried her drink in that hand and rolled her suitcase behind her with her free hand and headed up to her room. The room was nicer than she expected with a large king size bed centered in the middle of the room, a large tv mounted on the wall in front of the bed, an updated bathroom, and a view of the restaurants and bars lining Howard Avenue below. It was perfect.

She took Carole out of her carrier to let her get acclimated to their new home for the night. She took the beach bag and went back down to the car and put her litter box in the beach bag, and grabbed the backpack that contained Carole's food, bowls, and some snacks and waters for herself. She was happy with her hotel choice and was relieved she wouldn't have to spend another night at the El Rancho Motel.

After she fed Carole and got her litter box set up in the bathroom, she sat on the bed and ate her McDonald's. She turned on the tv and decided to skip the news. It had been stressful enough the last few days; she didn't need the news bringing her down. She flipped through the stations until she found a station playing reruns of Friends, one of her favorites, and was perfectly content for the first time since this crazy adventure had begun.

She thought about Billy. And the fact that he hadn't reached out to her or come back for her. Also, she was pretty sure he had drugged her, which was not nice at all. The more she thought about the last week, the angrier she got. He was so different than the person he had been in his letters to her.

Was it all an act? she wondered.

She was not going to be taken advantage of by another guy. And if Billy used her to get out of prison, he would pay. She would make sure of it. She never got the chance to seek her revenge on Toby.

If their paths ever crossed, though, well, she started to think before stopping herself. *Oh, fiddle-dee-dee, no sense thinking about that now.*

She thought about what her Mama used to always say to her, "Linda Lew, you're as sweet as molasses, until someone crosses you. And then you're as deadly as a moccasin," she'd laugh, shaking her head.

The court psychiatrist pretty much concluded the same thing, not in those words, of course, but the sentiment was the same. That was a long time ago, and luckily, she was a minor at the time. Those records had been sealed and nobody knew anything about the unfortunate accident with silly Donnie Morris, may he rest in peace.

He did get what was comin' to him, Linda thought, *and so will Billy, if he crossed me.*

CHAPTER FIFTY
HALLIE

Hallie loaded Juno and her overnight bag into the back seat of her BMW and followed Marcelo to his house. Marcelo unloaded Hallie's car while she brought Juno inside. They set up Juno's bed in the bedroom next to Marcelo's bed, and then went out to the kitchen to feed her and fill her water bowl with fresh water. Marcelo opened Hallie's wine, poured her a glass, and then poured himself a glass of bourbon on the rocks. It had been a rough night.

Hallie washed up and got ready for bed even though it was early, and they weren't ready to go to sleep yet. They got into Marcelo's bed, each with their nightcap, but didn't speak much the rest of the night, both pretending to watch TV. They were lost in their own thoughts, and Hallie resorted to uncharacteristically biting the skin off around her fingernails, something she hadn't done since she was a teenager while Marcelo anxiously checked his phone every few minutes. The tension in the room was palpable. Juno picked up on it, and, periodically got up to pace or go inspect the rest of the house, occasionally barking, causing Hallie to jump each time she did.

"Hallie," Marcelo said, breaking the silence, at the same time his phone pinged indicating he had received an incoming text.

They both flinched at the sound and looked down at the message at the same time.

"Garcia, Stephens has been spotted – in Tampa. Reliable source. Call when you can."

They sat in silence for another second while they both processed what they had just read.

"Do you think your colleagues will believe me now?" Hallie asked, rolling her eyes.

Marcelo called Detective Johnson without responding to Hallie's question.

"Got your text. I have you on speaker here with Hallie. What do we know?"

"Hey, sorry, wish I had better news. He was spotted in Ybor City by a witness who knew him before he went to prison. When she saw him, she called the police."

"Who is this witness?"

"Lauren Broadway. Attorney here in Tampa and, according to her statement, 'had her own issues with Stephens back in the day.' She said she was having dinner with her husband, Chris, at Bernini's, and were sitting at a table by the front window. She knew about Stephens' escape, so when he walked by and she recognized him, she called the police immediately."

"What happened? Did they get him?"

"Unfortunately, no. Broadway, the witness, hung up after reporting it and lost sight of him when he went around the corner."

"But she called it in? There're always units in Ybor, they should have been there in seconds," Marcelo said, exasperated.

"Yeah, that's where the problem came in. There was a new trainee on the phones tonight, and he didn't alert the regular dispatcher about the call. He didn't know who Stephens was and didn't realize the call was legitimate."

"Are you kidding me?"

"Um, no, I wish I was. Broadway continued to watch him, hiding behind her menu so he wouldn't see her. He had stopped on the corner, like he was waiting for someone, and then another man showed up a few minutes later, and they started arguing. When the police didn't show up, Broadway called 911 again. This time, the regular dispatcher took the call and immediately sent a unit out and escalated it, but it was too late. By the time they got there, he was in the wind."

"Okay, wait, back up. This Lauren Broadway is having dinner at Bernini's, Stephens walks by and, not only does she see him but recognizes him and continues to watch him? And we blew it?"

"Yeah, apparently."

"That's fucking great. How confident are we with this Broadway's ID? Any chance she's mistaken?"

"I don't think so. She seems pretty reliable. As she said, she had her own issues with Stephens when he was a judge. She said she was about to file a Bar complaint against him when he was arrested for murder, so she dropped it. As I said originally, reliable witness."

"Okay, thanks, Johnson, keep me posted if you hear anything else."

Marcelo hung up and looked at Hallie.

"Still thinking it's not Stephens who has a key to my house?" Hallie asked, taking a large sip of her wine as she looked away from him out the front window.

"I'm sorry, Hal, I never thought he would come back to Tampa, at least not now."

"Well, I told you he is a narcissistic, sociopath, who believes he's smarter than everyone else, so he doesn't think he'll get caught, despite going to prison in the first place. But he blames me for that, so here he is, to get his revenge and to prove he's smarter than everyone, including me, and especially the police."

"Do you know Lauren Broadway?" Marcelo asked.

"Yeah, I do, actually. She's an amazing trial attorney, brilliant, and extremely ethical. If she says she saw Stephens, then she saw him, and he was there. I'm sure the 'responding officers' will try to discredit her, maybe she was drinking a glass of wine, or maybe the front window of the restaurant wasn't clean, or maybe she's crazy, like all of us women are," Hallie started to say before realizing how angry she sounded. "Sorry, that probably wasn't fair. I'm just so angry and I know it's not your fault and I shouldn't be directing this at you. I'm just so frustrated and I can't believe Stephens is here even though I knew in my gut he was here. But getting the confirmation hit me harder than I expected."

"I know. And I don't blame you for feeling angry and frustrated. But now that we know for sure he's here, every officer on the force will be looking for him, and not only TPD and Hillsborough County sheriffs, but the department of corrections and federal officers, too. I bet he's in custody within the next 24 hours."

"I hope you're right."

"Me too. But I'm not just saying that; I really believe it."

Hallie remembered she had another training session scheduled with Jason the next morning followed by her final certification training session for her concealed weapons permit at the gun range. She wasn't going down without a fight this time, and she refused to live her life in fear or as a victim, especially from Stephens.

"Until Stephens is in custody, you shouldn't go anywhere," Marcelo said. "Stay here and when I'm not here, I'll have a patrol car stationed out front."

"No way. If that son of a bitch comes for me, I'll be waiting for *him* this time," Hallie said, reflexively clenching her hands into fists and gritting her teeth, as she thought about Stephens coming after her again.

"Hallie, you don't need to make yourself a target. Let us catch him and put him back in prison where he belongs."

"I'm working out first thing tomorrow with Jason and then going to pick up my gun. I'm not hiding."

"Speaking of Jason, what do you know about him, Hallie?"

"What do you mean? He's my trainer," Halie said, waiting to see what Marcelo was going to say next.

"He's been linked to the Martino family, doing private security for them. That family is bad news, as you know."

"But that doesn't mean he's bad news," Hallie found herself defending Jason. "There's nothing illegal about having a private security business."

"You don't seem surprised by this. Did you already know?" Marcelo asked.

"After the first break in, I told Jason about it, and he offered to protect me. He mentioned he had a side business doing private security, although he didn't say for who."

"Why didn't you mention that to me?"

"Because it wasn't relevant. I declined his offer, and we worked out. He's my trainer and that's all I've hired him to be. Whatever else he does is none of my business."

Marcelo was silent, and Hallie remembered Jason's comments about Marcelo's brothers being soldiers in the Colombian cartel along with Marcelo's possible connection, the irony not lost on her that both men were essentially arguing the same thing: each was distrustful of the other because of their affiliations, one to his family and the other to his employer, the Martino family.

Deciding to change the subject, Hallie said as casually as she could muster, "By the way, I forgot to mention that I took a few days off and booked an AirBnB in Siesta Key for this weekend. I need to get away and Paige agreed to go with me, you know, like an impromptu girls' weekend."

"Mmmm, Siesta Key, huh? Interesting pick. With all the beautiful beaches we have right here?" Marcelo said, looking at her suspiciously.

"Okay, fine, I'm going down to work on Charlie's case," Hallie confessed, unable to lie to Marcelo. "I found another AirBnB in Siesta Key owned by Ken Gardner, the same guy who owns the Treasure Island place where Dawn Owens was murdered. I just want to ask him a few questions, see if there are any connections."

"Wait, was the Siesta Key victim murdered in a place owned by this Ken Gardner?"

"No, that would be too coincidental, but unfortunately, no, that's not why I want to talk to him. I don't think he has anything to do with either murder, but he owns rentals in both small beach towns where women were murdered. He's probably familiar and maybe even friendly with the locals. And if someone gets murdered in your rental, you're definitely talking to anyone else you know who owns rentals in these areas."

"Okay, yeah, that makes sense. But a few randos gossiping doesn't equate to evidence," Marcelo said condescendingly.

"Yeah, I understand that, Detective. And I also understand that everything points to Charlie on the surface, so the police didn't even look for anyone else or at any other evidence. They have their man," Hallie said more accusatorily than she intended or realized.

"I'm sure they considered all suspects based on the evidence they had, but they have to follow the evidence where it leads them," Marcelo said defensively.

"Look, I wasn't saying that about you. I know you follow every lead and investigate every case thoroughly, but I'm just saying I don't think they did in this case. I get it why they're looking at Charlie: he was the last known person with her and his DNA and fingerprints were found at the scene, but I know he didn't do it. So that means someone else did. And no one else is looking for that person, so I have to. I want to talk to the roommate of the Siesta Key victim, too. There are a lot of similarities in the two murders, but no one is even considering that these cases could be related. And if there's a connection, I'll find it."

"I would try to talk you out of going, but I know that's impossible," Marcelo said, shaking his head. "Please be careful."

"I will, I promise. Besides, with Stephens in Tampa, I'll be safer in Siesta Key. With any luck, he'll be caught before I return on Sunday."

"I'm glad Paige is going with you, but seriously, stay together and don't let your guard down. Whoever murdered that girl is brutal and a sadist and he's still out there."

"I know," Hallie said. "But I know Charlie didn't kill Dawn Owens, so I have to try. I've read the entire discovery file sent over by the prosecution, so if I can find anything to connect the two cases, the police will have to consider other suspects as Charlie was already in custody when the poor girl in Siesta Key was murdered."

"Okay, I get it, but if you do find anything, please let the police follow up on the lead. I don't want you becoming a target for anyone else."

"I will, don't worry," Hallie reassured him. "I have enough psychos after me; any new psycho will have to wait their turn," Hallie joked, causing Marcelo to stare at her incredulously. "Sorry, babe, too soon?"

Marcelo shook his head, "not funny, Hallie."

Hallie poked him in the side, in the spot where she knew he was ticklish, forcing him to smile.

"Stop, okay, fine, it was a little funny. You have a sick sense of humor, Counselor."

"I'm not going to let these fucking assholes get to me, Marcelo. And I finally feel like I have a plan, rather than waiting around like a sitting duck for them to make their next move. I'm making the next move and I'll be ready if they come at me, whether it's Stephens or anyone else."

CHAPTER FIFTY-ONE
MONICA

Monica couldn't take another minute at her mother's house. She wanted to get back to Gulfport to her apartment, her artwork, her friends, Lily and Marge, and even O'Maddy's. Her mother triggered her in the worst ways and her anxiety was at its highest levels.

She sent her cousin, Tom, multiple texts like *'save me'* or *'break me out of this place'* or *'rescue me'* as if she was imprisoned and being held against her will. He responded with laughing emojis and promises of being there soon to rescue her. She felt claustrophobic in that house, despite the fact it was ten times the size of her Gulfport apartment.

She had been at her mom's for about five days. It was time for her to return to her apartment in Gulfport. She hadn't received anymore texts, and her uncle had someone change her locks and install a ring camera. Since it had been installed, no one had tried to enter her apartment, as far as she knew. Any notifications went directly to her uncle.

Jason Lane, the former detective turned personal train-er turned bodyguard was assigned to accompany Monica whenever she left her mother's home.

"Jason, can you please take me home?"

"Why, what do you need? We can swing by there to pick up some clothes and whatever else you need, but until we know who broke into your place, we think it's better if you stay at your mom's house."

"No, I need to go home. I can't stay here forever. The lock has been changed, the ring camera has been installed, and I have my Glock. I don't have any reason to be afraid or to stay here any longer."

Maybe it was just some weird rando with an underwear fetish, she thought, even though she knew better.

But she also knew it didn't seem like Christian. She hadn't seen him in many years, and she had no idea what prison could do to a man, but in her gut, she knew it wasn't him. If he was going to hurt or kill her, he would just do it. He wouldn't play games, like going through her lingerie drawer, to scare her.

So, who else could it be, she wondered.

And then it hit her: *Marlboro Man.*

"Jason, I thought of someone who might have broken into my place," Monica said, hoping she wouldn't sound crazy when she told him about their encounter.

After she finished, Jason said, "I need to check this out. Have you seen him since that first time in the parking lot of O'Maddy's?"

"I thought I did, maybe twice, but I can't be sure. Once I thought I saw him at this kava shop I went to, and then this other time, he may have been driving past my apartment."

"Okay, this is great, Monica. Do you think you can remember enough about him to give a description?"

"Um, I don't know. But I can try."

Monica sat in the living room with Jason, her uncle, and her mother. At Jason's prompting, she gave a full description of the Marlboro Man and told them about her initial encounter with him as well as the other possible sightings she may have had of him.

"Anything else?" Jason asked.

"Yeah, one more thing, he has a large tattoo running the length of his forearm that says '*Retribution*'."

Monica agreed to stay one more night to give Jason a chance to see what he could find out about him.

* * *

The next morning, Jason called to report what he had learned. Monica's uncle put Jason on speaker so they could all listen and in case Jason had any additional questions for Monica. Jason didn't believe the guy lived in Gulfport, and probably wasn't vacationing there either, but had been spotted lingering outside of Monica's apartment on the day it was broken into. The landlord approached him to find out what he was doing, but he walked away without engaging. He also learned through some buddies on the police force that there was a guy who fit the same description who tried to abduct a young waitress last Saturday night in downtown St. Pete, which wasn't far from Gulfport. She was walking to her car in the parking lot behind the bar after her late-night shift ended when he tried to pull her into his white Ford Explorer. She was able to break away from him and ran hysterically back inside the bar. Her manager called the police, but the guy was long gone and had not been spotted since.

After learning about the attempted abduction of the young waitress, Monica agreed to file a police report at Jason's urging, because she would never forgive herself if someone got murdered or raped by this creep when she could have done something to stop him.

Even though he hadn't been a detective in Tampa, Jason had made a few friends in the Tampa Police Department through his private security firm and personal training business. He called one of his buddies, explained what he knew about the break-in to Monica's apartment and her interactions with a guy who fit the description of the suspect in the attempted abduction in St. Pete.

"Thanks, Jason, I'll pass this information on to the detectives in the Criminal Investigations Division. Is Ms. Martino willing to talk to them and give a description if they come out?"

"Absolutely. Whatever she can do to help catch this guy and get him off the street, she wants to do."

"Thanks, buddy, see you at the gym tomorrow?"

"You got it. See you at the regular time."

* * *

A few hours later, two detectives arrived at Nina Martino's home on Davis Island.

"Monica, can you come downstairs? The detectives are here," her mother called up to her.

"Be right down," Monica said, checking her outfit, knowing they were going to judge her, especially when she explained her first encounter with the Marlboro Man took place after she left O'Maddy's.

She smoothed her dress and tried to breathe calmly. She was second-guessing her agreement to give a description of Marlboro Man. This was a mistake. She was drunk when she first met him, and had she really seen him since? It could have been anyone who broke into her apartment.

"Monica? Are you coming down?" her mother called upstairs again, more impatiently than before.

"Sorry, coming," Monica said, knowing she couldn't delay any longer.

Monica spoke to the detectives, describing their first encounter and everything she could remember about his looks, and how she thought she saw him on two other occasions, including once driving past her apartment.

"Can you tell us about the break-in to your apartment? Was anything stolen?"

"I unlocked the door with my key – it was definitely locked – and was heading into my bedroom when I noticed my drawers had been rummaged through. My underwear and bras were left cascading out of the drawers, and I knew I hadn't left them that way," Monica said.

"Did you call the police?" one of the detectives asked her.

"No, I was afraid if someone was still in my apartment, they would hear me, so instead I texted my cousin, Tom, and he called my uncle. My uncle sent Jason."

"Jason Lane does private security for me from time to time," Nicolas added. "He doesn't live far from Monica, and I thought he could get there faster."

"Okay, go on, Monica, anything else?" the detective asked, taking notes as Monica spoke.

She explained that after Jason got there and confirmed no one was in the apartment, she went into her bedroom to check to see if anything was missing. She explained that she had a license to carry, including a concealed weapons permit, so she checked for her gun first, which she kept under her bed. She told them that her gun clip had been emptied, including the one in the chamber, which made her think he was going to come back. Otherwise, he would have stolen the gun, not just emptied the bullets, she argued.

"Were there signs of a forced entry?"

"No, not that I could see, but Jason found markings on the key lock and metal shavings by the front door. He told me the lock had been picked."

"And you're sure it was locked when you came home?" the detective asked.

"Yes, I'm positive."

"Okay, so he locked it behind him on his way out."

The detectives took all the information down and seemed genuinely interested, especially the pretty auburn-haired detective named Johnson. Her eyes were kind and non-judgmental. Monica liked her.

"Was anything else out of place or missing other than what you've told us so far?"

"Yes, one more thing," Monica said. "He folded one of my nighties and a pair of my underwear very neatly and placed them at the bottom of my bed. It was creepy, like he was laying out what he wanted me to wear."

"Anything else from the night you encountered him outside of O'Maddy's?" the male detective asked her.

"Yeah, he said something to me that night, but it was the way he looked at me when he said it. It scared the shit out of me."

"What did he say, Ms. Martino?" Detective Johnson asked her.

"I made a joke about him looking like the Marlboro Man, you know, that commercial from the seventies or eighties with the cowboy who smoked Marlboros? Oh wait, you're way too young to remember that, but anyway, I made this joke, and he replied, 'yeah, I like to smoke things, maybe I'll smoke you,' but he wasn't joking. I don't even know what he meant by it, but he looked at me with the coldest, darkest eyes I've ever seen."

"Was he angry?"

"He didn't seem angry. He was eerily calm, but threatening at the same time, menacing actually. He wanted to scare me. That was clear."

"How did you get away from him?"

"Well, I was close enough to the door of the bar that I could run back in, and I got really loud, cussing him out. I think he walked away because I started to make a scene. But it wouldn't surprise me if he followed me home. That would explain how he knew where I lived, if he's the one who broke into my place."

"Is there anything else you can tell us about him that you think would be helpful?" Detective Johnson asked.

"He had really strong, muscular arms. Like the rest of him wasn't as fit, but his arms were. And he had a tattoo on the back of one of his forearms that said '*Retribution.*' I remember that because I noticed it when he was walking away."

"Ms. Martino, thank you for being so candid. This is really helpful, and we will convey it to the Gulfport and St. Pete police departments. Is there anything else you think we should tell them?"

"They need to catch this guy. He's dangerous. He's a sociopath, probably a serial killer. When I looked in his eyes, all I saw was evil. Pure evil."

"Thank you so much for your time, Ms. Martino. If you think of anything else, here's my card with my cellphone and email address on it. Don't hesitate to call me," Detective Johnson said, handing Monica her card.

As they finished the interview, Monica's phone pinged, notifying her of an incoming text. Her phone was in her pocket, but the sound made her smile, believing it was from either Tom or Lily, either of whom would make her laugh, she knew. Lily would tell her funny stories about the patrons of the kava shop who were trying so hard to be cool and original, even though most of them were neither cool nor original. Tom would tell her to meet him in the garden in five, which is what they often did when they were in the same room together at her mother's house but needed to sneak out back for a smoke. It became an inside joke between them that they would send to each other, regardless of where they were.

She walked away from the detectives as her mother and uncle walked the detectives towards the front door. She went into the kitchen and opened the text she had just received.

"*Meet me.*"

She looked at the sender. It wasn't from Tom or Lily. Another unknown number.

She texted back, "*Who is this?*" and bit her nails as she watched the screen light up with the little dots, signifying she was getting a response.

"Davis Island Beach, for old times' sake."

Chills ran up her spine.

In that moment, she knew who the texts were from.

Christian.

CHAPTER FIFTY-TWO
HALLIE

Marcelo had agreed to keep Juno for the weekend so Hallie could go to Siesta Key. She left her car at Marcelo's, and he dropped her off at her office. Hallie was looking forward to getting out of Tampa for a few days, especially to take a break from looking over her shoulder for Stephens. No one, besides Marcelo and Mike, Paige's husband, knew where they were going.

Hallie was becoming more confident every day. She had been training with Jason and practicing her shooting at the gun range, getting more accurate the more she practiced. She could deliver a mean right hook, and she had recently submitted her concealed weapons permit application to the State of Florida Bureau of Alcohol, Tobacco and Firearms.

Paige drove, and without anyone knowing they were going out of town, there would have been no reason for anyone, including Stephens, to be watching or following Paige. On the drive, Hallie told Paige everything she knew about Dawn Owens' murder, including a description of the crime scene photos, where Charlie's DNA was found, the cause of death, and anything else she thought might be helpful. She also told her about the other murders she had read about that shared some similarities. Paige asked a lot of questions, some of which Hallie wrote down to discuss with Mike and Charlie as she didn't know the answers and hadn't thought to ask them. Paige was a litigation attorney, and even though she wasn't a criminal defense attorney, it was interesting to hear her perspective on the State's evidence and possible defenses to explore.

Hallie and Paige arrived at their AirBnB on Siesta Key a little after 4:30 that Friday afternoon. They unpacked and freshened up.

"Ready to see if Cassandra, the roommate, will talk to us?" Hallie asked.

"Yup, ready. Do I get to be good cop or bad cop?"

"Neither." Hallie laughed. "We're just going to see if she'll even talk to us. We're not here officially, just as . . . wait, what's our story?"

"Um, good question. We shouldn't lie to her but if we tell her about Charlie being charged with a similar murder, she probably won't talk to us."

"I agree. I don't want to deceive her, but we can't tell her about Charlie and the Treasure Island victim. Okay, think," Hallie said, as she pondered what to say.

"What if we tell her the truth? Or mostly the truth. We're here because you're working on a case that seems similar to her roommate's murder, and you want to see if they're connected? You don't have to divulge that you're related to the prime suspect or part of his defense team," Paige said.

"Yeah, I guess that's true. We're not saying anything false, just maybe omitting my relationship to Charlie. She may not talk to us anyway," Hallie responded, as she thought about any other way to approach Cassandra.

"I think that's our best option to try to get her to talk to us."

"Okay, yeah, I agree. Let's go," Hallie said as she slipped the room key into her purse and headed towards the door. "Nothing ventured, nothing gained."

"Love a fitting cliché. Let's go gain some intel for Charlie. Um, since we're not actual detectives, we are having a drink, right?" Paige asked.

"Well, obviously, we are undercover, after all," Hallie laughed, only half joking.

Her brother's innocence and possibly his life was on the line, which she wasn't taking lightly, but she also had to keep her sense of humor and make the best of the situation, especially with all the craziness that had been happening in her own life. But they were there to see what information they could get from Cassandra that might help his case. As the sister of the accused in the Treasure Island murder and not being an actual private investigator, she wondered how they were going to get her to talk to them at all. She was beginning to doubt they should have come and that the trip may have been a mistake.

"Uh oh, I know that look. Don't go second-guessing yourself now, girl. We're here, let's do this," Paige said.

"You're right, you're right. Okay, let's do this. Worst case, we're in Siesta Key and we deserve to have a little fun."

They walked the few blocks from their AirBnB down Ocean Avenue until they arrived at the SKOB bar. They sat at the inside bar, noticing the thousands of mostly one-dollar bills and other currency completely covering the walls and ceiling of the iconic place. The pretty brunette bartender came over, placing waters and menus in front of them, and introduced herself as Cassandra.

After a few hours and a few drinks later, Hallie was relieved to see that the bar had mostly emptied out. The 'peak-season' on Siesta Key had long passed when the brutal summer heat set in, so the tourists were scarce and most of the patrons were locals. As Hallie was thinking about the best way to open the conversation, she heard Paige dive in.

"So, Cassandra, now that we have some privacy here at the bar, I think we should tell you why we're really here."

Before Paige could say another word, Cassandra exploded, "oh my God, if you two are fucking reporters, I'll have you thrown out of here. I'm so sick of you vultures."

"Whoa, whoa, no, I promise, we're not reporters," Paige responded in an unthreatening voice, her hands held up in defense.

"So, who the fuck are you?" Cassandra asked loudly enough for one of the busboys cleaning a table nearby to notice her distress and come towards them, ready to throw them out.

"We're investigating a case in Treasure Island, you know, up in the St. Pete area, that seems very similar to your roommate's case. The police haven't connected them, but we think there are similarities. We just want to ask you a few questions to see if there are connections that the police should know about. That's all, I promise," Paige explained.

"Are you detectives?" Cassandra asked.

"No, not exactly, and we're not with the police either," Paige admitted. "We have a personal interest in the case, and our only agenda is to see that the right perpetrator who committed this horrible crime is arrested and brought to justice. I'm sure you want the same thing, Cassandra, for your friend."

Hallie was impressed with Paige's calm demeanor and understood why she was such a great litigator. She was confident without being condescending, even keeled in her temperament, and non-emotional, whereas Hallie would have come across as confrontational or aggressive, she had no doubt.

"Cassandra, can we please ask you a few questions? Nothing more. If you can tell us anything that can lead us to the person who did this to your friend, isn't that what we all want? I think we're on the same side and want the same outcome," Paige said, gently, but suggesting if Cassandra didn't cooperate, she didn't want to find her friend's killer.

Man, she was good, Hallie thought.

"I already went through all of this with the police. I don't want to go through it again. Do you know how hard this is?" she asked, tears welling up in her eyes as she fought to keep them at bay.

"We do and we are so incredibly sorry to put you through this again, Cassandra," Paige continued, "but we're looking at this from an angle we don't think the police are focused on, and we think you can help us. We promise we won't take much of your time and your insight could be the key to catching this son of a bitch."

"Fine. Let's get this over with. You have five minutes and then I need to break down the bar."

Hallie let Paige lead with the questions, since she had developed a rapport with Cassandra, and only interjected when she felt it was necessary to glean more information based on Hallie's closer connection to the case.

"Cassandra, I'm so sorry to bring this horrible memory up again, but if you could back up a second. You mentioned you walked into the house you shared with Stacey and didn't see anything out of place until you opened Stacey's bedroom door. Can you walk us through what you saw when you first opened the door, besides Stacey herself? What did the room look like?" Hallie asked.

"Stacey was pretty neat, as far as roommates go, neater than me, actually. The first thing I noticed was her lamp was knocked off her bedside table and her bedding was in complete disarray, which was also unusual. We used to laugh about the fact that when Stacey went to sleep, she didn't move. The bed, and comforter, would look the same when she woke up as it did the night before when she went to bed," Cassandra said, a sad smile crossing her face at the memory.

"So that was the first thing I noticed, besides the lamp; the bed was an absolute shit show. And then I noticed the blood. Oh my God, so much blood. I hadn't noticed Stacey on the floor yet, but I was horrified and yet my mind wasn't registering what I was seeing. It was like I was seeing the scene in slow motion."

"Did you notice anything else before you found Stacey?" Paige asked gently.

"Yeah, one other thing. Her pajamas were folded neatly on the edge of the bed. Despite the chaos and everything else in the room, those were folded so neatly and left at the bottom of the bed. It seemed so strange to me," Cassandra said, looking up, "like my brain was asking, why would Stacey fold her pajamas but not make her bed? Such a stupid thing to notice when my best friend was lying murdered on the other side of the bed, right? But that just stuck with me," Cassandra said as tears welled up in her eyes, this time unable to keep them from streaming down her cheeks.

"Not stupid at all, Cassandra," Hallie said, "and, actually, it's very helpful. We are so very sorry for your loss, and we cannot thank you enough for talking to us. We won't take up any more of your time."

"Um, okay, yeah, sure, no problem. Um, if you find anything out, like who did this to Stacey, will you call me?"

"We will, I promise," Hallie said.

Hallie and Paige left the bar and didn't speak until they got a few blocks away when Paige broke the silence.

"Okay, so what's the deal with the folded pajamas? Your whole vibe changed when she mentioned that," Paige said.

"Oh my God, Paige, it's the same guy. It's the same fucking guy, no doubt in my mind. This might be the break we need to get Charlie off," Hallie said excitedly.

"Whoa, okay, slow down, explain."

"Mike gave me a copy of the discovery from the D.A.'s office in Charlie's case. When I looked through the crime scene photos there was this one thing that stood out to me, but I couldn't figure out if it meant anything. The victim's sundress was folded up very neatly at the bottom of the bed. It seemed strange to me because the rest of the room was in complete disarray and chaos: beer bottles, take-out food containers, and clothes strewn throughout the room, but there, on the corner of the bed where the victim was found, her sundress folded with military precision."

"Oh shit. We need to get a copy of the Siesta Key crime scene photos."

"Yeah, we do. Let's call Mike," Hallie said.

"Um, does this mean our beach weekend is cut short?"

"Not necessarily," Hallie thought. "So, we know Ken Gardner, the owner of our AirBnB, also owns the AirBnB where Dawn Owens was murdered, and SKOB, the bar where Stacey was the night she was murdered, is a few blocks from our AirBnB. What if Ken Gardner was down here that night? He could have easily followed Stacey home from SKOB and murdered her. He would have had plenty of time to leave Stacey's house to come back to the AirBnB or even leave Siesta Key to head back to Pinellas County before Cassandra came home and found her."

"Okay, but he had an alibi for Dawn's murder, didn't he? I thought the police cleared him in Treasure Island?"

"Yeah, true, but he had access to the Treasure Island condo before the police got there, as he was the one who called the police. I don't know. What if he lied about the time he got there? I just think we need to see where Ken Gardner was on the night Stacey was murdered."

"Hallie, I think we should turn this information over to the police and let them see if there are any other connections. You said yourself they already checked out Ken Gardner, including his alibi in the Treasure Island murder. Even if he was down here, it doesn't mean he killed Stacey. He does own a beach place down here, which would explain why he would be here."

"Yeah, I know you're right, but I can't shake my feeling that there is a connection between Dawn's murder and Stacey's, and Ken Gardner seems like too much of a coincidence. Let's go back to the condo and talk it through again."

They continued walking towards the AirBnB in silence as the bars and restaurants on Ocean were emptying out and closing up.

When they arrived, Hallie said, "What if we get him to come out here for some "issue" with the condo so we can get a vibe on this guy ourselves?"

"Hallie, I don't think this is a good idea. Why don't we call Marcelo and have him run his own check on Gardner?"

"Absolutely not. I want to do this on my own. Also, as you said, he's probably already been cleared. Let's at least call Gardner and see if we can get him to talk to us. Maybe he knows something he hasn't shared with the police."

"Girl, you're playing with fire, but fine, I'm in. Ride or die."

"Thank you, now let's think of a plan. We have his cell phone for emergencies. We can text him."

After they came up with their plan, Hallie texted Ken Gardner's cell number: "*We've been to SKOB and we think you left a few key facts out when you spoke to the Treasure Island police. Like maybe your connection to the Siesta Key murder?*"

They saw the text was read immediately and then the little dots appeared indicating he was replying.

In a few seconds they received, "*Um, is this some kind of joke?*"

"*No, we're very serious. I'm sure if you give us a few minutes of your time and answered a few questions it might clear everything up,*" Hallie texted back.

"Are you with the police? This seems very unconventional. I've already told the police everything I know. Who is this? How did you get this number?"

"Shit, what do we say now?" Paige asked Hallie as she read the text over her shoulder.

"Well, I think I admit we're his AirBnB guests, what we're doing here, and see how he reacts."

"But then we're leaving, right? I'm not comfortable staying here tonight after that," Paige said.

"Yeah, let's pack up. I'll just send this last text and see if he'll talk to us as we're driving back."

"Mr. Gardner, my name is Hallie, and I rented your Siesta Key AirBnB. I am trying to determine if the recent Siesta Key murder is related to the Treasure Island murder. I think you can help us answer that question."

"What the fuck? You rented under false pretenses! I am canceling your rental. Get the fuck out of my place. This isn't right. I will report you."

"Mr. Gardner, no need for all of that. I'm leaving, but I have some questions I think only you can answer. It's important."

After a few minutes, Hallie got back, *"Who are you? Important to whom?"*

Hallie wrote back, *"Please, Mr. Gardner, if you give me five minutes of your time, I will explain. If you're willing, please call me on this number in thirty minutes."*

Hallie and Paige packed up their stuff, which only took about ten minutes since they had never actually unpacked.

They left everything as it had been when they arrived and left, heading out of town on the one road that would take them back to the interstate and to Tampa. It had been about forty-five minutes since her last text to Ken Gardner, and they were beginning to think he would not be calling when Hallie's phone rang?"

"Hello?"

"Um, hello. This is Ken Gardner."

"Thank you for calling, Mr. Gardner."

"What is this all about? I told the police everything I know. I don't know what I could possibly add. And for the record I have no information about the Siesta Key murder. I heard about it, of course, but I had no idea that murder had anything to do with the one in Treasure Island."

"So, what did you hear about the Siesta Key murder? You know, other than what's been in the news?" Hallie asked.

"Nothing, I mean, how would I hear anything? I know who you are, by the way. You're not going to use me as the scapegoat to get your brother off."

"That was never my intention," Hallie said calmly. "Let me get right to the point, Ken. May I call you Ken?"

"Yeah, fine, just get to the point."

"We've discovered some things that we believe link the two murders, and we believe you can help us tremendously in determining if they are, in fact, connected. Yes, honestly, it will help my brother as he was already in custody when the Siesta Key murder happened. But we need to get to the truth."

After a pause, Ken said less defensively than he had been, "Okay, I understand. What do you want to know?"

"Ken, do you remember when you first opened the door at your Treasure Island place?"

"Oh my God, of course, how will I ever forget? That poor girl, oh my God, that poor girl. She was so young."

Hallie and Paige looked at each other. Ken's reaction seemed genuine and filled with despair.

"I'm sorry, I'm sure it's a day you'll never forget. But if you could try to focus on the details. Did you, by any chance, do anything with the victim's clothes after you discovered her?"

"What do you mean? I tried not to touch anything as soon as I realized she was dead."

"So, you didn't try to tidy up, for example, or pick up her clothes or anything else in the room, you know, to try to preserve her dignity, which is very common when people find victims of violent crimes," Hallie explained.

"No, absolutely not. I didn't touch anything. I could tell she was dead right away by the way her face and, oh my God, her eyes looked. I never even went inside. I can't get the image out of my head. She was facing towards the door, as I opened it, her eyes staring straight at me. I have never seen such fear and pain. The whites were stained with blood, which I now understand is the broken blood vessels from the strangulation, and all around her eyes her skin was swollen and purple from the bruises. I got out of there immediately and called the police."

"You didn't go into the room to check her pulse or give her first aid, like CPR?" Hallie asked.

"Honey, CPR was no longer an option, it was quite obvious. No, I didn't go into the room. I got the fuck out of there and called the police. There was nothing I could do for that poor girl."

Paige then asked, "Did you take any pictures before you backed out to call the police?"

Hallie looked at Paige, surprised by her question but impressed.

"Jesus, do you think I'm some kind of sociopath? This was the worst thing I've ever experienced. I'm seeing my therapist twice a week since it happened."

"So, is that a no?" Paige asked, the former prosecutor coming out in her.

"Yes, I mean, no, I mean, that's a no, an emphatic no. I did not take any fucking pictures. I'm done with this call now. You people, you have no idea," Ken was saying, exasperated, before Hallie interrupted him.

"I'm sorry, Ken, I can only imagine how difficult this has been for you. Just one last question, and we won't bother you anymore. Does your Treasure Island use a traditional key lock system on the door or is it an electronic lock system with a code like your Siesta Key place?"

"I went electronic on both properties a few years ago."

"Do you use the same access code on both properties?"

Silence.

Hallie's adrenaline started escalating. She knew she was on to something.

"Oh my God, how would he have gotten the co . . .," as his words trailed off, evidently realizing that the murderer may have been a former renter. "People are vetted before I rent to them. Like, seriously? Is that how he got in?" Ken asked, despair in his voice.

Hallie and Paige came to the same conclusion at the same moment as Ken did, and they looked at each other, nodding, before Hallie returned her eyes to the road in front of her.

"We don't know, Ken, but it's something we need to look into. It could be nothing, but we would appreciate it if you wouldn't discuss this with anyone until we have a chance to look into it."

"I should call the detective on the case. He told me if I thought of anything, I should call him. I need to tell him about this."

"I wish you wouldn't, Ken. If you could just give me a day or two to see . . ." Hallie said, trying to come up with a plausible reason for a delay that wouldn't result in a charge of obstructing justice or worse against her. "Actually, Ken, yes, of course, you should call the detective on the Treasure Island case right away. Someone needs to investigate whether the cases are connected."

Paige looked at Hallie and mouthed, "*what the fuck?*"

"Ken, I'm sure you have all of your business records in order, which is good," Hallie continued, smiling at Paige. "The police will go through everything you have with a fine-toothed comb, especially your rental history and bank accounts, to match rental income to the deposits in your bank account and the tenant information provided by AirBnB. It's a lot, but if you did everything through the AirBnB app and reported all the income on your tax returns, it shouldn't be too bad. I would start gathering it so you have it ready when they subpoena you."

"Subpoena me? What the fuck? I don't want to get involved in all this. I just own a few rental properties. They make enough money to pay my bills and allow me to have a few beers at the beach bars nearby. Can we just not report this right now? We don't even know if my Treasure Island place is actually connected to what happened in Siesta Key. I mean, it's not like that crime happened at my rental down there," Ken said, somewhat desperately.

"You're right, Ken, I get it. I mean, I think you should contact the detective, but you're right, there's no confirmed connection, I mean, other than you. Maybe you should wait. I don't know; I don't want to tell you what to do, but I would hate for you to open yourself up to all that scrutiny when it could be just a random coincidence."

"But aren't you going to call them? I don't want to seem like I'm hiding anything," Ken said, reconsidering, obviously still nervous.

"Who me? No, I don't like to feed the police anything until I figure it out myself. I feel like they look for evidence to fit the conclusion or story they've already come to. So I would rather find the truth before I bring in the police, which, of course, as soon as I have the answers, I will."

"Yeah, that makes sense. Okay, I would rather wait to see what you come up with before I contact the Treasure Island detective, if that's okay with you."

"Of course, I think that's actually a smart move, Ken. You haven't done anything wrong, so why have all that scrutiny and investigation into your business and personal life unless there is an actual connection to these crimes. Which, as you said, there probably is not."

Paige was smiling at Hallie.

"Okay, Ken, I have to go, but will you call me if you think of anything else?'

"Yes, but I can't imagine there's anything else. I've told you everything I remember. Will you call me if you learn anything else?"

"Of course, Ken, if we find anything that confirms the murder at your Treasure Island AirBnB is connected to the Siesta Key murder, we'll let you know. Thank you so much for talking to us tonight."

Hallie hung up and Paige said, "Wow, girl, you are good. You played that poor fool. And I'm convinced he had nothing to do with either murder now. There is no way that nervous Nellie could have murdered anyone," Paige laughed.

"Yeah, I agree. I came to that conclusion pretty quickly. But he did give us a lot of valuable information. I remember from the crime scene report in Treasure Island, there was no sign of forced entry, but I also don't remember seeing anything about electronic locks. I assumed, and I think the police assumed, that Dawn let her killer in. Of course, they think that's Charlie, but this is a game changer. What if this guy gets in by code? I need to get access to the Siesta Key murder scene reports. I want to see if she also had electronic locks."

"How are you going to get those?" Paige asked.

"I'm not. But Mike will."

"My husband, Mike?" Paige asked.

"I hope so. I'm going to present all of this to him and if he agrees there's enough here to connect the two cases, he can call the Siesta Key police department to have them investigate it. They'll share their reports with him."

"I hope you're right," Paige said as her phone started to ring. "Speak of the devil," she giggled as she answered her phone. "Hey, Mike, were your ears burning?"

Hallie was lost in her own thoughts as Paige chatted with Mike.

She knew there had to be more evidence connecting the Treasure Island victim to the Siesta Key victim, and she was going to find it.

CHAPTER FIFTY-THREE
LINDA

Linda slept better that night than she had in a long time and woke up with clarity. She realized that no man who truly loved her would have let her stay at the *El Rauncho Motel* for one minute, much less leave her there alone for three days. Billy had not tried to contact her once since he left her there in that roach-infested, crack hotel. It was obvious to her now that he had used her to get out of Starke and back to Tampa.

He was a bad man, Linda had come to realize.

He wasn't trying to protect her. He was trying to protect himself. She knew that now and felt so stupid for believing in him and pouring her heart out to him. She didn't know whether or not he had committed the horrible crimes they accused him of, but what she did know was that he had lied to her, about his feelings at least. And that was enough.

She heard her mother's voice in her head, "Linda Lew Mary Baker, when are you gonna stop letting these boys take advantage of you? You're gonna end up pregnant by the time you're sixteen and they're gonna be long gone, just like what happened to me. Thank God your step-daddy,

Luke, stepped up to raise you as his own. But you're not as pretty as I was; you won't be so lucky."

Linda didn't feel like it was a blessing having Luke "step up" to raise her as he was a violent, nasty and abusive drunk, and those were his good qualities. His other qualities were downright criminal. She didn't want to turn out like her mother, or her sisters, or her nieces, or so many other women in her family, who were thankful to be with an abusive, demanding and narcissistic man because somehow that was better than being alone. No, Linda had decided a long time ago that being alone was better than that kind of life.

But she also refused to be made the fool. And that's what Billy had done to her. Originally, she had wanted to find him so they could be together, and he could explain why he left her alone at that raunchy motel. But now, she didn't want any of that.

She wanted something else from him now.

Retribution.

And she would get it.

CHAPTER FIFTY-FOUR
HALLIE

They arrived at Marcelo's house from their brief Siesta Key trip just after 2 a.m. Hallie was surprised to see another car parked in Marcelo's driveway behind his truck.

"Whose car is that?" Paige asked.

"I don't know," Hallie said.

"Want me to come in with you?"

"No, it's fine. I'm sure he just has a buddy over," Hallie said, trying to sound convincing.

"Okay, well call me if you need me."

"I will, thanks for driving. Text me when you get home. I'll call you tomorrow."

After Paige drove away, Hallie walked to the front door and opened it, not knowing what to expect. Marcelo rarely had friends over and it was late.

"Well, that was a quick trip," Marcelo said, getting up off the couch as she came in the door. "Hallie, this is my good friend, Colin Rice. We were in the academy together, but after we graduated, he ended up being accepted to Quantico and has been with the FBI ever since. Colin, this is my girlfriend, Hallie."

Colin got up to shake Hallie's hand, "Hi Hallie, so nice to meet you in person. I've heard a lot about you. Sorry to impose, but I had to come into town at the last minute for a funeral, and this guy insisted I stay here."

"Oh no, I'm so sorry," Hallie said, trying to process everything, as she shook Colin's hand.

"Thank you, it's okay, it was my great aunt, Gladys. She was 97. Lived a great life and lived and died in her home in West Tampa – that's the way to go, ya know?"

"Wow, 97, that's amazing. It's very nice to meet you. I hope I'm not imposing on your reunion. I was supposed to be gone until Sunday."

Marcelo took Hallie's overnight bag from her as Juno got up from her bed to greet Hallie.

"Absolutely not. I'm the one who's imposing. I would never have taken him up on the offer if I knew you were coming home. Wait, that didn't come out right," Colin laughed awkwardly.

"Bro, we haven't hung out in like ten years. We have a lot of catching up to do. I'm glad you're here and Hallie doesn't mind, I promise you," Marcelo said, as he came out of the bedroom after bringing in her bag and looking to Hallie for confirmation.

"He's absolutely right. I don't mind at all. I'm glad you're here," Hallie said sincerely.

"Babe, what are you doing home so soon? Find anything out in Siesta Key? I told Colin about your brother's situation and what you were doing in Siesta Key. I hope you don't mind, but he's FBI, so maybe he can help."

Hallie explained why they cut their trip short and what they had learned, including what Cassandra had told them about the folded pajamas at the end of the bed and their conversation with Ken Gardner.

"Hallie, that sounds promising, as far as a connection between the two crime scenes go, but, playing devil's advocate, it could also be a coincidence. Is there any chance the picture or a description of the folded sundress from the Treasure Island scene ended up in the media? The Siesta Key murderer could have picked up on that and copied it, intentionally trying to throw the investigators off," Colin said, thoughtfully and non-condescendingly.

"I hadn't thought of that," Hallie thought for a second, feeling momentarily deflated. "No, that's not possible," she concluded. "Those photos haven't been released – they were too graphic – and I don't remember reading anything about the folded dress in any of the news reports. I'll check to make sure, of course, but I don't think so. I noticed the dress in the crime scene photos when Dawn's body was still on the bed, from the discovery in Charlie's case, but I don't even remember reading about it in the detective's reports. It struck me as strange when I saw it, but I didn't give it another thought until Cassandra mentioned Stacey's folded pajamas."

"Okay, so what do you want to do next?" Marcelo asked.

"I don't know. I need to talk to Mike Freeman. I don't want to do anything that could jeopardize Charlie's defense."

"Yeah, that's a good idea."

"I'm happy to run a search in the FBI database for similar crimes with that nuance, the folded clothes at the edge of the bed," Colin said. "I can tell you from experience, if it's a serial murderer, his crime scene is almost as important as what he does to his victim. He wants the investigators and others to see it a certain way, and nothing is random. It's purposeful."

"That would be amazing if you could," Hallie said. "I know my brother didn't do this, and I need to find anything I can to prove it."

Just then, Hallie heard Marcelo receive an incoming text.

Marcelo picked his phone up off the coffee table as Hallie and Colin watched him read the text.

He turned the phone around and showed them the text he had received:

"Hey, I don't know if you're up, but Campbell and I interviewed Monica Martino tonight about a break-in at her apartment and her run in with a creep who may have also attempted to abduct a waitress in St. Pete. Around the same time as that Treasure Island murder. Isn't your girlfriend's brother accused of that? She may want to know about this."

Hallie looked at the sender and saw that the text came from *Alicia*. Not Johnson, not Detective Johnson, not even

Alicia Johnson, just *Alicia*. Hallie found that interesting but didn't have time to process it.

"I definitely want to talk to her," Hallie said. "I'll meet her anywhere she wants tomorrow, whenever she's available."

"Let me ask her."

Detective Johnson agreed to meet Hallie the next day at 7:00 p.m. at Rome & Fig, a neighborhood bistro just south of downtown on the corner of Rome Avenue and Fig Street.

* * *

The next night, Hallie met Detective Johnson at Rome & Fig. The bar was filled with young, trendy UT students and young professionals. Hallie and the detective looked a little out of place, although no one seemed to pay them any attention. After being seated at a small table, they both ordered ice teas, and then waited for the waitress to leave before beginning their conversation.

"Thank you so much for meeting with me, Detective Johnson," Hallie started.

"Please, call me Alicia. And, of course, I'm happy to help. I don't want anyone who may be innocent wrongfully accused or convicted of a crime they didn't commit. There were some things that Ms. Martino said about the break-in at her apartment that struck me as odd and reminded me of what I knew about the Treasure Island murder your brother has been accused of. That's why I reached out to Marcelo."

"Thank you, I appreciate it. I'll tell you what I've learned and answer any questions you may have, too. Please, feel free to start," Hallie said.

Alicia opened her notebook and told her about her interview with Monica Martino, including about Monica's encounter in the parking lot with the man who 'gave her the creeps', in Monica's words, her description of him, subsequent sightings of him, and the break-in at her apartment. She also told her about the attempted abduction in St. Pete and the waitress's description of the assailant and his truck that matched Monica's description of the man who she had encountered.

"By the way, I know we're pretty sure that Stephens is the one who broke into your house, but you haven't seen anyone around your neighborhood or anywhere else that fits that description, have you?"

"No, I don't think so. I would have remembered seeing that tattoo, I think."

"Right, that makes sense. It's just in all of these cases, including Monica's break-in and your break-ins, there was no forced entry, so I want to rule out all possible connections between your break-in and these cases."

"I never considered mine could be related to any of these," Hallie said, confused.

"Well, you are connected in that your brother was arrested for the Treasure Island murder, someone broke into your house, and someone broke into Monica Martino's apartment, who you also have a connection to, so, we just have to explore and rule out all possibilities."

"Okay, I get it, what do you want to know?" Hallie asked.

"On the night you came home and found Juno locked in the bathroom, you took her and got out of there, and that's when we found the threatening note in your kitchen. But when you went back in, and specifically, when you went upstairs to your bedroom, did you find anything out of place?"

"I don't think so," Hallie said, thinking back. "Like what?"

"Well, like clothes, especially lingerie or underwear, pajamas maybe," Detective Johnson explained.

"No," Hallie said, her heart starting to race, "do you mean like lingerie or pajamas folded neatly at the bottom of my bed?

"Yes, exactly like that. Did you find any of your clothes that way?" Detective Johnson asked.

"No, but I know of at least two murder scenes where clothes were left that way," Hallie said. "Why did you ask me that?"

"Because what Monica described seemed similar to your break-in. He locked the door behind him and left other *messages*, albeit unwritten, to make sure she knew he was there, to instill fear in her and to suggest he would be back, like the note left in your kitchen."

"But why did you ask me about the clothes?" Hallie asked.

"The guy who broke into Monica Martino's apartment left a nightie and thong folded up neatly on the corner of her bed."

"Oh my God, okay, this is the same guy, no doubt in my mind," Hallie said, excitedly.

"Explain," Detective Alicia Johnson said.

After Hallie told Alicia everything she knew, she could tell the detective was as excited as she was.

"I'm going to contact my Chief immediately. Based on the information you've provided and what we've found, they need to look at all of these cases together, see if the same person committed them," Detective Johnson said excitedly.

"Can I ask you one more question?" Hallie asked.

"Of course, anything."

"How long have you and Marcelo been sleeping with each other?" Hallie asked, unemotionally, failing to abide by the number one rule as a lawyer: never ask a question you don't know the answer to.

CHAPTER FIFTY-FIVE
MONICA

Monica stared down at her phone as another text came through.

"*Moni?*"

Davis Islands Beach was where she and Christian went to be alone. It was "*their place*" and where she had gotten pregnant, no doubt. She would pack them a picnic, and they would stay out there all night. Monica's parents had no idea she would sneak out of the house almost every night to see him. She would bring a blanket, and they would make love under the stars. Monica had never been happier than when she was in his arms.

Monica often thought about how different her life would have turned out if her father had embraced Christian instead of setting him up and sending him to prison. They could have been a family and Pietro would have had a father. And they would have been happy.

Monica didn't know how to respond. She knew she shouldn't go but she knew she couldn't stay away either. She owed him that, at the very least. He had been out of prison for months. If he had wanted to hurt her, he already would have.

She typed, "*when?*"

"*One hour.*"

Her hand trembled slightly as she typed, "*Ok.*"

CHAPTER FIFTY-SIX
LINDA

Linda slept in on Saturday, appreciating the nice hotel room bed after the fleabag disgusting place she had been in. After lounging around all day in her hotel room, she headed over to the detective-boyfriend's house and was pleased to see the cars all there, especially the BMW. She had been watching for about two hours when the detective came outside with the dog. She hadn't seen Hallie Miller since she got there, but she felt she was there. As the detective went back inside with the dog, her intuition was right and Hallie came out, kissing the detective as they crossed paths and patting the dog on the head.

She got in her car and drove off.

Linda followed.

Hallie parked outside of a restaurant near downtown. Another car pulled up a few minutes later and the same pretty red head who had gotten out of the black sedan at Hallie's house now got out of a blue jeep.

"Hmmm, what's this all about?" Linda asked aloud before finding a parking space on the street where she could watch the door and both of their cars.

An hour later, they came out of the restaurant and walked towards their cars in opposite directions. Although it was starting to get dark, Linda could tell it was them and watched as Hallie got in her car and sped off, heading south. As soon as the BMW passed her, Linda saw another car that had been parked a few blocks away, turn its lights on, pull away from the curb and head in the same direction as Hallie. Linda ducked down but was able to look at the driver as he went past her, the streetlight illuminating the inside of the small gray car.

"Billy Stephens, got you, you son of a b-word," she said, feeling her adrenaline surge as she started her own car and did a U-turn to avoid losing them.

CHAPTER FIFTY-SEVEN
HALLIE

Hallie wanted to ask Monica Martino about the folded clothes and other details Hallie thought would connect the Treasure Island murder to the Siesta Key murder. She had no idea whether Monica would talk to her, but she had to try. This was her only chance.

She didn't have Monica's cell or any other way to reach her, but she knew from her conversation with Detective Johnson that Monica was at her mother's house on Davis Islands. She easily found the address on the Hillsborough County property appraiser's website and put it into her GPS.

She arrived on Davis Islands in less than fifteen minutes and easily found her way to the large house on Martinique Avenue, one of the southernmost streets on the island where all of the houses backed up to the water. She slowed down as she pulled up to the house and was about to park when she saw Monica Martino walking away from Martinique towards the Davis Islands Trail, which ran adjacent to the water and would eventually lead her to the Davis Islands Beach.

"*Hmm, where is she going?*" Hallie wondered, thinking it was too dark outside for a casual walk.

Hallie followed her.

She parked her car at the end of the street in front of a construction site and got out of the car. She was a good distance behind her, so she didn't think Monica could see or hear her, but every few minutes, she saw the glow of Monica's cigarette. She seemed to be heading toward the Davis Islands Beach just on the other side of the Seaplane Basin. The only things in that direction that Hallie could remember were a dog park, a boat ramp, and the beach.

* * *

By the time Hallie arrived at the beach, Monica was nowhere to be found. She couldn't see the ember of her cigarette anymore or light emitting from her phone.

Hallie called out to her, "Monica? Monica, are you out here?"

Nothing, no response. She listened but couldn't hear anything.

Hallie hadn't seen any other cars but was starting to think that maybe someone picked Monica up before she made it out there, possibly by boat. Hallie looked out at the calm water in the Basin as well as on the other side of the boat ramp, but she couldn't see anything or any boats on the water. It was very dark, the only light coming from the stars above, but on the cloudy night, the sky was an ominous gray.

Hallie shivered.

Something wasn't right, she could feel it. And now she was all alone at the beach, and she hadn't told anyone that she was going out there. She pulled her hoodie tighter around her as she turned to head back to her car. Stephens was still out there, somewhere, and she shouldn't have been so reckless.

She saw headlights in the distance coming down the road towards the beach.

"Shit," Hallie said, regretting that she had decided to follow Monica without her gun.

She looked around to see where she could hide. High school kids often went to the beach to party or make out, but she had no way of knowing. She would hide until they passed, and then she would jog the mile back to her car to get out of there. She ran back to the road, away from the beach area, and crouched down behind some trees and thick brush. As a lifelong Floridian, all she could think of was the possibility of a water moccasin or rattle snake being nearby or the voracious mosquitos that would enjoy the all-night buffet of her ankles and bare arms.

As soon as the car passed, she would make a run for it.

A small gray car passed by, slowly, as if the driver was looking for someone. It wasn't a car full of high school kids, but rather a car with a single occupant.

Was it Stephens? Hallie wondered. *Had he followed her there?*

The gray car kept heading towards the beach. Unless the driver had a boat docked there with late-night fishing or boating plans, he would have to turn around at the dead-end and head back from the direction he came, which was also the direction Hallie had to go to get back to her car.

As soon as he was a safe distance away, she started running towards her car. She could not outrun him if he turned around immediately, but she hoped, if it was Stephens, he would take his time to look for her on the dock and the beach before turning back.

She could run a mile, at her best time, in less than nine minutes.

Tonight, her life might depend on that.

CHAPTER FIFTY-EIGHT
MONICA

Monica left her house and headed towards the Davis Islands Beach, where she and Christian used to hang out. When they used to meet there, that's all there was out there, but now there was a dog park, a boat ramp, and the newly constructed pickleball court.

She arrived at the beach, heading to the familiar spot that they considered *their* spot all those years ago. The pickleball court was right next to it now, and she wondered if Christian would be able to find it. She sat on the sand, lit a fresh cigarette, and listened. It was quiet, the only sound being the lapping of the water rippling against the bank.

She heard a car approaching and figured that had to be him. The beach was usually empty at that time of night, unless a group of kids came to the Basin to party, which didn't happen too often. She nervously inhaled her cigarette, the glow from the tip illuminating her location. If he was out there, he would see it and know where to find her.

She was nervous. She still loved him. She had never stopped. But she knew he probably hated her. She couldn't blame him.

She saw a man get out of the car and head towards her. *It had to be Christian,* she thought.

She stood up, anxious to see him but terrified at what he was going to say and possibly do to her. She smoothed her slip dress, nervously, adjusting her breasts in her bra so they looked perky. She knew she deserved his wrath, but still . . . she held onto a shred of hope that maybe he could forgive her.

As the man approached, Monica was confused. He didn't look anything like what she expected him to look like. He was taller, thinner, lankier. When she knew Christian, he was stocky, muscular, *a presence.*

Had prison and the years changed him that much, she wondered.

But as he got closer, she realized he wasn't Christian and instinctively got up and started to walk away.

"Where's Hallie?" the man asked angrily.

"Hallie? Um, Hallie who? And who the fuck are you?" Monica retorted, confused at the stranger's sudden approach.

"Fucking cunt, always fucking with me. Did she put you up to this? I'm tired of these fucking games she's playing. I know she's out here. I followed her here, so I know you're helping her. You cunts think you're so smart, but you're not."

Monica was taken aback by his anger and realized his anger had nothing to do with her, but somehow, she was going to receive the brunt of it.

"Look, I don't know who or what you're talking about. I just came out here to take a walk. I'm leaving," Monica said as she started to head back towards the road.

"The fuck you are," the man said, as he grabbed her arm, twisted it behind her back, grabbed her other hand, and slipped handcuffs around both wrists in what seemed like seconds.

Monica cried out in pain from the yanking on her arms and the cuffs cutting into her wrists.

"Shut the fuck up," the man said as he dragged Monica to the pickleball court not ten feet away.

As he dragged her, Monica could smell the odor of sweat mixed with a hint of whiskey. She tried to resist but he was too strong for her.

"Do you know who I am?" Monica yelled, terrified, angry.

"I don't give a fuck who you are," the man answered coldly and calmly.

"Well, maybe you know the Martino name around this town. I'm Tommy Martino's daughter and Nicolas Martino's niece. Trust me, this is not a family you want to fuck with. If you let me go now, I won't tell my uncle about this, and you will live."

The man started laughing. Not laughing in a nervous or polite way, but laughing hysterically, as if Monica had just told the funniest joke this man had ever heard.

"How is old Nico these days?" the man said when he stopped laughing. "He has an unsettled debt with me he needs to pay up on. Maybe having his niece will incentivize him."

Monica backed up, looking around to where she could run, despite her handcuffed wrists.

But before she could make a move in any direction, the man had grabbed her again and dragged her over to one of the poles on the pickle ball court. He quickly, and despite Monica's struggles, easily secured the handcuffs to a steel ring affixed to the concrete.

She tried to resist and yanked and pulled at her restraints. But it was futile. She was secured tightly to the concrete with no chance of escape. She watched as her captor started pacing.

The man yelled into the night, "Haaalllliiieee, I know you're out there. Show yourself immediately or I'm going to kill your friend. You know I'm not bluffing."

Monica waled, "I don't have a friend out here. What the fuck are you talking about? If you so much as lay a finger on me, my uncle will have you chopped up into a million pieces and fed to the fish at the aquarium while he watches. That's the kind of guy he is. I suggest you let me go immediately!"

"Your uncle is an old man now. He can't do a fucking thing to me. But let me tell you what I can and will do to you – *are you listening, Hallie?*" he yelled again into the darkness. "I'm going to start cutting you and stabbing you all over your body, maybe starting with that beautiful face of yours. I want to make sure it hurts but doesn't kill you, at least not until I'm ready for you to die. You will start slowly bleeding to death, unless and until Hallie fucking Miller saves you by coming out of her hiding place. Do you understand? I have no beef with you. It's her I want."

"Hallie Miller? Are you fucking kidding me? This is about her? Oh my God, I am so sorry, God, I repent, I do!" Monica yelled up into the dark night. "I didn't mean to kill her father! I confess! Please make this stop. I have carried this burden for too long. I'm ready, God, please," Monica yelled and started to sob.

The man seemed confused by Monica's outburst and went silent for a moment, looking at her strangely. Then the anger returned to his face, and he lunged towards her. Monica instinctively jerked at her cuffs like a violent animal, kicking at him, spitting, and trying to force her petite wrists through the steel enclosures, trying to fight him off. As she fought, the cuffs lacerated her wrists, but she felt no pain, only a desperate urge to break free and save herself, like any wild, caged animal would.

As the man grabbed at her, his knife in hand, Monica fought violently, pulling back from him so abruptly that she slammed her head against the steel pole.

And then everything went black.

CHAPTER FIFTY-NINE
CHRISTIAN

CK watched from behind the mangroves that had become his cover as Monica came into view. She walked towards the area that had always been "*their place*" but was now a place where people played tennis, basketball, or some other sport played on a concrete base.

"*God, she's still so beautiful,*" CK thought as he watched her silhouette and had a yearning in his heart to immediately hug her.

He was rageful that she hadn't told him about their son. She should have. But as he watched the woman she had become, he realized how young she was when they were together. When he went away, she was pregnant with his child, and she was only seventeen.

Suddenly the lyrics of *Edge of Seventeen* by Stevie Nicks played in his head, and he felt a sadness he hadn't allowed himself to feel in a long time.

And yet, he felt hopeful, too.

He had sent her the text and here she was walking towards their meeting spot, to meet him. She showed up, alone, knowing she was meeting him and that he could kill her if he wanted to. He always admired her courage and tenacity. His anger subsided as he watched her, and all he wanted to do was take her in his arms.

He was about to come out from behind the wall he was crouching behind when he heard, "fucking cunt, always fucking with me. Did she put you up to this?"

CK crouched back down and watched, his adrenaline kicking in.

He heard Moni shouting back, arguing, and trying to back away from the guy. Next thing he saw was the guy grabbing her, subduing her, her hands behind her back, and then securing her to something on the court.

He saw Monica yell up into the sky, heard her screaming something about God and repenting, which stopped the man for a moment, confusing him. But it only lasted a few seconds before the man lunged at her again.

"What the fuck," CK whispered as his mind raced with what to do next.

Who the fuck is this guy, he wondered. From what he could hear Monica yelling, she didn't know him and was fighting back as best as she could, but the man was too big, too strong. Something reflected off of the little light in the sky onto something in the man's hand and CK realized he had a knife.

Monica struggled, kicking and yelling and fighting as hard as she could until her head hit the steel pole behind her and CK watched as her body instantly went limp.

CK had seen enough, and, in that moment, he knew how much he still loved her, could never stop loving her, no matter how flawed she was. They were both flawed. He had to save her.

He retreated in the darkness to the boat ramp, quickly assessing what he could from the boats docked at the small marina: gasoline cans, fishing lines, a tarp if he needed it. He grabbed two full gas cans and a crowbar and made his way back to the concrete court where Moni was handcuffed to the concrete pole. Her lifeless body was slumped against the pole, her head leaning awkwardly to one side.

He prayed he wasn't too late.

"*Mother fucker*," he said aloud, as he went into full attack-mode, catching the man who had attacked Monica off-guard, knowing he was about to kill again.

CHAPTER SIXTY
HALLIE

Hallie called Marcelo as soon as she got back to her car and had caught her breath. She was relieved the gray car she saw coming in had not followed her out. She called Marcelo but got his voicemail. She left him a message to let him know where she was, which she acknowledged she should have done before she headed out there.

"Hey, I'm out here on Davis Islands. I came out here to ask Monica Martino some questions about the break-in at her apartment. When I got here, she was walking out to the Davis Islands Beach, so I followed her, but then I lost her. A car showed up a few minutes ago, but I'm not waiting around to see who it is. I'm leaving now and I'll be there soon to pick up Juno. Call me when you get this."

Hallie hung up and was about to drive away when she saw headlights approaching in her rearview mirror. Before she could drive away, a blue Ford Escape pulled up, parking in front of her and intentionally blocking her ability to pull forward to drive away.

Hallie started her car, put it in reverse, and was ready to maneuver her way around the car when she saw a petite, plump blonde woman get out of the car. The woman looked like she should be heading to a PTA meeting rather than walking alone on deserted stretch of Davis Islands beach. Any relief Hallie felt at not seeing Stephens was short-lived as the woman started walking towards her driver's side door.

She didn't have anything in her hands, that Hallie could see, but, somehow, she knew that this wasn't a random encounter. Hallie opened her can of mace she kept handy in her car, ready to spray if necessary, regretting that she had secured her new gun in the trunk rather than her glovebox. She kept her doors locked and cracked her window so she could hear the woman, her finger on the nozzle of the mace.

"Ms. Miller? Hallie Miller? Can I talk to you?"

Hallie was taken aback at the woman knowing her name.

She pulled the can of mace up so the woman could see it, realizing if this woman had a gun, her can of mace was going to be useless. Hallie looked at the woman. She looked familiar to her, but she couldn't place her. She had definitely seen her before, and the woman knew her name.

"Do I know you?" Hallie asked.

"No, we haven't met, but I know a lot about you. You ruined Billy's life with that DNA nonsense about your daughter that they used against him at his trial, but I'm not here about that. That's between you and him."

"Billy?" Hallie asked, confused.

"Oh, you and the media call him William, William Stephens. I call him Billy."

"Oh my God, I know who you are," Hallie said, as she recognized the pudgy woman standing outside her car. "You were on the jury. You're the one who caused the mistrial."

"Guilty as charged," Linda laughed. "But it didn't do any good. He still went to prison."

Hallie started to reverse, ready to zip around the woman and her car to flee.

"Ms. Miller, wait, I'm not here to hurt you. I followed Billy here. Did you know he was following you? He was in a small, gray car. Did you see him?"

"What do you want?" Hallie asked, angrily, one hand holding the mace can, the other on the steering wheel, ready to take off.

"I have a matter to take up with Billy, but that will be between him and I. Or is it him and me? Whatever, anyway, I saw him follow you here and then drive over to that beach," Linda said, pointing across the Basin towards the beach where Hallie had just run from, her sweat-soaked shirt sticking to her body. "Did you see him?"

"No, and if I were you, I would get back in your car and drive away. He's a very dangerous man. You do realize he's a rapist and a murderer, right?" Hallie asked, looking at the woman's face, trying to determine if she was there to help or hurt Stephens.

The woman tilted her head back in a maniacal laugh, "Oh Lordy, honey, I'm not afraid of him. He's done me wrong and needs to understand that I don't take kindly to men lying to me or using me. So, I'm going to head on over to that beach and have a word or two with him."

"No, don't do that. Please, Miss, um, what's your name?"

"Linda," she said, at the precise moment they heard a small explosion from across the water.

They both looked over and saw a giant fireball that lit up the dark sky.

"What the fuck?" Hallie said.

"Oh my heavens," Linda said.

Hallie called 9-1-1 to report the explosion and requested EMT and fire rescue.

She also told the dispatcher, "My name is Hallie Miller. Please contact Detective Marcelo Garcia immediately and tell him that William Stephens is on the Davis Islands Beach. If you check your APB, you will see he is an extremely dangerous escaped inmate from the Florida State Prison."

The dispatcher started to ask her questions, but Hallie hung up. While Hallie was on with 9-1-1, Linda had returned to her car and was heading down Severn Avenue towards the Davis Islands Beach and the burning mass.

Before following her, Hallie retrieved her gun from its case in the trunk, placed it on the passenger seat, and followed the blue Ford Escape towards the beach.

CHAPTER SIXTY-ONE
MONICA

Fire is a curious thing, she thought, as the embers flitted around her like fireflies on a warm summer night. The flames crackled in front of her, taunting her, demanding that she notice them as she fought to regain consciousness.

Monica looked down and drew her bare legs closer into her body, the pins and needles a gnawing clue as to how long she had been there. As the sensation waned, she strained like a trapped animal against the handcuffs that kept her shackled to the concrete ground. She jerked every which way with every ounce of strength she had, more strength than she would've guessed, but it was futile, just as it had been before she passed out. The lacerations on her wrists had reopened from this last attempt, fresh blood seeping from her raw wounds, coating the unrelenting steel.

She never fully *felt* the danger of fire, had never been afraid of it, in part because she had always been captivated by its beauty, its ability to warm her, to cast a benign glow on her favorite portrait above the fireplace in her childhood home. These flames, though, were not those: these seemed otherworldly in their iridescence, in their incessant dance, flickering and cracking and whipping at the air above, as if hungering for something just out of reach.

She understood that yearning.

As the blaze grew and the heat with it, she believed – *no, she knew* – all the bad things she had done in her life had brought her to this night. She deserved this.

And now it was all too late.

As she struggled to slip her wrists, sticky from her own blood, out of the handcuffs, the wind shifted and an almost familiar smell drifted into her consciousness, vaguely reminding her of the barbeques her family used to throw when she was young, and her father was still alive, and she was happy. The fleeting memory almost made her smile, but the ache in her wrists and the dread in her gut wouldn't allow it.

Then, a horrid realization. It hit her so hard, the bile rose instantly from her empty stomach, and she wretched: *the smell was burning flesh.*

She screamed out into the night, but only a smoke-induced rasp of a cry escaped her chapped lips. No one would have heard that. She pressed her eyes shut to avoid looking at the heap smoldering a few feet away from her and choked down a new wave of bile. The odor of charred flesh, burnt hair, and gasoline would forever be embedded in her psyche the way the fragrance of white lilies and pink carnations evoked unsolicited memories of funerals and proms.

As she drifted in and out of consciousness, she thought of Christian. At one point, she thought she awoke and saw him but wasn't sure if she had been dreaming. Had he been there? Was it real? Had he saved her from the lunatic who had attacked her?

Her throat was raw from the fire and smoke, her body was sore, her head throbbing, her wrists bleeding, and she didn't know how much longer she could hold on. And then from somewhere in the distance she heard someone calling her name.

"Here, I'm here," she yelled with the only strength she had left before passing out again.

CHAPTER SIXTY-TWO
HALLIE

"Monica, where are you? Can you hear me?" Hallie yelled, running towards the outdoor pickleball court on Davis Islands Beach towards the smoke and fire, her gun drawn, looking around to watch for William Stephens.

She ran past Linda, who was starting to pant as she tried to keep up with Hallie.

Hallie couldn't tell what was burning, but the closer she got to it, the smell got stronger and more putrid. She stopped and started to gag. Linda caught up with her, out of breath.

"There's someone there, near the fire," Linda yelled. "Next to that pole on the court," she said, pointing towards Monica.

"Monica," Hallie whispered.

Hallie regained her composure, shielded her mouth and nose with her sleeve and resumed her run towards the court.

"Monica," she yelled again as she got closer.

This time she heard a faint, "here, I'm here."

In the distance, Hallie was relieved to hear sirens coming. She didn't know where Stephens was, but she believed the sirens would keep him in his hiding place, if he was even still out there. She knew he didn't want to go back to prison.

Hallie found Monica handcuffed to the court, her wrists and arms covered in blood. She was faint and sobbing incoherently.

Hallie cradled her head in her lap, "it's okay, Monica, it's going to be okay. The police are almost here."

She watched Linda standing near the burning heap, with a curious and confused look on her face, and a menacing smile.

"I'm so sorry, so sorry, Hallie. I'm so sorry," Monica cried, over and over again until the police and EMT finally got there and were able to unshackle her and load her into an ambulance to transport her the three miles to Tampa General's emergency room at the front of Davis Islands.

After loading Monica into the ambulance, Hallie stayed behind to give her statement to the police. As she was finishing, she saw Marcelo and Jason walking towards her.

CHAPTER SIXTY-THREE
MONICA

It would be a while before the Medical Examiner could positively identify the body that had been left to burn on the court but based on Linda's account and Monica's description of the man who had handcuffed her, it was believed to be the body of William Stephens. The M.E.'s initial examination determined he had suffered a blunt force injury to the back of his head before he had been doused in gasoline and set on fire. From the smoke in his lungs, he died *after* he had been set on fire.

Monica, along with Linda and Hallie, had been cleared of Stephens' murder as Linda and Hallie were together on the other side of the beach when he was hit on the head and set on fire, and Monica was unconscious and handcuffed to the pole at the time. Someone else was out there on the beach, but there were no witnesses, other than Monica before he was killed, and she swore she didn't see anyone other than Stephens.

When asked what she was doing out there, Monica explained that she often walked to the beach from her mother's house to clear her head, and that's when she was attacked by the man she learned was William Stephens. She told the detective he thought she was Hallie Miller at first and became violently angry when he discovered she wasn't her. She recounted everything that happened to her up to the point where she had been knocked unconscious. Her injuries corroborated her version of the events

"Ms. Martino, were you meeting someone on the beach?"

"No, I already told you, I've taken walks on this beach since I was a teenager. My mother's house is on Martinique, right near the path that leads to the beach."

She knew the detective didn't believe her, but he had nothing to prove otherwise.

"And you didn't see anyone else while you were out there?"

"No, no one," Monica lied.

CHAPTER SIXTY-FOUR
LINDA

After giving a full confession, Linda was arrested for helping William Stephens escape from prison. She was being held in the Hillsborough County jail until she could be moved to Union County to stand trial. If convicted, she faced up to five years in prison and possible fines, at a minimum. She could also be charged as an accomplice to any of the crimes Stephens committed while he was out.

Since her arrest, Linda had recanted her confession, claiming she was in shock and gave it under duress in a very stressful moment. Gloria Allred had taken up her defense, claiming Linda was just another one of Stephens' long line of victims. Linda loved being in the spotlight, even if some of the press was negative. Her picture was flashed all over the news, including the tabloid magazines in the checkout lines, and she felt like a celebrity.

She felt a little bad that Billy had died, but she knew in her heart that he had what was coming to him after using her to escape prison and leaving her in that horrible motel, as he did. As Gloria said to her, "you are a victim, Linda Morgan, and we will prove your innocence." Gloria told her when she got her off, she would likely get a television or movie deal out of it, of which Gloria, of course, was entitled to a percentage.

Even her boss, Karl Walters, had given a statement to the police and to the media in her support, "Linda has been one of my best employees. If she helped Stephens escape, I have no doubt she was coerced."

Her co-worker, Martha, on the other hand used the opportunity to disparage her once again, saying, "She was weird. She was always weird, sweating and smiling to herself, sometimes talking to herself. Seriously, there's something not right with that one."

Linda vowed to get even with Martha one day, but maybe she would bake a nice pie for Karl when she got out.

He always was kind of cute, she thought to herself, giggling. *Yes, indeedy, life had a way of giving you lemonade just when you thought you were being served sour lemons.*

And Linda knew this was just the beginning of the next great phase of her life.

She had been through worse.

A lot worse.

CHAPTER SIXTY-FIVE
HALLIE

After finally speaking with Charlie, Hallie reached out to Mike Freeman to provide all the information she had compiled about the murders that seemed similar to the Treasure Island murder, including dates, locations, what she had learned from Monica Martino and Detective Johnson, and the killer's signature of leaving neatly folded lingerie at the bottom of the victim's bed. Detective Johnson and Marcelo had given the same information to Chief Mastandrea.

During her call with Charlie, she had added a column to her spreadsheet to document where Charlie was on the dates of the other murders she thought were similar. Although he couldn't remember exact dates, when at least two of the other murders had occurred, he was either in jail or rehab, which would be easy to corroborate.

Chief Mastandrea contacted the chiefs of police in the other counties and together they created a state-wide task force to investigate the murders in Treasure Island, Siesta Key, Gainesville, and three other beach towns with similar unsolved cases. It wasn't long before the media learned of the possible serial killer and had dubbed him the "Beachside

Strangler." Many of the novelty and beach shops started selling t-shirts, in typical Florida-fashion, with the slogan "I survived the Beachside Strangler in ________" with the name of the town or beach in place of the blank.

Only in Florida, Hallie thought.

After a few weeks and the additional evidence discovered by the task force, Mike filed a motion to dismiss the charges against Charlie. Under pressure from the Chief based on the task force report, the State Attorney agreed to drop the charges against Charlie, and he was released. Slowly, he was making amends with the family and had even started going to church with Becky every Sunday. Hallie was happy to have her brother back in their life, proud of his sobriety, and even happier to see her mother so joyful.

She remembered her mother's question – *what wouldn't you do for Katie?* – and realized how hard these last few years must have been on her mother. She was relieved things had turned out the way they had, for her mother and her brother, and she was relieved she never had to worry about William Stephens again.

Hallie heard the sound of the incoming text on her phone. She picked up her phone and read it.

"Babe, I know these last few months have been tough. I know I screwed up and you need time. I'm here when you're ready. I love you."

She thought about her relationship with Marcelo. When she met with Detective Johnson, Alicia, she denied having any type of physical relationship with Marcelo but admitted they may have crossed the line via text, flirting and progressing in a way that likely would have led to a physical relationship. Alicia apologized, explaining that she stopped all inappropriate communications with Marcelo after she met Hallie. Hallie didn't know whether she was telling the truth or not, but she believed her.

When she confronted Marcelo, he didn't deny it, but said it was innocent, and he just enjoyed the distraction from the pressures of his job and everything Hallie was going through. He admitted it was nice to feel wanted, attractive by someone so young and pretty, but that he never intended to act on it. Hallie didn't believe him.

She knew they had been drifting apart for some time, and she didn't blame Marcelo entirely for that. She knew she was equally responsible for the breakdown of their relationship and his need to seek gratification or reassurance elsewhere. She didn't know if they could get back to where they had been at their happiest, but for the moment she needed to be on her own. She was stronger than she had ever been and had a new direction she was going. In the weeks since everything had happened, she had completed her PI course at HCC and had found a PI willing to mentor her.

She read the text from Marcelo again before putting her phone on silent. She poured herself a much-deserved glass of Faust and sat down on her couch to binge watch the latest season of *Bosch* with her beloved Juno at her feet.

EPILOGUE
THE HUNTER

The Hunter had been spending his weekends on the beaches along the west coast, making the two-to-four-hour drive, depending on how far south he went, before returning back to his home in Starke each Sunday night. Before he went inside, he removed his blonde wig and secured it in the locked toolbox he kept in the back of the white Ford Explorer together with his Japanese knife, condoms, plastic gloves, and other hunting weapons.

"Oh honey, you spoil me, that smells so good!" he said as he entered the small ranch home. "Sorry I'm late."

"Wash your hands, everything is ready. They don't pay you enough for all the overtime you been puttin' in lately."

"I know, hon, but somebody has to do it. Roger has young ones, and Marcia is a single mom. I'm the only one who can work the extra hours. And you know it's going to pay off for us. I'm making a name for myself."

"I'll believe it when I see it. I don't know. Seems like you're working almost every weekend now. It used to be like a weekend here and there every few months. Now it's all the time."

"Brenda, I'm tired, I don't need your grief right now," he said, his voice starting to rise. "I didn't work my ass off all weekend so I could come home to get shit from you. Should I go back to work?"

"Now, now, settle down, it's not good for your blood pressure. I just miss you, that's all. You been gone too much lately and I feel like the warden is taking advantage of you. But I'll stop bringing it up. I don't want to fight on your first night off in a week."

"I don't either, Brenda, but you're stressing me out. And I don't need this, ya know?"

"I know, I know, now, hush, stop getting yourself all worked up. Go wash up for dinner, my sweet. I made your favorite."

"Meat loaf?"

"Of course! And mashed potatoes with a stick of butter and some fresh green beans I picked from the garden. Don't you pay my complaining no mind. I just miss my husband, that's all. But enough about all that."

The Hunter leaned in and kissed his wife on the forehead as he headed to the bathroom to wash up for dinner. She was a good woman – very different from the women he killed. In some ways, he thought she would understand, although he could never tell her. He would never burden her with that.

"A new season of Yellowstone came out," Brenda called from the other room. "I've been waiting for you to start it. Want to eat dinner in front of the TV?"

"That sounds like a perfect evening, my sweet. My favorite meal and a new season of Yellowstone? I am truly living a blessed life," he said as he came into the living room, drying his hands.

A truly blessed life, Karl Walter thought.

THE END

ACKNOWLEDGEMENTS

To my front line and earliest readers: Pat Newman, Alice Siess, and David Gauthreaux. I cannot thank you enough for your patience, unwavering support, and ability to suffer through multiple versions of this book, some of which I have no doubt were more painful than others. Your constructive criticism, suggestions, and encouragement were instrumental in helping me arrive at this final version. It would not be the book it is without you, and it is by far better because of you (disclaimer: all flaws are solely mine, not theirs!).

To my second wave of advanced readers: Patti McLean, Amy Stoll, Jodi Trosclair Scott, Jason Lane, Karl Walter, Eden Feldman, Sheada Madani, and Deb Garding. Your feedback has been invaluable to me, and your willingness to take the time out of your busy lives to read my latest means more to me than you will ever know. Thank you for supporting me and staying invested in Hallie's journey.

To my brother, Matt: you are king among men when it comes to editing. With the stroke of a fine point pen (or a light touch on the keyboard), you see what I see in my head and am trying to convey on the page, yet you make it better while keeping true to my voice. I cherish your mad editing skills and ability to make me sound smarter and better than I am. Thank you, sincerely.

To my dear NOLA family and friends, thank you for welcoming me into your lives and making me feel like I belong. You truly know how to make a Tampa girl feel wanted. Whenever I'm in New Orleans, I'll be happy to fix any of you a drink to convey how much I appreciate you, if you're up to it. Ya'll know who you are! Love ya!

To David, one of the best reasons the next book will be set in New Orleans. I am so happy you came into my life and me into yours. I cannot wait to see where our adventures take us. I'm not sure where we will go, but I have no doubt we will have fun no matter what we're doing or where we are! Thank you for your unwavering support and encouragement – it is everything to me.

Thank you to everyone else who reads my books, comes to my book events, supports me on social media, in real life, or in any other way. I am eternally grateful to all of you!

Jen Murphy is a corporate and tax attorney in Tampa, Florida, where she lives with her two rescue German Shepherds, Sam and Vincent. She is the author of three murder mystery suspense novels, *When She Runs . . .*, *When He Watches*, and *When She Falls*, the third in the Hallie Miller series. She splits her time between Tampa and New Orleans, and when she's not practicing law, she's writing or spending time with her many friends and family, most often with a nice Cabernet in hand. You can read more about Jen and her books on her website www.JenMurphyBooks.com.